# ASSASSINS' ACADEMY

THE BOOK OF BAWB 1

SCOTT BARON

Print Editions:

ISBN 978-1-945996-68-9 Paperback

ISBN 978-1-945996-69-6 Hardcover



Cover by Jeff Brown

*"Little by little, one walks far."*
*- Peruvian Proverb*

# CHAPTER ONE

"Oof!" Bawb gasped, the utterance barely audible, as one of the nine guards he was fighting simultaneously managed to land a solid blow with a heavy wooden club studded with metal balls.

The impact hurt—more than enough to cripple a normal man—but Bawb remained focused, keeping on his feet and not letting the pain register. Not on his face nor in his mind. To any watching, he seemed calm. Inexplicably impervious to any hits his adversaries landed. It was impossible, and more than a little unsettling.

But this was Bawb's way. No matter the cost, he had a job to do and that was all there was to it. This was the reason he'd trained so hard for many years for. To be one of the deadliest assassins in the galaxy. Reaching this pinnacle hadn't come without a cost, however, and his blood and sweat were among the least of them.

Bawb ducked the flurry of sword strokes the Bandooki warriors swung at him, forcing him to dive aside and roll out of their path. The crunching sensation in his torso confirmed his self-assessment. One of his ribs was almost surely cracked from the force of the club's impact, but that was nothing compared to the damage the razor-sharp blades would inflict.

He lashed out with a dagger, the hidden blade appearing in his hand as if out of thin air, taking the Bandooki by surprise as one of his tentacles was sliced deep enough to prevent its use. More than the other guards, this one was proving to be difficult, not only because of its size—Bandooki were taller and broader than most bipedal races—but also because, in addition to having a set of relatively normal arms, it also possessed a pair of strong tentacles on each side.

The guard let out a cry of pain as its appendage dangled mostly useless at its side, blood pulsing in a steady flow. The blade it had been cut with was more than sharp enough to have removed it from its body entirely, but this was all part of the plan. Bawb had just made its own limb more of a hindrance than a help, and the Bandooki's flurry of attacks faltered because of it.

*"Mahtzoo augis!"* a stout guard shouted, sending a blast of invisible magical daggers flying at the intruder.

Judging by the volume with which he cast the spell, Bawb was fairly confident he was a novice spellcaster. It wasn't about how loud or how forceful one cast, but about the correct intonation, and most importantly, the *intent* backing the spell, directing the magic to do one's bidding.

*"Yampoh,"* the assassin countered almost effortlessly, his shield spell not only blocking but also deflecting the attack, sending the ill-cast magic careening off into the guard's companions.

Three of them yelled in pain, a fourth simply dropping to the ground, dead. Bawb took advantage of their momentary confusion to redouble the muting spell he had cast upon the room. No matter how loud things might get in the heat of this particular battle, not a sound would escape these walls. In this case, deep in the belly of a powerful emmik's compound. That was a good thing. A vital one, in fact. The magically induced silence was the only thing keeping an entire garrison of enemy troops from coming to their comrades' aid.

Bawb pulled from the tiny amount of magic stored in the band on his wrist, the konus still feeding his spells but growing dangerously low on power. He had drawn deep. Too deep. The enemy could sense it. One of the guards was a natural caster, her own magic nowhere near that of an emmik and certainly far, far below that of a visla, but she was strong in her own right. Strong enough to serve as one of the emmik's elite guards, in fact.

*"Mani Patzu!"* she cast, sending a cleverly cast freezing spell at the ground at Bawb's feet just as he drew another hidden blade and threw it hard at the nearest of the thick-skinned Omatzi warriors also serving as guards in the group, all of them coming at him with swords drawn.

The spell the caster used wasn't one normally employed in combat, but was rather intended to cool bodies of water on hot days. Even as his feet slipped on the thin sheet of ice, Bawb had to admire the woman's clever use of the spell.

The dagger flew slightly off course, impaling itself in the guard's chest instead of his forehead. The blade was only slightly enchanted, but that was all it needed to pierce the otherwise troublesome hide of the Omatzi.

"Agh!" the guard cried out, falling to the ground in a twitching heap.

It hadn't been an immediately killing blow as intended, but the Omatzi possessed several nerve plexuses normally protected under their thick skin. A cluster of nerves that had now been penetrated. The guard might survive, but he would be out of commission for quite a long time no matter what a healer might accomplish.

Two more guards were already down, and the others were all

injured to one degree or another, but this was taking longer than Bawb had anticipated. He was on a tight schedule and could not afford any serious delays. The emmik worked for the Council of Twenty and was only at this location because of the impending meeting with one of his superiors. It was the crucial weakness in his otherwise robust security that had made this the ideal location for the attack. But if the Council ships arrived before the job was complete things would take a decided turn for the worse.

A brutal force spell slammed into Bawb's side—the injured side, no less—nearly pushing through his defensive spells as it hurled him against the far wall. He was on his feet in a flash, counterattacking with a ferocity and calm that only served to reinforce what the desperate guards already knew.

He was more than just some random attacker. He had to be. This was a Wampeh Ghalian in their midst.

The fact that the intruder had managed to make it so far into their ranks without detection was the first clue, but it was his unusual fighting style, a mixture of so many elements from so many techniques, all flowing together in a way they'd never seen before, that reinforced their belief. They hoped they were wrong. That he was just a very talented assassin and nothing more. But they fought him as if failure would be their demise. And if he truly was a Ghalian, then odds were, it would be.

Bawb's internal timekeeping told him he had to wrap this up and move forward with his plans. He launched a dagger out of nowhere, shocking the guard into whom it buried its point, seeing as his visible sheaths were long empty. But Bawb had many hidden blades on his person, and the only time one would become aware of their presence would be when it was too late.

The guards formed a hasty semi-circle, protecting their casting member, and charged ahead. The magic would protect them from most, but not all of the killer's spells and attacks.

Bawb had to give them credit. Against a lesser opponent, their tactic might have worked.

Not so today.

His konus was running ever-lower on magic, and the caster could sense it as she probed his defenses. A perilous situation on the best of days, but given the injuries he was rapidly incurring as he pushed farther into the compound, it was worse than that. By the time he had reached these elite guards, Bawb had taken out no fewer than fifteen of the emmik's people, carefully hiding their bodies so his intrusion would remain unnoted until long after he was gone.

But he was clearly hurt. Lagging, even if barely detectable. The seemingly impervious man could be hurt, and that gave the guards hope.

"All at once!" the caster called out as she unleashed a twisting force spell, hoping to upend the killer in their midst.

Bawb dodged the spell as best he could, but it did require a small expenditure from his konus. The caster smiled. She created her own magic naturally, whereas this man, like the majority of people, relied on the power stored in a konus. And that device was running dangerously low.

Bawb twisted and spun, flinging his body into the midst of the guards, blocking their attacks with his blades and body as best he could. It was an impressive display, she had to admit, but he was outnumbered and weakening. She smiled to herself as she felt the tide of battle shift. This was just a man, and he was going to lose.

Her cockiness ceased abruptly, as did her casting when an expertly thrown dagger pierced her foot, nailing it to the ground. She cried out in pain, utterly shocked by the attack. Her defensive spells had all been firmly in place, a wall of force ready to stop whatever the man threw her way, but in the heat of battle the assassin had forced her own men back closer to her, and her magic recognized them as friends, not foes, as designed.

It hadn't been an outright penetration of her defenses, but a small gap had opened where one of the guards' feet had shuffled close to her own, and it was that which the killer had taken advantage of.

Her defenses were momentarily down, but they had trained for this. The others would increase the intensity of their attack while she regained control. Or so they had planned.

Brutal elbows, fists, and knees pummeled the guards, stunning them all and driving them aside as the intruder moved past them in a flash. Before anyone knew what was happening, a cold shift in power washed over the room.

"Oh, shit," the wounded Bandooki said as it realized what was happening.

The other guards turned to look and felt an icy chill run down their spines. Where there had been hope for victory—confidence, even—there was now despair. They were as good as dead, and they knew it.

The intruder's lips were pressed to the caster's neck, his fangs having extended the moment he reached her, shocking her with his speed before she could recover her composure. He was drinking her blood, and with it, stealing her power, draining her of her magic, making it his own. She only possessed a moderate amount of power, but injured as Bawb was, he was grateful for it. He had planned on finding other strong casters to draw from far sooner than now, but that part of the plan hadn't panned out, and he had been left dangerously vulnerable.

Bawb dropped the woman's body to the ground, allowing himself the indulgence of using some of the magic he'd just stolen to heal his most pressing injuries. He stopped short, however. He needed to keep the power he had just added to the other reserves hidden within his body.

He had drained his konus far more than he wanted to, but powering it up more beforehand would have conflicted with his disguise and possibly been noticed as he snuck into the compound grounds. So he improvised. He adapted. He overcame. Just as he always had. It was what made him one of the best.

He rolled his shoulders and wiped the blood from his lips, flashing a little grin. The fear that flooded the remaining guards was as short lived as they were. Moments later, cleansed of blood and with his disguise intact, the Ghalian assassin slipped from the room, cast a sealing spell on the door, and walked calmly down the corridor, assessing his remaining injuries as he moved.

He had power inside. Hidden power. But he would need to continue to hold it in reserve. Not until he had faced and defeated his final target could he risk expending any of it on himself. There would be other casters he could drain along the way. There had to be. And with them he would build his power further. At the end of the day, he had an emmik to kill, and reaching him was going to be a long, uphill battle.

# CHAPTER TWO

Bawb's disguise was perfect. It had required a minor expenditure of magic to freshen up his appearance after his most recent fight, one of many on this task, but compared to the amount of power he had taken from the group's caster, it was a perfectly acceptable use of the stolen magic.

He had shifted his look just in case the earlier victims were found by some fluke of bad luck. It was his third time altering his appearance since he had begun the mission, and this particular disguise was the easiest of all for him to cast. He now appeared to be a Tslavar for this part of his infiltration, the deep-green skin of the brutish, combative race staying in place with a simple spell.

He had chosen the Tslavar visage for the later stages as it required the least amount of magic to maintain, seeing as they were a bipedal race whose males were roughly the same build as the Wampeh Ghalian assassin. They were also one of the favored mercenary groups among the Council of Twenty's various factions, so his presence would likely not be questioned.

Bawb passed a pair of sentries, nodding just slightly to them as he walked, not even slowing his pace. They said nothing, as he expected. He was wearing the uniform of a higher-ranking guard, and from his reconnaissance of this particular compound's staff, they followed a top-down structure which featured some particularly insecure leaders. As such, underlings were very wary of upsetting the higher-ups.

This worked to his advantage. The emmik was powerful, but not extremely so, and as a result, he made a point to keep his fingers in everything happening within the ranks of his guards. Only a few were given any sort of autonomy to carry out orders utilizing their own judgment. The lower ranks, however, were essentially pawns, doing what they were told but not really thinking for themselves at all.

For his needs, it was perfect.

Bawb picked up his pace, trying to make up time without drawing attention. The emmik would only be vulnerable a short while longer. Once the Council of Twenty's ships arrived, he would be forced to abandon this attempt and regroup for another try at a later date. But he was a Master Ghalian, and he would only allow that to happen if there was absolutely no other option.

He stepped into a small room that smelled of fermented and smoked delicacies. He looked around. Cheese and dry goods were stacked high, preserved by skillfully cast spells. Several whole beasts hung from hooks, skinned and aging slowly, their pungent rot sealed in special dry-aging containment magic. The emmik had a reputation as a bit of a food lover, and this verified that tidbit of intel.

He was pleased to see the room was a storage locker of sorts. Not for daily use items, but for delicacies. As such, it was less likely to be visited on any regular basis. That meant Bawb had a moment to check his bearings. He was close to the kitchen, as the map he had committed to memory told him. That meant the emmik's quarters were just one level above him.

They would be heavily guarded, of course, but the kitchen possessed one feature most would overlook when fortifying their defenses. A gap between the walls where construction had simply left a space due to the layout of the addition. The walls were sealed, but the vertical passage still remained, and Bawb was a very skilled climber. All he needed was to access it without being noticed. In that manner he would be able to complete his mission and kill the emmik in his chambers without any of the guards outside his doors being any the wiser.

By the time they realized what had happened, he would be long gone and off this wretched planet.

Bawb measured out the paces in his head. The wall he would need to open would be hidden behind a shelf unit, but if he cast quickly and quietly, he could lift and move it without disturbing its contents. Then, he'd pull open the wall, slip into the forgotten shaft, and close it all behind himself before anyone noticed. If, that is, no one happened to be standing in the one spot with a clear view of the area.

He stepped out into the corridor and walked with purpose, pushing past the kitchen staff in the rude manner of a Tslavar guard.

*Damn*, he thought. Someone was preparing some aged Malooki steaks on the prep table. The prep table that was, of course, the one place with an unobstructed view of the shelf he would be moving. It seemed they were preparing food manually rather than with magic. Meals made without a trace of power. It was something the wealthy often enjoyed, though it was rather time-consuming. It was also how a great many regular citizens dined on a regular basis, but no one would point that out to the elite who took such joy in the novelty.

Bawb paused, surveying the ingredients on the table. He needed this person to leave, and that left very few options. He weighed the choices and made a snap decision.

"You aren't actually going to apply arranis powder to that before treating it with a fagarramin rub, are you?" he asked the young prep chef as he stepped closer.

"What do you mean?" the man replied, a little surprised that a guard would be so brazen as to make culinary suggestions. "Arranis is the seasoning of choice for aged Malooki. You should stick to guarding things and leave the cooking to the professionals."

"Professionals who forget that *aged* Malooki releases a toxin. One that is nullified only by fagarramin," the assassin replied. "That is, unless that is not *really* an aged Malooki steak. But if it is, I would hate to see you accidentally poison our employer. I do not think that would go over very well."

The prep chef blanched, realizing his error, scrambling to cover himself. "I already rubbed it with fagarramin," he lied. Anyone with a decent sense of smell could tell he had not.

"Oh, then it was my mistake," Bawb replied.

"Clearly. But I think I will give it a second rub, just to enhance the flavor," the chef said.

Bawb nodded but said nothing. He had given the chef an easy out, one that would not humiliate him. It would also buy him enough time to enter the shaft unnoticed, and as soon as the chef stepped away, the Ghalian master did just that, quick stepping across the kitchen, casting his lifting spell as he did. He then carefully pulled the wall apart, making sure to keep the section intact before slipping into the hidden passage and carefully sealing it behind him, the last strand of magic pulling the shelf back into place.

*Not exactly what I had planned,* he mused, then turned his attentions upward and began climbing the forgotten space.

It had been a while since Bawb had used his culinary knowledge for anything beyond whipping up a meal for himself.

But as a Ghalian master, he was versed in myriad skills that might seem benign to those not in his profession.

An assassin, however, would need to blend in, and sometimes that might mean infiltrating a location masquerading as staff, including the kitchen team. And as a result, all Ghalian learned a great deal about cooking, though Bawb had excelled more than his comrades. As he had in most things.

He could not use that disguise here, though. The kitchen staff was small, established, and close-knit. A new face would be noticed straightaway. A guard passing through, on the other hand, was just some annoying minion interrupting their flow, coming and going without drawing much attention. At least, that was the plan. The encounter with the prep chef was unfortunate, but it had been brief enough that it should ideally slip their mind in no time.

The shaft was a bit wider than he had expected, and it required a bit of a stretch to properly brace himself as he climbed. It slowed his progress, but only a slight delay. He would be in the emmik's chambers in no time, killing the man and departing long before the Council ever arrived.

Bawb froze in place as the faintest of sensations tickled his cheek from above. With the utmost care, he lowered himself back down a few inches and turned his head, cautiously studying the seemingly empty space above.

There it was, barely visible to the eye and nearly undetectable. It wasn't a web, as one of lesser skills might have thought. It was a fine length of filament running across the shaft.

*Clever*, he noted with an appreciative grin. Whoever had laid this trap had done so during the remodel. They had considered the slim possibility that someone might discover the shaft and had taken precautions. They'd clearly been a master at practical boobytraps. There wasn't a hint of magic on it. Of course, given how long ago the shaft had been abandoned, it made sense. Only the most powerful of spells would have been able to remain intact for so long without a refresher.

Rather than disarm the masterful tripwire, he cast a minor blocking spell to hold it in place, then shifted his position and moved past it, careful not to disturb the triggering mechanism. He had never encountered such an obstacle under circumstances like these. Bawb looked at the konus on his wrist and called up the secret display spell that none but he could see.

A long checklist of spells, skills, and other miscellany stretched out in front of him, only visible to the one wearing the unusual device. Every single item was maxed out. All but one.

*Still no?* he wondered.

The konus, its voice speaking inside his head, and quite chatty in the early years he had owned it, remained silent.

Bawb sighed. *Well, then. That wasn't it, I suppose.*

He was at the pinnacle of his craft, but one final thing was lacking. One gently flashing blank spot in the list. It really didn't matter, one more item checked off would not change who he was, but there was something about completion that nagged at him. After so many long years of training, struggling to become what he was today, it really would be nice to finally have that one last thing resolved.

But this was not the time.

Without so much as a sigh, he shifted his attention back to the exit looming above him. Bawb reached out with his senses, listening intently. His ears were sharper than most, and he heard the sounds of a lone person in the chambers. The emmik, it seemed, was all alone.

The killer cast a muting spell then created a hole in the wall. He then slid out of the shaft without a sound, crossing the room in a flash. His enchanted dagger appeared in his hand, deftly drawn from its hidden sheath, ready for action if the element of surprise failed him.

Bawb leapt out and grabbed them, his fangs in place, ready to drain them dry, but he stopped himself short, spinning the person and holding them at arm's length.

This was decidedly *not* his target. He cast a muting spell on the room immediately before the startled woman in the androgynous robes could cry out.

"Where is the emmik?" he asked, staring hard into her eyes.

"H-he is not here," she managed to say.

"I can see that. Explain," he demanded, hoping she would not require him to employ any of his more intense interrogation skills. There simply wasn't enough time for it. That, and she was a non-combatant.

Fortunately, the poor woman was so terrified at the sight of the dagger in his hand that she briefly lost control of her bladder, judging by the smell. Extracting information would not require any unsavory tactics.

"He left a little while ago," she blurted. "To the marketplace."

"Why is he at the marketplace? That is not his routine."

"He wanted to bring something special to his meeting today. It is a big day for him. The Council of Twenty is coming. They invited him to join them at the Council retreat."

This was bad. Worse than bad. All prior intel had pointed to them visiting the emmik at his own compound. The Council's estate could still be breached—anywhere could, given long enough—but Bawb simply did not have the time to begin from scratch. Once the emmik's fallen guards were discovered, security would be massively fortified, and things would get much, much more difficult.

"How long?" he asked. "How long until he returns?"

"He is going straight there," she replied. "I was told to prepare his chambers for when he returns tomorrow."

There it was. Confirmation. Confirmation that all the blood spilled, all of the pain and effort to get this far had been for naught. Bawb chuckled, though it was decidedly *not* a happy sound. But even he could appreciate the trick fate had played on him. Had he just waited out in the marketplace, this could have all been accomplished so much easier. If only he had known.

It was there he would now have to go.

"Please, don't kill me," the woman blubbered, tears streaking her face.

Bawb sheathed his blade. "You are an innocent," he replied. "You will be unharmed. *Boto pa.*" The spell dropped her to the ground, unconscious. She would remain that way until the following morning.

"But, since I cannot have you warning anyone," he said quietly, gently sliding her slumbering form under the bed. "Sleep well."

He then turned and headed back to the unused shaft, descending to the kitchen in a flash, changing his disguise to that of a young message courier as he climbed.

He looked around. The prep chef had returned but seemed very occupied with ensuring he did not accidentally poison his patron. Bawb slipped out and exited the kitchen without a sound.

Messengers were the lowest of the low. Unskilled labor. As such, they were ignored by all. No one said so much as a single word to him the entire walk to the exit. He stepped out of the compound and turned for the marketplace.

He preferred doing his work in private, but if it had to be done this way, so be it. What was paramount was that the emmik died today. And a public display by a Ghalian would certainly garner some attention of others who might be considering pushing back against the Council of Twenty in this region.

Once the Council arrived, even his shimmer-cloaked ship

might not evade notice if a powerful enough visla was present. The clock was ticking, and loudly at that.

Bawb ducked into a doorway and shed his disguise in a flash, reverting to his normal Wampeh visage. It wouldn't draw attention, as only a tiny fraction of a fraction of his race possessed the natural gift needed to become Ghalian assassins. Most were just people, living their lives. And no one in the compound had seen a Wampeh killer in their midst. At least, not anyone who was still alive.

Saving up his magic, Bawb stepped back out into the throng of people and began his walk to the marketplace. This was about to get ugly, and unpleasantly so at that. It was enough to make him pause and reflect back on how exactly he had wound up a master assassin in the first place.

# CHAPTER THREE

It all started in the most mundane and cliché of places. An orphanage.

The boy was built a bit smaller than the other children in the group home. He was relatively tall, but lanky and lean, his pale Wampeh body not yet filling out into that of the deadly man he would one day become.

He wasn't bullied, but he wasn't offered any special treatment. In this place, he simply existed, just another orphan in the system, albeit one with an anonymous personal endowment helping fund the facility. *That* worked to his benefit in ways he never realized, and as a result, he had been raised in far better conditions than many in similar circumstances would have faced.

Young Bawb was just ten years old when his life changed forever. Up until then, every one of those years had passed on the same quiet little world, either within the orphanage's walls or playing in the hills nearby. He always enjoyed those group outings immensely, reveling in the invigorating glory of the region's lush nature.

Bawb discovered early on that he had a way with animals.

They just seemed to trust him, venturing closer to him than with the other children. Perhaps it was his gentle nature and kind heart, or perhaps it was simply that he was the least threatening of the throngs of energetic youths unleashed into the wild for a few wonderful hours at a time.

Whatever the case, he was comfortable in this life, which was a good thing, because it was here he would remain.

He had realized early on that he was not likely to be adopted. In fact, when one couple seemed to take note of him, he had watched from afar as they spoke at length with the facility's corpulent overseer, the pair of would-be parents glancing his way with warm grins. Soon, however, those smiles wore thin until the couple ceased looking at all, shaking their heads slightly as they were led to meet with some of the other available children.

"It is just the way of things, Bawb," the rotund man had said at the time. "Those unable to conceive are very particular in what they want, and I am afraid you do not fit those criteria."

Bawb, understandably, was hurt by his words, the cold dagger of rejection twisting in his chest, making his eyes well up with tears.

"Do not let it get you down, lad. You are well looked after here and will never be wanting. And one day, when you are of age, you will head out on your own to make a life for yourself."

"But I don't know what I'll be able to do," the boy replied, tears welling in his eyes. "I'm not the biggest, nor the strongest or smartest."

"You are exceptionally clever, Bawb," the man corrected. "Do not let anyone tell you otherwise. But come, let us get you something sweet from the kitchen. I am sure that will help soothe your ails."

With that, he led Bawb down the long corridor to the kitchen workspace. Normally, the children were only allowed in the food preparation area when actively assisting the matrons prepare the house meals, and as such, the kitchen was eerily quiet. Bawb actually enjoyed it like this, for it afforded him the opportunity to take in the decades of layered smells baked into the walls without the distraction of a bustling crew.

Spice lingered near the ovens, sweet and smoky, ingredients having cooked and mixed and wafted up to the removal spell for years on end. The facility was well funded, and while they still prepared their meals manually, magic was used for some of the more labor-intensive aspects of the process.

Smoke and steam, for example, were captured by a constantly refreshed set of overlapping spells hovering above the cookspaces. There was no risk to anyone, though. The magic employed was not remotely powerful enough to affect a living being, though insects were known to get caught up from time to time. The spell would simply displace the clouds produced by the cooking food, transporting them via a magical link to an exhaust area several hundred meters outside the orphanage walls.

Whenever they would walk that direction on a daytime outing, the children would catch a whiff of whatever was being prepared for the evening's meal. It was a spell Bawb had found most fascinating. The idea of a spell moving something, even an item as benign as smoke or steam, and having it reappear a distance away was simply one of the coolest things he'd ever encountered.

Magic was something of a rarity at the orphanage, and none of the other children possessed any of their own that he knew of. If they did, they'd have almost certainly been adopted long ago. Natural magic users were a rarity, and as such, in high demand.

As for the staff, they utilized konuses, the slender golden bands worn around their wrists containing enough stored magic to power the spells needed to keep the facility running smoothly. The devices were incredibly commonplace throughout the galaxy, but to the orphans, the magic-storing wristlets were a marvel.

Had Bawb been on another world, he would have realized that magic was so ubiquitous that it was more unusual for someone to be totally without it in one form or another than to possess it. Illumination, fire-starting, transit upon floating conveyances via spellcasting, all were simply a part of daily life.

But here, in his quiet little bubble, Bawb had not been exposed to a great deal of magic, and as a result, any talk of its use was something he took great interest in.

It was late one evening as the sun hung low in the sky when a small ship of a design he had never seen before passed overhead then looped back before settling to the ground outside the compound. Bawb ran to the window with the other children to get a better look.

Like the others, he was always fascinated with ships but had never been aboard one. He did know of the powerful Drooks whose magic made them fly, however. A special race whose magic was specifically geared toward running spacecraft. Ships were normally crewed by anywhere from a small handful to several dozen Drooks, depending on their size, with the enslaved magic users working in shifts to drive the craft.

It was a life of servitude, but Drooks were looked at as something of a privileged class of slave. Yes, they were technically someone's property and were forced to work, but what they did was so unique and vital that they were treated with the utmost respect and afforded comfortable quarters and quality food and drink.

What's more, Drooks *enjoyed* using their power, and flexing that magical muscle to drive a spacefaring vessel was the pinnacle of their craft. One that, while technically work, was also a source of pleasure, making the Drooks almost a sort of symbiotic organism inhabiting their respective ships.

This new craft was small, but to Bawb it seemed as though it bristled with an invisible layer of power that was almost tangible. None of the others appeared to notice that aspect, but all were impressed with the sleek design.

Two people exited the ship and walked to the waiting facility overseer. The man was a bit older, his skin a deep gray and his hair ochre-red. He had broad shoulders, though he seemed a bit on the pudgy side. Not threatening in the least despite his apparent size.

The woman was younger and wore her hair pulled in a tight braid. Perhaps his daughter? Bawb wondered. It was not unheard of for a more romantic sort of relationship between disparate aged individuals, but the ten-year-old was as of yet unaware of that sort of thing and never considered the possibility for even a moment. In any case, the overseer seemed to jump to attention a bit as he read over the documents the man handed him.

That was something new. Bawb had never seen him act like that before. Whatever was in those words, it must have been something interesting. Unfortunately, while he and his companions were educated and could read and write, they lacked translation spells that would help them with foreign tongues, and the odds of the stranger having written in their backworld language was slim to none.

The overseer gestured for the visitors to follow him to the compound, and as they drew closer, Bawb could see the scaled ridges running down the arms of the pair from their necks to their wrists. He'd never seen this race before, and while they were bipedal and similar to many of the species he'd seen come and go from the orphanage, they were nevertheless a novelty.

The children all hurried back to the main gathering hall to see what news the visitors might bring.

"I bet they've come for one of the babies," an older boy named Otzik said, his eyes swiveling this way and that on their stalks. "They always want babies."

"Nah, look at them," Mirahn said, playing with her long green hair. "They don't look like they want to be changing diapers. They've clearly come for a well-mannered child."

"Like you?"

"Of course," she said, utterly free of guile.

The overseer stopped with his guests and looked across the gathered, curious faces of the orphans. He shocked them all when his gaze stopped on one boy in particular. One who was never going to be adopted.

"Bawb," he said. "Go to my office."

Bawb swallowed hard and did as he was told. He'd been sent to meet people before, but never in the overseer's office. Something different was afoot. What that could be, however, he had no idea.

He had been waiting quietly a few minutes when the newcomers followed their host into the room. They looked at Bawb as if he was just so much meat, none of the fawning and cooing normally found with prospective parents.

"This is him?" the man asked, his voice a deep, gravelly baritone.

"Yes. We have two Wampeh in our house, but this is the boy. Bawb is his name."

The man nodded and walked closer. "Boy, stand up."

Bawb did as he was told. Calloused hands grabbed his arms, assessing his musculature. Bawb couldn't help but shy away. The man and woman shared a look.

"He is a timid one. See the softness in his eyes?" she noted.

"Yes," the man agreed, grabbing Bawb's chin and turning his

head this way and that as if he was inspecting an animal for slaughter, not a child for adoption. "But he does possess the gift. Can you feel it?"

She squinted as if searching for a faint aroma in a bustling restaurant. "Yes, I believe so," she finally said. "Muted. Repressed. But it is there. It could be strong enough."

"Agreed. We may yet forge him into something more," the man said, then turned to the overseer. "As stipulated," he said, digging into his deep pocket and withdrawing a heavy bag of coin. "You know the penalty if you speak of this."

The overseer paled, but the coloring returned as he hefted the payment in his palm and nodded his affirmation. "Yes, of course."

"Good. Then we are done here. Boy, come along."

Bawb was beside himself, both with joy as well as fearful confusion. Someone had actually chosen him. It was a miracle. But for some reason, he didn't feel nearly as excited as he thought he would.

"I just need to get my things," he said, moving toward the door.

"You will not need them where you are going," the woman interjected.

Bawb felt a flutter of fear in his belly. "Wh-where are we going?"

A slight smile curved her lips, and it was not a comforting sight. "You will see soon enough."

# CHAPTER FOUR

With no more than the clothing draped over his lean frame, Bawb followed the man and woman to their ship. It was even more impressive up close, its lines flowing together in an elegant display of impressive designwork. Clearly, these people possessed wealth. What they wanted with him, rather than any of the other children, however, was a mystery.

"This way," the man said, ushering him into the craft's entryway.

Bawb hesitated. There would be no excited gossip about the amazing ship he had just seen up close and personal. In fact, he would quite possibly never see this place again, nor the handful of what he might consider friends he had made over his ten years there.

"He hesitates, Arvin," the woman scoffed. "My doubts about this one are growing."

*Arvin*. That was the man's name. Somehow, knowing that little tidbit of information made the situation feel less ominous. It was silly, of course, Bawb realized that. Nevertheless, he felt the knot in his stomach lessen, if only slightly.

"He possesses the gift, Soranna, and we have our task to perform."

"I realize that, naturally. But one must wonder if perhaps it would not be wiser to leave him to grow up in a normal life."

"We have our—"

"Yes, yes, we have a mission to complete. I hope it proves worth the expenditure."

Arvin glanced down at the boy, appraising his worth. "We shall see. Now, come, boy. We must be on our way."

He strode into the warm light of the ship without another word. Soranna stood by and waited for Bawb to follow.

"You heard him," she said. "Quickly. Do not make us wait."

Bawb forced down his uncertainty and stepped up into the hovering craft. It was the first time he had ever set foot aboard a spaceship, and the excitement of the moment quickly overcame his reticence.

The interior was bright and clean, the illumination emanating from the walls with an intensity he found just right for his eyes. Whoever had cast that spell had clearly been an expert. In fact, every single detail seemed just right to his inexperienced gaze.

The entryway closed, sealing with a simple spell.

"Come along. This way," the woman said.

Bawb fell in behind her, a pale shadow of a boy following in her footsteps. She led him through a pair of corridors heading forward in the ship. Arvin was in a seat in the command module, Bawb noted as they passed. At least, he was almost certain that was the chamber's purpose. He had read enough about space travel to know the basic designs of a fair number of ships, as was common with boys his age. But to see one in person? It was a thrill unlike any he'd ever experienced.

"Where are the Drooks?" he quietly asked. "Is their

compartment located in another part of the ship? I read that they are usually near the command center."

Soranna cast an amused look at him. "We do not have Drooks aboard this ship," she replied.

Bawb's eyes widened as he realized what that meant. "You have a *Drookonus*?" he marveled.

It was a device used by the wealthy to power some of their craft. Akin to a konus, it stored magic, but a Drookonus held Drook magic specifically, channeling it into a craft through powerful spells and carrying the vessel from planet to planet.

"I've never met anyone who had a Drookonus before," the boy said in awe.

The corners of Soranna's lips curved ever so slightly upward. "*Two*, actually, but the second is for emergency use only. You have an understanding of the device. Impressive, for an orphan."

"I read a lot. I mean, I've heard of them, but I've never actually seen one. Never been on a ship, for that matter."

"And yet you know what makes them fly."

"It's amazing. So much magic in such a small device. The amount of Drook power they hold is worth more than most normal people earn in a lifetime."

"You would be surprised, young one. Not all things are purchased with coin, and the trade of favors offers very attractive benefits, in the right circumstances. And Arvin and I? Let us just say we are not what one would call *normal* people. Now, come. It will be a few days' journey, and we have one additional stop to make. This chamber up ahead is to be your room for the flight."

Bawb felt a strange twinge in his chest, and his eyes threatened to grow damp as unexpected emotion flooded through him. Soranna looked at him with a curious gaze. He seemed overwhelmed.

"*My* chamber?"

"Yes. Is that a problem, young one?"

"No problem. It is just... I-I have never had a sleeping chamber to myself before. There have always been so many around me."

"And you are afraid?" she asked, her eyebrow cocked in judgment.

"No, not afraid," he replied, a weight lifted off his shoulders that he hadn't known he'd been carrying. "It is a luxury I never even thought to dream of. Solitude. Tranquility. Silence."

Soranna's brow relaxed, her sharp disapproval melting away, replaced by understanding and a hint of approval. "Well, do not become accustomed to such luxuries, young Bawb. This will be short-lived."

"I understand," he said, stepping into the blissful serenity of his own room.

"I will fetch you when it is time to eat," Soranna said. "For now, rest. You will need it."

Bawb found he couldn't drift off as he reclined on his very own personal bed in his very own private compartment. It was a strange feeling, being in a silent room. Something he'd long dreamt of but had never imagined he would be so fortunate as to experience, especially at so young an age.

But the reality was far different than he'd expected. The silence was too loud, if that made sense, the endless chatter deafening in its absence. Try as he might, Bawb could not fully relax. So, he turned his mind to other things. Namely, wondering what exactly his situation might be.

The strange couple didn't seem terribly parental in their demeanor. It was far more transactional than affectionate. And there had been a strange tension to the interaction with the overseer. Yes, coin had been exchanged, but despite his payment, the man had seemed ill at ease with Arvin and Soranna. For the life of him, Bawb could not imagine why.

They were wealthy, and they seemed kind enough, if a bit brusque.

A quiet chime pulled him from his thoughts. Bawb hadn't realized it but, while he had not drifted to sleep, he had fallen into a sort of meditative state as he contemplated his current situation. He'd been awake and alert to what was around him, but his mind had been churning with myriad thoughts.

"We are setting down on Moralia," Soranna informed him as the door slid open. "We will be gathering a package, which is of no concern to you. But as you have never been to another world, Arvin and I felt you would perhaps learn from the experience."

Bawb felt a surge of adrenaline flush through his veins. "Another world?" he murmured. "When do we go?"

Soranna smiled at his newfound enthusiasm. The timid boy was coming out of his shell, at least a little bit. The vibrations barely noticeable in the ship shifted slightly. They had settled into a low hover at the landing site.

"We go now."

She led him down the corridor to the open hatch. Arvin was already waiting outside. Forcing himself to show no hesitation, Bawb stepped out onto the deep-umber soil. The first alien world he had ever set foot on. He felt his emotions flare in his chest as he looked up.

The sky was so different from what he had grown up with. Red, with high, streaked-yellow clouds, the powerful winds at that altitude scattering them to the horizon. But as much as the environment itself took the youth aback, it was the variety of alien life the likes of which he had never seen that truly took his breath away.

They had landed in a cordoned off zone just beside a rustic marketplace, the tents and stands teeming with activity. In the distance, a modern city rose into the sky, the clean lines of the architectural style of this world contrasting sharply with the far less elegant feel of the surrounding low-rise structures. It was all fascinating and unlike anything Bawb had ever seen, and he loved it.

A tall, blue-skinned man—at least, he thought it was a man—moved past them on undulating tentacles rather than legs. He had sturdy arms and a broad chest and back, but his lower extremities were unlike any Bawb had ever seen before.

"An Ubaloo," Soranna said, noting his gaze. "Large, intimidating looking, but they have several weaknesses. Where the tentacles meet the body, the bottom side possesses thinner skin and is susceptible to attack. Below the arms, between the eighth and ninth rib, a vulnerable nerve plexus can be reached. And they are prone to momentary loss of sight when their noses are broken."

Bawb looked at her with confusion. "Why do you know all of these things?"

"Soon, young one. For now, take in the sights, but stay close. The city proper is safe, but the streets in this area are far rougher, especially for one such as yourself. Do not leave our sides. Is that clear?"

He nodded his understanding, even as he wondered what exactly his life had just become.

# CHAPTER FIVE

Walking through the marketplace was an experience the likes of which the young Wampeh had never imagined. The colorful fabrics, the dazzling array of goods he could only begin to guess the use for, and, of course, the smells. Oh, the wonderful smells of spices and cooking foods.

Of course, there were also *other* aromas wafting through the air that were less than pleasant, but those seemed constrained to the animal pens and butcher stalls. There was a fascinating collection of beasts of all shapes and sizes in that part of the dizzying maze of bustling commerce. Creatures of burden as well as livestock destined for processing as well as prepared meats. It was enough to make Bawb's senses nearly overload.

Arvin roughly yanked him by the arm, pulling him off his feet for an instant. Bawb looked up at the man, then down at the pile of steaming animal dung he had just avoided.

"Watch your step. We do not wish to soil our ship," Arvin said quietly.

Arvin's gaze had not shifted at all, his eyes casually looking ahead without interruption, scanning the crowd with a nonchalance that seemed as though he hadn't a care in the world.

But somehow, the deep-gray-skinned man had not only seen the obstacle, but had also been aware of the boy's location in relation to it, steering him clear without a glance. Bawb was impressed. Impressed and a little confused. What sort of person could do that? Clearly, there was more to these two than he initially thought.

Bawb had learned this particular lesson, and he made sure to watch where he stepped from that point on. He was still amazed by their novel surroundings, but he also now knew better than to be foolish enough to track filth into his new parents' ship.

*Parents.*

It was something he was just beginning to feel comfortable wrapping his head around. He had been an orphan for his entire life, but now, amazingly, he had somehow become part of a family. A somewhat odd family, no doubt, and one he would take a little time to get used to, but a family all the same.

For the first time in his life, Bawb felt like he might have a chance for a normal life, and the thought gave him an unfamiliar warm feeling in his chest. Arvin and Soranna had not asked him to call them father and mother, but he supposed that was only natural in the first stages of this sort of thing, though he was only speculating. However they wished to be addressed, he would do so happily.

They walked for a half hour, gradually making their way from the dusty, colorful marketplace into the cleaner, quieter, and more modern neighborhood at its outskirts. The city center with its towering edifices was still a fair distance away, but that didn't matter. Everything was novel to young Bawb, and he was enjoying every second of it.

The attire of the people in this part of town was different

from what they had seen previously in the marketplace. Cleaner. Crisp. Lines that fit their widely varying shapes perfectly and spoke to their elevated class status. It seemed the market was for commoners and laborers, not the upper crust. Here, however, the locals were above that sort of thing.

Floating conveyances ferried people along the open avenues, the magic powering them imperceptible as they glided silently past. Bawb was amazed. He'd never seen such a vast display of magic before. It was *everywhere.* The orphanage had employed only the most basic of spells, but here? This was a whole new world of possibilities.

His eyes darted every which way as they walked, making sure not to step in anything, of course, though the odds of coming across something fouling the walkway in this part of town seemed highly unlikely.

They soon stopped in front of a tall building that looked like a giant ring of glass towering into the sky. Bawb craned his neck and marveled at its height. This structure was taller than any building he had ever seen, its exterior clear and seamless. He peered through the glass and marveled at the magic-powered lift hurtling people up into its upper reaches.

"Wait here with Soranna," Arvin instructed him when they drew close to the solid sheet of glass.

It was even more impressive up close. Bawb had seen plenty of glass in his life, but never something so massive as this. The magic required to fabricate it, not to mention the sheer skill, was mindboggling. A great many structures used magic to seal themselves from the elements, allowing living objects the size of a person to enter but blocking anything else, such as dust or insects. It was a rather elegant way to keep the interior clean and climate controlled while allowing for a gentle breeze, but minus the dirty bits.

This, however, was something else. Bawb watched Arvin step

*into* the glass, the solid turning to liquid as he moved, flowing around his body without actually touching him.

"Whoa," the boy gasped.

"A simple entry spell," Soranna noted.

"I've never seen anything like it. They never taught us any spells."

Soranna nodded slightly. "It is unfortunate, but if you work hard, you will catch up."

"Catch up? I don't understand."

"Soon you will. Now, tell me, how many have passed our location since we stopped here?"

"I don't know. Ten?"

"Thirteen. And what were they wearing?"

"Clothes? I don't know."

"Then pay attention. Note details. *Everything* can be of significance."

"Sort of like a game?"

"Yes, like a game," she said with a little grin.

Bawb spent the next ten minutes doing his best to note the details of anyone who passed. Soranna would then quiz him a few minutes later, pointing out what he missed.

"But she had a red cloak," Bawb said when she corrected his recollection of a slender woman with multi-colored hair and the most angular features he'd ever seen.

"It was a loose coat, not a cloak," she said.

The glass wall rippled as Arvin stepped through, a small package held under his arm. "Debating the difference in clothing styles?" he asked.

"Teaching the boy the value in noting detail."

"Hm," he grunted, looking at their young companion. "The task is complete. We are on our way. Come, Bawb. We will procure food then depart."

Bawb hadn't realized his belly was rumbling, but now that

the thought of food had been put in his mind, he couldn't stop thinking about it. Arvin led the way, weaving down streets and alleyways until they reached the outskirts of the marketplace. He turned to the boy.

"Remember, while there are fancy dining establishments within the city proper, you will find far more interesting and affordable sustenance where the common folk dwell. There is a small tavern up ahead I have frequented in the past. There you will see of what I speak."

Bawb followed him on his winding path until they reached a dark and grimy façade. "*This* is it? But it looks abandoned."

A slight grin creased Arvin's lips. "You shall see."

He pushed open the door, and a tidal wave of smells and sounds washed over them. Spices and cooking meats. The tangy aroma of ale and sweat. This was a den of iniquity if ever there was one, and his new parents strode in as though they belonged. Bawb stuck close by and sat on a cushioned bench between them.

"Traveler's lunch for three," Soranna said to the passing wait staff, who acknowledged her order with the slightest of grunts and a nod.

"What's a traveler's lunch?"

"Ample sustenance for a long voyage," she replied. "Different from what you are accustomed to, no doubt, but I am confident you will enjoy it. Variants exist on every world."

Any concerns Bawb may have had vanished the moment the first fragrant plate was set down in front of him. A stew of some sort, and it smelled incredible. He took a bite, digging in with increasing gusto after the initial taste test. Arvin and Soranna shared an amused look and tucked into their meals.

Several more items were brought to the table, and the boy polished off each one of them until nothing but empty plates sat before him.

"I see you enjoyed it," Arvin said.

"It was amazing."

"Good. I am pleased to hear that. It will be some time before you will have a meal like this again."

Later, reflecting back on the moment, Bawb realized the true meaning of the man's words. But for the moment, he blissfully accepted them as a simple statement that there would be no need for a traveler's lunch as they would not be traveling much longer. About that, at least, he was correct.

The trio stepped out into the late afternoon air and began their trek back to their ship, following the winding alleyways of the neighborhood in the most direct path they could manage. Bawb was still minding his footing, but with a happily full belly and an overall sense of well-being, he was oblivious to other elements of their surroundings.

Five enormous thugs stepped out from a pair of doorways and blocked their paths, another two appearing behind the group. Seven bandits, and heavily armed ones at that. The biggest of them was of a race Bawb had never seen before. Broad shoulders and orange-red scales that shifted to a darker shade across the top of his elongated, flat-topped head.

Three of the others were Tslavars, long-limbed and tall, like dark elves, their deep green skin bulging with coiled muscle. Two of the remaining three had elongated arms with massive fists and red-brown hair running thick across their bodies. They walked in a slightly hunched manner, their upper body mass pulling them lower toward the ground.

The last of their little group was a yellow-green-skinned man with large eyes and fine teeth in his gaping maw. He appeared to have some sort of mucus oozing from his pores, almost like a fish or amphibian. He was also sporting a belt laden with a variety of sharp, dangerous-looking implements.

Arvin and Soranna stepped in front of and behind Bawb, respectively, blocking him with their bodies.

"Your coin, traveler," the largest of the group demanded.

"Of course," Arvin replied, tossing a small bag to the man. "We do not wish for any trouble."

The beast of a man opened the pouch and counted the coin. "That all you've got?"

"I assure you, we have no more," Arvin said. "Now, please, you have what you want. We would be on our way."

The thug stood still, blocking the way and his gaze fell to the package under Arvin's arm. "What's that?"

"It is of no value to you. Merely an item I have been tasked with delivering to an associate."

"Give it here."

Arvin tensed ever so slightly. "I am sorry, but I cannot do that."

The mugger laughed and looked at his comrades. "You hear that? He's sorry, but he can't."

They let out a hearty laugh, not a one of them stepping aside. Their leader leaned closer in the most menacing way possible.

"I think I'll be having that," he said, reaching out for the parcel.

Arvin pivoted aside, slapping the man's hand away so fast Bawb didn't even see his arm move. The robbers bristled and drew their weapons, but Arvin and Soranna remained perfectly calm, even in the face of such odds.

"Please, we do not wish for any further conflict," Arvin said. "You have our coin. That is a victory for you, so please, take your prize and let us be on our way."

The leader was having none of that.

"You *dare* lay your hand on me?" he bellowed. "You will regret your foolishness!"

Arvin sighed, his head shaking ever so slightly. "No," he said. "It is you who will."

Bawb played the whole thing back over and over in his mind later, but he still couldn't pin down exactly when Arvin and Soranna had flown into action. They moved impossibly fast, and in just a few seconds, six of the attackers lay motionless on the pavement.

Two were staring up sightlessly at the sky, their own weapons embedded in their bodies. The other four had limbs now bent at angles they were not intended to but still drew breath. The leader, amazingly, was the last standing.

"What are you?" he blubbered, waving his dagger wildly in front of him.

It was then that Bawb saw something amazing. Something he'd never known was possible. Arvin's skin and hair changed color in an instant, his build lessening slightly as well. He was no longer a foreign coloring. He was of the same pale skin as Bawb. He glanced at the boy and smiled, two pointed fangs sliding into place as he did. He turned back to his attacker, locking eyes with him, beaming wide and bright.

"Ghalian!" the man stammered as his bladder released its contents in a massive purge. "Please! Please, have mercy!"

Arvin stepped closer and slowly pulled his bag of coin from the man's pocket, his eyes locked with the helpless, massive man's the entire time.

"You had the opportunity to leave with profit," he said. "Yet you pushed your luck, overconfident in your numbers."

"I'm sorry! I'm so sorry!"

Arvin nodded once, then struck the man fast and hard on the side of his head. The man dropped like a sack of rocks.

Soranna had been watching Bawb during the encounter rather than her partner. "He did not flee," she said. "Nor did he flinch."

"But he did, a little. And he peed himself," Bawb blurted.

"Not *him*," she clarified. "*You*."

Arvin's appearance shifted back to the gray-skinned look Bawb was familiar with. "Perhaps there is something to him yet."

Bawb looked at the aftermath of the fight—if you could call it a fight—in awe. "How did you do that?"

"Someday, if you train your body and mind, you will also be capable of this," Arvin replied. "Perhaps, even more. Time will tell."

"Really?"

"Yes. If you survive."

"Survive? Survive what?"

"Patience, young one. As I have told you, you shall learn soon enough."

# CHAPTER SIX

Bawb was happy to find the remainder of the trip uneventful, but the events on Moralia, and what he had seen Arvin do, what he had seen him *become*, was in the forefront of his mind as he tried to rest in the wonderful quiet of his own room.

His thoughts raced. Somehow, Arvin had changed his appearance as easily as breathing. And the men who attacked them? He and Soranna had handled them without breaking a sweat. It was all over so fast. So smooth. Bawb had never seen *anyone* move like that. They were not the sort to be trifled with, yet they didn't carry themselves with any outward signs of the skills they possessed.

A comfort began to fill a void he hadn't thought about consciously in years. Ease of being, without fear. That Arvin and Soranna were now his new guardians made him feel truly safe and secure on a visceral level for the first time in longer than he could remember. And with that came rest, comfortable in his own quarters.

The trip was fairly long, and they flew to another solar system far from where he had grown up, making their way to one of the worlds more closely orbiting its sun. Cities large and small dotted the surface, but it was one of the smaller locales Soranna guided their ship toward.

They set down in a large open landing field, the sprawl of the city disappearing from view as they dropped below the buildings. The place was unlike any Bawb had ever seen. Most of the structures were relatively low compared to their last stop, perhaps five to ten levels above ground. Only a few stood much taller.

Several open-air markets sported colorful canopied stalls where farmers and vendors sold their wares to the bustling crowd, but without the lingering menace he had felt on the other world. The city's populace milling about was incredibly varied, with so many races of alien life that young Bawb had never known existed, let alone the wildly unusual physiologies that he had never thought to consider possible.

Some walked on legs, be it two, four, or even more. Others undulated along on sturdy tentacles, while still others floated on magic-powered conveyances that took them from place to place.

It was incredible. Overwhelming, truth be told. And if not for the pair guiding him through the city, Bawb would certainly have stumbled right into either a building or a person, so stunning were the new sights, sounds, and smells.

Cuisine he'd never heard of cooked in the many vendor stalls and taverns they passed, the intoxicating aromas of sweet, spicy, savory, and sour foods making his mouth water, though he had no idea what he was smelling. This place was a paradise, he thought, and one he was thrilled to learn he would be calling home.

"This way," Soranna urged, her firm grip guiding the youth through the throngs.

They walked for a good twenty minutes before reaching a block of connected buildings ranging from single to triple story. Arvin walked to a small door on one of the far buildings.

"Come along. We do not want to keep the others waiting."

Bawb hesitated. "Others?"

"You will see."

With that, Arvin disappeared inside. Bawb looked up at Soranna, unsure.

"Go on," she urged.

He took heed and pressed onward, walking into the building, ready to begin his new life.

Or so he thought.

The door closed behind him, leaving the trio in a sizable entry chamber. There were doorways and corridors leading off in multiple directions, but Arvin walked to an empty section of wall.

"*Impastus norata,*" he said quietly.

The door to the outside locked tight, and the wall seemed to shudder then suddenly disappear, revealing another doorway. He walked in without hesitation, Soranna pushing Bawb ahead of her, following him inside. Bawb turned to look back just as the wall sealed behind them. This was *not* what he had been expecting of his new home. Not one bit.

It was only going to get stranger.

They walked to a small room and stopped there. A large man, a Wampeh like he was, appeared out of nowhere. "This is the one?" he asked, looking down at the boy.

Arvin nodded. "He is."

The man stared at Bawb, sizing him up with a disconcerting lack of expression. Finally, he spoke.

"Strip."

Bawb felt a surge of adrenaline flood his body. "Strip?"

"The instruction was quite clear."

Bawb searched desperately for any sign this might be a joke. For a hint that they were all just playing a prank on him. The expressionless faces told him quite clearly he would have no such luck. Reluctantly, the boy began shedding his clothes, stopping at his undergarments.

"I said strip."

Bawb hesitated.

A fierce punch knocked him to the ground. A kick to the ribs followed. A knife flashed into the man's hand, though the boy didn't know where he'd drawn it from. Seeing as it looked like he was about to die, he didn't think he would ever find out.

The blade whistled through the air. Swiftly, the man sliced his remaining clothing from his body, his hands nothing but a blur. The knife then disappeared, though Bawb didn't know where it went. Covering himself modestly, he climbed back to his feet.

His so-called protectors didn't move a muscle.

"I will take him from here," the man said.

Arvin and Soranna simply turned and walked away without so much as a good luck or goodbye.

The man grabbed him by the arm and roughly hauled him down a cold hallway. Bawb struggled to keep up, tripping over his feet as the much taller man moved with long strides. Finally, they reached a door leading to a round chamber. A dozen or so boys and girls, ranging in age from around his ten years of age to their early teens, stood waiting. Bawb was shoved into their midst, confused and afraid.

"Begin," the man said.

Without a word, the children descended on the naked youth, raining blows upon him from all sides. The man who had brought him merely watched, silently observing with an impassive expression.

The boy tried to cover himself as best he could while protecting his vulnerable bits, but without clothing, alone and outnumbered, he quickly found himself knocked to the hard stone floor. Unfortunately, that didn't stop the onslaught. His assailants simply continued beating on him a bit longer as he curled into a ball, desperately hoping they would stop. And stop they finally did.

"Enough!" the man called out.

The attackers immediately stepped away, heading off down one of the attached corridors. A tall woman with a sturdy build stepped into view from the shadows of one of the doorways leading into the chamber, shaking her head.

"He has no natural instinct for it, Vallin," she said.

"I agree, Demelza. He appears to possess none at all. But we have our directive."

"Indeed."

The pair picked up the bloody and bruised youth roughly by his arms and hauled him down another corridor to a sparsely furnished bunk room. It was a decent-sized space, large enough to house twenty beds. Seven of the beds were vacant. Of them, one had fresh linen. The other children were all there, seated on their own bunks. Watching.

Shivering, the boy was dumped onto what was to be his mattress. Gingerly, he crawled between his sheets, his bloody, scuffed knees and arms sticking to the material as he curled himself into a tight ball.

The others said nothing for a long while until, finally, one of the younger boys in the group walked to his bunk. He looked down at the newcomer a long moment, his face unreadable.

"We *all* endured this," he finally said quietly, then walked away.

# CHAPTER SEVEN

The next morning the others leapt from their beds before sunrise. No alarm had sounded, but they nevertheless rose as one, attuned to some internal clock the newcomer still lacked. The boy hadn't slept a wink, however, and the sound of them dressing roused him to action. He slowly sat up in bed, his body aching from his rough welcome, remaining still as he quietly observed them.

Bawb swiveled his head around, getting a better look at the bunkroom that he'd been brought to the night before. He had been more than a little distracted and out of sorts, and to be fair, he still was, but at least he was no longer lying still in the dark, wondering what would become of him.

From what he could see, there were two sections to the bunks, a sort of separation of the beds, though he had no idea what the different areas represented. A door to an adjoining room opened, and a small group of older boys and girls passed through, heading right past the younger residents. All of them were pale-skinned Wampeh, just like he was. He'd never seen so many of his own kind in one place before.

Bawb craned his neck and caught a brief glimpse of a similar but more comfortably furnished chamber as the door shut behind them.

"They're the Aspirants," the boy who had spoken to him the night before said. "They've moved up and get a bit more comfort. Nulls and Novices like us stay in this room until they progress. *If* they progress."

Bawb was confused by the strange talk. "What's a Null?"

"You are. I am. Anyone with no skill to speak of."

"But why null?"

The boy looked over at his compatriots as they prepared for the day's labor, then back at the newcomer. "Because we are worth nothing. We are all zeroes. They gathered us from across the galaxy, but we're still of no real value. Until we prove ourselves worthy, our loss is negligible."

"What do you mean, our loss? What is this place?"

"The training house," he replied, turning to join the others. "Come on, get up. You'd best come with. I know you're sore, but if you remain here, things will be harder for you."

Harder. The newcomer couldn't imagine how they could be any worse than they already were. He'd left a boring life in the orphanage, but this wasn't remotely what he'd thought the outside world would be like.

"I don't like it here."

"It's tough at first. You'll get used to it. Come on, you need to get moving."

Bawb hesitated a moment, then rose to his feet. He wasn't sure why, but he chose to trust the only person who had shown him even a hint of kindness since his arrival. He looked around, but his clothing was nowhere to be found. *No* clothing, in fact. He was still nude, scabs crusting on the scrapes he'd received from his rude welcome.

"I just want to go home," he said, a deep depression welling up inside.

"You *are* home," the boy next to him said quietly.

Bawb shuddered, cold and a little bit scared. "My name is Bawb," he said, wrapping the sheet around himself as best he could.

"Zota," the boy said with a curt nod. "Good luck."

"Luck?" Bawb wondered aloud, but the other Nulls and Novices were already walking out of the room. Bawb followed on bare feet along with the others as they silently padded out.

The corridors were uniformly lit, the glow coming from illumination spells rather than torches. He was impressed at the display of power. The orphanage he had grown up in was not exactly a poor place, but they would never have dreamt of expending valuable magic on something like this.

Here, however, magic seemed to be just a fact of daily life, and one none of the others thought twice about.

Bawb hurried along, holding his sheet tight around his body. The temperature was mild, and the stone floor radiated a comfortable warmth that matched the air. That would soon change, however. The group split from the Novices and Aspirants, each of them diverging to a different corridor. The one the Nulls took led toward a grayish light coming in through an open door. Bawb felt the cool air harsh on his skin well before they stepped through it.

It was only worse outside.

His bare feet were cold on the ground, the early morning chill setting in as he stood with the others in what seemed to be a small courtyard set somewhere within the structure of the main building, though his sense of location couldn't pinpoint exactly where that might be. They all fell into place, standing in a line, none uttering a word. Bawb may have been new, but he instinctively knew to remain quiet as well.

Silent and cold, he looked around, gawking at his new surroundings. The walls were thick and high. He could have been anywhere in the building, from what he could see from this vantage point.

Without warning, he was pushed hard from behind, his sheet roughly yanked from his body as he fell to the ground. He rolled over to see who had shoved him. It was the same man from the previous day, he realized as he glared up from the ground, naked.

The hard expression on the man's face was terrifying. "I am Vallin, charged with intake of Nulls. You will do as I instruct. Stand."

Bawb did as he was told, covering himself as best he could. The man shook his head almost imperceptibly. He glanced over at the line of Nulls standing silently at attention.

"Usalla, if you please."

A girl Bawb thought looked about his age stepped forward. He didn't even have the chance to ask what was going on before she began throwing a flurry of attacks at the newcomer. Bawb was pummeled mercilessly, trying to block the punches and kicks as best he could while covering his private parts. Usalla did not seem to care, and blow after blow landed, until finally, they knocked him to the ground. Fortunately, the small, bony ridge all Wampeh had along their spines protected his back from injury, but the rest of him was not so lucky.

The girl ceased her attack as soon as he fell and stepped back a pace, staring right at him, waiting for him to rise. Slowly, he climbed back to his feet, his hands quickly covering his groin, a small cut on his forehead trickling crimson, the blood steaming in the cold air.

"Why do you stand as you do?" the man overseeing the fight asked. "Why do you place your hands in a position of weakness?"

"I'm naked," Bawb replied, timidly.

The man scoffed. "None care about your body other than

what harm they can do to it. But you have willingly taken your hands out of the fight. This leaves you vulnerable." The man turned to the girl. "Again."

Usalla did not hesitate, once more throwing punch after punch at the newcomer. It went on like that for some time, and Bawb took quite a few hard blows until, finally, his survival instinct overruled modesty, and he defended himself with both hands. He even tried to push her away.

"Enough," the man said, ending the attack at once. He stepped close, looming over the naked boy. "This is your first lesson, Null Bawb. A Ghalian feels no shame. No pride. A Ghalian is not self-conscious. Do you understand?"

"I-I guess? Maybe? What's a Ghalian?"

Out of the corner of his eye, Bawb saw a few of the other Nulls quietly shaking their heads. Wrong answer.

"What I am. What all of the masters are. The rare few of our race from across the stars who possess the gift. A Ghalian is what you too will one day become. If you survive, that is," he said. "Show him to the retrieval room."

Bawb wondered what in the world a retrieval room could possibly be. Following the others and stepping in from the cold, he almost didn't care. His body wasn't used to the elements like this, and the chill had set in despite only a relatively short exposure.

The retrieval room, it turned out, was a large chamber with a domed ceiling, illuminated by magic, like everywhere else in the structure. They had walked down several flights of stairs to get there, leaving Bawb with the distinct impression that there was a vast subterranean component to the compound entirely hidden from the world above.

He looked around the space, noting the various obstacles housed there. In the middle of the room was a slightly raised podium, atop which sat a simple red ball small enough to fit in one's hand. Before he could ask the obvious question, Vallin strode into the chamber, and Bawb was given his task.

"Retrieve the orb. Bring it back to this point. You will be timed."

"Is there—"

"The clock has already begun."

Bawb hesitated a moment longer, then raced into action. He was an active boy, and the obstacles didn't look like they would be too hard for him. He scaled a low wall, careful of his exposed flesh, and dropped to the ground, his bare feet already a little sore from the rough surface. He ignored the discomfort as best he could and tackled the next obstacles as quickly as possible.

He was nearing the podium when he felt the hair on his neck rise hard. Bawb froze in place, slowly turning around.

An animal, not particularly large but possessing long, spiny projections on its back and sharp claws, was snuffling about the area, agitated and erratic in its movements. Bawb panicked, turning and running behind a small hurdle wall.

The creature's head whipped his way, its mass taking off in a shot, chasing the fleeing boy. Bawb circled the wall to the opposite side and bolted, making for a series of angled logs, running up them in quick succession, gaining the higher ground.

The animal circled the wall and came charging out from behind it but stopped abruptly, its head turning from side to side. Bawb was easy enough to see, perched atop the obstacle, but the beast spun around, searching for him to no avail.

*It doesn't see me*, Bawb realized. *It must have really poor vision.* He glanced over at Vallin. The man, as well as the rest of the Nulls, were all watching him quietly. He would be getting no help from any of them.

The red ball was no more than fifteen steps away from his location, he estimated. All he had to do was get to it. Nude as he was, Bawb was far more concerned with the creature's pointy spines than he might otherwise have been, but he forced himself to calm down and think. Think of a way to get around it.

None presented itself. And the clock was ticking.

There was one option—the obvious one—but he did not like it. More than that, his legs didn't seem to want to obey his mind's command.

He sat up there, crouched and waiting, for a long while before he finally managed to force his body to do what he wanted. Slowly, he climbed down, moving deliberately and with no sudden movements. The animal was sniffing around but did not appear to notice him. So far, so good.

With painful care he began creeping toward the platform, exposed and in the open. If the creature decided to charge him, there was nothing he would be able to do to stop it. But rather than charge, the animal simply meandered around the chamber, oblivious to the boy's progress.

Bawb climbed the podium slowly and carefully lifted the ball.

A shrieking alarm rang out and the platform collapsed to the ground, the movement and noise drawing the animal's attention in a flash. Bawb watched in horror as it spun and ran, heading right for him. There was no way he could outrun it, and there was nowhere to hide or take shelter. He was screwed.

Fear froze him in place, and it was that unexpected failure of his fight or flight instinct that saved him. The creature raced right past him as he stood perfectly still, perceived as just a piece of the scenery and nothing more. He took the opportunity and ran the opposite way the moment his feet unglued themselves and heeded his commands.

Bawb ran hard and fast to the far side of the chamber, quickly ducking out of sight before the animal could stop its charge and spin around to see him. From there, he scrambled over the obstacles along the periphery, taking the long way back but one that kept him from the creature's view until, finally, he arrived at the starting point.

Bawb's heart was pounding in his chest so hard he thought it might burst.

He reached out, offering the ball to Vallin. The man took it from him without ceremony, uttered a few words that sounded like nonsense, then tossed it toward the collapsed podium, which snapped back together in a flash, the ball landing atop its original resting place.

"How did you do that?" the boy asked, amazed.

"A simple reset spell."

"You can do *magic*?"

"Of course."

With that, Vallin walked away, leaving the other Nulls to take Bawb with them to the next of their many daily tasks, each of them so grueling he thought he might drop from the exertion. But somehow, he made it through the day, filling his belly at the dining hall, bathing in their communal showering room, then passing out hard on his bunk, sleeping straight through until the following morning.

The next day it began again.

For a full week, Bawb was forced to remain nude.

He was allowed a sheet and blanket on his bunk, but aside from that, he ate nude, fought nude, did every single task he was ordered without a stitch of clothing. Where he had been so uncomfortable at first, awkward being naked around girls as well as boys, by the end of that week, bruised and exhausted as he was, he had finally forgotten to even think about trying to cover himself, let alone care.

*Then*, and only then, was he given clothing like the others.

But this was not a kindness. It was simply a lesson learned. And his rough welcome was only beginning.

# CHAPTER EIGHT

"Bawb, step forward," today's instructor, a fellow named Teacher Krallo, commanded.

Bawb did as he was told, standing quietly at attention while Krallo decided who his opponent would be this time.

He had been made to fight regularly, as had all of the Nulls, and by now he had faced each and every one of them multiple times. Age, gender, size, none of that mattered. What did matter was that when they were told to fight, they fought without hesitation.

Krallo walked along the line of Nulls, surveying the neophytes with a critical eye. Finally, he stopped at a particularly strong young girl named Elzina. She was tall for her age and excelled at the tasks they were given. She had also beaten Bawb soundly every time they faced one another. Krallo nodded to the older students brought to assist the younger ones on this occasion. Without a word they stepped in, binding the pair's hands behind their backs.

"Elzina. Bawb. You are to fight without the use of your hands."

"But how?" Bawb wondered.

"That is for you to figure out. *Begin*."

Elzina wasted no time, kicking out hard and fast. What she lacked in technique she more than made up for with aggression and drive. Bawb, however, managed to sidestep her attack, turning his body so her shin only glanced off his hip. He quickly shuffled backward, unsure how to react. He had never gotten in fights at the orphanage, but here he was being pitted in daily combat against the other Nulls. And he was losing every time.

"Stop running away," Elzina growled, landing a hard kick to his left leg.

Bawb stumbled, the muscle cramping from the blow, but still managed to avoid the follow-up kick that went whiffing past his face. Had he not recoiled as fast as he could, doing his best to ignore the pain in his leg, he might very well have had his jaw broken to go along with a sizable bruise on his cheek.

He tried to kick back, but his balance was horribly off and his leg swung through empty air. Elzina saw an opening and faked a high kick, opting instead to snap her lead leg forward with a quick shot to the groin.

Bawb felt pain explode in his belly, and he crumbled to the ground in a heap. Krallo nodded to the assistants who untied the pair. Elzina casually stepped back into her place in the line, while Bawb slowly pulled himself to his feet. He stood slightly hunched over as nausea flowed through him.

The first brutal nut shot he'd suffered a few days prior had left him curled in a ball, vomiting in pain. Now, at least, he managed to suffer the agony with a little less humiliation.

The others watched as he gathered himself, none offering to help, not a word of support sent his way. At first, he had thought they were an unfriendly bunch. Not exactly hostile, but not friendly by any means. After he survived the first week, however, he learned that there were a wide range of personalities among his fellow Nulls. They had simply learned to keep their mouths shut and do as they were told at all times.

It was self-preservation, and it was a lesson he had been learning one painful blow at a time.

Zota had spoken with him a few times back in their bunk room, and while the two had not exactly become friends, at least they could consider one another supportive classmates. Elzina, however, had seemed to take a disliking to him from day one. Or so he thought, until Zota informed him that she was just that way with *everyone* until she proved herself better than them.

She was hyper-competitive, and it showed in everything she did.

It was something Bawb witnessed firsthand over and over in the coming weeks. But no matter how driven Elzina might have been, she was still a Null, just like the others, and no amount of gumption and force of will could overcome that handicap.

The entire group was next taken to a deep underground chamber, an icy stream flowing lazily through it. It looked like some sort of cave, given the high, rocky ceiling far above them. And it very well may have been, seeing how far they had trekked down the winding pathways beneath the city to reach it. Interestingly, plants grew in the area as if they were out in the wild, though they all knew they were anywhere but.

Krallo was waiting for them when they arrived, standing on the shore of the frigid stream beside a cluster of small, prickly shrubs.

"You are likely wondering where you are," he began, surveying the youths like a drill instructor sizing up fresh meat in boot camp. "You have learned by now that the Ghalian have a vast network of training spaces deep beneath the surface. This allows us to train in private, away from prying eyes and ears. It also allows us to control the environments housed within. But do not let that make you lax in your attention.

There are dangers, and you *can* be hurt, or even die. Is that clear?"

The group nodded their understanding, a cold feeling of unease washing over them all as if they'd been dunked in the icy stream.

"Bawb, step forward."

Bawb did as he was told, wondering if this lesson would be easier for the first to attempt and fail or for the last. It seemed that nothing they did resulted in success, but in that regard, Krallo had been quite clear in the only words of encouragement he'd heard him utter.

"You are being pushed. Challenged. Forced to attempt things you do not know how to do. You are Nulls, and you *will* fail. But in your failure, you will learn. And a Ghalian never stops learning. That goes for all of us. Even the Five."

"The Five?"

"The masters who control the order. You will learn. But now you have a different lesson. Make a fire."

Bawb looked for a flint or something to use as a source of ignition. There was none.

"But there isn't anything here."

"Use magic."

"I-I don't have any magic."

"Correct. And this is a lesson to you all. Wampeh do not create their own magic. We must use the stored potential in a konus or other device," he said, showing the golden band around his wrist. "You will eventually learn to use a konus, to draw the power stored in it and use it in myriad ways. But what if you find yourself without one?"

He removed the konus from his wrist and placed it on a nearby rock. He then held his hand over a shrubbery. Strange words flowed from his mouth, and a moment later, the shrub burst into flames. Another word and it extinguished in an instant. Krallo picked up his konus and slid it back on and surveyed their stunned faces.

"How did you do that?" Usalla asked.

He turned to the girl and smiled. Sharp fangs gleamed where his canine teeth usually were. "We will get to that later. For the moment, you all must make do with what you have at hand. Make fire, if you are able. Keep yourselves warm. Make what shelter you can. You will be spending the night here. The other teachers and I will return in the morning."

"But this is a cavern," Bawb noted. "How will we know when it is morning?"

Krallo's eyes crinkled slightly with a rather frightening look of amusement. "You will know."

With that, he and the other instructors turned and left the Nulls to fend for themselves, utterly at a loss what to do. The ambient magical light in the chamber remained, but it seemed it was dimming, and at a fairly rapid rate. From what Krallo had said, this must be the underground version of nightfall, though how the Ghalian had achieved it was far beyond any of their understanding.

"What do we do?" Zota wondered aloud, voicing the thought all of them shared.

"We do as we've been instructed."

It was Elzina who spoke up, confident and taking charge, even if she didn't know what to do. Fake it until you make it was her way of blustering through life, and with her drive and ambition, it had worked for the most part. Up until now, anyway. But here, in this unusual situation, no amount of false confidence could start a fire.

Bawb looked around, taking in their home for the night as best he could in the dimming light. "He said we should make some kind of shelter."

"I know that," Elzina snapped. "You three, gather wood. The rest of us will build a shelter here."

"It's kind of damp, isn't it?" Bawb noted of the shoreline.

"We are close to fresh water. I've heard you can survive without food for weeks, but without water you won't last but a few days."

"But we won't be left here for days, right?"

She looked at Bawb but didn't dignify the question with a reply. She and the others had been Nulls a lot longer than he had, and while they had not yet graduated to Novices, they had learned one thing always held true with their teachers.

*Expect the unexpected.*

Bawb waited for a response, but everyone started working, pulling up shrubs and piling them together to act as a windbreak. There was a strange, cold breeze flowing through the place, and while it was tolerable, the night would pass much more comfortably if it was not a factor. He shrugged and set to his task, working up a sweat as he hurried about searching for more materials to use for their shelter.

Nightfall came, finding the group of youths huddled together, their bellies rumbling from hunger and their bodies chilled from the cool air. The lighting dimmed until there were just a few illuminated areas along the large cavern's walls, many of them blocked by tall boulders that scattered the landscape. The overhead lights had gone completely dark.

As the night wore on, the wind picked up in strength, the icy stream now blowing a freezing mist across the shivering Nulls. They pressed closer together, sharing their warmth, but the evaporative cooling of the water was taking its toll. Bawb was fortunate enough to be sandwiched between Marzis and Zota, but too much of him was still exposed to the elements to keep him remotely warm.

Despite having never spent the night outdoors, let alone

camping, Bawb had nevertheless instinctively felt certain they should not have made camp so close to the water's edge. But as he was the lowest of the low, to press the issue would have just brought ridicule, or worse. And now they were all suffering for it.

The night would have been longer and colder if not for the unexpected flash of light as their barely protecting shrubbery windbreak burst into flames in the wee hours, sending them scattering, grateful they were damp, the moisture sparing them burns from the unexpected fire.

A dark-clad Wampeh strode into the firelight. She was tall and lithe, a wicked-looking dagger riding on each hip and a long cloak draped across her back. She surveyed the group but a moment before she spoke.

"Your shelter has been compromised and you now face a hostile enemy. Flee, evade, regroup. You have until the count of ten."

The Nulls may not have been trained in the arts of war, but only a fool would not have taken her at her word. Immediately they scattered, running into the darkness, their eyes struggling to adjust after the brightness of the fire robbed them of their night vision.

One more lesson hard learned.

Bawb ran as fast as he could without crashing headlong into a boulder, recovering as quickly as possible and cowering behind a hunk of fallen rock. He strained his ears, listening for any sign of the imposing woman. Fists meeting skin, grunts and moans, and the occasional cry of startled pain were all he heard. He saw a strange light flicker for a split-second nearby out of the corner of his eye, pale blue and almost person-shaped, but when he turned his head to give it a proper look, it was gone.

He made a decision. He would run for the entryway to the cavern. If they were being hunted, no one would think to look for him there. Carefully, he stepped from cover and began creeping toward the barely visible tunnel entrance across the chamber. He was nearly there when a powerful kick knocked the wind out of him, followed by a leg sweep and punch sending him hard into the ground, flat on his back.

Bawb struggled for air, staring up at the strange woman looming over him.

"How did I find you?" she asked when he could finally breathe again.

"I don't know. I was being quiet."

"And doing a fair job for a Null. But what is that over there?"

He looked where she gestured. All he could see was the tunnel mouth, illuminated by the faintly glowing walls around it.

"It's the tunnel."

"It is, but what is around it?"

"Uh, nothing."

"Wrong. There is illumination. Your stealth was actually not bad, but you were backlit, making every movement blatantly clear."

"I-I didn't realize."

"You are a Null. Of course you didn't. *This* is how you learn. Commit this moment to memory, and do not let it happen again. *Always* be cognizant of your surroundings and use them not only to your advantage but to your enemy's disadvantage. Do you understand?"

Bawb nodded in the affirmative.

"What about the glowing person?"

The woman's face stayed neutral, but he could have sworn he saw a flash of something else there. A hint of surprise.

"You were seeing things, obviously. Now, stay here and be silent. You are no longer an escaped part of this group. You are now to play the part of an injured victim. Should they come upon you, it is up to them if they help you or not. Clear?"

"Yes."

"Good." She smiled at him then pulled her cloak up over her head, vanishing before his eyes.

"How did you do that?" he marveled, but the only reply was silence.

# CHAPTER NINE

Days later, healed and much warmer, Bawb sat quietly in one of the training rooms during a rare moment of free time, replaying his many mistakes over and over in his mind, a blush rising to his cheeks with each of them.

He had been rescued from a life in the orphanage, his age all but guaranteeing that he would remain there until adulthood, and brought into a new life, with a new family of sorts. But this had proven to be unlike any family he'd ever known, and the requirements placed on him were daunting, to say the least.

The Wampeh Ghalian, they were called. He was a Wampeh, just like all the others, with the same pale skin as the rest of their race. But, apparently, there was something different about them. Something special, though the teachers hadn't yet told them what, exactly. Apparently, the Ghalian were a secret order of some sort. Warriors? Mercenaries? He still wasn't entirely sure. And as a Null, he felt pretty certain they wouldn't be telling him anytime soon.

For now, at least, he would just do his best to make it through each exhausting day. Locked in here with the others, he had little choice in the matter.

Movement caught Bawb's eye as a lean, wiry man stepped through the doorway. The new arrival stood there a moment, staring at him quietly. He was a Wampeh as well, as were all inside these walls it seemed, but more than even the most senior of the teachers, this man had an air of absolute confidence and authority about him, accompanied by a tranquility that could only come with truly knowing oneself and one's capabilities.

He gave a little nod and walked over to the boy, his footfall utterly silent even on the hard floor. Bawb realized he was casting a spell to mute his footsteps almost as an afterthought. It was impressive, to say the least.

The man stopped directly in front of him, staring at him with a piercing gaze.

"I am Master Hozark."

"Uh, I'm Bawb."

"I know," he said with a little grin. "You are to come with me." He then turned and walked away.

Bawb rose and fell in behind him, following quietly. Hozark took him to one of the smaller training chambers and instructed the boy to stand tall and still. He did as he was told, though his eyes showed great uncertainty.

"You shall be training harder from now on, and it shall not be easy," Hozark said. "If you are to succeed in this endeavor, remember these words: Your mind is your greatest weapon. And it is yours alone to wield. Learn to control it, and you shall do well. Fail to do so and you will not survive." He paused, a slight hint of a smile tickling the corners of his mouth. "But between you and me, I think you have it in you. Do not prove me wrong."

The words were familiar to Hozark. They were the first, and only, words of kindness he had heard from Master Fahbahl when he had first arrived in a training house when he himself was but a boy. And now he was repeating them to this newcomer. This soon-to-be Aspirant Ghalian.

"I shall be here from time to time in this training house," he continued, "and I shall help you practice and grow, as best I can. Should you try your hardest, I am confident you can achieve great things."

"You really think I can make it?" the boy asked, coming out of his shell ever so slightly.

"I am certain of it."

"I don't understand. Are you a new teacher? Is there going to be another new class?"

"Not right now, no. I merely wanted to meet you. To welcome you to the fold, as it were."

"So you're not a teacher?"

Hozark's lips curled in a tiny grin. "I am, at times. But I am one of the Five, and as such, my duties often take me far away from this training house. We do have many others, you know. This is only one of our facilities."

"Oh. But you said you're one of the Five?"

"Yes. Do you know what that is?"

Bawb felt a knot form in his stomach. One more shortcoming about to be made apparent. "No, I don't," he admitted, his eyes cast low.

Hozark patted him on the arm. "Do not worry. You will learn. You will learn a lot in your time here. Time that will continue to be well spent."

"What do you mean?"

"I mean, congratulations, Bawb. You have passed the intake. You are no longer a Null. You are now a Novice."

Bawb looked at the man with confusion. "Passed? But I failed. I failed a *lot*."

"No, you did not."

"Really, I did."

Hozark chuckled. "Most of the trials the Nulls face are tests they have no chance of succeeding at. And that is the whole point. To help you learn to fail but not give up. To realize what it is you know as well as how much you do *not* know. Where your shortcomings are. And most importantly, to take away the knowledge that your enemy also quite often knows just as little."

"What do you mean, enemy?"

"The Ghalian live a dangerous existence, Bawb. One day, when you are older, you will face an adversary for real, and when you do, you will know that there are *always* shortcomings to exploit, be they in your enemy's training, preparation, or execution of a plan. And you will learn to seek out these opportunities and take full advantage of them."

Bawb's mind reeled as he tried to keep up with all this new information. It made sense, sort of, but he was still more or less in the dark. He'd been forced to fight as well as to make shelter and survive unpleasant situations. But now it seemed there was a method to this madness. A purpose for it all.

"Are you saying I'm going to learn how to do all of those things? The things I failed at?"

"Yes. Those and much, much more. Now, let me ask you a question. Do you know how to use a konus, Bawb?"

"No. I've seen Teacher Krallo use one, but I still don't know how he makes it do what he wants. He said something about spells requiring intent, but we're not allowed to use one."

"Not yet. One day, however, you shall have one of your own. All trainees receive a konus when they graduate from Novice to Aspirant. Of course, this is only after they pass the first two years of challenges and training."

"Two years?" Bawb gasped.

"It is what is required to weed out the weak of body, mind, and spirit. And make no mistake, it will be difficult. Just know that, when I am able, I will be watching. If you train hard and study your lessons, the time will pass faster than you would imagine, and you will soon enough have a konus of your own.

Remember, *a fire blazes but is dead without embers, and storms rage as a lone feather floats.*"

"What does that mean?"

"That, my boy, is for you to learn, in time. Now, off you go. I believe it is nearly time for Teacher Vallin's combatives lesson."

Bawb nodded and headed for the door but paused, turning back to the Master Ghalian who had, for whatever reason taken an interest in him.

"Thank you, Master Hozark."

"You are welcome, Novice Bawb. Good luck, and good fortune to you. I know you will do your best. Now, work hard. It will be arduous but worth the effort. You must grow strong before the *real* training begins."

Hozark smiled at the boy, genuine and bright, the expression of affection and care he had taken in the youngster's training giving Bawb a much-needed boost in confidence and motivation. Bawb turned and headed to his next class, excited to meet his next challenge head-on.

Hozark watched as he left the chamber, his lips slowly dropping back to their normal, stoic posturing. It would be the last time Bawb would see him smile for nearly two difficult years. Until the day he graduated to Aspirant. The day not just any master but Hozark, one of the Five himself, presented him with a konus of his own.

# CHAPTER TEN

Bawb was no longer a Null. He woke with that reassuring thought fresh in his mind.

Somehow, he had managed to muddle through the gauntlet of physical and mental challenges that had bombarded him and upended his life over the prior weeks and months and come out the other side a Novice.

Of course, a Novice was still near the bottom of the ladder, but at least he was no longer the lowest of the low. A Null was essentially worth nothing. A throwaway prospect whom the Ghalian had nothing truly invested in. If they failed to show the necessary drive and strength of will, ultimately resulting in their rejection, they would not be missed.

But a Novice was part of the team. The family. And while they were not afforded the comforts of the higher levels, they were, however, treated with a noticeable change in attitude. A modicum of respect. For while they still had many levels ahead of them, they had proven themselves worthy of the instruction.

Little did they know just how intense and challenging reaching those levels would be.

As a Novice, Bawb was at long last given a little insight into what lay ahead for him. The long road to reaching the higher levels.

There were seven, all told, starting with the Nulls and Novices. Once a student had spent roughly two years as a Novice, almost exclusively training their bodies to be ready for the *real* instruction, they would then rise to the level of Aspirant. At that time they would begin to truly learn spells and combat techniques in earnest.

While spells would be taught during the Novice years, they were more a matter of rote memorization of the unusual words that controlled the power stored in their konuses. It was akin to dryfiring a weapon to learn the mechanics and muscle memory but without the possibility of a misfire. The odds of one would be minuscule anyway, as not only the words, but also the focus of mind and, most importantly, the *intent* behind the recited spell all had to be perfectly aligned and cast as one.

Anything less and the spell would be no more than a collection of words. Sounds the elders had discovered could channel the magic flowing through the galaxy when intoned in a certain way. It had taken hundreds of years for the earliest casters to refine the most basic of spells. Thousands for the more complex and arcane ones. But now the entire galaxy functioned on this power, with magic a core part of daily life across the realm.

As only a few possessed natural magic of their own, a select few types of storage devices were filled with power and sold for a price, all to be employed by the populace for everything from making fires to cook, to flying massive spaceships.

While Bawb would not be learning the more complicated spells in his Novice years, as an Aspirant they would begin to instruct him in their use.

When he reached the highest degree of skill an Aspirant could achieve, he would then graduate as a Vessel, the term coming from the understanding that he was now a vessel holding the knowledge of the Ghalian, if not all of the skills just yet.

From there he would train long and hard to hone his abilities, learning to cast spells in all manner of conditions, all while put to the test physically and mentally, for in this line of work, casting in peace would be a rarity.

The training of a Vessel could take years. It varied entirely based on the individual. The most skilled could essentially graduate from trainee status and reach the level of Adept in only a few years, though that was the exception and not the rule. Once an Adept, they would be sent to work, though the contracts would be lower-level ones as they continued to train.

Real-world experience would hone their skills while their studies would continue until they achieved the rank of Mavin. This was the top tier of the rank-and-file Wampeh Ghalian, and at this level they would be afforded the opportunity to share their knowledge with the younger classes, assisting the teachers if they wished, or even becoming teachers themselves if they had the proclivity.

For most Ghalian, this sixth level was as far as they would progress. They would live out their days as elite assassins of the secretive order, carrying out contracts according to the Ghalian way, shaping societies and influencing political power struggles from the shadows, never taking sides. Often, though, their actions would also stymy the Council of Twenty, for whom there was no love lost.

It was a conflict of generations, and as the Council expanded their control across the systems, the Ghalian quietly pushed back against their most abhorrent efforts, their code of honor and justice guiding their actions. They may have been the deadliest killers in the galaxy, but they were not indiscriminate, and only a select few contracts were accepted, regardless of the amount of coin offered.

This degree of selectiveness, along with their notoriety for abhorring slavery and ill-treatment of the downtrodden, only added to their legend, and while they were feared by most, it also made them appreciated by many. It was the Mavins who carried out the bulk of the lesser Ghalian work, though people usually had no idea one had been in their presence.

There was still one level beyond Mavin, however. That of Master. The Highest level a Ghalian could attain. These were teachers and mentors whose innate skills and depth of knowledge surpassed even the brightest of their ranks. The assassins who could call up obscure spells on a moment's notice, all while fighting off multiple attackers, both physical and magical.

Their skills were things of legend, and from their limited ranks the Five were selected. The best of the best, charged with guiding the order through the centuries. Rare was it that all five were in the same place at once. Normally, they were spread across the systems, overseeing the pursuit of the overarching goals of the order.

As for the young boy who had only now proven himself worth more than nothing, it was daunting, to say the least. And his first trial as a Novice most definitely set the tone.

The other Nulls had all moved up in rank within a few weeks of one another, though a few had left their group earlier, having proven themselves already. Not all of them arrived at the same time, after all, and while they were given tasks as a group, each of them was being assessed individually, though they did not know that at the time.

Bawb saw familiar faces when he was directed to a new

training area deep underground. The network of tunnels and caverns was even more massive than he had thought, from what he had been able to discern. As a Null he had undoubtedly only seen a fraction of the hidden Ghalian compound's secrets.

Now, as a Novice, he was afforded a tiny bit more information, and with it, access to new areas formerly off limits to him and his classmates. This one was not a rough cavern but rather a clean and symmetrical chamber, tall and wide with ample illumination. In fact, it was so bright it felt as if they were outdoors in one of the compound's courtyards.

But Bawb looked up and made out the flat surface of the ceiling far above him through the layers of spells creating the impression of sky and sunlight. It was an impressive feat of casting, and one he had no doubt had cost a lot of magic. It was, however, something he would not have time to ponder. Not now, at least.

"Novice Bawb!" a gruff voice called out only moments after he had entered the chamber.

He spun, searching for the source. It wasn't hard to find.

A barrel-chested Ghalian stood towering over the other Novices, each of whom seemed to be performing some sort of odd task. He hurried over to join them, unsure what to make of the scene and wondering what might be required of him now that he had leveled up.

He needn't have worried. The teacher made that *very* clear the moment he reached him.

"I am Teacher Farpix."

"Hello, sir. I am—"

"I know who you are. I just called your name. Do not restate the obvious, and do not waste my time, is that clear?"

"Yes, sir."

Farpix loomed over him, something the teachers seemed to enjoy doing, though after his talk with Hozark, who was one of the Five, no less, Bawb had a sneaking suspicion it was all an act intended to apply emotional pressure along with the physical variety. Wisely, he kept this opinion to himself.

The teacher pointed to a spiral staircase that climbed all the way to the ceiling. At the base of it was a pool of water no wider than his bunk. The water appeared to be relatively deep, like a well, but from this vantage point he couldn't be sure. The other youths glanced at him with knowing looks. They had been through this before, it seemed, though he had no idea what lay in store for him.

He would soon find out.

"To the top," Farpix instructed.

Bawb took off at a jog, eyeing the tall staircase and small pool as he approached. He knew better than to hesitate by now, his feet transitioning to the steps smoothly with the spring of young legs. He took the steps two at a time, quickly making his way to the top. He stood there, barely out of breath, surveying the chamber from his high vantage point.

There were all manner of activities going on, so much for him to take in. Most of his fellow Nulls had leveled up and were working hard, though in his case, he wasn't sure what manner of training this actually was.

"What are you waiting for?" Farpix asked from below.

"Sir?"

"Come down."

Bawb turned to descend the staircase.

"Not like that. *Jump*."

The boy turned back, cautiously shuffling to the exposed precipice. It was a long way down, and the pool of water was not very big. Logically, he knew he only had to step off and he'd land in it, but this was high, and if he miscalculated he'd wind up with a pair of broken legs, if not worse.

"Do not wait. Do not think. Trust what you know and jump."

Bawb's legs trembled, unwilling to move.

"Overcome your fear. Your mind is your most powerful weapon."

"I know, but I just—"

"*Pohtzi Akkus,*" Farpix hissed, casting the spell under his breath.

Bawb felt a shove from behind. A moment later, he was falling through space.

The water was not cold, as he had expected it to be, but rather warm and almost pleasant to his body. The impact with it, however, was anything but. He landed awkwardly, missing the edges of the pool, but only just. Worse, his flank slapped the water hard when he hit, the wind knocked out of him from the impact. From that height, even water could hurt.

A lot.

Bawb climbed out of the water, holding his stinging side with his hand. Farpix strode over to him while the others carried on with their tasks.

"Let me see," he said gruffly, lifting Bawb's tunic.

The skin was red, but no bones were broken.

"Feet-first," he instructed. "This is not high enough to be fatal, but from greater heights, impacting the water with any large area of your body will be the same as striking the ground, is that clear?"

"Yes," Bawb managed, his diaphragm finally allowing him to draw normal breath.

Farpix nodded once. "Good. Now, again."

Bawb turned and jogged up the stairs once more, aching and certainly no longer taking them two at a time. When he reached the top, he hesitated.

"What are you waiting for?" the teacher called up to him.

Bawb's side ached, a painful reminder that his fear would hurt him more than overcoming it. Without waiting a moment longer, he stepped off into the open air, plummeting to the pool below. This time his feet hit first, and as Farpix had said, it was not painful at all.

A little boost of confidence trickled through his body. This wasn't so bad. In fact, it was almost fun in a weird way. Farpix seemed pleased enough at his performance. "Good. This is your task today."

"I am done?"

"Done? Not hardly. You are to repeat this exercise until you are told to stop. Now carry on."

With that, Farpix walked off to torment some other poor student. As for Bawb, he looked up at the steps above him and sighed.

It was only morning.

This was going to be a long day.

Later, after dinner, as he lay aching upon his bunk, his legs rubber from hours upon hours of exertion, he would find the memory of his overconfidence funny, in a morbid sort of way.

"So, this is being a Novice," he sighed to himself, wondering what else lay in store for him.

# CHAPTER ELEVEN

Bawb's introduction to the rigors of Novice-level training had been a rude awakening to what lay ahead. One that still did not remotely prepare him for just how grueling it would be.

He had been told it would take literally years for his body to grow strong enough for what Hozark had called the *real* Ghalian training, and if every day was like this, he almost dreaded finding out what would happen when he moved up to the higher-level rigors.

The logic behind it was sound, of course. They were all still children, undeveloped and weak. Even if they had the mental capacity and fortitude for the higher levels, their bodies would simply not be able to perform. And so it was that all of them would have to toil through years of hard labor.

None thought to leave, however. Firstly, because they didn't even know *how* they could get out of this place they now called home. But also because, suffer as they might, they were a part of something bigger than just themselves. And even for the ones who had come from normal family life, this felt different. More encompassing. It was like having family and friends all rolled into one, a feeling which was only strengthened by their spending every single day together, suffering through the same rigors side by side.

And what rigors they were.

Bawb had run up the stairs, jumping into the pool of water, then doing it so many times he lost track of the hours passing. His legs shook with every step, his body aching from not only the climb, but the impact and effort to lift himself from the water. And doing this in wet clothing meant he was carrying that additional weight with every climb.

He also found that while the warm waters were comfortable on his first few jumps, after hours of effort, he wanted nothing more than a cold dunk to lower his temperature and revitalize his spirits.

He would have no such luck.

The next morning he pushed himself up from his bunk with a groan and followed the rest of his cohort to the training chamber, his legs functional but still quite sore. It surprised him, actually, that he had recovered as quickly as he had. But then, all of the efforts in his time as a Null had apparently prepared him for these new trials more than he'd realized.

"Where are you going?" Farpix asked as Bawb trudged toward the looming staircase.

"I thought—"

"In this one setting, you do not think. You do as you are instructed. You are not climbing the stairs today. Go over there and wait with Usalla."

Bawb did as he was told, taking his place beside the girl. They both stood silently, watching as the others were assigned their tasks for the day. Finally, Farpix made his way over to them.

"Legs sore, Bawb?" he asked.

"Yes," he admitted.

"Would you prefer a task that is easy on the legs today?"

Bawb was unsure what the teacher meant to do to him, what manner of trick this might be, but he didn't think he could manage another full day of painful leg work.

"I would, if that's possible," he finally said.

"Very well. I offer you a choice. Heavy or light?"

Bawb glanced at Usalla. She'd arrived with a few other newly promoted Novices shortly before him and had already been through several of the exercises. He knew she felt his gaze, but she looked straight ahead, saying nothing. Bawb didn't take it personally. In fact, he figured it was probably the smart thing to do.

"Um, light," he finally said, hoping it was the right choice.

"Very well. Usalla, you are to carry those two buckets of water up that ramp and pour them into the drainage hole. When you have completed that task, return to the bottom of the ramp and refill them from the catch basin at the bottom."

She nodded once and took off at a run, swiftly grabbing up the full buckets and beginning the arduous trudge up the switchbacks of the ramp that would eventually take her almost to the roof of the chamber.

Bawb watched her muscles strain as she lifted the buckets and began her task with growing confidence he had lucked out and selected wisely.

"Bawb, climb atop this stump," the teacher instructed.

It was only one step up from the ground and was easily wide enough to fit both of his feet if he pressed them together. Balancing he could do, tired legs or not.

He watched Farpix pull a pair of small metal cups from his pocket. They were thin and light, capable of holding perhaps a mouthful of water each, but not much more. He filled each of them from a pitcher sitting on a nearby table laden with all manner of strange training implements, then walked back to Bawb.

The youth glanced up at Usalla as she descended from her first trip to the top, expecting her to be upset with him for leaving her the difficult task. But as she swung her arms, relaxing her shoulders and forearms on the trip back down, he noticed something that gave him pause.

She looked at him and winked. Worse yet, she was smiling.

*Oh, no,* he thought as her relatively happy demeanor registered. *What have I done*?

Teacher Farpix would make that quite clear.

"Arms out in front of you," he commanded. "Palms facing up."

Bawb did as he was told, holding his arms up at shoulder height. The teacher carefully placed one small cup in each hand then stepped back.

"You are to hold these in place. Do not lower your arms. Do not step down from that stump. Most importantly, do not spill any of the water." With that, Farpix turned his attention to the other students.

Bawb wanted to ask how long he would have to hold these little cups like this but knew what the answer would be. He would have to stay like this until he was told to relax and not a moment sooner.

He watched Usalla scoop up a new load into each bucket and begin the trudge uphill. Yes, it was a much heavier weight she was carrying, but she was getting breaks in between on the downhill walk. Bawb, on the other hand, would get no such respite. And while what he was holding weighed only a tiny fraction of those buckets, his shoulders and arms were already beginning to burn from the unrelenting effort.

Even the lightest of burdens could become overwhelming, given enough time. It was a lesson he was now learning in a most uncomfortable manner. One that would ensure he never forgot it.

. . .

The next day he kept his mouth shut, his poor body so sore he was barely able to raise his arms to face-height. Fortunately, or unfortunately, depending on one's perspective, the teachers were well familiarized with this phenomenon. Bawb was set to work on a different task. One that gave his arms a rest while taxing his core to the extreme.

He had to balance on a series of a dozen poles, each of them taller than he was and separated by the length of his extended arm. If he was able to extend it, that is. In any case, they were set close enough to allow one to move freely atop them if one's footing was sound.

Climbing onto one of the poles as he was instructed was hard enough, given the aches and lack of strength his upper body was suffering, but the balancing act he was about to endure made that look like child's play.

"Bawb, you are to remain atop the poles until told otherwise. You may move between them as you desire. Is that understood?" Farpix asked.

"It is," he replied, confident that at least this task would be one he could succeed at without too much pain.

He stood there for nearly twenty minutes, centered in his balance and finally relaxing into an almost meditative state, when the pole he was perched atop abruptly began to vibrate. At first, he thought it was his legs jackhammering from exhaustion from the other day's stair climb, but when the pole abruptly disappeared into the ground, leaving him hovering in the air for a split second, he realized this was different.

Bawb hit the ground hard, the unexpected fall knocking the wind out of him. As he lay there, the pole slid back into place, looming over him as if it were mocking him. It was an inanimate object, of course, but nevertheless, he felt an almost personal dislike for the length of wood.

"Novice Bawb, you were to remain atop the poles!" Farpix shouted from across the chamber. "Twenty laps!"

Bawb started running, making his way to the wall then following it all the way around. He knew better than to merely jog. The teachers would expect maximum effort in all that he did. As a result, when he completed the task, he was thoroughly winded. His body, he realized, actually felt better for it, the movement of his arms and legs helping force out the aches that had previously set in.

His lungs, however, were on fire from the exertion. His cardio endurance was growing, but it was nowhere near where it needed to be for Ghalian standards.

"Well, what are you waiting for?" Farpix demanded. "Back up you go."

Bawb nodded, unable to speak, and climbed atop the pole nearest him as best he could. Once he was safely on his feet, balancing on the slightly swaying piece of wood, he focused his attention not on merely settling into a comfortable position, but also on paying close attention to every thrumming vibration that might pass through his perch.

It was nearly an hour before the next incident, and he had very nearly slipped into complacency.

Bawb felt the vibration and tensed his legs, forcing himself to leap to the nearest pole. Or so he tried. He waited too long and once again hit the ground. This time, however, he was ready for the impact and landed without incident.

Teacher Farpix merely pointed at him then gestured with a sweeping circular motion. He was to run again.

Bawb ran his twenty laps and scrambled back atop one of the poles, unsure if he was supposed to run more or not. He figured the worst that would happen if he stopped short of the required number would be more running, but he wouldn't know until that actually happened.

Lucky for him, Farpix seemed pleased with this and continued focusing his attention on the failures of the other Novices.

Bawb had initially thought this would be a rest for his body, but now that he was remaining tense, on-edge, and ready to react, he realized that what looked like simply standing still was anything but. His lower back began to ache, as did his legs, hips, and abdomen. His shoulders and arms were somewhat free of those pains, but even they were still held ready to react at a moment's notice.

Bawb focused, his mind zeroing in on his feet, concentrating on the sensations he could perceive all while his body throbbed from the tension.

A vibration resonated through his feet.

Bawb reacted immediately, his coiled muscles springing into action as best they could. He leapt through the air to the pole to his right. His feet made contact just as the one he had been perched atop dropped into the ground. His arms windmilled wildly as he fought to maintain his balance, but somehow, he managed to keep his footing.

Slowly, he lowered his arms back to his sides, settling back into a waiting pose as the pole beside him slid back into position.

He turned and glanced around. The other Novices were too engrossed in their own training to have noticed what he had just done. Teacher Farpix, however, had been watching. It was almost imperceptible, the nod he gave, but Bawb saw it. Not a glowing seal of approval by any measure, but it was better than nothing, and the first positive feedback he'd received since climbing in the ranks.

There were sure to be many more challenges, he now

realized, and each of them would undoubtedly strain him to his limits. But if he could endure, if he could excel, the weeks and months would pass as his body grew in strength. And then, if all went well, he would graduate to the rank of Aspirant, and then the real training would begin.

# CHAPTER TWELVE

Two long years passed, just as Hozark had told him, and they were not easy ones by any stretch of the imagination. Bawb had been subjected to all manner of physical torments designed to test and challenge the will of the Novices as well as their bodies. They trained in speed, but also endurance. In heavy lifting but also fine motor skills. And that was not all.

Heat and cold, wet and dry, the Novices were subjected to all manner of discomfort heaped on top of the already grueling physical challenges. If it was cold, they were to wear thin clothing or none at all. If it was hot, they often had to layer up. All of it served the same underlying purpose. To prepare them for far worse in the real world.

They all worked hard, laboring through the pain, building callouses and muscles, their physiques growing from the effort, as well as the huge amounts of food they ate. Growing children could be ravenous under normal circumstances, but burning off thousands and thousands of calories a day, the would-be Aspirants ate enough to put even a glutton to shame.

And they used all of it.

Their muscles were growing stronger, thickening with

density even as their bones elongated in the growth spurts common to Wampeh of that age. They were getting taller, tougher, and most importantly, their bodies were nearly ready for the next level of training.

They were afforded some basic weapons instruction, but only with sticks and staffs rather than swords and spears. Even the wooden implements were too heavy for their young wrists at first, their inability to properly wield them a source of frustration to each and every one of them, even the strongest of their group lacking the muscle and control to properly swing a sword.

"It's too heavy," Bawb had griped after one particularly disappointing attempt.

"Then grow stronger," Teacher Farpix said matter-of-factly before fastening a pair of arm bands above Bawb's elbows.

Each of them was bristling with thorns. Normally, it would not be an issue—his shoulders had grown considerably stronger over time. But the thorns prevented him from lowering them to a resting position entirely. There was no temporary respite to allow him to recover and reset, and by the end of the day, his sides were damp with blood.

"See the healer," he was told. Words all of them had heard on many occasions.

It was one of the key elements of Ghalian training. Push hard and very possibly get hurt, but know that you would be healed and set right for the next day's training.

In the real world, there would be no healer standing by to tend to one's wounds, but having experienced injury and pain on such a regular basis, the Novices were learning to not fear it but to simply work through it. Hesitation could mean death in their line of work, and ignoring injuries, even serious ones, was something they would all have to learn as second nature.

Bawb was no better or worse than the other Novices at their

tasks, but having a master periodically keeping tabs on him, one of the Five, no less, gave him a little bit of much-needed additional drive. Of course, Hozark would only check in on rare occasions, and he would never interfere or disrupt the youth's training.

For two years Bawb was constantly pushed. Never past the breaking point, but always hard. If he thought he could defend himself, a stronger opponent was pitted against him, never allowing him the comfort of an easy win. It was a physical and psychological strain, testing his limits every single day. And he was miserable more often than not. But going home was not an option. This place was his home now, and there was no way out.

Most of his cohort pushed through the misery right along with him, and though he had initially thought they were a cold bunch who didn't like him, he quickly realized that he had simply been the new kid, and until they saw what he was made of, no one would be his friend. It was all about surviving to the next level, and they had all learned before his arrival that a friend made today might very well not be there the next.

Most had managed to sustain through those years, but a few failed out, young enough to still have their memories of the training house wiped before they were sent to wherever it was the order disposed of those who could not endure the rigors of Ghalian life.

At the end of it all, those who remained had become friends of a different sort. Bonded through shared misery and effort. Not all of them were friends in the truest, traditional sense, but there was a mutual respect even among those who did not always see eye-to-eye.

In an amusing twist of life, Usalla, the young woman who had been the one tasked with kicking Bawb's naked ass when he first arrived as a wide-eyed Null, had since become one of his dearest friends.

Elzina, on the other hand, had remained his nemesis of sorts, always giving him grief while making it abundantly clear she was the top dog in this group. It wasn't just Bawb, however. Anyone who challenged her standing in the rankings was bound to draw her ire.

But unpleasant as she could be, all would concede that Elzina was extremely skilled for her age and likely one of the finest students the teachers had seen in recent years. It was she who had first grasped the visceral ability that she and the others possessed. The thing that made them different from all other Wampeh. The skill that a fraction of a fraction of their kind could wield.

They could steal the power from a natural magic user.

But to do so required something Bawb found disgusting. They had to drink their blood.

Elzina had been able to will her fangs to slide into place almost immediately, while the rest of her classmates struggled with the challenge. It was the first time that the true nature of their future lives was fully laid out for them, and a few had a real problem reconciling what was expected of them.

They would become the deadliest killers in the galaxy. That, in itself, was a challenge, but to drink a power user's blood in the process was something none of them had dreamed of.

Mock battles pitting them against one another as if taking their opponent's power was the only way they could survive were waged in the final weeks of their Novice training, and while he was still smaller than many of his peers and was by no means a true fighter, young Bawb had shown that he could hold his own most of the time.

But while he would fight with vigor, Bawb still held back, even as the masters in charge of the training house came to survey the progress of the students.

"He is too caring. Soft," Master Orvus said with a

disappointed sigh after Bawb managed to get the better of Usalla. He had taken the dominant position but did not move to land a finishing blow on her. "He has the gift, but I fear he may not have the drive to use it."

"Do you think it is time?" Farpix asked. "Most of the others have already passed the test."

Master Orvus pondered a moment, sizing up the youngster with a cool gaze. "Perhaps. Let us find out. Bring the subject."

Farpix motioned to one of the muscular assistants standing near them. He hurried off immediately. A few moments later a scruffy man with deep red skin, stocky limbs, and six-fingered hands was hauled into the courtyard and forced to his knees. He was of a race Bawb had seen once before, but he knew little more about them other than they were among the races that often possessed a modicum of magic without need for a konus.

"Come here, boy," Orvus commanded.

He did as he was bidden.

Master Orvus nodded to the assistant, who pulled the prisoner's head to the side, exposing the thick vein visibly throbbing in the man's neck. "You possess the skill, young Novice. Now it is time for you to use it. You know what you are. What you are to become. What you are capable of doing."

"I-I think so?" he replied with more of an uncertain question than an answer.

Orvus was not pleased. Not one bit. "This man houses a modest amount of power," he continued. "If you feed on him, that power shall become yours. You have seen the others perform the same task. You know what you must do."

Bawb turned to fully face the prisoner, standing over the kneeling man.

"Please don't hurt me!" he blubbered. "I didn't do nothing wrong!"

The boy looked at him with compassionate eyes.

"Bawb, you were given a direct command from the master," Farpix reminded him.

Nevertheless, Bawb stood still, unable, or unwilling, to strike.

"He still will not," Master Orvus said, disgusted. "Fetch another."

"Usalla!" Farpix barked.

The girl stepped forward at once, extending her fangs and sinking them into the man's neck without hesitation. She drank, but not too deep, for her task was not to kill the man, but merely to feed on his power. Orvus seemed pleased at her performance.

"Enough."

She stepped back, blood on her lips.

"Now, fight again."

She nodded once, then launched into an attack, only now she was faster, stronger, and the magic she had absorbed from the man powered her, channeling into a flurry of minor attacks. They had only learned the words, practicing them, focusing on directing their intent, but now, with magic actually inside her, Usalla felt her will connecting to the power. It was a heady sensation, and one she was thrilled to give in to.

She cast her limited range of combative spells, most not working but a few directed with enough skill to properly form and fly true. Bawb found himself unexpectedly battered and tossed, the wildly cast magic knocking him off his feet. Usalla did not stop—the master had given no such command—instead sitting astride his chest, pummeling him until she was finally told to cease.

She immediately got off him and returned to her place with the other Novices.

Master Orvus walked over to the bloody-nosed boy. "Do you see? It is so simple, yet you deny your nature."

The boy said nothing, but quietly rose to his feet. If not for the magic Usalla had tapped into, he would have defeated her again, he knew it. But that wasn't what was expected of him. What was expected was something he simply couldn't bring himself to do. Master Orvus stared at him hard, as if reading his mind with such an intensity of gaze that Bawb found himself wondering if perhaps he actually could.

"Very well. Have it the hard way," the master finally said, walking away in disgust. "Farpix, you know what to do."

"Yes, Master Orvus."

Bawb felt a cold twist in his gut. He knew this meant more punishment. More brutal training. But he had become stronger. Tougher. He had survived this long. If he could just continue to persevere, to get through one day at a time, eventually, hopefully, he might finally find peace.

# CHAPTER THIRTEEN

Because of his reluctance to take blood, life as a Ghalian Novice had just gotten harder. A lot harder, and fast. All manner of unpleasant tasks had been immediately added to Bawb's daily routine. A routine from which there was no respite.

His concerns had not been unfounded.

But on top of that, his failure under the watchful eye of Master Orvus had caused more than a mere increase in his workload. Having been unwilling to present his fangs as commanded, Bawb was now viewed as a *probationary* Novice despite the years of training under his belt.

As a result, he was forced to train harder, longer, and under far more difficult conditions than ever before. And he had to do it with his fangs out much of the time. And when they were, he had to maintain that state of vampiric readiness. To retract them before he was allowed only led to further punishment. He had suffered aches and pains across every inch of his body before, but he had never thought his *teeth* would be exhausted as well.

It was impressive just how creative the Ghalian teachers could be when they *really* wanted to make a point.

Bawb also began abruptly losing confidants and friends.

While he toiled away, the rest of his classmates began graduating, entering the ranks of the Aspirants. And as they did, they departed the Null and Novice bunks for the more private and more comfortable Aspirant lodgings.

New faces were arriving in the Aspirant quarters as well. Apparently, enough would-be Ghalian failed out by the time they reached this level that the teachers would combine classes from many training house locations to bolster the numbers, while also allowing the students to train with new faces who possessed different skillsets.

One by one, his classmates left for the new quarters until, finally, only he remained behind.

A new group of Nulls and Novices would eventually fill the space to capacity, but for the time being, Bawb found himself alone. Alone, and after so many years always surrounded by others, strangely lonely.

The Ghalian worked solo once they graduated to the ranks of the active operatives, but training and living as a group had made him more attached to the presence of others than he had realized. The realization was like living with chronic pain; only when it was gone did you realize what you'd been living with all along.

Bawb was alone, but he also felt as though he wasn't.

It had been roughly two years since his first encounter with it, but the strange light he'd glimpsed during his earliest cavern survival lesson as a young boy had again appeared, albeit briefly, once the other students had moved on.

It was a crazy thought, but for a moment he felt like it almost seemed as if it had been waiting for them to leave. But though he saw it several times, Bawb never got a proper look at it. The dim light was always at the corner of his eye, flitting away in an instant whenever he turned for a better look, revealing nothing whatsoever.

But he was no longer a Null, and he had learned to trust his instincts. And his instincts told him there was something there. *What*, however, he had no idea. It seemed benign enough, but like all things in this training house, he knew that looks could be deceiving.

Weeks crept by as his training continued. He was pushed harder than ever before, each instructor now able to focus their attention fully on him and him alone now that his classmates had advanced. There were times he wondered if he could take any more, times when his body felt like it would simply give out on him.

It was in those moments his teachers would push him even harder, forcing him to adapt and overcome his shortcomings even when he didn't think it was possible. It was this additional pressure, as well as his focus and drive, that saw a surge in his abilities, his aptitude in the many skills increasing far more rapidly than ever before.

He was becoming a talented fighter because of it, and he was even allowed to practice with a konus on occasion despite remaining a Novice. It was a heady sensation, being able to finally cast spells he had been memorizing for years. Of course, most failed miserably, but he was starting to get the hang of it, drawing magic from the band around his wrist.

Bawb would have continued practicing in his free time, but the konus was collected from him at the end of every session.

"If you would just take power, you would have your own internal supply to utilize," Teacher Krallo told him. "You fight well, and you show proficiency with your casting. Put your emotions aside and become what you are meant to be."

Bawb, however, continued to refuse to feed on the prisoners presented to him.

It went on like this for weeks until finally Master Orvus finally had enough.

Bawb was pulled from his morning combative forms lessons and ushered down a corridor into a section of the compound he had never seen before. Of course, that didn't surprise him by now. He had learned long ago that this structure was vast, spanning far more area below ground than anyone in the city would ever have imagined. But today he went somewhere novel. An above-ground arena with open air above it.

Naturally, the Ghalian masters had cloaked and shielded the opening from detection or attack from the outside, but the feeling of a breeze—an actual breeze, not air moved by magic underground—was a wonderful sensation.

Bawb's moment of revelry was soon cut short. He looked around and found his former classmates were all lining the curved wall, as were the new arrivals to the Aspirant ranks. Across from them on the opposite side, sat not only Master Orvus, but several other masters he had seen on rare occasion as well as all of his teachers.

Whatever was going on, this was an all-hands-on-deck situation. A moment later, when a prisoner was walked out and forced to kneel, Bawb realized what was going on.

Master Orvus rose and stepped forward. "Novice Bawb, you have excelled in your training, yet you refuse to perform the one thing all Ghalian must learn to master to progress in the ranks. You *must* feed. Take this man's power and you will rejoin your cohort. It is as simple as that."

Bawb looked at his classmates but did not step forward. The idea was so distasteful to him, even now that he had learned to extend and retract his fangs at will, he had no desire whatsoever to drink anyone's blood, magic user or not.

All present stared at him, waiting for him to move.

He did not.

"Do you think you have a choice in this?" Orvus asked, not

expecting an answer. "Do you believe we have housed you, fed you, trained you, only to have you defy our ways?"

The boy stood silently, taking the berating, not saying a word.

Glances were shared by the masters and teachers. The students gazed straight ahead, fighting the urge to look anywhere but in front of them.

"This one is too soft," another master finally said with a disappointed sigh. "He will be of no use, and he has seen and learned too much of Ghalian ways."

Master Orvus raised an expectant eyebrow. "What would you suggest, Master Imalla?"

"Kill him," she said. "But do so without magic. Make a lesson of it that the others may gain some knowledge from this."

Orvus nodded, then gestured to one of the teachers Bawb did not recognize.

"Donnik, have you fed recently?"

"I have," he replied.

"Then I ask you refrain from using the power you have taken."

"It shall be done as you require," he replied, stepping forward and slipping the konus from his wrist. It was of no concern. He was full of stolen magic anyway and didn't need it, but that didn't matter. No magic was to be used. This was to be done the old way.

"You have squandered this opportunity," he said as he moved slowly toward the boy. "We are rare, our kind, and you had the chance to become one of the galaxy's most elite warriors. Yet you scoff at our generosity."

The boy said nothing. He may very well die this day, but he was not going to go without a fight. He watched the teacher carefully, noting his movements as he spoke, recounting every single technique he had seen his teachers perform. Every lesson he had been taught.

Obviously, there was an enormous amount he had *not* seen, but he hoped there might yet be a slim possibility he could live to see another day.

The man outweighed him by a significant amount, but Bawb had put on a fair bit of muscle in the years he'd been toiling within these stone walls. And as they taught him early on, size is not the determiner of success.

He doubted, however, that his opponent would make any mistakes of overconfidence.

In a flash, and without so much as a wink to say he was beginning, Donnik launched into a rapid attack, closing the distance faster than a man his size would ever be expected to move.

He pummeled the boy with punches, kicks, and elbows—none of them lethal—knocking Bawb to the ground.

The stubborn young man rose back to his feet, dusted himself off, a bit humiliated but mostly unharmed. He set his feet and prepared for the next onslaught.

He was being made an example of. This could take a while.

Donnik moved, and again, Bawb found himself beaten upon, though this time he did manage to land a few small blows of his own, to his attacker's surprise. Donnik seemed pleased by the development. It seemed the little one possessed some fight in him after all. He simply needed to be pushed to desperation to tap into it.

He smiled, then struck again.

Bawb reacted on pure instinct and actually surprised him with a kick snapped to the groin. Of course, Donnik had trained many years to ignore the pain shooting through his lower stomach, but the defensive attack had actually startled him a bit. He immediately spun, faking a low kick, then delivering a fierce hammer fist to the face, knocking the boy to the ground, blood leaking from his lips.

Donnik stepped back a moment, adjusting his trousers as he focused on shutting out the ache in his groin. He then lunged forward. Bawb was as ready as he could be. At least he thought he was, until a pair of blades appeared in the man's hands, slashing two deep gashes in his side.

Shocked, Bawb jumped backward, but that only gave his attacker more opportunities to strike, and soon enough, several more wounds were slowly draining his blood onto the stone floor. This teacher was making an example of him, all right. An example the others would take to heart long after their fellow pupil was dead and buried.

Donnik stepped back, flicking his blood off the blades with a twist of his wrists. He circled the boy, casually twirling the knives in his hands.

"You realize what you could have been. You're no fool. And yet now, rather than achieving glory, you will die like an animal. It is a waste. A stupid, stupid waste by a stupid child. You are a failure, and when your light has flickered out, your remains will be sold for Zomoki food, and none will even remember your name."

A flare of anger flushed within the boy's body. But something else filled him as well. Something hard, and cold. His eyes narrowed as the new sensation flowed through him.

Blades flashed once more, moving for a killing blow, but, miraculously, the boy bent and moved in impossible ways, ignoring the pain from his terrible injuries as he dodged the knives. He twirled through the air, landing just behind the larger man's line of attack.

Without hesitation, Bawb flung himself onto his back, his fangs springing forth as he dug them into the salty flesh of his neck without a second thought, instinct taking over completely as he sucked life-saving power from his teacher in desperate gulps.

The man staggered and nearly fell as his energy dropped dangerously fast, and for an instant, a flash of panic registered in his eyes. He dropped one of his knives, freeing a hand which desperately reached up behind him, barely managing to yank the youth free and fling him away. He then pressed his hand firmly to his neck to stanch the bleeding, staggering back several paces as he did.

Donnik brandished his other knife, but now it was to keep the boy at bay rather than attack. He felt incredibly weak. In fact, it seemed that more than half of his strength had been taken from him. And so quickly? It was unheard of. The power the boy possessed was incredible.

The teacher glanced at the Masters. His expression said enough. Ever so slightly, they nodded to him. Donnik lowered his knife, a slow upward curling shaping the corners of his mouth. In all their time in the training house, none of his pupils had ever seen him smile.

The boy wiped the blood from his lips with the back of his hand and waited for the impending attack that was, for whatever reason, not coming. It didn't matter. He was ready for more. The power he felt flowing through his veins was incredible. It had given him such wonderful strength that he wondered why he had resisted for so long.

Metal clanged, echoing in the silent chamber as the blade fell to the ground. Bawb eyed his attacker with confused but wary eyes. Donnik casually walked to him, his posture relaxed, his open hand extended. Rather than strike him, he clasped the boy's shoulder, looking at him not with anger, but with great approval.

"You have done well today. *Very* well. You have proven your worth." He made a sign with his hand, pressing three fingers to his chest, bowing his head slightly. The masters and other teachers did so as well.

Master Orvus stepped from the raised platform and strode to join them on the arena floor, stopping directly in front of the youth.

"Impressive. I hoped you had it in you. We all did."

"You're not mad?"

"Mad? Anything but. Welcome to the Wampeh Ghalian, *Aspirant* Bawb."

The master's words sank in. He had leveled up, and unlike his cohort, he'd done so facing a far superior adversary, not a weakened prisoner. It would be spoken of for years to come, even long after he was gone.

And so it was the Geist was born. Or at least the first hint of the legendary assassin he would one day become. It was a slow birth, and one that took many, many years, but from that day on, his *real* training began.

# CHAPTER FOURTEEN

Bawb didn't know what he was thinking, allowing himself the delusion that after graduating to Aspirant he would be allowed a break to celebrate with the others.

He couldn't have been more mistaken.

The training resumed pretty much the moment he left the healer, his knife wounds mended and his body ready for more abuse, albeit of a less deadly nature. He wasn't even afforded the opportunity to move his few belongings to the Aspirant quarters. Apparently, that would have to wait.

Interestingly, as he had taken a considerable amount of magic from Teacher Donnik during their fight, the healer had decided it was time to begin his instruction on self-care a little early. How to heal himself using the magic already there and at his disposal.

It was something all Ghalian would eventually learn, but this he could do now, without the need for a konus to make the repairs to his flesh. Also, as Bawb was an Aspirant, that meant he would have little to no control over his spells, and as such, his magic would quickly be squandered but in a way that would not harm others. What better use for it than to try to heal his injuries?

To her surprise, in that respect Bawb was actually a very quick study. Sure, his spells were more miss than hit, and he still had an overall air of barely hidden reluctance about him even after all this time, but nevertheless, he seemed to grasp the meaning of casting with intent on a visceral level. Whether that was because he was using the magic on himself, or that he was just more in touch with the feeling part of spellcasting than most, was unimportant. What mattered was the way he wielded power.

From what little she'd seen in the healing chambers, this young Aspirant would one day become a potent caster indeed.

He thanked her for her impromptu tutelage then hurried off to join the rest of his classmates, the new spells running through his mind. He had no idea what Aspirant training would look like compared to Novices, but he suspected it would be intense, and much more so than anything he'd ever experienced to date.

No sooner had he entered the training chamber when he was beset on all sides. Not one but three students attacked him at once, all of them clothed in masks and attire that hid their true size and shape. He had seen brief demonstrations of how Ghalian could confuse an opponent in such a way, forcing opponents to strike at decoy appendages and false silhouettes, but as a Novice, it wasn't something he had been trained in.

Apparently, as an Aspirant he would.

Bawb flew into motion, defending himself as best he could while trying to move in such a way as to position the attackers all in one general area. Not only would it make blocking and countering their attacks easier, it would also force them to stagger their attempts rather than come at him all at once.

At first, he was simply pummeled as the attackers bumped one another, but then fell into a rhythm, doing as he had hoped, staggering their attacks for maximum individual effect rather than overwhelming him all at once. It was still a dire situation, and Bawb nearly fell several times, but he kept to his feet. Deep in his gut he had a very reasonable expectation that going to the ground would in no way stop the assault.

There would be no respite to gather himself. No time-outs or breaks. He needed to fight back. To do whatever he had to.

Bawb lashed out with his fists and feet, creating a tiny break in the attackers' formation, allowing himself the briefest of moments to take in his surroundings.

He caught a glimpse of not only the other students, but also Teacher Krallo standing nearby, watching him with an amused grin on his lips. A questioning look must have flashed across Bawb's face just before an attacker's fist hit it, because the teacher's eyebrow arched slightly as he let out a laugh.

"You are an Aspirant Bawb. Do not expect help. In the real world Ghalian work alone. Do not expect mercy. Your enemies would not receive it, and neither will you."

Bawb ducked another punch from the nearest attacker, absorbing a kick from another as the third landed a painful elbow strike on his jaw. He saw stars but managed to keep moving, countering and fighting back as he'd been trained to do.

It was Elzina, he realized as she struck again. He had faced her many times over the years, and her movements were particular. Familiar. The way she moved there could be no doubt even with the mask. The other two, however, he did not recognize. They had habits none of his Novice cohort had ever shown. New arrivals from other classes, no doubt.

Whoever they were, they both landed powerful blows to his ribs just as that realization hit. A cracking sensation shook his torso and knocked the wind out of him, forcing him to drop his elbow to cover his damaged flank. Unfortunately, that exposed his face, which took another brutal punch.

This was not going well. Not well at all.

Bawb was hurting. A *lot*. But even as he fought off the multiple attackers, the lesson he had just learned from the healer somehow remained fresh in his mind, replaying almost instinctively, the spells forming on his lips effortlessly. Even as he received fresh injuries, it seemed the means to repair them presented itself to him, courtesy of his recent encounter.

Without realizing he was doing it aloud, he cast one of the healing spells just under his breath during a brief moment of opportunity while his opponents switched positions to better encircle him. A strange sensation washed over him immediately.

The spell wasn't well formed, not by a long shot, and the results were lackluster by most standards, especially considering how much magic he had just squandered, but, nevertheless, the intent behind the words was true, and the magic flowed through him.

Bawb felt his bruises and aches fade abruptly, the burn in his tired muscles retreating in a flash. He was healed. At least, mostly.

Yes, the magic he'd stolen was nearly gone, but he felt almost as good as new. And his opponents were getting tired.

He grinned at the three of them, a new spring in his step. The energized and unafraid look in his eyes made them abruptly question their strategy. They were uneasy with this development, and Bawb reveled in the feeling despite using up so much of his magic.

*Worth it.*

Bawb lunged back into the fray, his attacks fast and strong, fists, feet, and elbows scoring direct hits on his three adversaries in quick succession. He was driving them back with the ferocity of his charge, and his victory seemed assured to all present.

"Enough!" Krallo bellowed, ending the fight in an instant.

Bawb almost felt disappointment, the heady feeling of success washing over him.

He and the others lined up, silently standing at attention. He glanced over at Elzina, the dampness of her bloodied nose slowly seeping through her mask. The others had not fared any better. Their would-be victim, however, looked unscathed.

Krallo leaned close to the boy, examining his barely visible bruises. “Where did you learn to do that?” he demanded.

“I didn’t know. I mean, I only just found out how it all works today.”

“Unlikely. Give me your konus. There was to be no magic in this exercise.”

Bawb lifted his sleeves, showing his bare wrists. “I do not have a konus.”

This actually surprised Krallo, though you’d have been hard pressed to notice the nearly imperceptible dilation of his pupils that was the only outward sign. He held up his hands, muttering a quiet spell as Bawb stood silently at attention.

His eyes wandered, first across the stunned faces of his classmates, then to a small observation area across the chamber. Hozark stood quietly against the wall, plain to see once you knew he was there, yet nearly blending in with his still countenance. Beside him were two people who had just entered the room to join him, each wearing what looked a bit like pirateish attire. Outsiders, no doubt, and non-Ghalian at that.

The man was average in height, with a bit of swagger to him. The woman, on the other hand, was rather diminutive in size, but despite being small in stature, she possessed an air to her of extreme confidence, along with the aura of one prone to quite a lot of violence, should she be provoked. Even across the chamber, Bawb got the distinct feeling that of the two newcomers, she was the one not to mess with.

Krallo noticed Bawb's gaze and turned, nodding to the Ghalian master observing the session.

"Master Hozark, a pleasure," he called out. "What brings you to our class?"

"Merely observing the Aspirants," he called back. "Please, carry on. Do not let my presence interrupt. I would, however, like a word with young Bawb."

Krallo nodded and motioned for Bawb, then turned his attention back to the other Aspirants. Elzina's bruised eyes flashed a decidedly displeased glare at Bawb as she went to join the others for their next lesson. He ignored it. On this one occasion, at least, he had finally bested her, and soundly at that.

Bawb headed toward the master assassin and his visitors, their conversation becoming clear as he drew near.

"Sorry we were late getting here, Hozark," the woman said. "Nixxa's been at it again."

Hozark sighed and shook his head. "What this time?"

"She and a few of her crew took down a small transport convoy. Not a big deal normally; she does it all the time. But this time the ships belonged to the Council of Twenty. I'm sure you know what a mess that stirred up."

"Indeed," Hozark replied. "I assume their response was as swift as it was excessive."

"You can say that again," the man interjected. "I'm telling ya, Hozark, it's a mess for all of us. Any ship with a hint of pirating or smuggling to it has been coming under a ton of scrutiny."

The woman nodded her agreement. "Yeah, it's always something with Nixxa."

"True, that. She's always making things hard for us," her associate agreed.

Hozark chuckled, though he did not sound amused. "She makes things hard for *everyone*. It is a shame, really. She is misguided, yes, but quite skilled, and in general, her intentions are good. At least, to her way of thinking. But still, we may have to deal with her ourselves if she continues to cause these system-wide disruptions."

"She needs to keep her ass in check before she gets on the wrong people's bad side," the man noted with a wink.

Hozark shrugged. "We are well aware of her actions. In fact, she even attacked a Ghalian-allied resupply depot. We discovered the stolen goods spread among the local populace around the area, dispersed at no charge."

The man threw up his hands in a gesture of disbelief. "Sure, she likes to help the locals, but what kind of lunatic pokes at the Ghalian? I mean, that's just asking for trouble."

"Nixxa. *That*'s the kind of nut who would do it," the woman said with a groan. "I swear, I can't believe we actually used to raid with her."

"Yeah, me too. But you gotta admit, she *is* really good at what she does."

"Sure, but is it worth the headache? I mean, we had to dodge, what? Five Council checkpoints just to get here?"

She cut herself short when the young Aspirant joined them, eyeing the boy with quite a degree of curiosity. The man she'd arrived with also sized him up a bit more than he was used to, especially from outsiders.

"Uh, you wanted to see me, Master Hozark?" he asked.

"Yes, Bawb. An excellent display you put on just now, by the way. I am pleased to see you exceed your teachers' expectations. Quite a surprise, your use of magic, especially without a konus."

"Well, I took some for the first time earlier today. Teacher Donnik—"

"Yes, I heard. Very impressive," Hozark said with a proud gleam in his eyes. He turned to the pair beside him. "Bawb, I wish to introduce you to my dear friends, Uzabud and Henni."

Uzabud reached out and grasped him with a firm handshake. "You can just call me Bud."

"And you can call me Henni. Sorry, no fun nicknames for me," the woman added.

Now that they were close, Bawb could see her better, and what he saw was unusual to say the least. Henni had the appearance of a normalish woman, but her eyes sparkled as if they contained galaxies. He'd never seen anything like it.

"They aren't Ghalian," he noted with surprise.

"No, they are not."

"But how are they here at the training house? No one who is not Ghalian is allowed inside. We've all been taught that since as long as I can remember."

"Yes, that is normally the case," Hozark replied. "However, Bud and Henni are allies. They have proven themselves loyal friends of the Ghalian on many occasions, risking life and limb in the furtherance of our objectives. None of the Five possesses so much as a sliver of doubt as to their intentions or loyalties. As such, an exception has been made for them, and they may come and go freely."

"For the most part," Bud corrected. "There are occasions, after all."

"Yes, for the most part," Hozark said with a chuckle. "You are correct, my friend. Suffice to say, these two are trustworthy friends, Bawb, and are among the finest allies you could ever hope for."

"Aww, gee, Hozark. You're too much," Henni said with a sarcastic laugh. "You're gonna make me blush."

"As if *anything* could make you blush," Bud joked.

"Watch it, Mister. Unless you wanna sleep on a cot in the command room again."

"Sorry, sorry. Just kidding."

She shot him a wicked little grin and teasingly patted her rear. "That's right. Now kiss the *other* cheek."

"Oh, bite me, you ass!"

"Only if you ask nicely," she fired back.

Hozark raised his hands as if calming a pair of rowdy children. And to be fair, it almost felt as though he was.

"In any case," he said, "while Ghalian work alone, we do operate with non-Ghalian allies who are not in our order. I have traveled far and wide with Bud and Henni, and they have my complete trust, as they should have yours. They are as close to family as I have ever had outside the order."

"Yeah, kid. Us and your, uh, Hozark, here, are tight. And that friendship now extends to you. If ever the need arises, just reach out to us."

"Thank you, Mr. Uzabud."

"Just Bud, please."

"Thank you, Bud. But how would I even contact you?"

Henni reached out and smacked him on the shoulder. "Don't worry, kid. Hozark knows how to find us. And I'm sure when you're ready, you will too. Now, if you'll excuse me, I hear there's a mess hall buffet with my name on it."

Henni trotted off in search of food, leaving the somewhat confused boy at a loss for words.

"She's not kidding," Bud added with a friendly grin. "For someone her size, even after all these years, I still have no idea where she puts it all. I'd better catch up to her, otherwise there'll be nothing left for any of the rest of us. Hozark, a pleasure, as always. And Bawb," he said, turning to leave, "it really was a pleasure finally meeting you. I have a feeling we'll be seeing a lot more of each other one day."

# CHAPTER FIFTEEN

The Aspirant lodgings were quite similar to those in which Bawb had spent his Null and Novice days, but when he sat on his new bunk, he noticed it was a tiny bit softer. A modicum of comfort afforded those who had persevered and made it this far.

It was still a spartan lifestyle, but there were a few additional new amenities available to the trainees. For one, a small workspace was set up in a recessed area in one of the walls, cushions and low chairs available to those who wished to sit quietly after hours and continue their studies.

There was also a slightly larger bathing area that contained a small sauna room where Aspirants could sit and let the knots in their overtaxed muscles recover from the day's hard labors. Beside it were a series of individual tubs sunk into the floor. The cold water constantly flowing through them came from a source deep beneath the training facility and was not only just above freezing, but was also pure enough to drink, if one so desired.

After a long enough session in the sauna, a few would do just that once their salty sweat had washed away.

When the day's training was over, Bawb was finally allowed to gather his things from his prior lodgings, tuck them away, then rejoin the other Aspirants. Dinner would be upon them shortly, but at least he would have a short respite to see his friends and wash up.

He quietly entered the chamber and made his way to his bunk.

"Bawb, you are finally joining us!" Zota called to him, clearly happy his friend was now an Aspirant.

Usalla also came to greet him, along with several others from his former cohort.

"That was quite a demonstration today," she mused. "I did not realize you knew the healing arts."

"Nor did I," he admitted.

"Then how did you manage to do what you did? I've never seen the like."

He shrugged. "It was just something that came to me. The healer guided me in using the power I took from Teacher Donnik when I went to see her. I suppose the lesson was so fresh in my mind, I just used it instinctively."

"Your instincts served you well."

"I'll say," Zota agreed. "We were all shocked when you latched onto Donnik like that. I was sure you were as good as dead."

"As was I. But then something triggered in me."

Usalla chuckled. "I would say that is quite the understatement, wouldn't you agree?"

"I suppose so. I must admit, as soon as I began to drink, to take his power, well, it felt like I'd been a fool resisting my nature for so long."

Another one of their classmates heard the conversation and came over to join them. Finnia was her name. She had been singled out as not particularly suited for the assassin life in her first year with the Novices. She possessed a sharp mind and the drive to succeed, but the instinct to kill was weak within her, and that made her too much of a risk to send into the field as an assassin. But she possessed a number of other skills, all of which impressed the teachers.

And so, rather than being sent back to normal life, she was now receiving a specialized version of their training. In her case, less focus was placed on certain assassin skills while more was directed on her stealth and infiltration abilities. And at that, she excelled. With that, her course was set. Finnia was to be a spy.

"What was it like? Drinking from such a strong source like that?" she asked. "We all graduated using barely powered prisoners. But Teacher Donnik had recently fed. A fairly powerful emmik, I understand."

"How did you hear that?" Zota asked, joining the group.

"I have my ways. You do realize I *am* training to be a spy, Zota, do you not?" she replied with a grin.

She and Zota had something of a history of sniping banter between them, with him often taking the brunt of her quick wit. But the intent was never malicious, and the two were clearly fond of one another, though they had been told from their first days as Nulls that Ghalian did not bond and did not form unions.

Still, it seemed Zota at least entertained the idea in the back of his mind, even if he would never act on it.

As for Bawb, he found her personality quirks amusing. She had a nimble intellect and thought well on her feet and would make a fine spy one day, indeed. And it was no wonder she was curious about taking real power. Someday it could very well mean life or death in her line of work. All of theirs, for that matter.

He mulled over the sensation, carefully selecting the right words to describe the feeling. "It was a rush, not a trickle. Nearly too much in a way. As if I was drinking in energy from a great torrent rather than a stream. Almost overwhelming. Had he not pulled me off, I do not know if I would have been able to stop myself."

"Something we will all practice, I'm sure," Usalla noted, ever practical in her approach to their studies. "We cannot go draining people to their demise, after all. At least, not those who are not our targets."

"Indeed," Bawb agreed. "And those without power will be of no use to us anyway, so our natural magic user resources to feed from will be limited more often than not."

Others could not help but overhear the discussion, and soon enough, quite a few of them joined the small gathering. Bawb, it seemed, was something of a minor celebrity among the Aspirants, at least for the moment.

Everyone wanted to discuss what he had experienced. Everyone but Elzina, that is. Her broken nose had been healed, and she bore no lingering signs of her defeat, but the way he had managed to upstage her, and in front of her new classmates no less, left her feeling slighted. Challenged, even.

She was the top dog in this group, something she would work hard to remind them all.

"That. Was. Amazing!" an unfamiliar boy blurted, smacking Bawb on the back with a little too much enthusiasm for his taste. The youth didn't seem to notice, however, steamrolling on, having barely taken a breath. "I mean, the way you were all, *wham, bam*! And they were all, *oof!* It was the most fun I've had in ages."

Bawb glanced across the room and caught the sour look on Elzina's face. She clearly didn't like their new classmate. "It was combat. I do not know that I would necessarily call it fun."

"Well yeah, sure. Not *fun*-fun. But still, it was great," the boy continued. "Oh, I'm Albinius, by the way. Or you can call me Albi."

"I am Bawb, as it seems you already know."

"We all do. The last few days the others were telling us there was still one of you from the original group in this training house who was being held back. I thought they were going to boot you out, or worse!"

"It was very nearly the latter."

"I know! But now you've jumped to the head of the class. It's fantastic!"

The enthusiasm, while appreciated, also rubbed Bawb the wrong way. The very public outburst would only serve to draw Elzina's ire even more, though, to be fair, he would undoubtedly already have had to deal with her because of this anyway. In any case, it was too late. The die was cast, and he would just have to roll with the punches, figurative as well as literal.

"Don't mind him," a serious-faced young woman said. "He talks. A *lot*. But it's all part of his act. He's been developing his undercover persona for the last year, and it is a bit exhausting."

"You know you love it, Martza," he shot back.

Her attention remained on Bawb, though her head shook side to side. "One day, I fear he will forget who he really is and irritate the teachers for the last time."

"Good thing I'm such a hard worker, then."

"Because you lack the proclivity for spell casting, you have no choice but to work harder," she shot back.

"Low blow, Martza."

"And well-deserved. Now, if you'll kindly keep your exuberance under check, I think we would all like to hear more about Bawb's experience with not only real power, but also using it for healing. The master observing the fight seemed quite impressed."

"That was Hozark," Bawb said.

The newcomers had apparently never met him but knew him by reputation. "You know one of the Five?" Albinius gasped. "What's he like?"

Bawb hesitated. "Uh, he is a teacher. A master. One who gives guidance and counsel."

"Yeah, but he's one of the *Five*."

"And you would never know it to speak with him," Bawb noted. "A matter which I believe is the whole point."

"Aspirants! On your feet!" a deep voice boomed, the command echoing off the walls.

The owner of the voice was a stocky man, a pair of blades strapped to his hips, a thick konus on his wrist. He bore several large scars even though a healer could have easily repaired them. But some of the teachers who no longer needed to blend in for public contracts chose to leave them be, wearing them as trophies as well as cautionary reminders of the seriousness of their work.

"I am Teacher Rovos. You will all be getting to know me *very* well in the coming months and years. I will train you in many aspects of Ghalian ways, but none so important as the use of magic. You will all become deadly in the martial ways, but wielding magic with skill can, and will, be the difference between a long life as a Ghalian and a quick fate. And let me assure you, dying without permission is not allowed."

"But if we're dead, how can—" Albinius foolishly began to say.

"I did not tell you to speak!" Rovos barked. He stormed over to the boy, his face pressed almost against the poor student's. "You're a joker, are you?"

"Uh—"

"Albinius, isn't it? Yes, I've been informed of your tendencies. That mouth of yours is going to get you in trouble one of these days."

"I didn't mean to—"

"Twenty laps around the second-level sparring field." He stared hard at the boy. "What are you waiting for?"

"I thought—"

"Do not think. Go!"

Albinius lurched into motion, running for the door before additional punishment could be piled on. Rovos glared at the rest of them, walking through their ranks like a dangerous predator just waiting for someone to be foolish enough to present him a reason to react. The rest of the students, wisely, stood stock-still, eyes forward and mouths shut.

"Does anyone else have anything clever they wish to add to the conversation?"

No one said a word.

"You are learning. Good. This is not a dialogue. This is a monologue. I teach; you listen. I command; you obey. Do so and maybe one day you will actually become proper Ghalian. Fail to do so at your own peril. Now, your friend will be occupied for some time. The rest of you are to come with me. Today we begin digging into the *real* lessons that will set you on your path to becoming Ghalian. That, or you will fail miserably and lose limbs, if not your lives."

Teacher Rovos turned and stormed out of the room, the students quickly falling in behind him lest they draw his ire. Bawb glanced at Usalla and Zota, sharing a brief look of concern. The expressions on their faces said it all. They were in for a whole new kind of training, it seemed.

Life was about to get a lot more interesting. Whether that was good or bad, they would find out very shortly.

# CHAPTER SIXTEEN

An older woman with warm, round cheeks was waiting in the sparring field when the Aspirants arrived, watching Albinius with a little grin creasing her lips as he ran and ran.

"Keep it up. You've got this," she called out to him as he passed her. "Ah, Rovos, there you are. After this one showed up on his own, I was beginning to wonder if you were just going to send the students one at a time."

"Pallik," he replied with a curt nod.

She walked past him, surveying the ranks with a pleasant smile on her face. "So, let us have a look at these Aspirants, shall we? Give them a little trial by fire. I am Teacher Pallik. Today, Teacher Rovos and I will be guiding you in the use of a konus and the casting of basic spells. You have been practicing them, I know, but the difference between memorizing the words and actually putting them to use is quite challenging at first."

"Bawb already cast a healing spell," Zota blurted, his cheeks darkening the moment he caught himself.

"Yes, I was made aware of that," she noted. "And which one of you is Bawb?"

Uncomfortable being the object of this unexpected attention, Bawb stepped forward. "I am."

"Pallik, you already know who he is," Rovos grumbled. "Can we please dispense with the games and get on with it?"

"I just wished to see how he would respond to the situation. Not a shy one, I see."

"We cannot afford to be shy," the young student replied. "We are training to be Ghalian. Shyness is not an option."

Teacher Pallik nodded her approval, and even crotchety Teacher Rovos seemed pleased by the reply, though his face was far more difficult to read than hers.

Pallik stepped close and placed her hand on Bawb's head. "Ah, yes. I sense there is still a little of the power you took from Donnik remaining in you. An impressive display. Donnik is quite skilled and certainly no pushover."

"I didn't really mean to—"

"No, of course not. But yet you did, and under great pressure, no less. That is admirable. But for now, you will all be learning to draw power from a konus. While we Ghalian are the few of our kind with the ability to take power from another, it is not something to be relied upon."

Teacher Rovos stepped forward and lifted his hand, a moderately ornate golden band held aloft. "A konus such as this, on the other hand, is consistent. Predictable. A source of magic that we can fill and empty time and again, always knowing exactly how much magic is at our disposal. It is one of these you will be utilizing to begin your journey into spell casting."

He nodded to the table near the closest doorway to the chamber. On it lay a selection of basic konuses.

"You will soon be given your first konus. The masters will confer and select one they deem appropriate for each of you. This will then remain with you for the duration of your training. Skill, attitude, strengths and weaknesses, all will be taken into consideration during the process. For the time being, however, you will be afforded the use of one of these basic konuses. They are functional and charged, but of low enough power that you will not be at risk of accidentally causing any real harm. For now you will learn the basics. How to make fire. How to cast an illumination spell. That sort of thing."

A hand shot up.

Rovos gave a slight nod of his head. "Yes, Marzis?"

"I was just wondering, what about the other spells? The fighting ones."

Rovos sighed. "Pallik? Would you care to answer that?"

"You see, Marzis, there is much more to the art of casting than merely reciting the words. Even if you have the intent fully formed in your mind, combining the vocalizations with the internalized direction is something that can take years to become proficient in. This is why you have been practicing the verbal portion only for so long. To master the basics upon which to build. But as you are well aware, the words and intent are nothing without a source of magic to power them. And as you also know, only emmiks and vislas contain truly significant levels of naturally occurring power within them."

"What about Drooks? Or Ootaki?" Usalla asked politely. "They make their own power."

"Yes, they do, but you should already know that Drooks possess only one kind of power, and it is specific to the flight and control of various sorts of vessels. They funnel their power to charge a drookonus to do the job in their absence, but that is essentially all they can use it for. They still require a konus for even the most simple of spells outside their natural abilities. Now, as for the others, what do we know about Ootaki?" she asked.

Finnia was the first to speak up on that front. "They are essentially storehouses of power, absorbing it not only from the sun of the system they are in, but also from any power user who would want to save some of their power for later use. Their capacity is supposed to be almost limitless, and they can hold way more than a konus can."

Pallik seemed pleased. "Very good, Finnia. But what else do we know about Ootaki? Anyone?"

"It's their hair," Bawb said quietly.

"What was that?"

"Their hair. It's where they store their power."

"Good. And what more do you know?"

"If you cut it, the hair loses a lot of power. Less if it's given freely, but they still lose a bunch."

Teacher Pallik nodded her approval. "Correct, Bawb. Ootaki hair is a valuable commodity, and as a result, they are often hunted and kept enslaved specifically for that purpose. Ootaki cannot use the power they contain, making them the safest way to store power. Unfortunately, they are treated as livestock for that reason. Something all Ghalian find abhorrent."

"But what about Drooks?" Usalla asked. "They're kept aboard ships for pretty much their whole lives."

Teacher Rovos cleared his throat. "Drooks are a different matter entirely. They are treated exceptionally well, for starters. The best food. The best lodging. And they work in close-knit teams to power ships. But more than that, they *want* to live life aboard a ship. It gives them a sense of purpose, of satisfaction, being able to use their powers like that. Without a ship to guide, they would be living the plainest lives imaginable."

"He's right," Pallik agreed. "We have even freed teams of Drooks in the past only to have them immediately seek out another ship to call home."

"Exactly," he said. "It is what they desire, and it is not our place to tell them to do otherwise."

A curious look spread across Elzina's face. "Teacher Rovos, I understand they may wish to remain aboard a ship, but what about their power? We can take from those who naturally produce it on their own. How does Drook power work when absorbed by a Ghalian?"

Rovos's countenance darkened slightly. "We do not take from Drooks. We do not take from Ootaki. This is simply how things are done."

Elzina looked as though she had a follow-up to that question but thought better of it.

Bawb took her words to heart, as well as those of their teachers. Yes, he had been taught that very few people actually possessed power of their own, but it had never really been important to him. He was just a normal kid, or so he thought.

But now that he had experienced the surge of power in his body from drinking magical blood, he was forced to reassess the whole power dynamic from top to bottom.

"Another question, if I may."

"Yes, Bawb?" Rovos replied.

"We can take magic from people. But what of other sources? Some animals possess magic of their own."

Disgust briefly flashed across the teacher's face, quickly pushed away, replaced by his usual stoic expression. "Yes, many animals do, in fact, possess power to varying degrees, and it can be used in the most dire of situations. It can be enough to keep you alive. To heal basic injuries. But this sort of power generally does not sit well with our kind and is to be avoided unless there is no other option. Animals and Wampeh Ghalian should not mix."

"Well, that's not *entirely* true," Pallik noted. "There are Zomoki, after all."

"You know as well as I that the truly powerful Zomoki have not been seen in hundreds of years. Not since the destruction of Visla Balamar's home. All that remains is a wasteland."

"Visla Balamar?" Bawb asked. "I've never heard of him."

"Nor would you. He has been dead since long before you were conceived. But since the subject has been broached, I will spend a moment on something you would normally learn later in your studies. The visla was a powerful man. Extremely powerful, in fact. So much so that the Council of Twenty had to band together as a single force to destroy him."

"It took that many to fight this one person?" Usalla marveled.

"Yes. But that is because of two factors. One, he had befriended the Wise Ones. Ancient, powerful Zomoki who possessed more than just exceptional power, but also the ability to utilize it to jump not only from planet to planet, but from system to system, spanning the galaxy."

"A Zomoki could do that? But they're just aggressive beasts," Elzina marveled.

"What we have left of them today, yes. But the Wise Ones? They were great intellects. Animals with the power of speech as well as deep reserves of magic. And Visla Balamar was their ally and source of the greatest restorative in the galaxy. The Balamar waters."

Elzina's attention sharpened. "What are they? Some kind of elixir? How difficult are they to acquire?"

"Oh, you do not ever wish to come across the Balamar waters, Elzina. For while they are a powerful healing concentrate when applied to the scales of Zomoki and the skin of other races, they are fatal for Ghalian, reducing us to ash in an instant."

The girl's confidence faltered. "If we get splashed, we *die*?"

"Yes."

A murmur rose among the students. This was a weakness none of them had ever known they possessed, and the revelation that something as simple as being splashed with this Balamar water could end them was disquieting, to say the least.

"Now, students, do not panic," Pallik said, attempting to settle them down. "The Balamar waters were destroyed along with Visla Balamar and the Zomoki he called his friends. Now, so many centuries later, only a tiny amount still exists anywhere in the galaxy. And we Ghalian do all we can to procure any trace we learn of."

Zota shook his head, confused. "But you said it would kill us."

"And it would. But we take precautions, sealing it up tight with layers upon layers of spells before tucking it away in our most secret of vaults. The more we control, the less likely we are to encounter it used against us, you see. But this will all be gone over in detail when you are older. This is not a lesson for today. Today, we will begin with basic spell casting. Each of you, please take a konus from the table and put it on."

The students all did as they were told, quietly talking among themselves as they did, shocked at the revelation they had just heard. Their training to date had been preparing them to be what they'd been told were invincible assassins. But this? A simple fluid that could end them quicker than any sword? It had set them all ill at ease.

Bawb put on a konus and got back in line with the others, unable to put the idea of bursting into flames out of his mind. It was disconcerting, to say the least, but it made sense that the Ghalian would acquire the Balamar waters whenever they could, frightening as it was. He forced his mind to calm as best he could. It was out of his hands. All they could do was train. Train, and be ready.

"Before we begin, there will be an exercise at the start of every session," Rovos announced as he walked past the row of Aspirants. "You will practice extending your fangs. This is to be a daily task. You will practice until this becomes as natural as breathing. They will be ready when you need them, but safely tucked away when not. This skill could be the difference between survival and failure." He looked at the young students, blank canvases ready to be painted. "What are you waiting for? Begin!"

The Aspirants jumped into action and quickly did as they were told, each of them forcing their fangs into place with varying degrees of success.

Bawb's appeared with ease at once. He looked at the others, all of them having a bit of difficulty. He retracted them and extended them again.

"Well done, Bawb," Rovos said as he walked past him. "Elzina, all the way out! Do not be lazy in this exercise! Martza, retract faster! Come on, let me see some effort here. All of you know this can be done. You would not be here if you did not."

The practice went on for several minutes, during which time Bawb was afforded a rare bit of a respite of a sort during which he had the realization that his earlier failure, and the rough treatment he had received as a result, had actually set him ahead of his classmates in this particular skill.

Failure could still lead to success. It was a lesson he was going to be sure to take to heart.

Heavy breathing and a whiff of fresh sweat met the ears and noses of the Aspirants.

"What did I miss?" Albinius asked, huffing and puffing from his run.

Rovos simply stared at him. "Was that twenty laps?"

"Yes, Teacher."

"Then you may rejoin the others. We are practicing the extending of fangs, after which we will move on to basic spells, starting with a simple illumination spell."

"But what about the cool stuff?" he asked, a hint of a whine in his tone.

Bawb felt his body tense and sensed the others doing so as

well. Albinius really needed to learn when to keep his mouth shut. Fortunately, Rovos had already punished him and was more likely to be a little bit lenient.

The teacher locked his gaze on the boy, unblinking. "Listen well, Albinius. I will tell you this once. You are an Aspirant. While that is a step up from a Novice, you are still among the lowest of the low. And as such, you must walk before you run. More complex spells will not be taught until you are proficient with the basics."

Albinius let out a disappointed sigh. Bawb winced at the sound.

"But can't we try just one? I mean, what's the harm in it?"

Rovos's expression shifted to a glare. He was not amused.

"You master the basics first. They are the basis upon which you build the rest of your knowledge."

"I get it, really. I just thought it would be fun to—"

Rovos held up his hand, his jaw muscle twitching. "You wish to run before you walk? Fine."

"Really?"

"Oh, yes. Really."

"Wow. Great. What do I do?"

"Do? You will run. Another twenty laps."

The look on the boy's face was priceless, and Bawb and his friends had to fight hard not to chuckle, knowing full well if they did, they would join their classmate. Somehow, they succeeded as Albinius jogged away, leaving them to hide their mirth and continue with their training.

# CHAPTER SEVENTEEN

Following breakfast the next day, the Aspirants were afforded a rare bit of quiet time to themselves. Under any other circumstances the students would have rejoiced at the unexpected respite, but they had been training under the watchful eyes of the Ghalian instructors for long enough to know full well that where there was rest, there was sure to be increased work shortly thereafter.

The question was, what form would it be in?

Sometimes physical tasks were presented to them. Those, while tough on the body, were relatively straightforward in nature. Overcome and push through adversity and pain to reach your objective.

Other times, however, they were required to solve puzzles while engaged in their training, draining mental power as well as physical. Bawb had long ago learned that using his brain firing on all cylinders was a surefire way to burn through everything he'd eaten that day, so taxing were those lessons.

Today, whatever lay ahead of them was still a mystery. And since there was nothing he could do about the unknown, Bawb decided to simply use the free time to get in a little practice on his own.

He made his way to one of the smaller training rooms on the same floor as the bunk house. All he needed were thick walls and a bit of privacy to experiment with what little power still remained inside of him.

He attempted to cast the spells he had learned the prior day but found himself unable to produce fire after several attempts. Illumination, however, seemed to be relatively easy, and he repeatedly generated a tiny bit of light without the benefit of a konus.

Interestingly, he could now recognize the sensation of his internal magic stores draining. He didn't have much left, and far less than he'd thought initially.

"Better to use it in training," he reasoned, fully cognizant of the fact that if he didn't burn through the power on his own, the teachers would surely find a task to drain him completely soon enough.

His being able to cast the healing spells without the benefit of months of practice had both impressed and disquieted them. He had been no prodigy up until this point, and anyone could get lucky on occasion. But for an Aspirant to be able to cast with stolen power, and at such a young age, no less, the situation held the potential for problems, if not disaster.

Bawb decided it was time to try something else. Something the teachers had not instructed him in the previous day. He walked to the wall and dragged his arm along a rough edge, pressing just hard enough to draw a thin line of blood.

*Good.*

He then focused his mind on mending his flesh. Repairing the damage from within, as he had done the previous day. The door abruptly opening stopped his attempt.

"Bawb," a familiar voice called in greeting.

"Master Hozark. How did you know I was here?"

"The Five make it our business to know all that happens within our walls."

"Wow."

Hozark chuckled. "That, and I simply asked your classmate." He glanced at the trickle of blood on the boy's arm, one eyebrow arching slightly at the sight. "You are injured?"

"Not really. I was just, well, I wanted to see if I could still heal myself like I did yesterday."

The master assassin grinned wide. "Then please, do not let me interrupt. Carry on."

That was easier said than done. Previously, he had done it without thinking about it. Instinct in the heat of battle when he couldn't afford to be distracted. But now here was a master, one of the Five, no less, quietly watching his attempt. It was more than a little disquieting.

"Breathe," Hozark said, noting the boy's discomfiture. "You know how to do this. Focus on that one spell. Put all else out of your mind."

*Easier said than done*, the boy mused.

He tried his best to envision the spell's purpose, pulling from the little magic remaining within him as he uttered the words that would heal his wound. "*Maktus olara*," he said, forming the words with their intent burning in his mind. "*Maktus olara*."

An itch sprouted on his arm, the sensation of pins and needles making him lose focus. And just like that, the last of his internal power was gone.

Hozark nodded, seemingly unconcerned by the failure. If anything, he appeared almost pleased.

"That was a very good beginning, Bawb. You nearly accomplished your goal, and with almost no formal training in the healing arts and only a fraction of the power normally required for one your age."

"But I failed."

"At the end result, yes. But learning is failing. Everyone has done so, from the lowest Null to the head of the Five."

"I know, but it still feels like I'm letting myself down. Letting you down."

"Nonsense. Look how far you have come. You have passed the initial phases and are no longer a Novice. You are a full-fledged Ghalian Aspirant now. How do you feel?"

Bawb hesitated. "I don't know. The same, I guess."

He expected to be corrected, given some words of inspiration and a pat on the back, but instead, Hozark's reaction was altogether different.

"And you are correct," he said, pleased with the youth. "You *are* the same. So many suffer from the false hope that by simply leveling up in the order, they will suddenly experience a paradigm shift in their training. Those people are always disappointed. But in a way, you are different, just not one that you can notice with the passing of just one day."

"What do you mean?"

"I mean, you have entered a new phase of your training, and your prior years have prepared you for it. You have worked hard, Bawb, and now the *difficult* part begins."

"You mean all that was supposed to be easy? Those years of hard work?"

"No, of course not. But that which was hard to a Null is simple to an Aspirant. Second nature, even. You are gaining in abilities you don't even realize, and soon enough you will discover which aspects of Ghalian life you are most suited for."

"But we all train together."

"Yes, but each of you has a strong suit. Take Finnia, for example. A talented young woman with stealth skills unrivaled in your cohort. But she is a middling fighter and lacks the psychological makeup to be an assassin. But she is still a Ghalian, only her gifts will be focused on spy craft more than combatives. And it seems you two have a good rapport. That is pleasing. In our world you always want to keep your spies close. They can be the difference between success and failure. Strengthen that relationship and it will serve you well."

"I will."

"Good. But also remember, our Ghalian brothers and sisters cannot always disguise themselves to avoid scrutiny, no matter how skilled they are, and as such, we sometimes rely on agents from outside the order. Those who are not Wampeh Ghalian, but who ally with us if the coin is good and the task within their reach. Those you must get to know for yourself. Never give your full trust to an asset until they have proven themself to you."

"Like Bud and Henni?"

"Yes, like Bud and Henni. I trust them with my life, as they trust me with theirs, but I did not come to this assessment lightly, and not without all of us facing and surviving great danger together."

"I will commit your advice to memory."

"May it serve you well. Now, there are others in your class who I believe will be formidable in their own right one day. Take Elzina. A strong fighter and driven to the point of being almost *too* zealous. She is firmly afoot on the killer's path."

"And can be a bit of a bitch, if I may speak freely."

"Of course. Do not worry, Bawb. Most of us suffered from a nemesis of one sort or another as we rose through the ranks. But ultimately, they made us stronger for all their difficult behavior. I hope she will prove the same for you."

"And me? What about me?"

"We will see. You are emotional, Bawb. *Too* emotional, many would say. And while that can be overlooked in Nulls and Novices, as an Aspirant, you must endeavor to keep your feelings under wraps where they cannot be used against you. Now, on to the reason I came here. I have something for you."

Hozark reached into his cloak pocket and pulled out a slightly dull golden band. Ornate runes and design work had been inlaid into the metal, but all of it seemed to have been worn flatter over time. This was a konus, and a sturdy one at that, but it had seen better days.

Hozark held it out to the boy. "This is to be your konus from this point on."

"They said we'd be getting one of our own. I didn't expect it this soon. It looks a little different than what we've been using."

Hozark leaned in, speaking in a conspiratorial hush. "Well, that is because this is no ordinary konus, Bawb. Crafted by a rather curious race, it has some, shall we say, *unusual* quirks. But it will not fail you. It may be old, and clearly not designed for Ghalian use, but what it lacks in flash, it makes up for in both power as well as some rather unconventional features."

"What do you mean, unconventional?"

"You will soon find out," he replied with a knowing smile. "This konus will communicate with you and you alone. No one else will be able to see or hear what it presents you. Its messages are for your eyes and ears only. Do you understand?"

"Not really. You're saying it talks?"

"In a way. Konuses do not speak, not normally, and they cannot be enchanted as some weapons. But those who fashioned this particular konus did something different with it. Something marvelous and quite unique. And though it is not Ghalian in origin, it has been adjusted to heed our kind. It has seen a great amount of magic flow through it over time, and as a result it has developed a bit of a personality of its own. Not a truly independent life form, but it is far more than just a tool."

"It's alive?"

"Yes and no. Suffice it to say, this konus will guide you

through your studies and help you achieve more than you may think yourself capable of. It is also incredibly powerful. One of the strongest I've ever seen, in fact."

"But I'm an Aspirant. Why give it to me? What if I hurt someone?"

"Eventually, that will be the point. You are training to be an assassin, after all. But none of that power will be accessible to you until you have reached the appropriate level of training. For now, it will simply appear to all as a trainee's konus, nothing more. You may consider that a safety feature of sorts as well as a roadmap to help you progress."

Bawb reached out and touched the metal with tentative fingertips. It wasn't hot or cold, but simply a comfortable, neutral temperature. Strangely enough, it almost felt familiar, as if it was always meant to be his even though he'd never seen it before today.

"Go ahead. Put it on," Hozark said, releasing his grip.

Bawb slid it over his hand and onto his wrist. The band shrank slightly, fitting itself to just the right size once in place. He knew some konuses could do this, but the ones they had trained with the previous day were bare-bones models lacking any such features.

He felt for the power it contained but came up empty. So far as he could tell, it was no more than a powerless piece of metal. Hozark watched him try to connect for a moment before stopping him.

"It needs to be activated," he said. "A phrase that will only work for you. To anyone else it will appear to be no more than a drained konus."

"Another safety feature?"

"You could say that. Now, to activate it, simply say the word *Mozgas*. It will do the rest."

Bawb held his arm a little bit away from his body, unsure what might happen next. "*Mozgas.*"

Nothing.

"Um, Master Hozark? I don't think that worked."

Hozark chuckled to himself. "Oh, it did, I assure you. Give it a minute to connect with you properly."

"Connect?"

"I told you, it is for you and you alone. And it will guide you, but to do so, it first needs to establish your baseline. Trust me, you'll see. And now I will leave you to it. Oh, and for your first exercise, perhaps you might try drawing from it to heal that scratch on your arm. I'm confident you can do it."

With that he turned and walked out, leaving a very confused Aspirant alone in the chamber.

Bawb held up his wrist and looked at the band. It wasn't glowing or doing anything else out of the ordinary. In fact, it still seemed to be quite inert.

"Well, this is going to be interesting."

A tingle vibrated in his wrist then stopped.

"Uh, hello? I am talking to an inanimate object. This is ridiculous."

*Greetings, Aspirant Bawb* a voice said.

Bawb spun around. He was alone.

"Hello?"

*Again, greetings, Aspirant Bawb.*

"Wait, is this my konus?"

*Very perceptive. Clearly, you are a great intellect and will fly through the levels*, the konus said sarcastically.

"A snarky konus? Oh, Hozark, what have you done to me? I never thought leveling to Aspirant would lead to *this*."

*Levels. Displaying now.*

A translucent image leapt from his wrist, appearing right in front of him. It took a moment, but he quickly realized what it was. It was a list of the levels in Ghalian training. Or he was pretty sure it was. Only Null, Novice, Aspirant and Vessel were legible. The remaining levels were blurred out, barely visible.

"Why can't I read the others?"

*You are an Aspirant. You can only perceive levels you are on or are directly working toward.*

"And these other things floating off to the side?" he asked of the minimized icons hovering at the periphery of the display.

*Your skills.*

"My skills?" he wondered, reaching out for the symbols.

His hand passed right through them.

*These are not tangible items*, the konus reminded him. *Nor can any but you perceive them, just as only you can hear me. Worth noting, it would be advised you don't try to touch them. You would draw undue attention to yourself, reaching out and grabbing nothing like a fool.*

"You think?"

*Just stating a fact. I've been doing this far longer than you have drawn breath.*

"So how do I see them?"

*Like all things magical, it relies on your intent, though in this particular instance, verbalization of a spell isn't required. Think it and so it will be.*

"Think it, huh?" *Okay, show me the skills.*

*With intent, Aspirant Bawb. Come on, don't be lazy. You don't need the same focus as casting, but it requires more than just casually thinking to yourself*, the konus said.

"You read my thoughts," he stated more than asked.

*A solid grasp of the obvious. Clearly, you will go far, young Ghalian.*

Bawb was tempted to say something back when the absurdity of arguing with a barely sentient piece of magical metal around his wrist struck him. He calmed himself and focused instead, turning his mind to the intent of his desire. *Show me the skills,* he thought again.

A flash of icons displayed in front of him, threatening to block the entire room from view. There were so many of them, and most were still blurred out. Too advanced for an Aspirant, it seemed. But some were clear, and most of them had a zero next to them.

"This says agility is at one."

*Yep. That's correct.*

"But I've been training for years."

*That is also correct. But while you may have become relatively agile for a regular man, you're still a toddler by Ghalian standards.*

Bawb wasn't going to argue. Instead, he just scanned the icons and words, trying his best to make sense of it all.

"This is ridiculous. How am I supposed to do anything if this image blocks my field of view?"

*Make it so it does* not *block your field of view.*

"I can adjust this?"

*You can adjust everything.*

"But how?"

*Please rephrase the question.*

"What's the trick to adjusting them?"

*Please rephrase the question.*

Bawb felt his ire start to rise. "You just don't want to tell me, do you? You want me to figure it out on my own."

A chime sounded, and one of the blurred icons suddenly became clear. The number one slid into place next to it. Bawb read the words. "Perception of deceit?"

*Well done. You have just ranked at the lowest level that is not zero,* the konus said with a healthy dose of sarcasm.

Without really thinking about it, Bawb envisioned the sprawling image going away.

It vanished.

He stared at the konus a moment then pictured it reappearing. The image once more filled his field of vision.

"Ah," he muttered. "Okay. Now I understand."

He tried again, this time picturing it shrinking and becoming almost transparent. The image did as he wished. He then tried rearranging the icons so at least the unblurred ones he could see were all grouped together. It wasn't perfect, but it was a start.

"I suppose you're not going to be giving me any helpful tips on how to level up, are you?" he asked.

*What would be the fun in that?* the konus replied.

Bawb looked at the band on his wrist, slowly shaking his head. "Fun? This is going to be a *long* several years."

# CHAPTER EIGHTEEN

Bawb spent far too long arguing with the device on his wrist before joining the others for their next lesson. It was maddening, the way it almost taunted him with half answers and obfuscated replies. Hozark had said the konus was not truly sentient, as a living entity would be, but so far as Bawb could tell it was about as close as anything could come while remaining inanimate.

In any case, there would be plenty of time to learn the strange device's ins and outs. For now, he had training to attend, and he was almost late.

He headed to the ground floor meeting area they had been told to gather in. All the others were there, waiting patiently, wondering what today's lesson would be. There was an excited vibe to the group. Apparently, they would be meeting several new teachers in the coming days and weeks now that they were Aspirants, but no one knew who they were or exactly what they would be teaching them.

One thing was for sure, they would be challenged and pushed to their limits, as they were pretty much every single day.

A young man they did not recognize entered the chamber some time later and took a quick head count. All were present.

"Aspirants, this way," he said, leading them out into the hallway.

He marched them in a rather circuitous route until they reached a heavy door. "Through there."

"What are we supposed to do?" Albinius asked.

"You wait for your teacher," the man replied, then walked away.

The youths looked at one another. Normally, they received at least a bit of an idea what was expected of them, but this was something new.

"You heard him," Elzina said, fearlessly taking the lead.

She opened the door, bright sunlight flooding through, illuminating her in its warm glow. She stepped out into the street. She was outside. Outside the training house for the first time in years.

"Come on!" she called to the others.

One by one they followed her, finally closing the door behind them when the last of their group exited. With surprised eyes, they looked around, taking in their environs. It was a relatively small street, curving at both ends. From what they could see, the ground floor of the buildings surrounding them all contained storefronts of one sort or another.

There was a bakery nearby as well, and they could smell the hot bread on the faint breeze. A mercantile depot was also close by, offering up a variety of wares, some in displays outside the entrance. More than the stores, however, it was the people milling about that really caught their attention.

So many of them, and of a wide variety of races. Having been surrounded exclusively by Wampeh for so long, it was something of a shock to them all.

"Are we actually outside?" Zota gasped.

Bawb looked around, spinning in a slow circle as he took it all in. "It appears that way."

"But we're only Aspirants. Are we supposed to be out here? Maybe this is a mistake."

"Quiet, idiot," Usalla hissed. "No one knows what we are. We're just kids, nothing more."

"She's right. Just act normal," Bawb agreed.

"I didn't mean to—" Zota began.

It was too late.

"Aspirant, huh?" a gruff, red-skinned man with thick wrists and a thicker neck growled, pushing off from the wall he'd been leaning against, his heavy boots crunching on the ground as he approached them.

He was tall and broad, easily outweighing any two of them combined. Three even, if you were counting the smaller of them. His dark orange hair was coarse and wiry, sprouting from his head and shoulders almost like the spines of a beast rather than the hair of a man.

He moved with an air of aggression about him, and his eyes burned with hate. "You're some of them would-be Ghalian, ain'tcha?"

"N-no," Zota blurted. "You have us mistaken with someone else."

"Nah, I heard ya. Aspirant, you said. Only one sort of Wampeh would say that. Damned Ghalian killed my brother. And now I'm going to kill you!"

He lunged, a meaty fist swinging at Zota's head in a wide haymaker.

Without hesitation, Bawb jumped in front of his friend, using both arms to block the attack, but he was too small to stop him entirely. He slid backward as the meaty fist continued to its target, the force of the blow diminished but still hitting Zota with a solid thump.

A little chime rang out, and Bawb's new konus briefly flashed a one next to an icon briefly visible with his peripheral vision.

*Level up: Initiative*, the konus informed him.

Bawb had little chance to respond or even think about the announcement as the man had already turned his attention to Bawb and moved to attack, his focus apparently shifting to whoever happened to be in his sights. The ferocity of the assailant was frightening, and his strength was overwhelming. There was no way they could overpower him.

Nevertheless, Bawb stood his ground, fighting back as best he could. Or, defending as best he could, was more like it. The others watched in shock, unsure what to do.

Out of nowhere, a stocky but smaller man with gray-green skin and light brown spots leapt into the fray. He was smaller than the attacker, but the way he moved somehow nullified the larger attacker's advantage. The two fought, the strange newcomer's technique countering the raw strength of the enraged man.

Punches met with gentle redirection rather than force-on-force blocking. Kicks were avoided entirely, the gaps in the man's defenses taken advantage of to the fullest by the smaller defender. Whoever this man was, he was not only skilled, he was fearless as well. At no point did he show a flicker of hesitation, and the sword strapped to his back remained sheathed.

Clearly, he had no need for it in this situation.

The red-skinned man bellowed and leapt high in the air, an enormous fist poised to rain down damage on the smaller adversary. It missed its mark, pushed aside with ease.

"Enough," the smaller man said.

Incredibly, the attacker ceased his assault.

The green man surveyed the stunned faces of the students, staring hard at each and every one of them before turning to the gathered onlookers. "We are done here. Thank you for your time."

All of the people in the street, including the formerly angry attacker, turned and walked away, exiting via the door the students had just arrived through.

"But that leads—" Zota began.

"Into the training house. I know," the man replied. "And you are still within its walls."

The man uttered a spell, his body shifting in shape, his coloration returning to his usual pale state. The students were stunned. He was a Wampeh, like them. And with the disguise shed, it was clear that he was a she.

"I am Teacher Demelza," she said, striding up and down the line of Aspirants. "And this has been your first lesson. I will be instructing you in the use of disguises and swordplay. What you have just experienced was a test. A test all of you failed." She paused in front of Bawb. "Why did you intervene?"

"I-I saw that Zota was unprepared for the attack and sought to assist him."

"And in so doing, placed yourself squarely in the attacker's attention." She looked at their confused faces. "What did Bawb do wrong?"

Elzina spoke first. "He entered a fight that wasn't his."

"And?"

Bawb reluctantly stepped forward slightly, his cheeks slightly flushed. "And I jeopardized myself and the others when the man's attention was solely on one person. I made him take notice of the rest of us."

*Negative one for stealth,* the konus announced, and Bawb could have sworn he heard amusement in its tone.

Demelza simply nodded. "Very good. Perhaps you are not as hopeless as I initially thought. But the rest of you? You stood gawking while this situation unfolded. You were not only vulnerable, but drawing attention to yourselves when you could have been taking steps to disperse, altering your appearance in the presence of someone keyed into our kind. Of course, you do not yet know how to properly disguise yourselves. That will be rectified soon enough, at least the basic elements. But the rest? You already possess the knowledge to protect your identities."

She spun toward Zota. "And you. I assume you recognize your error?"

"Yes, Teacher."

"In a real situation you could have gotten yourself, as well as your classmates, killed."

"I understand. It will not happen again."

"See that it doesn't."

Albinius timidly raised his hand.

"Yes?"

He gestured at the street around them. "I'm still unsure about something here. How are we still inside the training house?"

"This is all a fabrication designed to offer you a real-world experience without the risk of public exposure."

"But the street—"

"Ends just around the corners."

"And all the people. None of them were Ghalian."

Demelza grinned. "And *that*, my young student, is your second lesson. I was not the only one in disguise. In fact, *all* of them were Ghalian."

The students were abuzz with shock.

"All of them?" Albinius marveled.

"Yes. And you will learn to detect the spells we all used, in time. Magic can both hide you but also make you easy to pick out. It also requires years of training to be able to maintain the spell while engaged in combat. For that reason, you will also train extensively in the application of practical disguises that utilize little or no magic whatsoever."

It made sense, especially to the minds of the Aspirants. They had only just begun learning to cast spells—properly cast them, that is—and it was hard enough to perform even the simplest of tasks. But to maintain a complex and power-hungry spell while doing anything difficult, let alone fighting? It sounded impossible.

Of course, Demelza and whomever had been fighting her in disguise, had just shown them all that it was anything but. Just one more level to achieve as they struggled in their studies.

"Teacher?" Elzina asked.

"Yes, Elzina?"

"You said you would also be teaching us swordplay," she said, gesturing to the blade strapped to the woman's back.

Demelza reached over her shoulder and effortlessly drew forth a beautiful weapon with a long, dark-blue blade. She looked over the assembled students with an amused glance, then focused her energy. The blade flared bright, its blue glow startling the Aspirants.

"You will learn the use of a sword," she said, sheathing the weapon as its glow dissipated. "But not like this. A Vespus blade is not for the uninitiated."

Bawb felt something deep inside him stir, almost tugging him toward the weapon when she displayed it to the group. Even now, sheathed and dark, he still felt an attraction. One unlike any he'd felt before. He couldn't help but wonder if this was just some Ghalian thing. If the others felt it too.

There would be time to inquire of his friends later.

"Come," Demelza commanded. "There is no time like the present to begin your training. Today you will learn the basics of swordplay."

She walked out into the hallway, the students following like eager ducklings, excited to train, for once, in something more exciting than torturous physical labors. Bawb, Usalla, and Zota trailed behind, quietly marveling at their new teacher's skills.

"Did you see how she did that?" Zota asked. "I was right there near her and couldn't tell she was a Wampeh."

"She's very impressive, I'll say that," Usalla agreed, picturing herself perhaps being as skilled one day.

"More than most," Bawb added. "I heard Master Hozark's friends speaking about her one day. Teacher Demelza used to go into battle with him."

Zota seemed a little confused. "But they have always taught us that Master Ghalian work alone."

"Apparently, there was some sort of huge conflict that required coordinated efforts. And from what I've heard, she was a crucial part in it all. It's said there are not many better than her with a blade."

"But Master Hozark is, of course," Usalla noted.

"Yes, but that's to be expected. He's one of the Five, after all. But Teacher Demelza?" Bawb said. "He was the one who taught her."

# CHAPTER NINETEEN

Demelza led the students to a familiar place. The main sparring room on the first level of the compound.

A great deal of sweat, and occasionally blood, had soaked into the dirt floor over the years they had spent training there, learning the basics of hand-to-hand combat while the teachers devised new and cruel ways of making their muscles ache. It had to be the least favorite place of nearly all the Aspirants, but now, rather than dread, they felt something else.

Excitement.

Something new was there. Something that held the promise of an exciting change of pace.

A long wooden rack upon which hung dozens of swords awaited them. Demelza walked to it, giving them a quick once-over, then turned to her students.

"Each of you is to select a weapon from the rack. Do not let ego get the better of you. A smaller blade may serve you far more efficiently than a more impressive-looking, large one. Find what feels good in your hands. Take a few moments to make your selection, then line up against that wall."

Elzina was the first to choose a sword, happily twirling it

about in her hands with ease. She had been practicing with sticks in her free time, as had they all, and having an actual sword in her grasp was a heady feeling.

Albinius rapped the edge of the blade he had chosen against his arm. "Hey, these are dull!"

"Of course. You did not think we would allow the use of deadly weapons on your first day of sword training, did you?"

Albinius seemed to be about to say something clever, then thought better of it. He had no idea if Demelza was the sort to make him run laps, but he really didn't want to find out. At least, not so soon into their first use of real swords.

"These are swords," she said, pacing along their ranks. "These are not toys. They are not playthings. While the material they have been constructed with is far lighter than a real weapon, and though the edges have been dulled, they can still cause significant harm. Is that understood?"

"Yes, Teacher," they replied in unison.

"Good. We have talented healers here, but it is a waste of their skills and your time if you visit them without a very good reason. Now, pay attention." She picked up a dull sword from the rack. "This sword is the same as the weapons you are wielding. You saw me take it from among the others. There is nothing special about it."

She ran the dull blade across her hand without so much as a scratch, then, without hesitation she turned and swung it hard, the dull blade cleaving the rack easily, sending the remaining blades to the ground in a loud clamor. She surveyed their surprised faces.

"Just because a weapon lacks a sharpened edge, does not mean you can allow yourself become complacent. A club or war hammer can cause massive amounts of damage to a body, and even a dull sword is quite deadly in the right hands."

Demelza spun the sword, the weapon flowing around her

body as if it were an extension of her limbs, so easily did she wield it. Over her head, behind her back, figure eights in front and behind, the dull blade was a blur of deadly kinetic motion. She spun and threw the weapon across the chamber, where it embedded in a wooden training dummy. Somehow, the students kept their shocked gasps to themselves, but only just.

"There are many ways you can use a sword, and not all of them are what you would normally think. But for the moment, familiarize yourself with the weapon you have selected. The weight, the balance. Feel how it moves in your hand, how the grip presses against your fingers and palm depending how you grasp it. This is the first, extremely important, step on your very long path to mastering swordplay. I will leave you to practice on your own for a while. Familiarize yourselves well."

"What's next?" Zota asked, awkwardly twirling his sword. "Are we going to learn to throw them?"

"Not for some time, I am afraid. No, first things first. Once you are comfortable with your blade, you will learn to fight."

"But we only just started."

"True, but there is no time like the present to begin. Ghalian do not shy away from adversity and hardship, after all."

The Aspirants looked at one another, a little unsure. She said they would fight, but she had also just said these swords were dangerous and they were not to waste the healers' time.

Bawb looked at Zota and shrugged. It seemed they would find out what exactly she meant soon enough.

The students spread out, giving themselves enough room to practice and move without fear of striking one another. Bawb proceeded to do what everyone else was doing, namely, performing movements with a sword that he had only pretended to do with a stick in prior years.

It was odd at first, the balance of the weapon being different than a wooden rod, but after a few minutes it began to feel more natural. Normal, even. In fact, Bawb was starting to feel rather comfortable with it.

He glanced at his konus and focused on one icon he had seen in particular. A large image flashed in front of his eyes. Bawb concentrated, forcing it to minimize according to his will. Now it was just a small icon with one word and one number.

*Swordplay: 0*

"Well, that's just great," he muttered.

"What was that?" Usalla asked. "Were you talking to me?"

"No. Just musing over my lack of skill."

"We are all in the same situation," she noted. "But with a teacher such as Demelza, I am sure we will soon learn many exciting techniques."

"We shall see."

They practiced for what seemed like a long time, but in reality was likely far less than they imagined. When Demelza returned, she had another teacher with her. The pair observed them practicing for a few minutes then finally called them together to the middle of the room.

"Observe," Demelza said, then nodded to her associate.

The other teacher leapt into action, swinging his sword at her head. Demelza blocked the attack and delivered a counterstrike, the blade slapping his torso harmlessly.

"Do you see?" she asked the group. "We spar to improve our skills, but in so doin we must never intentionally miss our target. Teacher Warfin was attempting to hit my head, and it fell upon me to prevent him from achieving his goal. We have healers here, and this is how we train. To do otherwise is to develop bad habits, and those will get you killed."

Warfin slid the dull blade into his belt and walked down the row of students. "You and you, over there. You two, there. You and you, to that side."

He continued like that until everyone had been paired off

with an opponent. Some duos were friend pitted against friend. In Bawb's case, he now stood a blade's length away from his nemesis.

Elzina grinned, reading his expression as easily as a book. "Do not worry, Bawb. I will try to defeat you in a manner that is not *too* humiliating."

Without another word, she launched into an attack.

Bawb awkwardly swung his sword to meet hers, the impact ringing out loud in the chamber. She slid her blade along his, pulling free, then jabbing him in the torso with the dull tip. It was not sharp, but the impact hurt, nevertheless.

"Touch!" she teased, then started again.

Bawb moved as best he could, but Elzina was faster. More flexible. And most importantly, she had selected a much smaller, lighter blade that she could maneuver much easier than the larger weapon he had chosen.

Time after time she pierced his defenses, striking him all over his body with the blade until his flesh began to ache. He was glad of one thing, however. At least these weapons were dull. If not, he would have been slain many times over.

"Line up facing one another," Demelza called out. All the students did so, forming two lines. "Now, switch. Move one step to your left. The end student will come around to the other end. This is your new partner. Return to your training area and begin."

Bawb was paired up with Usalla, who had also opted for a somewhat smaller blade, though not to the degree Elzina had.

"Are you ready?" he asked.

The metal swinging toward his head was all the reply he needed. Bawb reacted immediately, blocking the attack hard, the blades shaking from the impact. Usalla smiled and took a step back to prepare her next assault.

Her sword flew fast and low, aiming for Bawb's thigh. Again he blocked, but this time he stepped in close, preventing her from shifting the blade higher. Bawb pushed her with his shoulder as he spun, knocking her off balance and creating space between them.

His sword flew true, striking her on the neck before she could move to parry the attack. Usalla's legs buckled momentarily from the blow. Bawb immediately dropped his guard and rushed to her. "Are you hurt?"

"Aspirant Bawb, what are you doing?" Warfin barked. "You do not drop your guard."

"I was just concerned she was hurt."

"She *will* get hurt. You will all get hurt. It is part of life you must accept." He glanced over at Demelza. She gave a slight nod. "Bawb, pair up with Elzina, and do not ever let me see you drop your guard like that again."

"Yes, Teacher Warfin," he sheepishly replied. "May I change my weapon?"

He eyed the student curiously then nodded his approval. "Very well. But be quick."

Bawb hurried to the pile of swords and selected a new one, lighter than his original one and a bit shorter to boot. He felt the balance as he swung it around his body, taking care to move it slowly as he had before despite this new blade wanting to go faster.

"Ready for another beating?" Elzina joked as she watched him prepare. "I will go easy on you."

"Do not bother," he shot back, a ball of anger growing in his belly.

Demelza and Warfin watched the two square off from a distance, far enough away so as not to distract them but close enough to observe the nuances of the exchange.

"He is too emotional," Warfin noted quietly. "I do not see how he was allowed to advance to Aspirant."

Demelza's eyes remained on the two youths battling it out. "He is a boy, Warfin. He will grow, and he will learn."

"He showed a timid nature. He would not finish the attack."

"Usalla is his friend. Remember when we were their age, even in the throes of training, we still did not wish to inflict true harm upon one another."

"Maybe so, but the Ghalian are not timid. He will either learn to overcome his nature or he will never succeed."

"Give him time. I think this youngster may surprise us yet."

Warfin shrugged. "We shall see."

Bawb and Elzina were locked in a sloppy but energetic engagement, the advantage the girl had possessed now nullified by Bawb's new weapon. At first, she had been overconfident and attempted several of the moves she had used previously to land blows on him. This time, Bawb was ready, the lighter weapon in his hands moving faster than the larger one he had ill-advisedly taken to start the exercise.

He blocked her repeatedly, forcing her to retreat as he pushed forward with his own attack. Elzina's arms moved fast, blocking him, but only just. This was different than before. She was being forced to expend a lot more energy, and more than that, out of the corner of her eye, she saw the other students were watching.

Elzina's anger at her top spot being challenged in front of the others flared. She took great pleasure in the comfortable solidity of her position, but now Bawb was making her look bad. She would have none of that.

With a surge of energy she charged ahead, her sword a blur of attacks. Bawb pushed himself hard, countering most but taking blows from some. He was losing ground and suddenly felt sure he would lose this engagement. But he wasn't about to make it easy for her.

He held back, feigning injury, allowing Elzina to move in for a powerful strike. At the last moment, he spun out of the way, slamming the hilt of his sword into her ribs hard enough to hear a crack.

*Swordplay: Level One,* his konus informed him upon impact.

Elzina yelled out in pain and surprise, dropping her sword and grabbing him hard, then leaping on his back, her fangs fully extended.

"Elzina! Enough!" Demelza shouted, her voice booming in the enclosed space.

The girl let go and stepped back.

"What were you thinking?" Demelza demanded.

"To win."

"And you would win how, exactly? Bawb is a Wampeh. Our kind has no power of our own. And as he has not taken any from a power user, if you bit him, you would get a mouthful of blood, nothing more."

"I—"

"And furthermore, this is sword training, not free-for-all combat. You will stick with the lessons at hand, is that clear?"

"Yes, Teacher."

"Good. Now, take ten laps to think about what you have done."

Elzina flashed an angry look at Bawb, then started running.

"Bawb, you will switch out with Zota."

"Yes, Teacher," he replied.

Bawb walked over to where he had been told to go, marveling at what had just happened.

"Konus? Are you there?"

*I'm always here.*

"How many levels are there, anyway? Do they go to ten? Eleven?"

*The number of levels varies depending on the skill in question.*

"That is not exactly helpful."

*Perhaps*, the konus agreed. *But cheer up. At least you are no longer a zero in this one.*

# CHAPTER TWENTY

"Pathetic," Elzina grumbled as she and the others returned to their bunkhouse after what had become a very long, very trying day of swordplay and more. "I am punished for being better? It is not right."

Finnia shifted course so she could walk closer to her. "Let it go, Elzina. These things happen. You know this as well as all of us."

"These things do not happen to *me*. I am the best of us. I should not pay a price for superiority."

The spy in training shook her head. "A touch of modesty might serve you better than anger."

"Says the one who can't hack it as an assassin. You're too soft, Finnia."

"Soft? Who says I'm soft? I may not possess the bloodlust you have, but I excel in other things. Areas of training in which even you do not surpass me."

"*Yet*," Elzina said with an arrogance that the teachers had noted on more than one occasion.

She shrugged off her sweaty garments and headed for the

shower room along with the others. It had been a difficult session, and the warm water would feel quite refreshing. But as she took her place beneath the flow, Bawb and Usalla stepped in to join the group, finding open spaces and letting the warm water wash over them.

Elzina glared at Bawb, but he paid her no heed.

"Hey. *Hey*!"

He continued bathing, ignoring her calls.

"Bawb. You know you'll never amount to anything, don't you? You should not have even been allowed to join the Aspirants. It was just blind luck you reacted the way you did. You're soft. Weak. You don't have what it takes to become a true Ghalian."

He turned and cast a calm glance her way. "You are entitled to your opinion, Elzina," he said in an even tone. "And I am entitled to prove you wrong."

With that he turned back to his shower, scrubbing himself clean as if he hadn't a care in the world. Of course, he actually *did* feel the sting of her words. He *was* emotional, and he knew it. And the points she brought up echoed doubts he had felt on more than one occasion. But he had learned many things in the difficult years leading up to this moment. Among them was how not to react when goaded.

Elzina had gotten a reaction out of him plenty of times in his early days among the group, but over time he had developed a system for dealing with her verbal barrage, essentially disarming her with his refusal to react.

Naturally, that enraged her even more, and though her varied attempts typically failed, Elzina never stopped trying. She was talented, yes, but her ego was something that concerned her teachers. She would require close supervision if they were to mold her into the finest version of what she could become.

For the time being, she was still a girl. A skilled one with impressive drive, but also one prone to the tumultuous reactions that accompanied that age.

Elzina stared daggers at Bawb's back as he ignored her, the frustration of the day prickling her ire more than other occasions. This had been her chance to shine. To show their new teacher just how skilled she was. And Bawb had ruined it.

She looked around, glaring at the others. When Elzina was in a mood like this, it was just common sense to let her cool down, and even though all of them had seen what happened, they wisely kept their mouths shut and gazes averted.

All but one.

Usalla had turned to watch the exchange between her friend and his nemesis with some interest. Bawb had always been ranked somewhat toward the lower end of their cohort. He wasn't bad at the tasks assigned them, but he wasn't exceptional by any means.

But now it seemed that, for whatever reason, he had begun to come into his own. To get comfortable in his own skin. And for him to have not only held his ground but actually overcome Elzina in combat? It was a paradigm shift, and she wondered whether things would continue in that vein.

It was that curiosity that led to her error. She forgot to look away.

"What are you looking at?" Elzina spat, vitriol in her words as she latched onto someone else to berate.

"Nothing, Elzina. I am just bathing."

"Bathing and staring, is more like it." Elzina stepped out from her shower and stormed across the wet stone floor until she was face-to-face with her classmate. "You think this is funny, don't you?"

"Nothing is funny, Elzina. Please, go back to your shower."

"Are you telling me what to do? Do you think that just because I was made a fool of today you are now somehow superior to me?"

"I did not say that."

"But you were thinking it," she growled, giving Usalla a little shove.

Bawb was all for avoiding conflict when it came to Elzina. They would be spending many more years training in the same class together, after all. But Usalla was his friend, and there was no way he would stand for this uncalled-for aggression.

"Leave her alone, Elzina," he said with a calm strength to his voice that surprised even himself.

She spun on him, the original object of her anger finally engaging, providing her a more suitable target for her rage. "You cannot tell me what to do, Bawb. You're barely an Aspirant. You should go back to the Novices where you belong."

With that, she shoved Usalla again. The girl was no pushover, figuratively as well as literally. She was a Ghalian trainee as well, and she easily maintained her footing, though she did slide back from the impact.

Bawb reacted without thought, instinct alone driving him as he leapt from his shower, his fist driving hard into Elzina's jaw.

She stumbled back a step then engaged him head-on, the two of them exchanging attacks in a flurry. Bawb shifted, pivoting on his lead foot. He ducked under Elzina's hastily thrown elbow and drove his own into her chin.

She took the impact well, spinning and dropping a solid hammer fist across his face. Neither was fazed by the blows. Their adrenaline was far too high, and this fight had been brewing between them far longer than merely today's training incident.

There was a score to settle, and it seemed this unlikely moment was the time for it.

The other Aspirants quickly exited the showers whether they had finished bathing or not. The two combatants were going at it hard and fierce, and they wanted nothing to do with that fight. Only Usalla remained, standing back, trying to get them to stop but to no avail.

"Bawb, let it go!" she urged.

He ignored her, driving his fist into Elzina's solar plexus. She let out a gasp but stayed on her feet, snapping out a kick that grazed his exposed groin.

Bawb grit his teeth, doing his best to ignore the nausea in his gut. He lunged forward, faking a low kick. Elzina fell for his feint, moving to block it. Bawb's feet slid on the wet floor, and he found himself too close to deliver the punch he had intended. It seemed he would have to improvise.

Elzina's nose let out a terrible crack as his forehead butted her hard enough to open a small gash on his own face. The two of them staggered back from one another, the concussion of the impact stunning them both momentarily. They eyed one another, each of their fangs sliding into place on instinct.

The blood from their injuries ran freely, quickly mixing with the flowing water all around them, swirling down the drain like a bloody Fibonacci spiral.

Neither was hurt badly, though. The head simply possessed more blood vessels than other parts of the body, making even superficial injuries appear worse than they were. But to anyone not in the know, the two bloody-faced teenagers would have looked like gladiators in a bout to the death. *Naked* gladiators, but enraged combatants, nonetheless.

"***What do you think you are doing***?" Teacher Rovos's deep voice bellowed as he charged into the showers, echoing off the stone walls. "Stand at attention! ***Now***!"

Despite being in the thrall of combat, Bawb and Elzina immediately stopped in place and snapped up straight, backs rigid and eyes forward, ignoring the rivulets of blood tickling their faces.

Rovos turned and glared at the other students peering in through the doorway, sending them scattering with a glance. He redirected his ire back at the two standing in front of him, pacing back and forth, ignoring the water splashing around them as if it didn't even exist. The two students were the only thing that mattered right now. The center of the universe. And it was *not* a place they wanted to be.

"A fight in the bunk house? Have you lost your senses?"

"No, Teacher," they both replied.

"Oh? Are you certain? Are you sure you two have not suffered a head injury? Because you must have lost your minds to even consider something as foolish as this." He stared at them hard, his displeasure clear. And for a Master Ghalian to show emotion, he had to be *truly* angry.

That, or he was putting on a show to make his point.

Whatever the case, he had the pair's undivided attention.

"Not acceptable. Not acceptable at all under *any* circumstances. You are no longer Novices. Emotional outbursts might have been tolerated before, but no more. You are Aspirants now, and you will be held to a higher standard. Is that clear?"

"Yes, Teacher."

Rovos glared at them a moment longer. "Let me see your teeth."

Bawb and Elzina opened their mouths. Their fangs had retracted fully. Though he would not say it, Rovos was pleased to see them gaining such control over their fangs so early on. Unfortunately, this was not how he wanted them to display their newfound skill.

He loomed over them a long while before breaking the

uncomfortable silence. "You are both to dress and come with me."

He strode out of the showers, not waiting for a reply.

Elzina found herself directed into a room she'd never visited before. It was much smaller than the others, not intended for combat or training, it appeared. And the only people inside were Master Imalla and Teacher Warfin. Bawb fought the urge to stare as the door closed behind her. He had enough to worry about of his own.

In the next room they came to, a master and teacher were also waiting for him. Two he knew, one better than most.

"Sit," Hozark said, gesturing to the empty seat.

Demelza stood silently beside him, observing the youth with a judgmental eye.

Hozark stepped close, examining the cut on Bawb's forehead. "This does not appear to have been caused by a fist."

"I was cut when I broke her nose."

"Oh?"

"I slipped and was too close, so I improvised."

"He used his head," Demelza noted with a hint of amusement in her eyes.

Hozark stifled a chuckle. This was a serious matter. That said, he could not help but be proud of the boy for thinking on his feet. It was that sort of instinct that could elevate him from the ranks of the ordinary Ghalian into something more.

Time would tell.

"I understand Elzina has been tormenting you again," he finally said.

"It is nothing."

"She has been doing so for years, but you have learned to ignore her provocations. What changed?"

"You know about that?"

"We are the Wampeh Ghalian. We know about *everything* that takes place in these walls."

Bawb swallowed his pride. This was Hozark. If there was ever a master he could speak plainly with, he was the one.

"She was attacking Usalla," he admitted. "She had no part in our quarrel. It was wrong for her to be drawn into it."

Hozark nodded, glancing at Demelza. "Ah, I see. An emotional response when a friend was in distress. Admirable for most, but unacceptable for Ghalian. Do you understand that?"

"I do. It will not happen again."

"I hope it does not, Bawb. We do not fight among our own."

"I understand."

"Good. Now, go get cleaned up, then go back to your bunkhouse. Get a good night's sleep. You will need it."

Bawb rose and gave a slight bow then exited, leaving Hozark and Demelza alone. Demelza looked at her mentor and friend. "He is too emotional, Hozark. He feels too much."

The master assassin could not help but agree. "It is true, yes. But if he can find it within himself to channel that energy into a calm, driving force, I believe he could have truly exceptional potential."

"I find no fault in that assessment. But he is reactive. He feels deeply."

Hozark let out a frustrated little sigh. "On this we agree. And passion does not agree with our lifestyle."

"No, it does not," she replied, her brow raising slightly, the corner of her lips twitching ever so gently upward. "But then, he is not the first to overcome such a thing, is he?"

Hozark did not grace her with a reply, but she felt his amusement percolate despite his dour expression. She could make comments like that to him only because they'd been through a lot together over the years and trusted each other with their lives. But beyond that, unlike almost anyone alive, Demelza had caught glimpses of parts of the enigmatic master's persona that he kept tightly under wraps.

# CHAPTER TWENTY-ONE

Master Hozark wasn't kidding when he said Bawb would be needing his rest. The following morning started earlier than usual with a two-hour run through an interconnecting maze of underground tunnels and obstacles that none of them had ever seen before.

Vast as the hidden facility had already seemed, the Aspirants now realized it was so much larger than any of them could have imagined. In fact, it was entirely possible that it spanned far beyond the city's limits with the tendrils of the Ghalian cavern network even leading deep into the wilderness.

Of course, underground, they couldn't tell. But given the distance they ran in a relatively straight line, it seemed entirely possible. What's more, there had been talk among the teachers of upcoming training as they grew in strength and skill. Outings deep beneath their feet where they would be challenged to their limits.

For now, however, they were getting no more than a passing look as they were led on a forced run at a pace that taxed even the fittest of them.

On and on they ran, hurrying through tunnels, clamoring

over rock bridges spanning rushing rivers and bubbling hot springs. The variety of environments was breathtaking, with no two of the caverns exactly alike.

Many of the chambers they passed through were incredibly expansive in their size, while some were more intimate. This wasn't magic, though. The planet's volcanic birth was what had created the perfect network of subterranean realms for the Ghalian to claim as their own and outfit for their needs. It was likely why they had selected this planet in the first place, well before it had been populated by vast cities.

Buildings, obstacle dungeons, and assault courses had been constructed over the millennia, as had a wild array of simulated environments, all of them carefully molded under the order's watchful eye. Bawb and his fellow students were amazed at the fraction of the network they were able to see as they ran by, huffing and puffing from the effort.

"Are those Adepts?" Zota asked as they ran into a large, brightly lit chamber that rather resembled a parade ground.

Bawb looked where he was gesturing. There was a group of older teens, all of them engaged in sparring, spell casting, and demonstrations of skill and endurance.

"They look like it," he replied. "But I can't say for sure."

Zota seemed perplexed. "Why would they allow us near Adepts? I mean, we haven't even moved up to Vessels yet. Those students are way above us."

Bawb looked closer at the group as they ran past. They were drenched in sweat, training at full speed without respite. It was impressive, actually, but also more than a little intimidating. One day, if all went to plan, he and his friends would be training at that level.

That realization gave him pause. There were quite a few less of the Adepts than in his group of Aspirants. It made sense, of course. Not all trainees could succeed, and many would wash out or die in the pursuit of higher rank as they moved to more difficult training. One day, many of the faces he'd been toiling beside all these years would not be there, and that was a reality he had only now really understood.

"Bawb!" Usalla hissed. "Look at the observation stands!"

His gaze shifted to the small group seated quietly in the nondescript stands. It took him a moment, but he soon realized what she was so excited about. It wasn't just teachers. It was a group of masters, and a lot of them to be in one place.

In fact, it had been made clear to them as they progressed in their studies that teachers would be their main adult contact and only on occasion would masters join in their training.

"What about the Five?" Bawb had asked shortly after he learned of the existence of the leadership of the order.

It had been Teacher Krallo who clarified things for him. "You will rarely see many masters gathered in one place. Most are far too busy undertaking the most difficult of missions for the order. But, from time to time, you may see a few of them together. But the Five? They do not gather in the same place, as a rule."

"Why not?"

"The Five possess certain knowledge. Secrets of great importance. If one or even two were to be killed, we could fill their positions with relative ease. The surviving members would pass on the requisite knowledge, as was done for them when they ascended. But if more than that were to fall, it would leave the order in a precarious situation with greatly diminished leadership and compromised mission planning. The Five oversee far more aspects of Ghalian activity than just one or two training houses. They are the minds putting into action plans that may have taken years to mature and cultivate."

"How do they get to be one of the Five? Is there some sort of special class?"

"Hardly. The newest addition to the Five is selected by the others. It is more than difficult to achieve that level of skill. But beyond that, it is not something you can specifically train for. Your abilities and demeanor are assessed over many, many years, and then, if you are one of the few to be considered worthy, one obstacle still remains."

"What is it?"

"One of the Five needs to die."

Bawb had been taken aback. "Die?"

"Do not act surprised, Bawb. You know the nature of the Ghalian life. And skilled as the masters, and even the Five may be, death comes for us all eventually. Rare is the Ghalian who dies of old age."

Bawb didn't know what to say at the time, so he had just gone back to his training rather than dig deeper. But as he sweated and toiled, Krallo's words replayed through his mind. The conversation had really impressed upon the boy just how secretive a life he was going to live. That is, if he progressed in the ranks as Hozark said he believed he would.

But what if he didn't? What if he failed out? How would they handle someone who knew too much about them to be set loose into the outside world? It was something he supposed he would learn the answer to one day, but for now he would just have to work hard and keep his nose to the proverbial grindstone.

And today he would be pressing it hard.

"Aspirants, at attention!" Teacher Warfin called out.

They stopped running in unison and snapped up straight, backs rigid, forcing their heaving chests to still and their racing hearts to slow. It was something they had trained in since their early days. An unlikely skill that would one day serve them well.

Running was part of an assassin's life, like it or not, but so too was blending in, and if pursuers were running after an escaping killer they would be unlikely to suspect a seemingly relaxed bystander who was not the slightest bit out of breath.

Bawb kept his head still, but his eyes glanced toward his konus with curiosity.

The display faintly projected from his wrist. *Recovery: Level one,* it said. His lungs still burning from the run, Bawb had to wonder what it would take to reach the higher levels. Another icon unblurred, making itself visible for the first time. *Fleet Foot,* it read. *Level one.*

He wondered what exactly that meant, but with a group of masters taking a seat before them, now was certainly not the time to ask. Bawb used his peripheral vision to see who they were as best he could. There were more masters here than he could have imagined, all of them observing the different level students as they demonstrated their skills.

In this group, however, one stood out. Hozark sat quietly with the others, watching with a casual gaze. Bawb knew it was anything but.

Teacher Warfin looked them over. "Students. Aspirants. Ghalian. You are to be tested today. Not only your skills, but your mental fortitude and drive. Prepare yourselves."

He glanced at Hozark, the ranking Ghalian. Hozark gave a little nod, and now the very long, very difficult day *truly* began. In no time at all, one thing was made clear to all of the Aspirants. The brutal run had only been a warm-up.

It was near nightfall when the exhausted students finally stopped their demonstrations. They had been run through the ringer, made to perform every skill they had ever learned over and over while faced with a seemingly endless stream of tasks pushing their bodies and minds to the limit. And that was the whole point.

They worked straight through what would normally have

been a lunch break and well into the dinner hour before Hozark raised a hand.

"Aspirants! That is all," Warfin called out. "Back to the training house." With that he led them on a run through a new set of tunnels and caverns. There was a shorter way back, apparently, though he still made them push the pace for a solid hour before diverting to it.

By the time they reached their quarters, even Elzina was too tired to gripe. They stripped, showered, and dressed in clean clothes then proceeded to the dining hall, where the famished youth ate their fill and then some, having burned off more calories than any of them would have thought possible.

"Did you see?" Finnia asked as she and a few others trudged back to their bunk house.

"See what?" Albinius asked.

"All the masters who were there today. They were testing *everyone*, not just us."

Zota shrugged. "We all saw, Finnia. What of it?"

"We had Master Hozark watching us. *Us*! We're just Aspirants, yet one of the Five personally observed our performance. It was inspiring."

Albinius, exhausted, just shrugged. "Inspiring?"

"Yes, inspiring. Didn't you try harder because he was there? All of you?"

"I guess," Albinius admitted.

"Yeah, sure," Zota agreed.

Even Bawb had to admit that yes, he did push himself to the limit knowing Hozark was watching his every move. But now, with exhaustion as an excuse, he slowed his walk back to the bunk house, allowing his friends to pull slightly ahead of him, and turned his attention to the band around his wrist.

"Konus?" he asked.

*Yes, Aspirant Bawb?*

"How does one really become so skilled as to become one of the Five?"

There was a pause, as if the supposedly inanimate device was mulling over the best reply. *Practice,* it finally said.

"Practice? That's all you have for me?"

*It's not my place to tell you what to do, only to report how well you are doing it. And for the moment? Your performance is lacking.*

"Gee. Thanks."

*My pleasure. Now, one day, if you somehow discover the marvels of discipline and effort, perhaps I will have more that I can display for you. I do hope so. Being stuck with a base model Aspirant is so very dull.*

"I am sorry to bore you," Bawb snarked at the opinionated device.

*It is to be expected*, the konus replied. *But please, do make an effort. Otherwise, it will be a long union for both of us.*

# CHAPTER TWENTY-TWO

The next morning the Aspirants assembled in a spartan training room, but this one was lacking the torturous devices they had grown so accustomed to toiling with in their quest for advancement. All that was present were basic weapons, and not even the truly difficult ones at that.

It seemed the teachers, while not giving them a day off, were sympathetic to the extremes the group had gone through the day before. A theory borne out when Demelza entered the chamber.

"A tired body can very quickly become an injured body," she began, walking up and down the line of students. "We train hard. Harder than anyone, and as a result of our hard work, we Ghalian are the most respected and feared order of assassins in the galaxy bar none. It is that reputation preceding us that often opens doors and causes surrender without a fight. We do all we can to see that reputation remains untarnished. I am sure you can see why."

She was not wearing the Vespus blade typically riding on her back today, nor were there any other weapons that they could see, though a Ghalian *always* had a few secreted on their body somewhere. But the lack of her usual accoutrements piqued their interest. What was her plan for the day?

They would soon find out, and, for once, the day's labors were a relief.

"Today you will be working with these," she said, uncovering a rack of weapons. Only these were not ordinary ones.

The weapons, while having the general shape of what they had trained with all this time, appeared made out of some extremely light material. It wasn't wood or metal, but rather a tightly woven reed of some sort, lending them not only feather weight but also added flexibility. She picked up a reed sword and began spinning it around her body.

Faster and faster she went, the sword no more than a blur as it circumscribed arcs around her in all directions. Demelza leapt forward, the reed blade stopping mere inches from Elzina's face. She stepped back and gave a little nod.

"Good. You controlled your reflexes. Any fool can swing a blade, but a master is in control of their body as well as their weapon." She placed the sword back on the rack.

"Your bodies are resilient and you have proven yourselves worthy of continuing on in your education, but even the toughest of warriors need to recover. For that reason, you will only be using these for the next two days. Yesterday's exercises pushed you all to your limits and beyond them, but now you will be allowed to regain your strength and heal. It is, however, an *active* recovery. A time to focus on form over brute force. We have healers at the ready here, as you all know very well by now, but someday you will not be so lucky as to have that option, and your bodies must remember how to heal themselves."

Demelza pointed to Bawb and Usalla. "Pick up a weapon and step here," she directed.

The two walked to the rack and selected their tool of choice. Bawb opted for a mid-length sword while Usalla chose a spear.

The real versions were both deadly weapons in the right hands, but these were almost incapable of causing true harm. Yes, impact would sting and possibly even break skin, but beyond that the risks were negligible.

"Take a few swings with them. Get a feel for them in your hands. You will notice that these move differently than the real thing in many ways, but in others they are quite similar. They are light, and they are fast, but if you are struck they will not cause any real damage. But that is no excuse for sloppiness. Always maintain form. *Always*. Maintain your control."

Bawb and Usalla began moving their weapons, slowly at first, as they'd been directed. Demelza had not been kidding, these were incredibly light, and the effort required to wield them was minimal. The two sped up as they became more comfortable with the way they handled.

"Begin," their teacher instructed.

Bawb and Usalla launched into action at once.

The girl's spear grazed Bawb's cheek as she feigned a swing then opted to thrust it forward instead. Had he been using a real sword there would have been no way Bawb could have moved to block it in time. Even with the lightweight weapon, he only barely managed to deflect it from a direct hit.

Usalla's eyes crinkled with a hint of amusement. They were training, yes, but for once they could almost have a bit of fun with it. Almost.

Bawb twirled his sword, swinging at her head with crisscrossing swipes. Usalla batted them away, her spear held high, taking the bait. Bawb shifted his weight to the left but dove to the right, his aching body not thrilled with the torsion he was subjecting it to. Bawb ignored the discomfort and dove into a roll, closing the distance and rendering Usalla's spear useless as he sliced the reed weapon across her thighs before rolling to his feet a safe distance away.

"Stop," Demelza said, nodding her approval. "Did you see what Usalla and Bawb did? Both embraced the traditional principles of combat while also taking advantage of the benefits of these lighter weapons. The spear, while already a fast tool, is made even more so with the reduction of weight. And the sword can be maneuvered much faster and easier from off-balance positions and even while in motion."

Bawb glanced at his konus, willing the display to appear, although minimized, but was met with disappointment. There were no changes.

"This training," Demelza continued, "is to prepare you for a series of spells you will be learning in coming months. These spells, while existing in similar forms elsewhere, are a particular version known only to the Ghalian. They will bolster your strength in combat, aiding you in the performance of your missions even when your body feels it can take no more."

"What if we are at full strength?" Zota asked. "Can we make ourselves extra strong?"

Demelza smiled. "Many have asked this question, and all have heard the same reply. No, these spells are not capable of making you overly strong when you are rested. They only replenish weakened muscles, but the quirk of these spells is that they will provide a boost that will, for a short time, make your limbs and the weapons they wield feel slightly lighter than normal. That is why we train with the lighter weapons today. To familiarize you with the feeling but without yet using the spells you have not mastered. I know this sounds like a fantastic advantage, and it can be in the right circumstance, but remember, the spells are short lasting and only function on already exhausted bodies. And if you do not replenish your energy and let your body heal afterwards, you can wind up incurring even greater damage you may not have even realized you were suffering."

The warning was a worrisome one, but the thought of having a secret power-up spell at their disposal was too exciting to allow the students to worry about that. At least, not for the moment.

"What if our konus runs out of power before we can cast the spells?" Albinius asked. "I mean, if we're on some big mission, it's possible we'll drain our konuses before we have the chance to use them, right?"

"Indeed. But you must remember, the konus is not your only source of power. You are Wampeh Ghalian, and you can take power from others and make it your own."

The Aspirants shifted slightly at the thought. All but Elzina, that is. They had taken power only once, and that had been a test to progress to become Aspirants. But to use that ability in combat? It was a daunting concept but one they would have to embrace if they wished to fully excel in the order.

"What if we willingly allow ourselves to deplete our strength?" Elzina wondered. "To fight hard enough against lesser adversaries to then prime ourselves to utilize the benefits of the spells when we encounter a more difficult foe?"

"An interesting idea, and not one that has not been attempted. But the issue, which you will learn first-hand one day, is that things often do not go as expected, and you may find yourself facing all manner of adversary at all points in your mission. If these contracts tended to be so straight-forward I assure you it would have become a standard practice among the Ghalian."

"Expect the worst, hope for the best, and prepare for both," Bawb said.

Demelza turned and fixed a surprised look on him. "Very wise words. Where did you learn them?"

"Master Hozark mentioned it to me one day."

"Ah. Well, he would know better than most. You know, he is

rather legendary for the impossible scrapes he has somehow gotten out of. A very difficult man to kill, though many have tried. Something I know he credits to the philosophy you just quoted. It is a lesson all of you should take to heart. Expect the absolute worst, and you will almost never be surprised."

She gestured to the rack of lightweight weapons.

"The rest of you, arm yourselves and pair up. Familiarize yourselves with the weapons, then practice. This is open study. I will be observing but not instructing at first. I wish for you to move instinctively. Let your training guide you. From there, we can then adjust and improve your technique."

The others did as she requested, arming themselves and separating into groups of two spread across the room.

They fought hard, then rotated to another partner, each using the techniques that felt natural to them. It made for something of a free-for-all sensation, not being so strictly regimented in their movements for once. Of course, one day they would hope to pass the examination to level up to become masters, but before they could do that, they would have to devise a fighting system that was entirely their own.

All Ghalian masters did it, and while some were a bit similar and even derivative of one another, some of them came up with wildly novel fighting styles, employing weapons, magic, diversion, and anything else they found worthy of including in their technique.

It made for a fighting force that no adversary could fully prepare for. There were no standard routines, no predictable patterns for which to train defenses. Facing a Master Ghalian typically meant one thing.

Death.

The only question was how quickly.

. . .

The following weeks and months the Aspirants began practicing the spells, and while they were by no means proficient, they did see some of the benefits of having magic bolstering their tired bodies. But when that magic failed, a trip to the healer was almost inevitable. In fact, at this point the healers all knew the students on a first-name basis, along with the ever increasing list of injuries they had sustained in their pursuit of excellence.

Ghalian training was many things, but there was one thing it was not.

It was not forgiving.

Elzina seemed to take great pleasure in pitting herself against Bawb, and her superior skill and strength led to his taking a beating on a regular basis as the training intensity increased with every passing week. But Bawb, battered and bruised as he was, was nevertheless growing in confidence.

He could take a shot and keep fighting. He was rapidly learning just how much abuse he could push through and still stay on task. In that regard, Elzina was unintentionally giving him an advantage that would one day push him to the front of the class. But for now, Bawb had an issue or two that had to be addressed.

Not long after receiving his unusual konus, Bawb had developed something of a bad habit, checking the device many times a day to see if he had leveled up in any areas. It had gotten to the point where he was finding himself distracted from his training more often than not, constantly pulling up the display.

Finally, the konus let him have it, dishing out a tongue-lashing that only a semi-sentient, magic-storing, shit-talking training aid could. It had told Bawb in no uncertain terms that he would be risking his standing and possibly fall behind if he did not focus.

Bawb and the konus had a rather unusual discussion at that point and came to an arrangement. The konus would actively alert him if there was anything truly noteworthy involving his skills, but Bawb would have to restrict himself to checking on his own no more than twice a day.

It was hard at first, the urge to check just one more time after completing a difficult task often proving almost impossible to ignore. But Bawb toughed it out, forcing himself to not even think about the konus unless he was drawing power from it for his lessons.

In just a few months he had reached the point where he almost forgot to check it for days at a time. And it was then that he excelled. It was then that he leveled up. The konus, however, waited, biding its time before announcing his progress.

*You have leveled up in swordplay, knife work, as well as several styles of fighting,* it informed him as he headed off to the showers one evening.

"Which styles?" Bawb asked.

The konus flashed up its display. Several things that had been blurred out were now visible. Bawb scanned them, noting he was only level one for nearly all of them. He also noted that a new spellcasting icon had appeared, and while he felt shaky with his casting, this tangible proof he was making progress lit a fire inside him.

He was getting better. They all were. The rigorous training was working. And that left a lingering question on all their minds.

What was going to come next?

At least they would have a good night's sleep to prepare for whatever it might be.

# CHAPTER TWENTY-THREE

"Up on your feet!" Teacher Rovos yelled at some ungodly hour in the middle of the night.

Bawb and the others were moving immediately, scrambling from their bunks in a hurry. To dally was to face punishment, typically of the painfully exhausting kind.

Their regular training was punishment enough.

Zota cast an illumination spell.

"*Phallistos!*" Rovos growled, extinguishing the lesser spell in an instant. "Aspirant Zota, what were you thinking?"

"I-uh, I thought—"

"You were *not* thinking, and that could have gotten you and all your classmates killed." Rovos stalked the line of students, surveying them in the dark. They'd all learned basic night-vision spells a few weeks prior and a few had managed to cast them to varying degrees of success. The rest, however, were left in the dark as to what was going on, literally and figuratively.

Teacher Pallik was there as well, standing off to the side, silently watching the youths as Rovos made his speech. Judging by the look on her face, it was one she'd heard many times before.

"Ghalian operate in the dark," he continued. "We thrive in it. And we do not fear what may be hiding in the shadows, for we *are* what is hiding in the shadows. And you go casting an illumination spell? Not only giving away *your* position as well as that of your classmates, but also ruining the night vision of anyone not ready for the spell."

"Forgive me, Teacher Rovos. It was dark, and I only wished to know what—"

"You have other senses, do you not? Other spells to draw upon? Yet you chose the one option that made you an easy target for any who would want you dead."

Zota's head hung, but only slightly. He had learned not to show weakness around Rovos under any circumstances. The man would berate him, forcing him to recite spells until his traumatized mind could fire them off in whatever order he demanded by rote. It was a miserable way to learn, but it certainly did make the lessons stick.

"I'm sorry, Teacher," the boy said quietly but with enough firmness of voice to not draw his teacher's ire.

Rovos seemed satisfied with his response. "As you should be. You reacted foolishly. Learn from this. Drill it into that thick skull of yours. Never cast when you are unsure of your situation. You may do far more harm than good."

Teacher Pallik took this as the moment to address the students.

"You are not the first young trainee to make this mistake, and you won't be the last. Just ensure you do not make it again. You'll do that, won't you?"

"Of course, Teacher."

"Good. Then, with that out of the way, we would like you all to dress and arm yourselves and assemble in the fifth lower level training chamber at once."

Even Albinius knew better than to mention it was the

middle of the night. Erratic hours and surprise training were the norm for them, though they were typically afforded a full night's sleep to recover. But not always.

Training would simulate real-world situations with increasing regularity as they grew older, and one such circumstance was the unfortunate reality of sleep deprivation. As Ghalian, they would sometimes be forced to abstain from sleep for many days in pursuit of their objective, all while remaining alert and operating at the highest levels of skill and stealth.

For now, however, a little sluggishness would be overlooked. There were still plenty of years left in their training and ample time to suffer and endure those rigors until they each faded from the forefront and became just one more discomfort they didn't even think about as they completed their tasks.

"What weapons?" Elzina asked, already clothed and securing a few daggers on her body.

"That is up to you," Pallik replied with a knowing twinkle in her eye. "You are going into an uncertain situation facing creatures that may cause you harm. But it will be a long approach, and you may require speed, stealth, and agility. Or you may not. Such is the nature of uncertainty. In time you will have developed your standard go-to set of weapons. For now, however, you are learning what works for each of you. For that reason, this decision is entirely up to you."

Elzina seemed satisfied with the response and added a few items to her kit. Bawb was also already clothed and armed, but he chose to bring a lighter load. Others would have more weapons, and if they were moving as a group, he could rely on them to handle whatever might come their way that required such tools.

For himself, he had been paying close attention to Pallik's words. While she stressed there would be dangerous beasts along the way, she also mentioned, although with minimal emphasis, that the approach would be long. And if one of their teachers said it would be a lengthy effort, it was sure to be even more than anticipated.

He chose to keep his muscles fresh, or at least as fresh as he could, carrying a lighter load on whatever this task might be.

The teachers departed, leaving the group to quickly finish preparing then hurry down the stone staircase to the training chamber on the fifth level beneath the surface. It was a fairly large room, carved out of the stone rather than naturally formed. All manner of equipment was set up in it, and it had become one of the training rooms they knew the best.

Or so they thought.

When they entered the room, they found a surprise was awaiting them.

"Is that a door?" Zota marveled as they fell in, forming a single line.

"It is," Bawb replied.

"Where did it come from?"

"I honestly have no idea."

All the other Aspirants were marveling at the same thing. There, cut into the wall, a wall they had seen, leaned against, stood near, and observed for a few years now, was a door. A door they had never seen before.

Bawb squinted, searching for any sign of how this opening had appeared. To the naked eye it was impossible to detect. A master craftsman had built the passageway, and the seams were so perfectly blended with the rest of the stone wall to such a degree he doubted anyone would have been able to find it if they didn't already know it was there.

"All this time, right in front of us. How many other secrets like this might be around us and we have no idea?" Bawb wondered quietly.

A faint light appeared in the darkness of the tunnel the door led to, growing brighter as it drew near. Teacher Pallik walked out, extinguishing her illumination spell, while Teacher Rovos arrived through the other doorway.

"How did she get here before us?" Albinius whispered. "They barely left before we did."

"Shh," Finnia hissed, her eyes forward and back straight as she stood at attention.

Teacher Rovos walked around them from behind, taking note of how each of them had kitted themselves for the excursion. He paused at Bawb, eyeing the boy up and down.

"That is all you are bringing?"

"Yes, Teacher."

"The others are much better armed than you."

"Yes, Teacher," he replied, still confident in his choice.

Rovos didn't say anything more but simply stared at him a moment then continued down the line.

Pallik stood by quietly, a cheerful look on her face, as there pretty much always was. But the students knew better by now. While she appeared happy and sweet, she was both cold and deadly. On first glance, an outsider would have thought she was probably too soft on the students. Going easy on them for fear of harming the poor children.

They would have been wrong.

Rovos, on the other hand, for all his gruff attitude, seemed to actually care for them and truly wished them the best. With a hard fist, if need be, but he was always on their side in the end. It was just one more lesson that things were not what they seemed when it came to the Wampeh Ghalian.

Teacher Pallik walked to a table and pulled off the cover, revealing a selection of water bladders and foods. "You have quite a journey ahead of you," she said. "So we took the liberty of providing you options to take on your trek."

Rovos moved to the tunnel entrance. "This is the way to what will become a familiar new training area. The path there, however, is unlike any you have faced thus far. The tunnels are long and winding, passing through many caverns and traversing obstacles along the way. And, if you are unfortunate enough to happen upon them, you will be forced to deal with the creatures that dwell within. There is no fixed structure to this exercise. No time limit. You are simply to make it to the end, at which point you will be given your task and begin the day's training. Questions?"

Silence.

"Very well. Gather what you feel might be of use from the table, then depart. Know that once you have entered the tunnel, the door will seal behind you. There is no turning back."

It was ominous sounding, but then, so were most declarations made in the course of their training.

Bawb grabbed a medium-sized water bladder and a few pieces of dried meat and tucked them into his pockets. Albinius took a much larger quantity, loading up until it looked as if he might tear his clothing at the seams.

"What are you doing?" Finnia asked, shaking her head.

"If it's as long as they say, I'm going to get hungry. Just you wait and see. You'll wish you brought more."

"You are a fool, Albinius. Have I ever told you that?"

"Once or twice," he replied with a grin.

A high-pitched yowl wafted to their ears from the depths of the tunnel, causing all conversation to cease.

"What was that?" Albinius asked.

Rovos let out a rare chuckle. "*That* is one of the creatures that lives within these walls. Perhaps you will meet it on your trek."

The Aspirants checked their weapons quickly, reassured by their heft on their bodies. They were no longer Nulls. They had trained long and hard to reach where they were today, and no beasts were going to stand in their way.

"Come on," Elzina said, heading into the tunnel. "No sense waiting."

The others hurried after her, following her natural display of leadership. All but Bawb. He paused at the entryway, noting a faint marking just inside the doorway.

"Are you not joining the others?" Pallik asked.

"I am. I was just admiring the craftsmanship of this hidden door."

"Master Olafitz made this many generations ago. A master among masters, many would say."

"Seeing his work, I would tend to agree," Bawb replied.

"You had best be on your way before the others get too far ahead," Rovos grumbled.

Bawb did as he was told and stepped inside, but as the door slid closed behind him, he took a good long look at the internal structure embedded within the rock itself.

Wood. Wood and metal, both melded with the stone walls. He cast an illumination spell and took one more look before moving to join the others.

"Wait a moment. Where did the marking go?" he wondered.

It had been there but now was gone.

"Impossible." Bawb extinguished the illumination spell and focused hard, drawing from his konus as he cast the night-vision spell he had yet to master.

Slowly, some details began to appear where blackness had formerly been. Down the corridor in the distance, he could see the lit-up dot of his classmates as they moved ahead, but here, in the dark, he saw something else. The markings on the wall were only visible without the aid of light spells to illuminate them.

"I wonder," he mused, taking note of the marks and the wall

they were etched into, then began on his way, following his classmates deeper into the bowels of the tunnel system.

*Night Sight: Level one*, his konus quietly announced as he walked. He wondered how many more levels there were to that spell, knowing his konus would almost certainly not tell him.

# CHAPTER TWENTY-FOUR

A short distance down the corridor, Bawb noticed another transition from stone to wood then back to stone. Not long after that, a metal reinforced section appeared. Both were very small in the scheme of things, no more than a few paces long, but they did break up the continuity of the lengthy stone walls.

Bawb's night-vision spell was beginning to fail. He had only just learned it and had by no means perfected even the most rudimentary aspects of it. Fortunately, he was closing in on the others, and their combined illumination spells would allow him to save his konus's magic for later. He had a sinking feeling he might need it.

Before his vision returned to normal, he noticed that there were again markings etched into the walls. Different than before, but clearly cut by the same hand. He made careful note of them to ponder later. The size and shape as well as location had to have some sort of meaning. Why else would they be here? It wasn't as if Master Olafitz needed to sign his work every few hundred meters. They were deep within a Ghalian compound, and no outsider would ever see his work.

"Where were you, Bawb?" Usalla asked as he rejoined the

group. "I was beginning to wonder if anything had happened to you."

"No, just looking around."

"You sure about that?" Elzina chimed in with a snort. "Maybe you were afraid of what lies ahead in the dark."

"No such luck, Elzina. I was merely securing my gear and getting my bearings."

"Bearings? We are in a tunnel, Bawb. There are no bearings. No decisions to make. We follow this to the end. You heard the teachers."

"Of course. But that does not mean I cannot find beauty in the construction of this place. It was masterfully crafted."

The overconfident and overeager girl snorted a laugh. "There is no time for sightseeing. We have a task waiting for us at the end of this trek, and I, for one, would see that we get there sooner than later."

"I am not disagreeing, Elzina. I am merely pointing out that there are still things to see even while in a hurry."

The girl scoffed and pressed on, singular in her drive and relishing the position of leader she had so easily assumed. The others were following her, and in her opinion, that was how it should be.

They walked for nearly a half hour in the dark tunnel, the walls only illuminated by the spells the youths were casting. No flames were to be had here; there was nothing to make a torch with even if they wanted to. Fortunately, illumination was a spell they were all becoming proficient in.

A bend in the tunnel brought with it a narrowing of the walls as well, forcing the group to move ahead single file for a short while. When the pathway straightened out again they saw why.

The tunnel opened into a large, natural cavern through a fissure in the rock wall. It had been formed by nature, not a

Ghalian, and thus the tunnel had been modified to fit the stone's natural shape.

A faint glow illuminated the ground from above, the moss on the stalactites glowing with some sort of natural bioluminescence. The Aspirants let their spells fade, saving magic by using the ambient light.

Albinius abruptly disappeared from sight.

"Oof!" he exclaimed with a gasp as he hit the ground.

"Watch your step!" Elzina chided, easily hopping down to the trail below.

It was a short hop, no taller than a grown man, and all of them quickly made their way to the cavern's floor.

"Where now?" Zota asked, looking around at the unusual plants growing tall in the cavern.

"There's a gap in the vegetation that way," Usalla noted. "We should probably follow the openings."

"Obviously," Elzina said, stepping in front of her and pressing on. "Follow me."

Usalla glanced at Bawb, shaking her head but saying nothing. If the teachers had been telling the truth, they had a long way to go, and there was no point in riling up their classmate if they could avoid it. Once Elzina got in a mood she could make things difficult for all of them, and part of their Ghalian training had been learning to sidestep potential issues that could affect a mission. They just hadn't expected to be applying that lesson to one of their own.

The air was damp, which explained not only the stalactites and moss but also the plants that had sprung up surprisingly dense in the cavern. The space was spacious enough to allow for ample air flow, and the ambient light must have had enough of the right spectrum to help the vegetation grow.

A sound reached their ears.

"What is that?" Zota wondered.

"Shh," Usalla hissed, drawing the short sword she'd strapped to her back.

The others drew their weapons as well. Bawb pulled out a single blade, not particularly long but one he was very comfortable handling, and stood ready. Something was down here with them. Or, by the sound of it, something*s*.

*Griiik!*

A group of tiny, furred creatures with short brown hair and oversized feet charged at them, fangs bared. There were at least a dozen of them, and while they were no taller than knee-height, their teeth looked more than capable of taking a decent bite out of anyone they managed to latch onto.

The group scattered, spreading out to give them each space to fight and maneuver without running into one another. The animals didn't even pause, continuing their advance.

*Griik! Griik!*

More of them were coming from the other direction. This was rapidly becoming out of hand. Bawb looked across the cavern, noting a narrow opening like the one they had arrived through up on the wall.

"There's an exit!" he called out. "Let's go!"

He sheathed his knife and took off running. Usalla and Zota followed at once while the others looked to Elzina. An angry look flashed in her eyes, but she turned and ran as well. The entirety of their group was making a dash for the far wall, all of their agility training paying off dividends as they kept ahead of the pursuing herd.

Bawb got to the wall first and leapt high, grabbing the edge and pulling himself up with a fluid motion. Then he turned and reached down, ready to help the others.

Usalla's hand grasped his, her momentum carrying her up with ease. Zota was next, joining them on the ledge.

"Check that the tunnel is safe," Bawb urged.

Usalla and Zota drew their weapons and hurried ahead, casting illumination spells in the dark passageway.

Elzina threw her sword up onto the ledge, narrowly missing Bawb, then scrambled up, ignoring his outstretched hand. She snatched up her blade and sheathed it, watching from the side as the others raced up to safety.

The last of them made it up, but not before suffering a few bites from the fastest of the animals. They'd drawn blood, but not caused much harm.

"Why did you make a run for it?" Elzina demanded, spinning on Bawb with an angry glare.

"There was a way out. Elevated. These creatures are fast, but they have short legs and do not appear well suited to climbing."

"So you ran? We could have taken them."

"We could have, but to what purpose? We would have wasted energy and time when we could just as easily avoid the conflict."

"He's right," Albinius agreed. "No sense scrapping with angry critters if we don't have to."

Elzina scowled at them both, then turned and stormed into the tunnel.

"Well done, Bawb," Finnia said as she passed him, following Elzina into the passageway.

"Yes, nice job," Albinius agreed. "You may have angered Elzina in the process, but that's pretty much unavoidable, isn't it?"

A little smile creased Bawb's lips. "That it is."

Bawb allowed himself to slide to the rear of the group once more, searching the walls for any more signs of Master Olafitz's handiwork, but he found none. And so he trekked. They all did. For hours and hours they moved ahead, transitioning from tunnels to caverns to precarious walkways spanning flowing subterranean rivers and boiling thermal springs.

The variety of environments astounded Bawb, and he could not help but enjoy the welcome change from the routine they had all settled into for so many years. Yes, this was a challenge, and they were forced to deal with extremes of temperature as well as strange creatures, but at least it was something different. And different was good.

There was no sun to judge the length of time they had been trekking, but it must have been most of the day, and there was no end in sight. All of the Aspirants were bruised and sore from not only climbing rocks and pushing through narrow spots in the tunnels, but they had also received a few minor injuries fighting off the various creatures they had been warned about.

Albinius was faring the worst of them, but that was a mess of his own doing. They had stopped in a hot, open cavern devoid of any plants whatsoever when it happened. The wildlife had been small up until that point, but a much larger creature was stalking this chamber. Too big to force itself through the openings on either end, it was here it was forced to remain, feeding on smaller animals that passed through.

One larger one, however, caught its attention.

Albinius.

The young Ghalian had been overzealous in packing food for this trek, and in so doing, some had fallen from his pockets as they traversed the cavern. The creature, while poor of eyesight, possessed an excellent sense of smell and hearing, and Albinius had just given it a whiff of a fresh meal.

"Run for it!" Elzina commanded when the beast rounded a boulder and charged.

She hurdled over the hot stones and bubbling springs in a dash to the safety of the next section of the tunnel network. Several others followed, but this path was too narrow for all to go at once, and the tunnel opening was only big enough for one at a time.

Bawb and Usalla moved close, weapons ready, as a second creature joined the first, drawn by the noise and smell of this novel source of food. They were bipedal and shaggy, long green hair hanging matted from their bodies. They possessed long arms with long claws, and their jaws looked as though they could crush bones with ease.

Albinius threw his food at them, but the animals, while initially interested in the novel little morsels, were now quite taken by this larger meal that had presented itself. The two bellowed as one and charged.

The three of them dove aside, avoiding the swiping claws while doling out attacks of their own. But their blades seemed to slide off the wiry hair. Whatever they were, these creatures possessed a natural defense in their cut-resistant hair. Hair that, judging by the scorch marks on it, was also highly flame resistant. A useful trait in this volcanic chamber.

The beasts charged again, a claw scratching Albinius on the arm but not enough to slow his frantic roll in the opposite direction. Bawb let out a fierce kick, catching one of them in the jaw, forcing its head back hard from the blow.

"The abdomen," Bawb yelled, spotting a weakness.

Usalla moved at once, heeding his call and driving her sword into the nearest beast's belly. The hair was thinner there, and though it required great force, her weapon penetrated, and once it had, it only required a shift of pressure to open the thing up from belly to chin.

It cried out once then fell silent with a wet, bloody thump.

The other beast sniffed the air and leapt backward. Apparently, the scent of its own kind being slain gave it second thoughts about its attack. Without looking back, it turned and fled, leaving the trio alone and relatively unscathed.

"Your arm. How bad is it?" Bawb asked, pulling a water skin free.

"I don't know," Albinius said. "I think there's some kind of numbing agent in their claws."

"Hopefully not poison," Usalla said, driving her sword through the animal's head, making sure it would not rise again.

Bawb poured copious water over Albinius's arm.

"Ow!"

"Good. The pain means whatever was on their claws washes off easily. Likely not a poison. And your arm does not look too bad. A bandage should suffice until we can have a healer look at it."

"I have dressings," Usalla offered, pulling a few strips from her pockets. Bawb looked at her with surprise. She chuckled. "You never know what may come in handy."

"Truer words have never been spoken," he agreed.

Albinius's arm was wrapped by the time the others left the safety of the tunnel and rejoined them. Elzina was not amused.

"*This* time you choose to fight? Why didn't you run?" she demanded.

Bawb shrugged. "There was no way we could have all made it in time. It seemed best to fight on terrain we could control."

Elzina looked at the dead beast and had to admit she couldn't find fault in the reasoning. Not that she would ever tell him that to his face, let alone in front of the others. "We should get moving."

Usalla bent over the animal and began cutting pieces off, using the sturdy hair as a hand hold. "Actually," she said, "we have just been provided a meal."

Bawb joined her, helping cut chunks of meat which they then placed atop one of the hot rocks near a molten spring. Disturbing as the sight may have been, the smell of sizzling flesh made the group's mouths water. They'd been trekking all day and had not stopped for more than a cursory snack. And now a meal—a hot meal at that—had just presented itself.

Bawb pulled the first fully cooked piece off the hot stone, using the hair as a handle, and offered it to Albinius. "It seems your foolishness led to a beneficial outcome after all," he said, gathering portions to hand the others as well. "Eat up, everyone, and regain your strength. Who knows how much farther we have to go."

## CHAPTER TWENTY-FIVE

"Messy, but you managed to arrive in one piece. More or less."

Teacher Rovos was standing at the tunnel's exit, looking extremely well-rested. The Aspirants, on the other hand, were dirty, bruised, bloodied, and an all-around mess.

"How did you get here before us?" Albinius asked.

Rovos snickered. "For once, a good question, Albinius. And one you will not get an answer to. So, Teacher Pallik, what are your thoughts?"

Pallik rose from the small boulder she was perched atop and leapt into the air, executing a perfect flip, landing effortlessly without a sound, her cheerful smile and disarmingly sweet demeanor never faltering.

Of course not.

Pallik looked them over, straightening the one hair that had slipped out of place as she dropped down to survey them. "Not bad, I would say, though a few of you are more worse for wear than others." She lifted Albinius's arm. "Not a bad field dressing. Who did this?"

"I did," Usalla replied.

"Well done, for an Aspirant," she said, unwrapping the

wound. "Oh, it seems a Zikik got you. How do you feel, Albinius?"

"Fine. A bit sore, but that's to be expected."

"No loss of sensation?"

"There was, but Bawb flushed it out. Said there was probably some kind of toxin on the thing's claws."

"It is a Zikik. And yes, they do possess a mild toxin on their claws. It can disable smaller game, but for one the size of you it would be far less effective." She turned to Bawb. "Who taught you to flush the wound made by a Zikik?"

"No one, Teacher Pallik."

"No one? Then why did you do so?"

Bawb shrugged almost imperceptibly, catching himself before he might offend the teacher. "It seemed the logical thing to do. There was a wound, and the reaction was pretty much immediate. Given no one else was suffering in a similar manner, direct contact causing it was the most likely option. The creature must have had something on it that triggered the reaction. I didn't know if it would work or not, but flushing the wound made the most sense given our limited resources."

"And yet you wasted valuable water, speaking of resources," Rovos noted.

"Yes, but I thought it a reasonable risk."

"Why is that? Water is vital, and you did not know how much farther you had to go."

"True, but if the toxin spread and Albinius became unable to walk, the effort of carrying him would slow us down even more, and the exertion would cause us to use up just as much of our water, if not more."

Rovos gave a satisfied nod, looking at his counterpart with approval. "The boy makes good sense."

"Yes. He did perform admirably. Well done, Bawb. You as well, Usalla. You both exceeded our expectations. And I am pleased to see that, despite your run-in with the Zikik, none of you require the healer's attention. At least, not yet."

Rovos tossed each of them a small, compressed ball of a foul-tasting concoction. It was one they knew well. A specialty of his that gave a boost of energy and endurance for a short while without the crash of some of the more potent spells. The one downside was that it tasted horrible.

"Eat up and restore your energy, then follow me."

*It was messy,* the konus said as Bawb forced down the disgusting snack. *But you have leveled up in several areas.*

"Show me later," Bawb said, swallowing hard to finish the last bite, then rushing after their teacher.

Rovos strode off across the small cavern, stopping at an ornate doorway, sealed up tight. It was twice as tall as he, and three times as wide. Whatever it was designed to accommodate, it was massive. The students quickly gathered around him.

"What is that?" Elzina asked.

"This is your task. What you trekked here to experience. Through this doorway is the expansive Molarian dungeon. Designed by Master Molarian herself, this task will test you to your limits and beyond. You have improved in your training and are well on your way to leveling up and becoming Vessels of the Ghalian order, but that is still some time away, and you will have to work harder than ever to earn that title." He paced back and forth, as was his habit, staring down at them like a serpent eyeing its prey. "You will come to know this place well and will train here often. It is a shifting thing, this dungeon, and the tasks may change unexpectedly. You will have to adapt accordingly. Are you ready to proceed with the next level of your training?"

"Yes, Teacher!" the Aspirants replied as one.

"Good. Teacher Pallik will explain your task."

Pallik stepped to the front with a warm smile. "I am so proud of you all, making it this far. Now you shall have a new task to test your mettle. One I am confident at least some of you may hope to succeed at."

Bawb did not like the sound of that.

"Today's task is a simple one. Enter the Molarian dungeon and locate the Orabis fruit. Be wary, things are often not as they seem. Once you have acquired it, bring it to the exit, whereupon you may eat it, should you so desire. This is every pupil for themselves, so act accordingly. You may work together or alone; the choice is yours."

The Orabis fruit was rumored to have restorative powers on most species. Given the beating they'd taken today, whoever managed to claim it would have a much easier trek back to their bunkhouse than the rest. It was enough to put all of them in a fiercely competitive mindset.

"With that, I will leave you to it," she said, then began walking away.

"Teacher Pallik?" Zota called after her. "The door is sealed. How do we enter the dungeon?"

She turned and smiled. "*That*, my dear Zota, is part of the exercise. Good luck! See you at the exit."

Pallik and Rovos walked off, leaving the confused students at a loss.

The door towered over them, ornate and quite solidly locked. There was a keyhole, but none had a key, nor did they possess anything with which to force it open. And as this had been crafted by a Master Ghalian, they very much doubted simple force could achieve that goal anyway, just as they were sure there had to be another way in.

"Give me a hand up," Elzina ordered two of their cohort. The pair leaned on one another, providing her a living ladder of sorts to climb up and examine the door from on high.

"You are not going to find the answer up there," Bawb called up to her.

"Oh? And what is it you think you know, Bawb?" she replied, jumping down in front of him.

Tension crackled between them, all of it originating from Elzina. Bawb simply wanted to get this part of their task underway as quickly as possible. He pointed to the door.

"This was created by a Ghalian. A Wampeh, like us. Putting the opening mechanism out of reach would make no sense."

"So, where would it be, then?"

"I didn't say I knew that bit of information, only that it would have to be somewhere we could reach unaided."

Elzina didn't want to admit it, but he had a point. "I say we each pick a section and start looking. You two, take that panel there. Albinius, you work on that bit there."

"But I—"

"Just do it," she snapped back, then quickly divvied up tasks for the rest of them. All but Bawb, that is. "We've got enough to cover the parts we can reach, like you said. I guess you can just wait for us to open it."

Bawb, rather than being angry or even annoyed, simply shrugged and stepped away, leaving them all to crowd around the door, inspecting every inch of it for some clue how to get in without a key.

Bawb took the opportunity to walk around a bit and properly take in the area. The cavern was not natural, and every aspect of it was carefully crafted, the stones aligning just right, the spells generating the ambient lighting keeping a steady glow but not too bright.

"Oh," he said as a realization hit him.

Bawb glanced at the others. They were all hard at work. Perfect. He turned from them and studied the blank stone of the walls around them. The door had been so big, so ornate, that it couldn't help but catch anyone's eye who made their way to this chamber. But he thought back to how the day had begun. How

Master Olafitz had hidden the tunnel entrance in plain sight in a room they frequented regularly.

*What if*—he mused, quietly casting his night sight spell under his breath. It was illuminated here, and he had no idea how to extinguish the lights, not to mention doing that would anger his classmates to no end. But perhaps if he stood close enough to the wall, any markings normally hidden would make themselves visible.

Bawb strained his eyes, searching for anything out of the ordinary.

Nothing.

"What are you doing?" Elzina shouted to him.

"Just looking at the craftsmanship that made this chamber," he replied. It wasn't a lie. Not exactly. He just wasn't telling her the entire truth. And he *was* admiring the craftsmanship. He just happened to be looking at it for a particular reason.

He walked back and forth several times, examining both sides bordering the doorway. Nothing was making itself clear to him, but there had to be something there. Frustrated, he stepped back, moving to the spot atop the small boulder where Teacher Pallik had been crouched.

It was a comfortable vantage point, he realized when he ascended. Odd that in a carefully designed chamber they would leave a boulder just sitting there. Still, one could see pretty much everything from this height. No wonder she had chosen it for her perch. It afforded a view of the whole chamber, not to mention a clear view of the—

"Oh!" he exclaimed quietly to himself, shifting his position.

He looked at the shadows of the other boulders and rocks in the chamber and how the magical lighting formed them. This was not some haphazard illumination spell. It had been placed with great care and at great expense. And now he saw something else. Something he had missed—they *all* had missed —from up close.

The shadows aligned with architectural details of the door, the smoky dark lines reaching all the way to the door's frame and face, intersecting in such a way that could not have been accidental. Bawb studied the shapes and realized what he was looking at. It was an elongated doorway, only part of which was on the wall. The shadowy bit, the part that was made up of no more than the careful absence of light, formed the rest. And it was there that he saw it.

Bawb hopped down from his perch and walked to what seemed like any other shadow now that he was standing on ground level. He crouched down, running his fingers over the stone floor, sensing the subtle shifts in texture. He followed them with his fingertips, drawing a faint pattern in the dust until they came to rest on an embedded rock.

It was lodged firmly in place, but Bawb sensed there was something different about it. He cast his night sight once again, the faint markings scratched into the rock revealing themselves to his enhanced vision. Just as he'd seen when they first entered the passageway when they began their trek, there were several very deliberate shapes, four of which looked to be almost perfectly spaced for a hand's span.

He reached out and carefully placed his fingers atop each of them. A brief surge of power flowed from his konus into the stone, as if it knew what to do without him having to tell it. A moment later a cracking sound erupted from the wall next to the door.

"Look out!" Zota shouted, scurrying away from the door.

The others followed immediately, unsure what was going on.

Bawb, however, remained crouched, his hand now locked in place, powering this mechanism. The wall to the right side of the door abruptly vanished, swinging open to reveal a clear path inside. It was just like the sort of entry Master Olafitz had made.

"What happened? Who did that?" Elzina demanded.

Usalla looked at her crouching friend with surprise. "I think it was Bawb."

"What did you do? That is not Master Molarian's door!"

Bawb released his grip and stood. "No, it is not. The key was what Teacher Pallik said. That not everything is as it seems. This door, this massive, incredibly ornate door is buried far beneath the ground. In a Ghalian stronghold no less. Who from the outside would ever see it? The answer is no one. And if that is the case, why create something like this? The answer is clear once you step away from the problem. This is designed to distract. To divert attention. To waste time. That door is not the entry to the dungeon, it is *part* of the dungeon and its tricks."

Usalla and Zota were grinning, proud of their friend's accomplishment. Elzina, on the other hand, had been upstaged yet again, and that was putting her in a most foul mood. More than she already was, and that was saying something.

"Fine. Bravo," she said with a condescending smirk. "I will still be the first to the Orabis fruit, so in the end, it won't matter who opened the door."

With that she rushed inside, heeding their teacher's words. It was everyone for themself, and she wasn't about to share the prize.

"What are we waiting for?" Albinius blurted, scrambling after her.

Bawb turned to his friends and shrugged. "It is undoubtedly full of traps and obstacles. There is no sense in rushing."

"I agree," Usalla said. "But I also do not wish to see Elzina win."

"Fair enough," he replied with a chuckle, stepping into the open doorway. "Very well, my friends. Shall we?"

# CHAPTER TWENTY-SIX

While Elzina elbowed her way ahead of the others as they first rushed into the new training dungeon and chose their paths, Bawb held back a moment, casting his night-sight spell again, even though he was pretty sure it would not help in this situation.

He was right. It didn't do a thing.

"It was worth a try," he mused, wondering what manner of obstacles and traps the Ghalian masters had laid for them. Surely, there would be many, in whatever form they might be.

Albinius, Dillar, and the others hurried along, but Usalla and Zota had stayed with him at the rear at first, stopping at the junction just inside the door where they were offered a choice of routes, allowing the other more eager of their cohort to discover the first round of boobytraps. Painfully, on occasion, judging by the grunts and cries that reached their ears.

"Which way, do you think?" Zota wondered, staring at the three tunnel mouths that now lay ahead of them.

"I would assume all of them will eventually reach the end," Bawb replied. "The only question is which of them will be the least difficult to pass."

"There is but one way to find out. I'll take this one," Usalla said as she trotted off into the dark passage on the right, her illumination spell glowing bright.

"I'll try this one," Zota added, heading to the opposite side.

That left the center tunnel. One that was illuminated, but only just, before tapering off into darkness as the passageway curved up in the distance. Bawb stepped carefully into the opening, his ears straining for sound, his eyes constantly moving, scanning for traps. He took a deep breath, noting the slightly damp quality of the air. There was water here. Whether it was part of his route he was unsure.

He walked on, feet quiet on the stone floor. This section was simply a tunnel, its stone walls carved by a steady hand, the ground worn smooth from centuries of trainees walking these same steps.

The dungeon had to be an expansive space judging from what the air flow felt like. A cold breeze told tale of vast chambers and long corridors winding through the underground. How long this task would take was anyone's guess, but knowing the Ghalian, each path would require roughly the same amount of time if an Aspirant was skilled and sure of foot.

Bawb moved ahead and rounded the corner, entering a mid-sized chamber with a relatively low ceiling. It was both light and dark, depending on which part one was in, and the other Aspirants who had come in before him were using their illumination spells as needed as they spread out in search of the correct path.

Marzis lay squirming off to Bawb's left, his leg firmly snared in a hole in the ground. From what Bawb could tell by the dirt patterns, the boy had stepped on a trigger stone, the trap pulling his leg down then slamming onto it from all sides. It was a snare trap and nothing more, but the boy, in his haste, had somehow triggered a secondary spell meant for those who managed to pass the trap. One that slammed him against the stone wall.

His leg, however, remained behind.

Bawb did a quick assessment of his classmate's injury. The leg had been severed just below the hip, a horrible shattering of the bone and destruction of the flesh encasing it. An injury like this was too much for even the most skilled healer to repair completely. Marzis would never become a full-fledged Ghalian. Not minus a leg.

As an adult and Master of the order, the injury could be worked around, an injured person's style adapted to accommodate their injury. But a mere Aspirant? He had only just begun down the long road to mastery. And now that road had been cut short, and not even in a situation any would have anticipated being *this* dangerous. It was a lesson they would both remember the rest of their days.

Bawb felt a twinge of sadness for his classmate even as he noted the boy's quick thinking. A strip of cloth was tied tight around the stump, the makeshift tourniquet applied even in his dazed and agonized state.

"Have you stopped the bleeding?" Bawb asked.

Marzis nodded, doing his best to deal with the pain.

Bawb rested his hand on his shoulder a moment, then gave a nod and continued on. He could not help him, nor would the teachers want him to. This was training. This was their life. Injuries happened to one's traveling companions, and in the real world, even death. None of that could be allowed to stop a Ghalian from completing their task.

Bawb moved forward, scanning the floor. The layer of dirt that had accumulated made it difficult to see any traps. He pulled a little magic from his konus and cast one of the few spells he had been playing with in his spare time. It had been something safe he could work with to help him better grasp the feeling of casting with intent, nothing more. But now the harmless little wind spell could come in handy.

"*Flarius ekto,*" he said, envisioning the breeze as he intoned the words. His intent was clear and present, and a slight gust of wind blew across the floor in front of him.

*Oh, now he's thinking outside the box,* the konus announced. *Who'd have guessed? Well, that was surprising. You may have some potential yet. Level up: Unconventional spell use.* A formerly blurred icon briefly flashed clear in his hidden display. Unconventional use of spells? Apparently, that was a thing. He was most curious to pursue that line of logic further, but that would have to wait. For now, he had a task to complete. And the spell, it seemed, had just made that a little easier.

The gaps were almost invisible to the eye, the spacing between the stones just a little wider than the others. Pitfalls. Triggers. Whatever they were, they were now clear to him. It was an intricate and random pattern that lay ahead of him, but it was all visible now. Rather than hurry ahead, however, Bawb paused, committing their location to memory. The teachers had said they would be training here a lot, and taking a moment to prepare himself for future trials could pay off one day.

He reached the middle of the chamber and climbed atop a low obstacle rather than racing for the tunnel so close by. He looked around, wondering why, exactly, this elevated position was even an option. The fact that it was here at all made him suspect it was of importance. He looked up.

There, barely extending from the ceiling, were a set of small handholds colored to blend with the stone. Had he been at ground level he would certainly have missed them.

"Hmm. I wonder."

Bawb climbed back down and picked up a small rock, then resumed his elevated position. He tossed the rock into the open floor ahead of him.

*Whoosh!*

A series of thick ropes lashed out, flying from one side of the chamber walls to the other. Anyone who had been standing there would have been pinned, and quite likely concussed as well.

"A trap spell using actual ropes. Clever," he had to admit.

The path, difficult as it was, now presented itself. Bawb jumped up and grabbed the first handhold. It was solid. The distance was such that he would be unable to skip one if he felt it was another trap.

"I suppose I am committed," he said, then began swinging.

From hold to hold, he moved quickly until he softly dropped to the ground on the far side, unscathed. He did not bother looking back as he hurried into the tunnel ahead. Elzina would surely be making good progress, as would the others. It was going to require more effort than this to catch up.

The next chamber was full of water. It wasn't a still pool, but neither was it a raging torrent. Nevertheless, he had no desire to fall in. A series of hanging ropes and precarious walkways presented themselves. There were also dry rocks jutting from the water at various points. It was all rather self-explanatory. Cross however you could. Just know that it was all but certain that some of the seemingly stable areas would be anything but.

Bawb surveyed the area and made his choices. He would begin with a long leap to a rock rather than a much closer rope, which most would be tempted to use. From there he would assess as he moved, jumping up and down, alternating his stability points as needed.

His feet landed on the rock solidly. It did not budge. He held his breath, waiting for something to happen. Nothing did.

"Looks as though that was the right assumption."

Bawb leapt high and grabbed the bottom of a nearby suspended walkway and hauled himself up. Had it been rigged to fail, he would have triggered it as soon as he grabbed on, so he hurried along with steady steps until he reached the end. There was one choice.

He jumped hard, barely grabbing the dangling rope just within reach. He swung wildly at first but kicked his legs, forcing himself into a more controlled trajectory. Bawb then continued this pattern, dropping to rocks, climbing up to platforms or ropes, repeating until he reached the far end.

Dry and intact, he hurried into the waiting tunnel but skidded to a halt. Something was making the hair on his neck stand on end. He cast his illumination spell.

Nothing.

He picked up a small rock and tossed it ahead.

Again, nothing.

Bawb was about to move forward when an idea flashed through his mind. He returned to the water and cupped his hands, scooping up a handful. He stepped to the tunnel entrance and threw it, the water spraying high and low.

A few tiny droplets hung in mid-air.

"Aha," he exclaimed, leaning in to examine the magical tripwires. "Clever."

They were invisible to the eye, and he had not yet learned the spells to detect them. Clearly, this was meant as a lesson most would fail, and in that failure, they would learn the hard and painful way and likely never do it again.

Bawb, however, had managed what most Aspirants would not at this age. He had detected the magical trap without using magic of his own. He had relied on something else. Something that did not trigger the mechanism.

*Trap Detection: One*, the konus said. *You may not be as bad at this as I thought.*

"Aren't you supposed to be *quietly* noting my progress in the background?" he asked.

*Normally, sure. But I thought you could use the moral support.*

"From an inanimate item."

*Now that's just rude. I suppose I'll just keep quiet, then.*

"At last. I must concentrate."

The konus ignored the verbal jab and kept true to its word and didn't say another thing.

It was a somewhat tenuous situation, the path through the tripwires clear enough, but with the time it would take to carefully ease past them, the water would evaporate before he could possibly make it through them all. That meant a memorization drill. One that would have more serious repercussions if he failed.

Bawb splashed more water on the tripwires but did not begin his attempt. Instead, he stood still, just staring at the pattern, allowing his eyes to disengage and unfocus from anything but the task before him. He was new to this, utterly green, but something seemed to click in his head. This made sense. *Difficult* sense, but it was clear all the same.

The water evaporated, as he expected, but Bawb didn't gather any more. He would rely on his memory rather than his eyes. To do anything else would likely lead to fixating on the visual cues, throwing him off the mental roadmap he had more or less locked in place.

He edged forward, bending and twisting, stepping at odd angles, his body contorted into all manner of positions as he progressed. To any who might observe him, the lack of visible reason for his actions would make it seem as though he was simply partaking in some strange manner of dance. But this was far more than that. And while likely not fatal, the trap would undoubtedly hurt, and pain avoidance was always a good motivator, no matter how much the students were reminded that a Ghalian often had to overcome discomfort and even pain in the course of their contracts. But that didn't mean one couldn't avoid it, especially if it was in the furthering of their goal.

And so he continued on in his silent dance, spinning and twisting, following the mental map he had formed until he was clear of the last tripwire. Or he thought he was. With so many moves, he couldn't be entirely sure.

"Konus? Was that the last one?"

Silence.

He didn't bother asking again. If the device was going to throw attitude, so be it. He would do this entirely on his own. He took a step forward, then another, then one more still.

Nothing happened.

Bawb breathed a sigh of relief and continued on with his task, passing through chamber after chamber, doing all he could to note hidden traps and tripwires, and occasionally finding another of his fallen classmates who had been caught up in a snare or who had tumbled to the ground hard from an unstable boobytrap. All were hurt, and a few were concussed, but nothing was fatal. At this stage of their training the perils were not of that variety. Eventually, however, that would change.

Bawb's body was exhausted by the time he exited yet another tunnel into a vast cavern, illuminated by the flowing lava that streamed across parts of the surface in several areas. The orange glow made everything waver from the heatwaves, but there, up ahead, was the final challenge, and at the end, the Orabis fruit resting atop a small pedestal.

If he could make his way across the tops of the towering poles to the platform at the end, he would win. Tired as he was, he knew it would be difficult. His balance was good, but his muscles shook from the continued exertion. He eyed the prize just one final series of obstacles away.

It would revitalize him, Bawb knew, and it was so close he could almost taste it.

Motion on his right caught his eye. He turned.

Elzina.

She had just exited from one of the other tunnels that led to this chamber and was assessing the final obstacle just as he had done. She took it all in then surveyed the rest of the chamber. Her eyes fell upon Bawb. They had arrived before the others. And they would be making their approach at the same time.

She leapt into action at once, scrambling up the lower poles, making her way to the tall ones. Bawb moved as soon as she did, doing the same until they both stood perched high above the ground. The poles were just big enough to hold two feet pressed close together, and they were spaced out just close enough to step from one to another.

Undoubtedly, some would be rigged to either tip or fall, or perhaps something even worse, but that didn't matter right now. What did matter was making it to the end. A goal that the singular focus of both Aspirants.

Bawb and Elzina began hopping from pole to pole, balancing as they landed, the poles swaying from the weight. Bawb was moving slower than she was, but he was doing so on purpose. Some of the poles seemed to have faint markings on them. He just had to figure out what they meant.

One fell away as he tried to step on it, only barely adjusting his course to an adjacent one, narrowly averting the tumble.

"Got it," he said to himself, his confidence surging.

He moved faster now, closing the gap with Elzina until they were side-by-side. He kept his momentum, pressing his pace until he edged past her. They were close to the end now, down to just a small series of poles.

"We cannot move ahead without tripping one another up," he said. "If we work together, we can finish this task. I see the path. Will you join me?"

Elzina cocked her head slightly. "You've found the key to the traps?"

"I have."

"Then lead the way."

Bawb didn't hesitate, jumping forward with conviction as Elzina fell in behind him, unafraid and sure of foot as the two of them moved together. He made quick work of the last few poles. They were almost there, an end to their struggle finally in reach.

Hands slammed into his back, knocking him from his pole, sending him tumbling to the ground far below. Bawb hit hard, bruising his ribs from the impact. At least nothing was broken. He looked around, dazed. He thought he saw a boy down there with him for a moment, a flicker of pale blue light tricking his eyes where there was clearly nothing but darkness. His senses cleared quickly, and with them the realization that there were two choices. Try to make it back to the beginning, hopping over lava as he did, or climb the pole as best he could from where he was.

The choice was a simple one.

He wrapped his arms around the pole and began climbing. It hurt, his ribs aching with every movement, but he was not going to give up. Up he climbed, forcing his body to move until at long last his hands felt the top of the pole. He hoisted himself up, careful as he found his footing, then completed the last few hops until his feet were once more on solid ground.

The pedestal was empty, the Orabis fruit gone.

He jogged out of the dungeon's exit to find Elzina merrily eating the prize, keeping it all to herself. The other students were there as well, bruised and bloody, having failed the course and been removed to be healed then given space to sit and wait, thinking about their mistakes. A few were missing, though. Likely those too injured for a quick healing to put right.

Bawb glared at Elzina. "You cheated," he growled. "You pushed me off."

Elzina laughed. "There is no such thing as cheating for a Ghalian. You should know that. We succeed by any means necessary, period."

"But we were going to finish together. I was showing the way."

"And it is wise to let another take the risk so we can benefit from their actions. Isn't that true, Teacher?"

Rovos nodded, though he did not seem particularly pleased with Elzina. "She is correct. We can and should utilize the efforts of others to ease our path."

"See? I told you."

"*But* we must also protect and nurture our allies, for we never know when we may be required to call upon them."

Usalla limped over to Bawb and handed him one of the foul-tasting energy balls. It was nowhere near as restorative as the Orabis fruit, but it would boost his energy considerably.

"Don't mind her, Bawb. Just because we work alone, it doesn't mean we needn't support one another. We are all on the same team. We all aspire to be Wampeh Ghalian one day."

Bawb nodded, fighting the urge to gag as he took a bite of the nasty restorative. He glanced at his konus, mentally calling up his skills display. Despite Elzina's treachery, he had at least made progress in a few areas.

*Sure you did,* the konus said, reading his mind. *But are you really going to be satisfied with mediocrity?*

"I thought you were going to remain quiet," he grumbled.

Usalla's warm eyes hardened slightly. "What was that?"

"Uh, nothing. Just talking to myself. I didn't mean you, of course. I am grateful for your help, Usalla. You are a good friend."

Her eyes relaxed. "As are you," she replied.

*Level Deduction - Tact and Stealth.*

"Those are even things?" he thought, rather than said aloud.

*They are. And more will be revealed as you progress.* If *you progress.*

Bawb bit his tongue. It had been a long day, and arguing with his konus would not make it any better.

Rovos paced among the weary students, surveying their degree of hurt. "With me," he commanded, taking off at a jog down a tunnel.

The students lurched to their feet and followed, soon finding themselves back at the ornate doorway once more. Rovos cast a spell then turned to the students.

"The paths have been shifted," he said, opening the hidden entry for them. "Learn from your mistakes."

Albinius looked at the open door then back at their teacher. "You don't really want us to go back in there, do you?" he whined.

Rovos glared at him a moment then looked at the others, pausing on each of their faces to see if anyone else wanted to mouth off. Wisely, no one did. He stepped back, motioning to the opening with a sweeping gesture.

"Aspirants. Again!"

# CHAPTER TWENTY-SEVEN

Three times.

The Aspirants had run the gauntlet of the brutal training dungeon three times, back to back to back, and even Elzina, winner of the Orabis fruit, was utterly drained by the end.

This, of course, as usual, was the point.

Rovos and Pallik showed the tiniest bit of mercy to the exhausted students, allowing them to make an improvised camp at the dungeon's entrance and sleep there rather than trek all the way back to the training house. It had taken them nearly all day to get to the dungeon, and even the most stoic of them doubted they could make it back. It wasn't a question of willpower; it was a matter of physics. Their energy was simply no more.

While Rovos had watched them run through the course, Teacher Pallik had apparently summoned to have one of the upper classes bring sustenance for the Aspirants. How she did it was a mystery until she showed them a small device she kept in her pocket.

"This is a skree," she told them by way of explanation. "It uses a modest amount of magic when in proximity to the intended recipient, allowing for economical communication, even through stone, water, or space."

"Space?" Zota marveled. "How far can it reach?"

"A long-range skree can signal quite far. Systems away, in fact, but the power required is significant. But in this circumstance, the message to the kitchens was instantaneous. A good thing too. You all look famished."

They were, and as soon as they were allowed, the students filled their bellies, then curled into whatever spot they had chosen to spend the nigh. They all quickly fell sound asleep.

The following morning—or whatever time it was, as underground there was no way to tell—saw Teacher Rovos in good spirits, ready to lead the class in the further use of magic.

The students, however, were slow to rise despite their best efforts. The previous day had done a number on them, and it took longer than usual to get their limbs to obey their wishes.

"Come along," Rovos said. "We are going to work with magic today, and there is a perfect chamber for such exercises not far from here."

The Aspirants shook off the cobwebs of sleep and followed him as he set off at a casual jog down a nearby corridor.

Nearly an hour later they arrived at their destination.

The first twenty minutes had been misery, but once their limbs finally warmed up, the group found that the pain was pretty much gone, their bodies having regained their usual flexibility and most of their strength.

"Gather around," Rovos instructed.

The Aspirants formed a semicircle in front of him.

"You all have received your konuses and have learned the basics of spell casting. Today, we are going to delve into the topic in greater depth, going so far as to discuss the use of slaaps and even claithes, though odds are none of you will ever wield one."

"I have heard that a slaap is essentially a higher-powered

konus that also fits over the knuckles as well as the wrist. They say it is usually favored by military types," Finnia noted. "But I have never heard of a claithe before."

"For good reason, Finnia. The claithe is an incredibly powerful weapon. One that has been known to kill its user as well as their enemies if they are not fully in control of it. That is why none but the most powerful would even attempt to wield one, and even then, only in the most dire of circumstances. But we will come back to that later. For the moment, I wish for you all to connect with your konuses, but do not cast. Simply feel the power stored within. Gauge it. Note its intensity and readiness to be deployed according to your wishes. How it reacts to your intent."

He waited while the class did as instructed. Some were able to dial in their konuses pretty easily, while others were still struggling to control and direct the magic they contained. Bawb was both lucky and unlucky in that his konus would tell him if he was doing something wrong, though typically in a berating, sarcastic manner. It was motivation to do it right, no doubt, but also an annoyance that could really grate on his nerves.

Of course, that was also part of the process. To learn to tune out anything that might distract you from your task.

"Now, you all know the spell for basic force casting," Rovos continued. "This can be used in both offensive and defensive roles. You can attack and unbalance your adversary, but also use it to deflect an attack thrown your way. Space out a bit and practice casting that spell."

The group did as he said and spent the next twenty minutes getting the feel for wielding magic like this. It was becoming almost easy when he changed things up, having them cast pulling spells instead, then eventually combining the two, alternating from one to the other.

"These are basic spells, but sometimes the most basic can

take an opponent off guard. Once you gain proficiency in high-level spells, your enemy may very well prepare to counter that level of attack. This could lead to them being open to the most simplistic of spells. Do you understand the concept?"

"Yes, Teacher," they replied.

"Good. Now, before our next practical lesson, I would like to talk to you about two other forms of magic. One that can benefit us, and the other being instantly deadly to our kind. You have heard of the Ootaki and how their hair stores magic, and one day, you may even possess some yourself."

Bawb shifted uneasily on his feet. "I thought the Ghalian were against the trade of Ootaki hair."

"We most certainly are, and the Wampeh Ghalian do all we can to protect them. But in the case of hair that has already been shorn by another, we claim it and add it to the Ghalian coffers. On occasion, it is used, a powerful addition to our agents' tools." He noted the look in Bawb's eye. It seemed the boy was not entirely satisfied with the explanation.

"Let me put it this way, Bawb. Do you throw away fruit that has already been picked or do you try to use it, adding it to a meal so it does not go to waste?"

"I would eat it or give it to someone who would."

"Precisely. And just like any other harvested item, it would be a waste of the poor Ootaki's sacrifice to destroy the hair they labored to grow for so long, regardless of the circumstances that brought it about. Even a lone strand of their golden locks can be a great boost to your own power in times of need. To tap into it, you need only cast as you would with a konus, drawing its magic to power your spells. As for the other form of stored magic, I think you have also already learned about the Balamar waters."

The group stood fast, but the mood among them grew decidedly uneasy at the mention of the Balamar waters.

"It kills us on contact," Elzina noted. "But while it is deadly to us, it is a powerful healing agent for other species, so long as it is only applied topically."

"And if ingested?"

"They also die, right?"

"That is correct. Only the oldest, strongest Zomoki could ever ingest the waters, but they have been gone for a long, long time."

Albinius raised his hand.

"You do not need to raise your hand, Albinius. Simply ask your question in a concise manner."

"Right. Sorry. Uh, I was just wondering. If we do get splashed with Balamar water on say our clothes or something, will we still die?"

"Of course," Elzina snorted.

"No, it is a good question," Rovos countered. "If the water is somehow stopped from actually contacting your skin directly, be it by one or several layers of clothing, then, in theory, if you can shed it quickly enough to avoid touching it, you could survive. But even the slightest contact will result in instant immolation."

"Immo-what?" Elzina asked.

"Immolation," Bawb chimed in. "It means burning to death."

Elzina shot him an annoyed look.

He shrugged it off. "What? I read."

Rovos nodded his approval. "Very good, Bawb. That is correct. Fortunately for us, very little still exists anywhere in the galaxy, and the Ghalian have managed to obtain control of a great deal of it."

"Deny our enemies their most potent weapon," Usalla noted. "A logical tactic, though it must be prohibitively expensive."

"That it is. Even the smallest sample of the waters fetches a fortune these days. When Balamar's grand cistern was destroyed, the small amount that had been sold outside his realm instantly became priceless. Fortunately, more often than not, we steal it from a target during a contract. That, or our agents and spies do the leg work and we come in to finish the job."

"Is there any defense against it?" Bawb asked. "Could one use a fire spell as protection?"

"In very limited circumstances that might work, but Balamar water is unlike regular liquids and is quite hardy. A simple fire would do little. The heat required would be immense. That said, I would not rule out the option should you ever find yourself in a situation calling for it. Better to try and fail gloriously than not try at all."

Rovos cracked his neck, shifting his thoughts back to the real task at hand. Their little discussion had gotten him a bit derailed, though he didn't really mind. These were good questions. Valuable ones. And they showed that a few of the Aspirants were already thinking like Ghalian. At least in some regards.

"All right. It is time for you to put your casting skills to the test," he said. "Follow me."

The group was expecting another long run but was glad to find they were merely directed to an adjoining chamber. This one had a large circle etched in the ground, the stone scarred from what looked like it might have been lightning or a firestorm. Along the edges were seats, in front of which a strong magical barrier had been cast. It was transparent, but more than robust enough to stop any errant spells from injuring an observer.

Rovos strode to the center of the circle and looked over the students.

"Elzina, step forward."

She did as she was told, stepping into the ring then standing quietly at attention.

"Bawb, step forward."

Bawb did likewise, quietly wondering what might come next.

*Oh, you're in for it now,* the konus jeered, flashing his stats without his wishing it. *You need to level up a lot more in your spell casting for this.*

"For what?" Bawb wondered.

*You'll see.*

Rovos gestured toward the protected seats. "The rest of you, take a seat."

They hurried to the observation area and did as they were told. Only when all were safely behind the barrier did Rovos turn his attention back to the pair standing alone in the ring.

"It is time to test your mettle," he said, a hint of amusement in his voice. "Are you ready?"

"Yes," Elzina replied, a fierce look in her eye.

"Ready for what?" Bawb asked, expecting the worst as he had been taught, yet desperately hoping for the best.

No such luck.

Rovos grinned. "It is time for a duel," he said, stepping back and casting a protective spell in front of himself. "You know the spells. You know the defenses. Prepare yourselves, get the spells straight in your minds. In one minute we begin!"

# CHAPTER TWENTY-EIGHT

All eyes were on the pair facing off for their very first magical duel. So intent were the Aspirants that none even noticed when Hozark and Demelza quietly entered the chamber, sliding to the back of the viewing area with the stealth that would be expected of masters of the order.

Even the combatants, out in the open and separated at opposite sides of the ring, failed to see their arrival. Only Teacher Rovos noted the two as they entered, giving the slightest of nods but nothing more.

Though they had a clear line of sight to the entryway, the combatants were so focused on their opponent, preparing the spells they would attempt to launch at one another, that they failed to notice the obvious. It was a lesson they would reflect on, but after the duel.

"*Pallinus!*" Elzina shouted, her arm raised, aimed in Bawb's direction.

A whirl of turbulent air launched across the room, ruffling Bawb's clothing but nothing more.

"Had that been a properly cast attack you would have fallen. Defend yourself next time!" Rovos barked.

Bawb was already casting his own attack. "*Malovicta!*" he yelled in return.

It should have been a force spell, pushing Elzina to the far wall, but Rovos had distracted him, causing his intent to falter. As a result, no spell at all was cast. Bawb realized his error and quickly ran through the spells he had been practicing. Elzina was already casting her reply, and he had no time to waste.

She fixed him in her sights, an aggressive fire in her eyes. "*Innix Mahl!*"

"*Yeltza!*" Bawb cast in reply.

Hers was a variation of a force spell, while his was a lesser version he intended to deflect it with.

He failed. The attack was too strong, blasting right through his defense.

Her spell hit him hard, forcing him backward. If not for the little energy the counter spell had caused it to lose, her attack might very well have flung him into the far wall.

"*Pallinus!*" he cast, this time with his intent holding fast.

The spell flew true, and while Elzina's attempt had been rather pathetic, Bawb's actually had some force behind it. She dug her feet in hard but was pushed back, nonetheless. Bawb grinned. He had actually done it. His spell had worked, for the most part.

"*Acalla tox!*"

Elzina's spell hit him like an invisible fist in the gut, doubling him over and dropping him to the ground, his wind knocked out from the blow.

"*Innix Mahl!*" she cast again, this time with growing confidence.

Bawb tried to speak the words to his own attack, the phrase dangling on the tip of his tongue, but he was still having trouble drawing breath. Elzina's spell hit him square as a result, with no defenses up whatsoever.

Bawb was driven off his feet, lifted high before landing hard on the stone floor.

He lurched up, sucking in air as his diaphragm finally unclenched enough to do so. He was hurting and on the receiving end of attack after attack as Elzina's doubts about her casting faded with every spell. As a result, they flew fast and true, if not terribly powerful.

Bawb was battered over and over as he desperately cast his own attacks. They were to no avail. Elzina was on a roll, and he couldn't cast fast enough to land a solid hit on her.

"*Porata!*" she yelled, using the most powerful spell she knew.

Bawb's own attack spell was leveled by its power, leaving Elzina untouched as he was flung hard out of the circle and into the far wall.

"Enough!" Rovos called out. "Elzina is the winner. Usalla and Finnia, you are next."

Elzina jogged over to the viewing area, beaming, happy to be number one. Bawb pushed himself up to his feet and dusted himself off, then trudged to join the others.

*Not an impressive showing*, his konus chided. *Not at all. Crude. Inartful. Brutish. You are aware you do not need to yell to cast a spell, yes?*

"I was just trying to give it more power."

*And you disappoint me yet again. You know full well that it's the intent behind the spell that drives it, not the volume of your voice. How do you think the Ghalian carry out their contracts without being noticed? It's because they are quiet about it. Operative word being* quiet."

"I wasn't thinking—"

*Clearly not. Be better*, the konus said, then mercifully fell silent.

Bawb took a seat and watched as Usalla and Finnia prepared themselves. Having just watched him getting his ass handed to him, it seemed they had both been coming up with a game plan as to which spells they were going to be using.

Of course, at this stage in their training, they all knew the same small selection of spells. In some ways, that made things easier. There was less to remember in the heat of the fight. But conversely, that also meant one's opponent would be far more likely to adjust and counter since both were working from the same playbook.

The two girls stood ready, waiting for the command. Rovos looked at Usalla then at Finnia. Neither seemed hesitant.

"Begin!"

Each launched a spell the moment the word left his mouth. Usalla's was a pushing spell while Finnia's was a pulling one. Both of them cast and quickly moved, diving out of each other's spells as they flew past harmlessly.

Bawb almost smacked himself for not thinking of that. Of course he could have moved around. He had been so caught up in the whole duel concept that he completely forgot he had non-magical options at his disposal. Instead, he and Elzina had just gone toe-to-toe, slugging it out. And she was a better caster. It had been foolish and ill-advised. A mistake he would try not to make in the future.

He watched as the two girls scrambled around the ring, casting attacks, dodging them, throwing up defenses while on the move. It was impressive, actually, and it made him reassess his own instincts in his first ever magic fight.

He would have to learn to be fluid. To shift according to the needs of the battle. Around and around the two went, casting and dodging, relying more on their physical skills than magical. After only a few minutes, Rovos called for them to stop.

"What are you doing wrong?" he asked them.

They stood quietly, unsure.

"Anyone? Do any of you know what they are doing wrong?" he asked the spectators.

He was greeted by the silence of a class that desperately did not want to be called on for an answer they did not possess.

"This is a casting exercise," Hozark's voice declared loud and clear from the back row.

He and Demelza rose and strode out to the center of the ring. Rovos gave a slight bow and stepped back. One of the Five was going to be an impromptu part of this lesson, it seemed.

"You both possess great agility, and your casting is not bad for ones your age. Your instincts to move and avoid head-on magical combat were wise. However, your casting suffered for it. The spells you cast were successful only in that you maintained enough intent to make them work. *Barely*. But in true combat they would have been entirely insufficient. Now, can you see where you erred in your choices?"

"Is it because we didn't focus entirely on magic?" Finnia asked.

"Not exactly. While you diluted your potential, that happens in the heat of battle. But the real issue lies in a habit most fall into in their early years. You resorted to the skills you felt most comfortable with rather than focusing on those you need to practice. Those appropriate for the situation. In training this can be detrimental. In real combat it is often fatal."

"Master Hozark? Our konuses are not terribly powerful. Would it not make more sense to utilize other skills when faced with that problem?" Usalla asked.

Hozark slid the konus from his wrist and unsheathed his Vespus blade, the metal flaring bright for a moment before returning to normal. He handed both to Demelza and held his hands up for all to see.

"I am not in possession of any magic-storing items. Now, if you would please, allow me to see your konus."

Usalla pulled hers off and handed it to him. He slid it onto his wrist and stepped to one side of the ring. "Teacher Rovos, would you be so kind?"

Rovos strode to the other side and stood in a loose fighting stance. They had seen him demonstrate before, but never with this sort of body language. He was working with Hozark, and that meant taking things up a notch at the very least.

Hozark nodded to him. "When you are ready."

Rovos began casting attacks immediately. His konus was far more powerful than the one Hozark was wearing, but the master assassin countered and blocked the spells with only moderate effort, moving as the girls had done but also using the limited magic available to him to the fullest.

Rovos pushed the attack, moving closer as he peppered Hozark with attack spells. Hozark responded with far weaker attacks, all of them blocked with ease. It appeared as if it would be a stalemate when Hozark did the unexpected. He stood still and allowed Rovos's attack to land. He cast a defensive spell that absorbed much of it, but he was still hit, nonetheless. But as soon as he cast the defense, he immediately cast a flurry of small offensive spells that sprayed out the moment Rovos's spell hit.

The result was an unexpected counterattack where one would normally expect a momentary pause, one that could be taken advantage of, pressing the attack. Rovos did just that, seizing the opportunity and casting on the offense. The spell was just leaving his lips when he realized his error. It was too late to cast a defensive spell.

The little spells hit him in rapid succession, pushing and pulling, hitting and jarring until he was knocked off his feet. Rovos scrambled back upright at once, but the point had been made. Hozark held up his hand to stop the demonstration.

"Now, do you see what just happened?" he asked Usalla as he handed her back her konus. "I was using a far-lesser powered konus against a skilled opponent, and yet I did not resort to physical maneuvers alone. I leveraged the situation, using the konus in a way that was not expected, thus landing several attacks. Of course, had this been true combat Teacher Rovos and I would have employed our other weapons in the process, combining bladed attacks with magical ones. But the point remains. It is not the power you have at your disposal but how you choose to wield it."

Demelza handed him his konus and Vespus blade. Bawb again felt that strange tug when the blue sword flashed for a moment, as if the power was somehow reaching out to him.

"Thank you for the demonstration, Master Hozark," Rovos said.

"And you for your assistance, Teacher Rovos. I will leave you to it." He turned and walked to the Aspirants on his way to the exit. "Bawb, I would like a word with you."

The others looked at their classmate with a bit of envy as well as confusion as he rose and followed Hozark and Demelza into the hallway.

"Stop your staring," Rovos growled. "You've just learned a valuable lesson. Now, let's see if it sank in. Albinius, Zota, you're up!"

Outside the chamber Bawb stood at attention, a little uneasy at being singled out like that.

"Relax, Bawb," Hozark said. "I merely wish to ask you something."

Bawb felt the tension release from his shoulders. "What is it?"

"Do you know why you lost your match?"

"Because Elzina is more skilled at magic than I am. She knows her spells better."

"Perhaps, but that is not the reason you lost."

"It wasn't?"

"You were almost entirely focused on attacking. On being on the offensive."

"But the point is to win, isn't it?"

"Of course, but you saw how I fought Teacher Rovos. That konus did not possess the power to face him head-on, so I adjusted. Do you see what I am getting at, Bawb? Sometimes, defense is the best offense. You allow your opponents to show their cards. To reveal patterns and habits. And in true combat, to use up their valuable magic while saving yours for when the opportunity is right."

"I think I understand. I'd never seen anyone fight like that before. It was just so, well, *different*."

"And now you have learned a useful lesson. Fight smart, not hard. While you are young and resilient, there is no longevity for those who do not learn this lesson. Old members of the order will all tell you the same. Practice defense as well as offense, learn to use technique to counter force. And on top of that, know that unusual spells can be used to great effect in place of normal combative ones. *Anything* can make the difference between success and failure. You just have to open your mind to the possibilities. Now, go join your classmates when it is safe to enter. I expect you to take these words to heart."

"And I will see you in class," Demelza added.

With that, Hozark and Demelza walked away, leaving the young Aspirant to process and absorb the wisdom shared with him.

# CHAPTER TWENTY-NINE

The duel sessions went on for hours, with each student facing a different opponent until they all had the opportunity to try their skills against each other. As expected, they all improved dramatically as the day progressed, and they gained muscle memory experience with their spellcasting.

The point was to wear them down. To exhaust them. To make it so they were reacting without thinking, and by the end of the day, it worked.

Once the act of intent finally became something they simply did rather than stopped to think about, *then* they truly began to understand. And Bawb, who had been rather humiliated in his first duel, proved to be one of the better casters in the group once he got the hang of it.

Hozark's words also helped, of course. Sometimes the slightest adjustment could make all the difference, and his notes had made Bawb see things much more clearly, especially when he was falling into a bad habit like being too aggressive, when allowing his opponent to press the attack and stumble into an opening was a better option.

They finished class relatively early, tired and sweaty. But just because they were done with the training portion did not mean the endurance part wasn't still in play. The bunkhouse was hours away, and if they wanted to sleep in their own beds, they would have to make the long trek there despite their exhaustion.

It was a long distance, but the group ran together, helping their slower members by surrounding them and making them keep pace. It wasn't the fastest they'd gone by any measure, but they were consistent in their progress. By the time they reached the training house it was dinnertime.

Voracious might be an appropriate word to describe their appetites after the last two days of exercises. Between the dungeon and the duels, they had been pushed much farther than they'd imagined they could withstand. This was all done to show them by forced example rather than words that what they thought was impossible in reality was not.

"Sleep well, Aspirants," Rovos said as he made the final evening's rounds at their quarters. "Tomorrow will be an easier day."

No one believed him.

Funny enough, the following day actually *was* easier. Sure, it was mentally taxing, but physically, they were being afforded something of a break. A respite to allow their bodies to recharge and recover.

They were brought to a small room full of worktables and stools, the surfaces covered with all manner of seemingly random items. Teacher Warfin was there, as was Demelza, though she was there in a purely observational capacity.

"Good morning, Aspirants," Warfin greeted the students. "Today, we have something different for you to sink your teeth into. Figuratively, of course." He walked over to the nearest table and picked up a seemingly normal dining plate. "Today's class will focus on crafting skills."

Albinius raised his hand. Warfin's gaze intentionally flew right past him as he continued. "Now, I know what some of you are thinking. Crafting is boring, and how can it possibly be of use to a deadly assassin? Let me assure you, proper preparation can prevent poor performance, and crafting plays a role more often than you would think. Take this plate, for example."

"You made a plate?" Albinius asked.

"I did not make it, no. But I did modify it for my purposes."

"I don't understand. How does one modify a plate? It looks like any other plate, from what I can tell."

Warfin stared at the boy a moment, one brow slightly cocked, then spun on his heel, throwing the plate hard. The plate embedded deep into the wooden cabinet on the far wall. He turned back to Albinius.

"Does that answer your question?"

The boy just nodded.

"Good," he said, retrieving the plate with a strong pull. "I hope this illustrates the most basic principle of crafting. Namely, that just about anything can be made into a weapon. And in this class, you will learn how."

He handed the plate to the nearest student so they could examine it and pass it around. While it was a metal plate, the edge was not sharp to the touch. At least, not normally. But when torque was applied to the edge as if it had been thrown, the false edge encircling it retracted, revealing the razor-sharp business end.

It was an extremely clever design, Bawb had to admit. Cutlery could be a weapon, obviously, but he'd never even considered dishware being used in this manner. But now that his eyes had been opened, the possibilities spread out before him.

"All of these items can be worked with to become lethal in one way or another," he said, walking among the tables, picking up seemingly benign items at random. "Not all are intuitive, of course. We expect a sharp edge such as you just saw demonstrated with the plate, but the protective covering concealing it was, I think you would all agree, something most would not think to look for."

He sat on a stool, slowly spinning to look at the students. Warfin stood up and picked the stool up. "Is this a weapon?"

Elzina piped up immediately. "Yes. You can batter with it, or if need be, you can jab with the legs for more focused impact."

"And you would be correct. But only partly correct. This is a stool I have modified from its original design. To your eyes it seems to be no more than a place to sit, but what if I do this?"

Warfin tossed the stool in the air in front of him, grabbing two legs and twisting them simultaneously, unlocking the hidden catches that kept a pair of slender blades concealed within. He twirled them in a dazzling display of skill while the rest of the stool bounced away on the floor.

"If I had hit someone with that stool, they would likely have grabbed the seat, thinking to disarm me. But in so doing they would expose themselves, occupying their hands and leaving their torso open. By the time they realized what was happening it would be over. Items of use hidden in the open. That is the essence of this class. To craft tools you can utilize without detection. And not all may be lethal. Some may be designed to aid in entry or egress, others decoys or alarm trips meant to divert attention. There are myriad configurations and uses as varied as your imagination can conceive. And now comes the fun part."

"Fun?" Albinius asked.

"Most find it to be. This is where you get to try your hand at coming up with a design of your own. All the items on these tables are here for you to experiment with. See what you can think up. Unlike many disciplines, crafting is a bit more flexible, so be bold, and do not fear failure. It is how we learn. If you have questions, I will be working on a new item over in the corner."

Warfin moved to a worktable set off from the others and took a seat. It looked like there was no more than a pile of junk in front of him, but from what they had just witnessed, something lethal was likely on the cusp of creation at his hands.

"Well, this should be interesting," Usalla said as she rummaged through the random things on the table before her, picking up a small teapot. "I understand the task, but I must admit, I fail to see how *this* could be made into a weapon."

"It can't," Elzina replied. "Much of this has to be junk meant to distract us from the task."

Usalla nodded her agreement and tossed it back onto the table. But rather than land and come to a rest, Bawb watched as the faintest of flashes of pale blue illuminated a small area on the side of the teapot, seemingly nudging it off the table. Bawb picked up the fallen item, the metal unusually cold to his touch.

"I don't know about that," Bawb interjected, putting it back on the table. "I do not believe Teacher Warfin would set us up to fail in that manner. We might not succeed in the task, but he would not sabotage our efforts."

"At least, not on our first try," Finnia added. "We all know too well how the teachers enjoy throwing chaos into our activities."

"But a teapot?" Elzina repeated, picking it up once more before handing it back to Usalla. "No way."

Bawb looked at the pot, an idea starting to blossom in his mind. Maybe, just maybe, he could make it work.

"I'll take it," he said. "I'll make something out of it."

Usalla and Elzina both looked at him with clear doubt. Usalla handed it to him with a shrug. "Suit yourself. Good luck."

Elzina snort-laughed. "He'll never do it."

Bawb ignored her and took the pot and moved to a different table, looking over the tools each workstation had available. Without giving Elzina a second thought he sat down and began studying the details of the teapot.

The others scattered, opting for more clearly weapon-like items they found at their disposal. Elzina was already hard at work finding a way to hide a blade within a thick serving platter. Usalla and Zota were each working with travel items one might find in luggage, while Finnia had her attentions on a decorative brooch.

Bawb's interest in the teapot had shifted since his initial assessment. The metal seams would be difficult to alter in the way he had in mind, especially with no practical experience to draw on. He opted for an easier modification. One he hoped he could manage to fashion.

Warfin left them to it for a few hours, letting the students fall into a deep contemplative state as they focused on their tasks. All of them had gotten into the spirit of it, he noted, and that was a good start. After the third hour he called on them to stop.

"Okay, that is enough," he announced. "I know you are likely not finished with your work, but I would like to take a pause here to examine your designs and offer guidance if you feel you need it. Elzina, what are you working on?"

"A hidden blade," she said, handing him the serving tray.

She had been carefully cutting into it, creating a space to hide the blade she had chosen. It wasn't the greatest of designs, but the concept was solid.

"Would it not be better to utilize the carrying handle of the platter in some way?" he asked. "Perhaps to lock the weapon into place while also serving a practical purpose?"

"But I thought someone might accidentally pull it out if I did."

"Of course. But if you included a safety feature to secure it, only those who know how to release it would be able to free the blade. And it would make for a better handle as well. As you have it now, you would be forced to hold the weapon in a somewhat awkward manner when you pulled it free."

He handed the tray back to her.

"Thank you, Teacher."

"How about you, Finnia? What have you there?"

She handed him the ornate brooch.

"Ah, you opted for entry tools rather than a weapon, I see. Logical, given your spy path within the Ghalian. The design is somewhat crude, though. A lesser guard might miss it, but any with experience would likely see this part here. Can you see how it could be better hidden from sight? The principle is sound; you just need to work on execution of the idea."

He handed it back and moved on.

"Bawb, I see you have a teapot. A very unusual choice, I must admit. Not one most would make."

"That is why I selected it," he replied. "I thought most people would feel that way, making this more likely to slip past unnoticed."

Warfin picked up the teapot, turning it over in his hands. He studied it a long while, uttering a little, *hmm* every so often before handing it back to the student.

"Interesting design, Bawb. Truly, this is unexpected given the heft of the tea pot. Yet, this is not a brute force weapon, as most would opt for with something such as this. A pummeling tool, perhaps. But you selected a different tack. Marvelous idea. Very original. Would you please show the others how it works?"

Bawb fought to keep a prideful blush from his cheeks. It wasn't every day, or nearly *any* day, for that matter, that he received praise like this from a teacher.

"Of course. Whom would you like me to demonstrate with?"

Warfin looked at the students, his eyes resting on Bawb's nemesis.

"Elzina, I think you would appreciate Bawb's creation. Please, help him with his demonstration."

Elzina was already annoyed that Bawb was receiving more attention than she was, and adding insult to injury, he seemed to have truly impressed Teacher Warfin. Now she had to be his guinea pig? It was infuriating. She bit her tongue and stepped forward, ready to make him look like a fool if she could.

"All right, let me see it," she said, reaching for the teapot, intending to turn the tables and use it on him instead.

Bawb held the teapot out for Elzina by the handle, holding it opposite the spout end as one would do to balance it while pouring. She snatched it from him, grabbing the middle section firmly. It was then that she realized her mistake.

The handle detached from the back, the front part pivoting in a snap, pressing the spout firmly against her wrist while the handle wrapped around the other way, trapping her hand, the tip of the spout cutting into her skin slightly.

Elzina shook her hand angrily, but that only made it tighter.

"Get this stupid thing off me!"

Bawb looked to Teacher Warfin. The man gave him an amused little nod. The boy quickly depressed the locking mechanism and freed Elzina's bleeding hand. In under a second the teapot looked just like it had before, save the blood on the spout.

"Let me see," Warfin said, taking Elzina's hand. "Hm, yes. Not bad. I'll cast a basic healing spell. That should tide you over until you can visit one of the healers should it still bother you."

"I'm fine," she lied as he mended her flesh.

The others looked at Bawb with a mix of awe and envy. He had actually made a real weapon, and he'd totally embarrassed Elzina in the process, though Teacher Warfin also played a role in that. The point was, Bawb had just shown a proficiency in something most everyone found hard at first. For once, he was at the head of the class.

"Just a drop of poison on the edge there and you could incapacitate someone without having to be in the chamber. So clever, Bawb. And in the attack, it also removes one of your enemy's hands from the equation, at least momentarily. Very out-of-the-box thinking."

"Thank you, Teacher, though, admittedly, it was also an odd trick of the light that helped me select this item."

"Oh?" Warfin said, a hint of interest in his eye. "In any case, well done, indeed. Now, let me take a look at what the rest of you came up with."

Warfin moved through their ranks, examining their projects, offering commentary and critique as he did. Elzina just stared daggers at Bawb, her real injury far worse than her hand. He had hurt her pride.

*You actually have a knack for this,* his konus announced. *Crafting: Level two.*

"You skipped level one."

*You surpassed and excelled. You are a level two crafter now.*

"Out of how many?"

*Time will tell,* the konus replied with amusement.

Bawb didn't mind the cryptic reply. Not this time, anyway.

Warfin took his time, using each Aspirant's efforts as a learning experience for the entire group. There was to be no shame in making mistakes, for, as he said often, mistakes are how you learn. That is, unless the error is of the fatal variety. But today, nothing so dire was at stake.

He walked back to Bawb and patted his shoulder. "Truly, that was a delight to see you devise, young Bawb. Not just some brute force weapon, but a subtle manipulation of the expected. Less is more, as Master Hozark often says, eh?"

"I guess so," he replied. "So, can I make something else?"

"Not now, I am afraid. You have another task at hand."

"I do?"

"You all do. Aspirants, gather your things and come with me. Your day has only just begun."

# CHAPTER THIRTY

Teacher Warfin led the group through the usual network of vast corridors they had grown so familiar with since their arrival in the training house. It was more than just that, of course. This compound was a Ghalian sanctuary and safe ground for any of the order to visit when in the area and in need of a comfortable place to lay their head.

There were still many areas left unexplored, but for the most part the Aspirants knew the compound. It had become something of a comfort, in a way. Knowing they could rely on the consistency of a Ghalian-controlled environment. Even the dangers they faced in their training were carefully planned and implemented.

"Bawb, walk with me," the teacher said, moving a bit ahead of the others. His young student did as he asked, following close. Warfin walked silently for a moment, as if somewhat conflicted. "Bawb, you made mention of a light back in the crafting chamber."

"Yes. But it was nothing."

"Nothing? Perhaps. But tell me, what did you see?"

"Just a hint of a pale blue glow that seemed to—it's silly."

"Never dismiss anything out of hand as silly. What happened?"

"Well, it looked as if the light almost nudged the teapot off the table."

Warfin's face remained neutral. His tone, however, was one betraying a hint of curiosity. Perhaps more than a hint. "Hmm. Anything else?"

"No. I mean, when I picked it up, the metal was particularly cold, but that—"

"*Cold*, you say?"

"Yes."

At that, Warfin actually nodded slightly to himself. "It is as I thought. I believe you have encountered Porrius. You are the first in many years to do so."

"Porrius?"

"A former student. Well, the geist of him, anyway."

Bawb felt a flash of confused excitement flow through his veins. "Those are real? An actual spirit?"

"Of a sort, though very rarely encountered. Porrius was a Vessel, and a rather talented one at that, always putting in extra work and studying well in advance of his rank in hopes of excelling further. But one day he went missing. The Masters and teachers searched for him everywhere but found no trace. It was initially assumed he had fled the order, but upon review of the exit wards and monitoring spells, it seemed clear that he never left the training house. It was only when strange occurrences began happening that the Masters surmised what had happened."

"He died?"

"Clearly. But in so doing, he must have been wielding one of the unfamiliar spells he was in the habit of practicing in his free time, and right at the moment of his demise, no less. As such, somehow, though incredibly rare, the magic went awry, and his core essence did not pass on from this plane. At least, not entirely. Ghalian do not believe in an afterlife, Bawb, but we are nevertheless quite certain that what animates our bodies is more than mere flesh and blood. A trace of that is what you saw. Held here, unable to completely dissipate until the spell is released."

"But why not let him go? Is it some sort of penalty laid upon him for a transgression despite his death?" Bawb wondered, horrified at the thought of such a punishment.

Warfin chuckled. "No, Bawb. We would do no such thing. Not even to the worst of students, which he certainly was not, though his extracurricular studies did push his teachers' limits at times. But no, this is not a punishment. Merely that without possessing his body to release the twisted magic, what is left of him remains trapped. And to this day, none can say for certain how or where he perished. Our own robust Ghalian warding within this facility has been a double-edged sword in that regard, and has stymied those who sought him out, the inherent security magic permeating our walls keeping him quite hidden."

"But Porrius still visits us?"

"Yes, in a way. Passing through the walls unseen, as only a geist can. Entering and leaving without a trace, only the occasional disruption of a project or rearranging of items ever confirming his presence. A sighting such as you had almost never occurs."

Bawb marveled at the idea. An actual spirit existing within these walls. Now he realized what he'd caught the tiniest of glimpses of on rare occasions over the years. It hadn't been a trick of the light; it had almost certainly been Porrius. And, somehow, Bawb was able to see him, or at least traces of him, where others could not. But rather than frighten him, Bawb felt a surge of excited interest in his belly.

Training was fascinating, but this? This was a whole new level of the excitingly unknown to ponder. And unlike his studies, *this* had his teachers just as perplexed as he was. The thought was tantalizing.

"How long ago did he die?"

"Well before my time," the teacher replied. "But we have arrived at the junction, so this is a discussion for a later time. Now, as this would be quite a distraction to your class, I must request you keep this to yourself. Can you do that?"

"I will," Bawb replied, ready to focus on the lesson at hand, but tucking away this new information to ponder further at a later time.

"Good." He turned his head, looking over his shoulder. "This way, class," Warfin called to the students following behind them, then uttered a phrase under his breath, opening a section of thick stone wall where no door had previously been visible.

This time, however, the existence of a secret passageway in the walls didn't take the Aspirants by surprise. After facing the training dungeon and its unusual entrance—not to mention the obstacles contained within—they didn't think much could.

They would be wrong.

"Is that grease?" Zota wondered as a scent wafted past their noses.

"Yeah, something's cooking," Albinius agreed. "But we're nowhere near the dining hall. And there's something else."

"Body odor," Bawb realized with a degree of shock as the acrid tang hit his nose. "The sweat of non-Ghalian."

He looked at the corridor more closely. It was not subterranean, it lacked the invisible feel of all that dirt and stone pressing down from above. And what's more, though they had ample fresh air in even the deepest of corridors, this felt different. The slight breeze smelled like something he and the others knew from occasional lessons in one of the many courtyards.

Bawb looked at their teacher expectantly. "We are going outside, aren't we?"

"Very good, Bawb. A Ghalian uses all of their senses."

"But this is different. I smell things. New things."

"Ah, yes. I suppose it is time I told you all what today's test will be." Warfin stopped and waited for each member of the group to gather close. "Listen up, Aspirants. Today is an important day for you. A test of your abilities and how well you adapt and improvise to accomplish your goal. And for it, you will be leaving this training house."

The students felt a jolt of excitement one and all, but they maintained their stoic façades as they had been trained, Warfin noted to his satisfaction. They were getting better.

"You will be taken to another Ghalian facility. One off-world."

"We're going in a spaceship?" Albinius blurted.

"Yes, Albinius. You will be escorted to the training facility by masters of the order, flown in their shimmer ships in small groups."

"A shimmer ship?" Finnia asked. "I've heard of the shimmer cloak used to hide ourselves when infiltrating or lying in wait, but a *ship*?"

"Yes, a ship. Several, to be precise. Far beyond the skills of most, but Master Ghalian possess the requisite abilities to power the spells and cloak their vessels from detection for at least a short while."

Bawb was in awe. They had all heard of shimmer cloaks, of course. Students talked, after all. But the existence of an entire ship that could vanish from sight was something altogether different. The magic it would require must have been immense, and the spell to power it unlike anything he'd ever dreamed of.

"It is going to be a tower siege attack and infiltration," Warfin continued, jarring Bawb from his reverie. "It is a low tower, so you have that to be thankful for, but it will be difficult, nonetheless. This fortified compound is part of a remote Ghalian training facility not too long of a flight from here, so your first foray outside these walls since your arrival will not be an overly lengthy one."

"We're going outside for real?" Albinius marveled. "And to another planet?"

"As I said, yes. I know this is exciting after so many years. From this point onward, you will be training and operating out in the real world more and more frequently. But for today, you must focus on the task at hand. Prepare yourselves mentally for the challenge, and you will do fine."

"You said we will be training there more?" Elzina asked.

"There and other places. Today's destination is but one of many such locations you will visit as your skills improve and you progress through the levels. But enough talk. The masters flying you there are waiting. But remember, you are not Ghalian in the outside world. You are just a group of Wampeh youths and nothing more."

He continued along the corridor and out the thick door leading to the outside world.

The group stepped out and breathed deep, the scents and sights of real, normal, non-Ghalian life bombarding them from all sides. They had each arrived as children under varying circumstances and at different times of day and night, but one thing held true for them all. It had been years since they had seen the outside world.

The area around this particular exit from the training compound abutted a small marketplace. Outdoor vendors were selling their wares, colorful tapestries and awnings covering them from the sun and elements. Food carts were cooking up a wild assortment of delicacies the likes of which the Aspirants had never even thought to miss. But now, out in the world again, the memory of many of these came flooding back. At least to those who had grown up outside an orphanage.

For Bawb, it was *all* new. He'd lived such a secluded life even before being taken by the Ghalian that just about everything was novel and amazing.

"Come along, children," Warfin said, his typically stern expression warm and glowing, a bright smile plastered on his lips. "We have much to do, and we wouldn't want to be late!"

It was all an act, of course, but it was almost spooky how convincing he was once he slid into this character. He may have fooled all the commoners with his charm and cheer, but the Aspirants knew better.

They hurried along, passing the temptations of the stalls with eyes looking but hands not touching. One day they would graduate out into the world and could explore to their hearts' content, but not yet. For now, they had a test awaiting them.

Warfin was merry and jovial, warmly greeting those they passed as he led them through the streets. Soon enough the throngs of people thinned out as they moved farther from the marketplace. A short walk later they were on the outskirts of one of the city's landing areas. There were a fair number of ships there, their crews loading them with cargo or heading out to take shore leave, but the overall feel of the place was quite mellow.

Several small ships sat parked among them, arranged in no particular order, seemingly just another vessel amongst many. Only the pale Wampeh relaxing beside them hinted at their true nature. These were shimmer ships, apparently, though Bawb found himself wondering if the appearance of the vessels themselves weren't magically altered in some way as well. It would make sense, after all, to disguise a Ghalian craft from casual observation.

Whatever the case, he would find out soon enough.

"Okay, children. Enjoy your field trip," Warfin called after them, then walked away.

The Wampeh from the ships walked over to the group.

"You, you, and you, with me," a particularly wiry woman with a long scar on her neck directed, leading her passengers to their waiting ride.

In short order the other pilots did the same until all were split up and aboard one of the shimmer ships. From there it was just a matter of shuttling them to their destination.

"So that's where you put your Drookonus?" Bawb asked, eyeing the small rod inserted into the control panel of the ship he had boarded.

"It is. You've seen one before?" the pilot asked as he intoned the spell to engage the device.

Bawb listened carefully and did his best to memorize the words.

"I have, but it was years ago."

"Ah. You are an Aspirant. It has been, what? Two? Three years since your arrival?"

"Closer to three."

"So you are progressing on schedule. That is a good sign for your future advancement. On occasion, some less adept students are forced to be held back. It is not a good situation."

"I can imagine."

The pilot engaged the ship, casting the flight spell and setting their course. He then turned to his passengers. Usalla and Finnia had been selected to come on this flight with Bawb, and he was glad for it. The way he'd been paired up with Elzina of late had made things quite unpleasant.

"I am Master Kopal, but you may simply address me as Kopal. We are far less formal when away from the compound."

"But when we arrive at the training facility?" Usalla asked.

"Then we go back to formalities, I am afraid. But come, ask

questions. I know this is your first time aboard a shimmer ship. Surely you have many, and I am here not only as your ride but also your teacher for the short time we have together. Of course, you will not be flying a ship yourselves anytime soon, but that does not mean you cannot begin to learn about the intricacies of controlling one."

Finnia looked around, taking in the interior of the craft with an eye for detail. The same trait that made her stand out as a potential spy protegee if she should prove herself. "This isn't a very large craft," she noted. "How long can you go without landing?"

"Ah, the question I would have expected from this one," Kopal said with a chuckle. "You are already well on your way, I see."

"Just curious."

"Of course you are," he replied with a knowing grin. "But to answer your question, there is ample accommodation for two. Three or four, if need be, though sleeping arrangements would be a bit cramped. But with just myself aboard, I could spend many months in space in relative comfort. And I have had to do so on occasion. Anything it takes to complete the contract, as you know."

"But food? Water? Air?"

"All accounted for prior to departure. You see, being a Ghalian has some benefits, including access to rather pricey magic. For example, air is recycled, the water vapor from our breath pulled out and added to a reserve tank. A simple spell, really. The same with waste fluids. All are separated to constituent parts and preserved in case an extended flight is required."

"You drink your urine?" Usalla asked.

"Oh, yes. But at least in this case, it is transformed back to water. I have done it the other way a few times when there was no alternative and it was not pleasant. Normally, I would build a solar still to catch evaporation, but at the time, that was not an option."

"Solar still?" Bawb asked.

"A means to collect pure water from tainted using the sun's heat without relying on magic, or only a fractional amount at most. A fluid source is placed in a depression with a collecting vessel in the middle, then a seal is laid across with a small rock or similar in the middle to create a low point over the collection site. As it heats, the water evaporates from the soil and whatever you put in there, and that then it collects and trickles down to the middle. It is not a terribly efficient means of gathering water, but it can mean the difference between life and death. But you will learn about this in survival class. Let us talk more about spaceships."

Bawb was still fascinated by the idea of creating water out of waste, and without magic, no less, but the opportunity to learn about flying was a greater appeal. "How does the shimmer work?"

"Aha, getting to the good stuff, I see. This ship, along with other variants, has a powerful konus melded to its frame. It is from that, working with our Drookonus, which we power the shimmer spell cloaking it."

"Can't you use a regular konus?"

"You could, yes, but the drain would be enormous. The Ghalian learned a long time ago, though that happened to be by happy accident, that bonding a konus with a vessel dramatically increased the efficiency of certain spells. Not all, mind you, but some. And among those was the shimmer spell, which required very advanced, very specialized magic."

Usalla cocked her head, perplexed. "You are saying this konus, it is truly part of the ship?"

"Are you familiar with Ootaki?" Kopal asked.

"Somewhat."

"Then you know that their hair, when taken by force, loses much of the power stored within. But if given freely, somehow that same hair retains magnitudes more magic. It is the same with the ship. Somewhat, anyway. The point I am trying to make is that when the konus is correctly made into part of the ship itself rather than separated from it, its magic transfers with much greater ease, much like the difference we see in Ootaki hair."

Usalla was still amazed by the revelation of a ship that had a konus built into its framework, but then she supposed she had seen many other strange things since joining the Ghalian ranks. As for Bawb and Finnia, they seemed to be thoroughly enjoying the impromptu lesson.

"What about jumping?" Bawb asked. "We're flying normally now, but how do we jump to another world?"

Kopal's smile grew. "Glad you asked, Bawb, because that is what we are about to do."

# CHAPTER THIRTY-ONE

Bawb watched with not only youthful fascination, but also a keen eye for detail as Kopal cast the jump spell, sending them on a near-instantaneous leap through space. As he had promised, his passengers were getting a command chair view of the process. It seemed so simple to their eyes, but they had been in training long enough to know that looks could be, and in fact, more often than not were, quite deceiving.

The talent to connect with the ship's konus was one to be learned over months, or even years, of practice, as was controlling such a powerful device. To do so while wearing one's own konus was one of the few times an average person could double-wield, in a magical sense.

One would normally only wear a single konus at any time. Even low-powered ones were typically not stacked, though some could get away with it if they were extremely careful. The issue was they had a tendency to dangerously cross magic if not carefully managed, and for all but the most powerful of naturally powered casters, this could be an incredibly risky proposition.

Still, some could manage, and Ghalian had done just such a

thing on occasion when no other option was available, but that was attributed to their years of devoted training, in addition to having recently fed on the magic of a powerful natural magic user.

In any case, before ever being allowed to touch a konus the Aspirants had received a very clear lecture on the dangers of stacking them. Apparently, when flying a shimmer ship, those rules did not apply.

Kopal cast, and they popped out of existence, reappearing in dark space nowhere near the planet they had just departed. Bawb had no idea how far they had traveled. He had felt nothing. But looking outside, it was clear they had crossed space to what looked like a small moon.

Kopal brought the ship in toward the atmosphere. Apparently, this moon was habitable, though it did not appear to have any large cities from what Bawb could see from above.

"Typically, we do not cast a shimmer spell when flying into the atmosphere," Kopal informed his passengers. "The magic is extremely hard to maintain during the entry phase."

Bawb watched as the color shifted to orange outside the craft as they hit the edge of the atmosphere. "Noted."

The descent quickly shifted to a slightly bumpy ride when the ship transitioned to flying in air. A moment later Kopal adjusted his flight spells, and they slipped into a smooth glide down to the surface.

From above they caught a glimpse of what seemed like a fairly extensive network of structures. A compound, or fortress of some sort. It was beside the outmost of the structures located far across a muddy field that they finally set down.

"You will meet with the others in that building and receive your instructions on the day's exercise."

"You are not coming with?" Usalla asked.

"No, this is for the teachers to handle. I will be here to fly you back when you are finished." He opened the door. "Good luck. And please, rinse off before you board. I would rather not have to perform a deep clean of the ship when we return."

Bawb hopped out, his boots squishing in the damp ground. He breathed deep, the verdant wet of the growing fields and woods lending a welcoming air to the new arrivals. This was the air of a new world. He had only ever been on two, the one where he was born and the one where he'd spent his years of Ghalian training. This was something different. New. Exciting.

"Hey," Kopal called after them.

The trio turned back.

"I thought you might enjoy seeing this," he said, then closed the door. A moment later the shimmer ship seemed to vanish from existence, hidden by the powerful spell.

The students walked to the meeting point with an excited buzz about them.

"That was *amazing*," Usalla all but chirped, her Ghalian cool slipping in her excitement.

"I know! And we will be able to do that one day," Bawb added, equally jazzed.

Stepping into the building, they pushed their emotions aside, their attitudes calm and focused as they had been trained. A lone teacher was waiting for them and the others to arrive. One Bawb recognized.

"You are the first to arrive," Teacher Donnik informed them. "Take a seat. The others will be here momentarily."

In just a few minutes the rest of their cohort joined them, all of the anxious Aspirants readying themselves for whatever would come next. Donnik looked them over and gave a satisfied nod.

"Good, you are all present and ready, I see." He walked to a large cabinet that stretched the length of one wall, sliding it open to reveal all manner of weapons on racks. "You are to select the weapon, or weapons, of your choosing. Be wise in your selection, as you will not be able to change once the test begins."

"What are we facing?" Elzina asked, her eyes locked on the sharp swords and knives normally saved for the upper-class levels.

"You will be laying siege to a fortified tower. You will devise a plan and approach as a group."

"But Ghalian work alone," she replied.

"Normally we do. But you must also understand how others work together. In this way you may overcome them without their knowledge, for someday you may be forced to infiltrate a large group, and knowing how to function in such a setting will be key to maintaining your disguise."

The students nodded their understanding. It made sense. While Ghalian were lone killers, that did not mean they would not be interacting with others, and in large numbers at times, as their teacher had said.

"You are to work together," he continued, "but there is an ultimate goal to this test. One that the most skilled of you will benefit from. Somewhere in this tower is an enchanted dagger. It is only moderately powerful, but one of you will find it and claim it as your own. This is how Aspirants begin to assemble their own collection of weapons."

"The one to find it keeps it?" Bawb asked.

"Yes. But there will be more than just obstacles. There are guardians as well."

"Guards?" Zota asked.

"*Guardians*. You will see. Now, step outside and head toward the tower. Take care to observe all around you and remember your lessons. And above all else, take note of each other's successes as well as mistakes. You may save yourself much future effort and suffering in so doing."

The Aspirants armed themselves as they saw fit then exited

the structure and trekked out toward the tower in the mud, their boots sticking as they walked.

It was a rather wide tower, but only five levels high, though that did not mean there weren't underground levels as well. Given the shape, each level was likely divided into multiple areas. There would be no simple central stairwell to take them to the top. And, for all they knew, the prize could be hidden on the first level rather than the fifth.

Odds were, however, that it would be secreted on the uppermost portion, as the teachers undoubtedly wanted them to have to work their way through as many obstacles as possible to reach it.

"What is that?" Zota asked quietly as they drew near.

The group slowed, each straining their eyes to see better. It was difficult to make out against the dark stone of the tower, but there, affixed to a long chain, was a fearsome-looking beast guarding the front gate.

"Does anyone know what that is?" Usalla asked.

Bawb squinted hard, taking in every detail he could. "Not a clue. But look at its eyes. They seem to be tiny for its size."

"But its ears are large, as is its nose," Zota added.

Bawb realized he was right. "It likely relies more on sound and smell than sight. If we're quiet, we can make it around to the opposite side without it knowing."

"Or we could sneak through the gate," Albinius opined. "We just need a diversion."

"A diversion would raise an alarm, fool," Elzina hissed. "Look at the chain. It can only move so far. We go around and scale the wall to the windows."

She didn't wait for anyone to reply. She just started moving, confident in her leadership.

With a shrug, the others followed her. It wasn't exactly her idea, but they knew well enough by now to let her think it was.

They all had the same goal, and that would require getting around the beast and finding another way in.

Bawb, however, hesitated. "Wait," he called after them.

"What is it?" Elzina growled, pausing her approach.

"The breeze. If you go that way, you will be upwind of the beast. We should go the other way around."

"Of course we will," she shot back. "I was merely getting a better look from this angle. Come on."

She changed course, ignoring Bawb as she passed him, the others following her lead.

"Good thinking," Usalla said, stopping beside him. "We are so used to training in the caverns, I had not even thought about wind."

Bawb was full of surprises, it seemed. "Come on," he said. "We need to keep up."

The Aspirants were forced to walk far wider than they'd have liked, and as they finally moved closer to the tower, the sucking mud was becoming an issue. It was making a stealthy approach difficult despite being downwind.

The beast seemed to sense something was out there, cocking its head, its hackles raised as it listened, sniffing the air. The students stopped in their tracks, holding still until the animal trotted off to inspect the other side of the gate.

"Quick, before it comes back," Elzina whispered, hurrying ahead.

She made good time but stopped abruptly, nearly falling into the moat that blocked their access to the tower wall.

It was not terribly wide, and not very deep from what they could see. The waters were clear, likely fed by a spring, and sure to be cold. The way the ground had sloped upward toward the tower base made it appear as if the obstacle was not there from a distance. Only now did they realize what lay before them.

"Do we go back to the gate and kill the beast?" Zota wondered. "Or do we try to jump across?"

"It is much too far to jump, idiot," Elzina hissed. "But you should take a few others and try the gate." She gazed upward at the low windows dotting the tower then down at the water. "I will go the hard way and swim across and enter through one of those."

She didn't wait for the others to chime in with their thoughts on the matter. Without hesitation she slid into the water, the cold making her shiver involuntarily, then quickly swam across.

"We can take it," Zota said, turning for the gate. "Come on. If we move fast, we might keep it from making too much noise."

He hurried off toward the animal, the small sword he had brought with him held low and ready. Several others looked at the water then at the gate and followed him, having decided that was the best option.

Bawb and Usalla stood together, watching the others make their choices. Most were heading for the gate, hoping the sheer force of numbers would speed their progress. Others were following Elzina, who had already begun the slow climb up the slippery stones.

"Your thoughts, Bawb?" Usalla asked.

He wasn't watching either group. Bawb's focus was on the water. It had become muddied when the others lowered into it, but he had gotten a fair look beforehand.

"You have something in mind. I can see it," she said.

"Have you noticed, there are no creatures in the water. Not even fish."

"I had. As did Elzina, I am sure, otherwise she would have convinced someone else to swim across first."

"I would expect no less from her," he agreed. "I saw something down there while it was still clear. A structure of some sort. I think it is the source of the spring from which this moat is fed."

"How does that help us?"

"A tower would be built with its own water supply, meaning atop the spring. The moat would be filled by a channel constructed specifically for that purpose."

Usalla saw where he was going with this. "And that channel would lead to the spring, *inside* the tower walls."

"Exactly."

"We do not know how far it is, Bawb."

"No, we do not."

He looked up. Elzina was moving slowly, but she was making progress, as were the others who had decided to follow her. Without another thought he slid into the water, swimming across to where he had seen the opening. Usalla swam up beside him, treading cold water.

"Together, then?" he asked.

"Together."

They took several deep breaths, filling their bodies with oxygen, then dove, swimming down as smoothly as possible to conserve the limited air in their lungs. The opening was wide enough for them to both enter easily, but it led off into the unknown darkness.

Bawb swam ahead, his hands sliding along the stone sides, guiding him forward. He chided himself for not thinking to cast a minor illumination spell before they submerged, but it was too late now. He had no way to utter the words, even if he did somehow have enough air in his lungs for it.

All of their training was paying off, however, as the pair's lung capacity and cardiovascular fitness made the swim relatively easy. They were fighting a slight current, but it was nothing insurmountable.

Bawb's hands abruptly smacked into metal. He heard the

faint clang as Usalla did as well. He felt around and realized it was a set of bars blocking the way. But were they? There was an edge to them. A rim they were all mounted on. He tapped Usalla and guided her hand to a bar, then gave it a tug. His meaning clear, she pulled hard just as he did.

At first there was only a tiny creak, but slowly the bars began to move. Bawb's lungs were starting to burn, but they were so close. He forced himself to ignore the pain and kept pulling. Usalla stuck with him, inching the grating open until they could fit through.

He tugged her arm and slid through the opening, swimming ahead into the dark. He felt Usalla beside him and wondered if her lungs were on fire as much as his. There was no light anywhere, no change in the flow of water. And even in the black, he realized his vision was starting to go dark. He could very possibly die if he continued on.

Instinct kicked in.

Bawb grabbed her arm and changed direction, heading back for the grating and the fresh air above the moat. She followed close, brushing against him as their movements became more frantic. They swam and swam, heads dizzy from oxygen deprivation. There was a light up ahead, they just had to make it.

He felt Usalla twitch beside him, then go limp. His lungs aflame in agony, he grabbed her by her arm and dragged her ahead, his head spinning, his body screaming at him to take a breath. Near the point of blacking out, he gave a final push, driving them from the tunnel and up to the surface.

Bawb sucked in air, his body pins and needles from the strain. He took another breath, then remembered his friend in his arms. He pressed Usalla up against the stone, her head above water. She was breathing, albeit shallowly. Abruptly, she coughed, water spraying as she took a deep breath, her eyes wide with disorientation.

"You are safe," he said, holding her up while she regained her senses.

"What—we almost died, Bawb."

"But we did not." He looked up at the tower. "Can you climb?"

"I do not think I can."

"Then swim to the other side and wait. I have something I must do."

Bawb pulled the twin daggers he had opted to carry on this test and jabbed them into the gaps between the stones, pulling himself up out of the water. While most had opted for longer weapons given the teacher's warning about beasts, Bawb felt more comfortable with something lighter and maneuverable. And in this case, that proved to be a wise choice.

Up and up he climbed, his muscles aching but his lungs happy to be breathing air instead of water. He scrambled through the first window he could find. It would be a more direct route to climb straight up the exterior in the same manner, but he simply didn't have the energy for it.

Bawb hit the floor and rolled to his feet, daggers ready. Nothing came for him. He did, however, notice blood on the stone floor. More as he progressed to the nearest staircase.

Long-toothed animals that would have stood as tall as his thigh lay slain on the ground, the pair of them dispatched with brutal efficiency. Someone had cleared a path. He wondered how far ahead they would be.

He ran up to the next level to find a few more slain beasts. These were different, though. Long and twisty, as if they were serpents, but with long arms bearing sharp claws. They had been dispatched as well, but judging by the signs of struggle, they had not gone without a fight.

Bawb hurried onward until he reached the uppermost level. As expected, there was a pedestal where the prize had been placed. Only, the enchanted dagger was nowhere to be seen. Someone had already claimed it.

Noise was coming from behind him. Noise that sounded a lot like the clacking of claws on stone.

"There is no sense in further bloodshed," he muttered, then stepped out the nearest window, plummeting into the moat below with a mighty splash.

Bawb circled back to retrieve Usalla, then the two made their way back toward the shimmer ships waiting to take them home. The others were following the same course, weary, muddy, and some even bloodied. At the head of the group, Elzina walked with a spring in her step, despite the minor wounds she had suffered.

A faintly glowing dagger was in her hand, to the victor the prize.

Zota looked at it with disappointment. He and the others who had opted to charge the gate had not only been forced to fight the beast guarding it, but also all the other creatures their foolish attack had drawn to them as well.

"Thank you for providing such an excellent distraction," Elzina said with a grin as she eyed his many minor injuries. "You cleared out many of the beasts from the tower."

"You knew that would happen," he grumbled.

"Knew? I would not say I *knew*. Anticipated, perhaps."

Zota was too tired to argue and just let it go. Elzina had gotten the better of him and that was all there was to it.

Bawb watched the exchange with interest but was unsurprised. She hadn't forced them to do anything. She had merely played them with a well-placed suggestion. Much as he disliked her, and much as he hated to admit it, it was clear that Elzina would become a very talented Ghalian one day. But seeing how she treated others, Bawb found himself feeling an unusual sensation.

He didn't just want to get by as he always had. Something was shifting inside, in part driven by Elzina's unrelenting attitude. He found he wanted to excel in this life, not merely progress normally. A new goal was fresh in his mind, and it would be a challenging one to say the least.

He wanted to climb the ranks and beat her to the top.

# CHAPTER THIRTY-TWO

The ride back to their home had been a time to quietly reflect on what they had, and more importantly, had *not* done right. Finnia had followed Elzina up the tower wall and related how she watched her deftly avoid most of the beasts inside, leaving them for those trailing behind her to deal with. It was actually quite well done, and as a result, she had won herself a shiny new prize. Odds were they would likely never hear the end of it.

At least they were on a different ship for the trip, so there was that to be thankful for.

Bawb and Usalla were a bit less talkative than on the way to the training grounds, and Kopal could tell something was bothering each of them. He wasn't a teacher, at least not in any formal role, but he could still sense when perhaps a few words might do a youngster some good.

"So, it was a tough one, I take it?"

"Yes," was all Bawb replied. Usalla just sat there quietly, her mind a million miles away.

"I hear one of your classmates tricked some of the others to make a try at the front gate," he persisted. "That was a poor choice. Admirable skill that she could manipulate people who should know better, though. Judging by your demeanor, I assume you were in that group?"

"No, we were not."

"Interesting. Then tell me, what happened?"

Bawb really didn't want to give the play-by-play of their failure and near death, but this was a Master Ghalian speaking, and even if he was treating them casually, there was still a matter of respect in play.

He took a deep breath and began the story. He told Kopal how they had watched the others either try for the front gate or follow Elzina up the wall. How Bawb had seen the underwater tunnel. How they had made it in past the protective gate. And worst of all, how they had nearly perished from his foolishness.

"It was not a foolish choice, Bawb. I hope you both realize that. Yes, you failed in the attempt today, but you tried something that hardly anyone else would have dreamed of. You took a risk, made your judgment call, and you might have succeeded because of it."

"But we did not succeed."

"No, but a Ghalian often takes risks, not only of injury but of possible death. It is what we do. And to do so at so young an age? You should rise to the head of your class based on that merit alone."

"But it doesn't work like that. Elzina holds that position."

"For now. Listen, Bawb. Usalla, you too. I want you to take heed of what I have to tell you. What you did was the same choice I would have made."

Usalla's gaze shifted. "You would have?" she asked.

"Yes. Given the situation, it was the best option to possibly overtake the others. The only difference is, I am older and know the spells that would have allowed you to travel much farther underwater, even casting one or two along the way if you had to. You were punching far above your weight and still nearly made it, and that is admirable."

"What do you mean, nearly made it?" Usalla asked.

"That tunnel? I swam it as a boy too, though older and more experienced than you are now. There is another grating just below the spring's source. It is that final obstacle that takes you into the underground cistern where the tower gets its water. Without the right spells you would not have made it, that is clear, but you nevertheless got farther than anyone at your level should have been able. Be proud of that. Keep that achievement in your minds. You have the drive, and you both did not so much fail as you simply lacked the tools to succeed."

Both Bawb and Usalla felt the weight of their perceived failure lift, for the most part, anyway. For the remainder of the flight, Bawb even felt up to asking questions about the operation of the ship. Seeing the boy's interest return pleased Kopal. He liked these three and wished them the best, and if a few pointers could help them along the way, well, who was he to deny them information?

They landed on the outskirts where they had been picked up, their teacher waiting to collect them. Warfin saw Elzina walking tall, her prize in her hand. He flashed her a stern look.

"Do not flaunt your weapons in public," he said with a glare in his eyes, the quiet force of his words as good as a slap.

She blushed and quickly tucked it away in her garments, and there it remained for the rest of the walk back to the training house. Once inside, however, it emerged again, a new wonder to show off to the losers.

"For the last time, put it down, Elzina," Teacher Pallik said when she continued fiddling with it during their post-dinner class.

She did as she was told, tucking it back into its sheath, leaving it on the table rather than putting it in a pocket. A silent brag, of sorts, but one Pallik would allow. This time, anyway.

"Now, where was I? Oh, yes. The hidden art of codes and riddles. Very tricky for even the most astute, I must warn you. You will have to pay great attention to details, sometimes calling upon knowledge of things you learned many years ago. But that is how riddles often work, and the greatest of them endure through the millennia."

She propped up a stone tablet. It was blank, just a smooth sheet of stone, ordinary in every way.

"Do you see the message?" she asked.

The students stared hard. There wasn't so much as a mark on it.

"Where?" Albinius asked.

"I assure you, it is present," she replied, then cast a minor fire spell, holding the ball of flame in her hand. "Now, you can also do this with a candle, but in my experience, I have found the control I have over the flame is greater in this way. And if the message is written on something flammable such as parchment, control is key."

She moved her hand closer, allowing the fire to heat the stone but not scorch it. At first nothing happened, but then, right before their eyes, runes began to appear.

"The heat activates them?" Finnia asked.

"It does."

"How long do they remain visible?"

"That varies. Some last minutes, others mere seconds. This particular piece is a test item and thus lasts a bit longer than most to afford you a better view. The key here is two-fold. One must not only find the message, which is a puzzle in and of itself, but then must decipher what it means. Sometimes, the messages are maps or clues, often spoken in plain words but with a hidden meaning."

For Bawb, it was starting to make sense. "So what it needs is a key for the cipher."

"Exactly. Ordinary words can have entirely different meanings. Sometimes only certain letters are to be paid attention to. Other times the words are a decoy, the pattern they form providing the actual information. But Bawb is right. Most often you will simply require a key to decipher the message."

She pulled out an ancient-looking scroll and unrolled it for them to see. It was ornate, covered in detailed, fine writing, the borders decorated with gilding and designs.

"This belonged to an ancient society. And there lay a secret order hidden within their numbers. This particular group tended to hide messages in the artwork, not the words themselves."

The students leaned in, examining the art for whatever message it might contain. They saw nothing.

"This was a star chart," Pallik clarified, pointing out sections of what appeared to be simple ornamental filigree around the edges. "Directions to a burial trove only known to a select few. But there was always the risk of those who knew the location perishing, so rather than losing the location forever, the elders immortalized it, hidden in plain sight where only those in the know would find it."

"But how does this help us as Ghalian?" Zota asked.

"Because we perform many tasks in our duties. We kill, yes, but we also acquire the unacquireable. Steal the unstealable. It is part of what makes the Ghalian not only feared, but also respected across the galaxy."

"That, and we kill a lot of people," Elzina added.

"We do at that," Pallik replied without so much as a chuckle.

"You must take these lessons seriously. Apply what you learn to every aspect of your Ghalian training. Remember *everything*, even if it seems insignificant, for in the heat of battle, it is those small details that might save you. It is for this reason we train your minds as well as your bodies. Push you to your limits and beyond in scenarios designed to speed your recall. We have long records of ciphers and traps, and what has already happened are lessons that can be learned from. An unfortunate repeat of mistakes can be avoided. Scenarios that have played out before can be recognized before they happen again. Of course, there are those doomed to repeat history no matter what tools are at their disposal. Ghalian are not among them."

Always something of a bookworm, Bawb's interest was piqued. "You said there are records?"

"Yes. And those are now open for you all to read at your leisure should you so desire. Mythologies and facts, a great many of which can overlap. Studying ancient cultures can be quite useful," she noted. "Deactivating traps is something we do regularly, and on many occasions, I have personally come across obscure obstacles that my book learning helped me overcome."

"What about using magic to detect or deactivate traps?" Finnia asked.

"You are still learning. The phrases needed to power the right spells are older than recorded history, so do not expect to master them easily. But while the words are old, the means of channeling the power and shaping it to your will, your *intent*, is well documented. And it is that you will practice in abundance."

Finnia's eyes brightened. "So we will learn to defuse traps?"

"I did not say that. I said you will practice intent and casting. The basics, young Aspirant, come first. You walk before you run. And so it is with magic as well."

Bawb's mind raced at the possibilities. There would

undoubtedly be spells included in the texts. As Aspirants, they would not be able to cast them, but that didn't mean Bawb couldn't make the effort to learn them. And, in so doing, perhaps begin to understand a little more about what might have happened to the elusive wraith haunting his home.

# CHAPTER THIRTY-THREE

The chamber Pallik led the group to was one they had never visited before. It lay deep underground, but the bright illumination and spaciousness of it made it feel like being outside on a sunny day. What also added to that illusion was the dense violet grass that grew throughout the entire cavern.

The students walked in, following Pallik to the center. Their footfall was muffled by the grass, each step crushing some blades, releasing a healthy, outdoorsy smell that only enhanced the feeling of the place. A few areas seemed to have suffered a scorching of some sort, the grass growing back over charred and browned patches. Bawb and the others wondered what might have caused it.

"You will be practicing spells," Pallik informed them. "Much more powerful ones than you have used before. Today you push your limits. There will be mistakes made, so have no illusions about that. You will not complete the lesson without several abject failures. But that is part of the process."

Bawb realized now why there were scorch marks on the ground. Why this chamber was so deep underground as well. It was the safest way they could do as she asked without jeopardizing others. And the system clearly worked. Some other class had been using this chamber, and they must have had some spells go awry, but none of his compatriots had been any the wiser.

"You may also be distracted as you cast. Be alert."

"By distracted, what exactly do you mean?" Zota asked.

"It could be physical. It could be something else," she replied with a low chuckle. "You will see soon enough. The important thing for you to remember is to keep your focus and complete your casting. Being able to cast under duress could mean the difference between success and failure. And as you know, for a Ghalian, that also means life and death. Now, spread out and face that direction. Do you see the wooden targets before you? That is where you are to aim your spells. Begin with a force spell, then proceed to the more advanced ones. I do, however, wish for you to attempt fireballs last. We had a few problems with that particular spell not so long ago, so let us be sure you are ready for it first."

"You hear that?" Bawb quietly asked his konus. "We get to cast some of the advanced spells."

*Whoopee for you. Let's hope you don't take a limb off,* the konus said, utterly unimpressed.

"That is the plan," he replied, turning to face his target. "Just be sure to give me the power I need."

*I always provide what you need. Now, whether you have the skill to use it is another thing entirely.*

"Fine. Just do what you can. Here we go."

He took a breath and cast. The first few spells came relatively easy. He pushed the target back a few feet, then pulled it forward before nearly knocking it over with an overly enthusiastic punch spell. The others were having similar success to varying degrees.

Bawb glanced at Usalla and Zota. Both were doing quite

well, all told. Albinius, on the other hand, was having some difficulties. As always, Elzina was excelling.

Teacher Pallik let them practice for nearly an hour, stepping in to fine-tune their casting as each of the group gradually worked their way up to the more violent of spells.

"Enough," she announced. "Enough with the practice. It is time to pit your skills against one another."

She paired up the students, spacing them apart, then had them begin practicing casting and defending, back and forth, until it started to become second nature.

"Good. You must always have a defensive spell ready. Minimizing damage to yourself and preservation of your magic are key points for all Ghalian. This drill will make that instinctive. Muscle memory, if you will."

The Aspirants continued, taking turns, the speed and power of their spells gradually ramping up until they reached the point where slacking off and not casting a defensive spell could result in significant injury.

"Aspirants, line up," Pallik commanded.

They did as she directed at once, standing motionless at attention.

"You likely know what is coming next. It is once more time for sparring. One-on-one combat. A magical duel, if you will. You have done this before, but never like this. Two will face off at a time in the center of the field. Bawb, Elzina, I think it is time for a little rematch. Step forward."

They did as she directed, each taking a place in the empty middle of the grassy area. Pallik assessed them each as they walked, gauging not only their magic, but also how they carried themselves. Both seemed confident. That was good enough for her.

"You may begin."

As before, Elzina's aggression showed, her spell cast the

moment they were given the all-clear. This time, however, Bawb was ready for it.

He dove aside, rolling clear of what seemed to be a rather violent force spell. She wasn't pulling punches. But then, neither was he. His own attack was already on his lips, and rolling as he did, he was able to cast it before he even completely regained his footing.

"*Acalla tox*," he said, not yelling, but rather calmly picturing a ball of energy pulling through his body and out of his konus. His intent was clear, aided in part by Elzina's overzealous attack motivating him.

The spell flew true, hitting her with a powerful blow, knocking her clean off her feet, tumbling backward on the grass.

Elzina jumped to her feet and launched a flurry of counters, simultaneously casting little shielding spells in the mix. Bawb fought back, remembering Hozark's words and focusing on defense until an opportunity presented itself.

"*Porata*," he cast, the throwing spell snuck through in between his defensive ones.

He had timed it with Elzina's casting rhythm, and it almost took her by surprise. However, at the last minute she managed to sprinkle in a quick defensive spell just as it hit her. Normally, it would have thrown her from her feet, but instead, she only slid aside.

Bawb, on the other hand, had paused to take a breath, something Elzina was counting on.

She sent out a wave of spells before he could properly counter them. Bawb ran to his left, but one caught his leg, allowing two more to strike him, knocking him to the grass.

"Think beyond what is expected," Pallik called out to them. "You are both too rigid. Be like water. Flow with ease as new obstacles arise."

Bawb had heard similar advice from Hozark and Teacher

Demelza on occasion. Unfortunately, it was easier said than done. Maybe when he was more experienced it would come naturally. For now, however, the effort of trying to make himself relax and flow like water was, in itself, causing him to tense up.

Elzina was having some difficulty with the instruction as well, and while her casting was still superior to Bawb's, that little delay in her spells gave him occasional opportunities he might not have otherwise been able to take advantage of.

The two pummeled each other for nearly two minutes, casting and blocking, moving around rather than staying still, their feet not remaining rooted in place as so many beginners tended to be. Bawb realized that Elzina was simply better at this than he was. If they kept going like this, she would eventually win.

Bawb called up the display of his skills, focusing on spells. It was not an impressive site by a long shot.

"Konus, I'm not strong enough. My casting skills aren't as good. What should I do?"

*Do I have to do everything?* his konus griped. *You heard her. Think beyond what is expected.*

"What does that even mean?" he asked in his mind while his mouth cast a hasty defensive spell.

The konus did not seem to feel like replying.

Bawb and Elzina were moving all over the place, attacking and defending, adjusting accordingly. But what could he use that was not expected? They all learned the same spells. Starting back when they first learned the most basic—

It came to him in a flash, and he could almost *feel* his konus smile as his mind clicked into place. He immediately brought an entirely different sort of spells to mind.

"*Scopara ligto*," he cast.

Elzina sensed a spell coming for her and cast a defense

against attack. The spell, however, sailed right past it, to her surprise.

It was a simple thing. A cleaning spell. Sweeping, to be exact. Only this time it was sweeping the ground at Elzina's feet. The magic hit her ankle-high, sweeping her, quite literally, off her feet.

"*Pallinus,*" Bawb followed up, his intent driving far more force into the wind spell than ever before.

Normally, it would have blown a pile of swept up leaves away, but now it was blasting Elzina with forceful wind, dust and grit stinging her eyes. Bawb saw his opportunity and ran. Ran as fast as he could, taking her flank before she could wipe her eyes clean.

Elzina was no fool. She realized she was vulnerable, so she cast nothing but defensive spells as she worked to clear her vision. Unfortunately, Bawb was nowhere near where they were directed.

"*Malovicta,*" he cast, sending a force spell slamming into her undefended side.

Elzina tumbled hard, the wind knocked out of her.

"Enough!" Pallik called out, ceasing the activity. She walked to Bawb, an amused grin on her face. "Well done, Bawb. A clever use of your limited resources, utilizing those spells. And you remembered your lessons on movement. Taking your opponent's side rather than battling head-on. What inspired you to use the wind spell?"

"As you said, *anything* can give an advantage in the right situation. I saw she was on a patch of ground with more exposed dirt and capitalized on it."

*You didn't know it was going to do that, though, did you?* his konus mocked.

Bawb didn't dignify the comment with a reply. He had won. Finally. And while it was unconventional, a win was a win.

Pallik turned to the rest of the group standing a safe distance away.

"Next up will be—"

"I want a rematch!" Elzina blurted, anger clear in her expression and tone.

Pallik turned, allowing the interruption, but not amused by it.

"You are reacting with emotion," she pointed out. "Emotion is something the Ghalian leave behind."

Elzina took a deep breath, calming her demeanor. "I am *not* emotional. I am merely wishing to prove that he simply got lucky. I am a better caster than he is."

"Even luck can decide an outcome in matters of life and death. Some of the greatest warriors have fallen for just such a reason."

"Let me prove myself. *Please.*"

Pallik looked over at Bawb. "Are you willing to face her again or would you rather rest?"

A little cocky from his unexpected win, Bawb's ego spoke before his mind could catch up. "Yes, I will face her again."

"Very well. Perhaps things will be more *interesting* for both of you this time."

"I look forward to it," he replied.

The konus, however, was not so enthused. *Are you sure you don't want to ask what she meant by that?*

Bawb ignored it and walked to his starting point across from his opponent. Elzina's expression was calm, but the vibe coming from her was fierce. *She* was the best in the class, and she would make that abundantly clear to all present.

She launched her attack as soon as Bawb stepped into place, not waiting for any further instruction. Take your enemy by surprise, they were taught, after all.

Bawb took the hit full-on, barely keeping to his feet. He cast defense spells, but Elzina was already on the move, running toward him in a serpentine pattern, peppering him with spells to keep him off-balance.

Bawb dove aside, rolling out of her line of fire for long enough to cast a few spells of his own. Elzina blocked most and only intensified her attack.

She charged him, swinging punches and kicks as she cast. This was something different, something they had not trained in, but in the moment, in the heat of battle, both Aspirants stopped thinking and started simply fighting, going with the flow of combat, letting their bodies and magic do what came naturally.

Teacher Pallik was a bit shocked but also pleased to see them take so great a leap. Normally, she would have saved this sort of sparring until at least a few months from now, when they had better refined their casting. But Elzina was a protegee, and Bawb, well, the overly emotional boy had turned out to be something of a surprise as well.

Elzina's frustration was beginning to show as Bawb took her beating but managed to stay in the fight. He was losing, no doubt about that, but his determination facing her onslaught had him pulling deep from a well of resolve no one would have thought he possessed.

Elzina sensed it, her anger growing.

"*Barriacto!*" she blurted, an ill-formed fireball blasting from her hands.

It missed Bawb, hitting the grass beside him, leaving a nasty scorch mark but the boy unharmed. Pallik was decidedly not amused by this. Elzina was playing with magic she could not yet control. It was time to change the playing field and force her to focus on something else and rein in her wild casting.

Pallik quietly spoke the triggering words. As soon as she did, the ground at the combatants' feet shook violently. So much so, they almost stopped fighting.

Almost.

Elzina's fist managed to connect with Bawb's jaw, staggering him backward a step. She moved toward him, but as she did, the ground at their feet began to fall away all around them, crumbling and dropping into a chasm beneath. One so deep they could not see the bottom.

"What are you stopping for?" Pallik called out. "Do not fear heights. You train to ignore them. The ground you stand on is solid enough. Continue!"

They did as she commanded, but the entire air of their battle had shifted to one of cautious sparring rather than an all-out fight. They had several paces of solid ground in all directions to work with, but they clearly feared the fall, limiting themselves to attacks they knew would not put them in jeopardy.

"I said *fight*!" Pallik bellowed, startling them both. "You wanted this rematch. There is no excuse. You must perform to the best of your abilities, or I will crumble the rest of the ground at both your feet."

Elzina and Bawb didn't need any more urging than that. Their attacks increased in fury and intensity until they were both fighting at full speed. The spells had pretty much dried up by this point, both of them breathing too hard to properly cast. But in hand-to-hand combat they had trained to fight when exhausted, and that was what they were very quickly becoming.

Elzina pushed Bawb hard, his feet sliding on the grass toward the edge. On stone or dirt he could have dug in better to stop her, but the grass was just too slick. He realized he couldn't stop her. He was going to fall.

*Are you really going to go down alone?* his konus asked.

His foot at the drop-off, Bawb acted before he could think,

grabbing her hard and pivoting, throwing her over his hip toward the void.

Elzina's grasp on him tightened, pulling him with her as she flew over the edge.

Both landed with a thump, hovering in mid-air.

They let go of one another and looked down, confused. They were suspended over empty space, but it felt solid beneath them. They could even feel grass. Teacher Pallik walked to them, right across the gap without hesitation.

"*Marbus ekto,*" she said, the ground suddenly appearing beneath them once more. She stood there looming over them, shaking her head.

"What was that, Elzina?"

"I was attempting to win."

"By pushing him? So inelegant. Brute force is not the best option, especially against a skilled adversary. You must use leverage. Technique."

"But this is Bawb."

"Yes. But Bawb, young as he may be, is training to be a Ghalian nonetheless. And as evidenced by his assessment of the situation and self-sacrifice to take you with him in the face of defeat, he has learned that lesson, whereas you have not."

Elzina wisely bit her tongue.

"This danger was just a spell. A simple one at that, yet one that is not expected and may one day cause your pursuers to falter. You will all learn this, and much more, as your training advances. Come along. Up, you two," she said, urging them to their feet. "Your turn is over. Step to the observation area. Now, who will be next?"

# CHAPTER THIRTY-FOUR

For the next several days things changed in their training. Magic was taken off the table entirely for the time being. Instead, the Aspirants were either cold and wet, warm and wet, or some variation thereof. They were also just plain *tired* and wet by the time they were finally allowed back on dry land at the end of each day, and most ate and slept hard as soon as they were released from class.

Bawb, however, had something of an itch he felt compelled to scratch. The itch for knowledge, partially triggered by the interesting story of the poor spirit living within their walls rattling around in his head.

*You know this is a bad idea,* the konus warned him.

"I am only examining what would soon enough be made available to me anyway," he replied, perusing items in the small library of spells and magic the teachers had recently made available to them to study at their leisure.

Normally, he wouldn't have even dreamed of reading texts so far above his level. Bawb's skills were growing, sure, but he was nowhere near being ready for those spells, and he couldn't cast them even if he knew how. He simply lacked the training and requisite focus of intent to come close to making them work. What he could do, however, was scan the texts for ideas on what sort of magic might have caused Porrius to wind up in his terrible state.

Bawb was tired at the end of each and every day, and he knew full well he needed his rest, but he nevertheless managed to put in at least a little bit of extra study before passing out with his cohort. This he did for several days, skimming a great many books and scrolls, observing the notes some had scribbled in the margins over the centuries. It was there that he came across one particular note that caught his eye. It wasn't the words that stood out, however. It was the odd yet familiar hint of light that appeared nearby when he read them.

"This is it," he realized. "It has to be."

*No way. You couldn't possibly know the spell out of all the thousands contained in these volumes. Even the Masters couldn't figure it out, so there's no way you could in just a few days.*

"Say what you will, Konus, but I feel it in my gut. This is the spell."

Bawb turned and looked around, but the light was, yet again, gone. But this time he felt something different. Rather than frustration, he felt hope. Why, he wasn't sure, but the sensation was there, though its origin was uncertain.

"*Pallus Orvix Imanna* with counterclockwise *Rommus*." It was a curious inscription that made no sense. *Rommus* was a tension spell used for tools, but Bawb had no idea what the other spell was. He continued reading.

Beneath that handwritten combination was another. "Cast *Horkus Axiota* with *Maxeliovicto* spell to boost potency," the scrawled note read. It was a relatively straightforward combative spell, but if the boy casting had truly mixed it with another spell, the resulting magic could have been understandably unstable. Bawb had to wonder, what could have made him attempt the dangerous spell amalgam. There was no way to know, but in any case, he wasn't ready to mention it to the teachers. Not yet, at least.

This simply wasn't proof, not in the slightest. And there was no way any teacher or Master would give any credence to his supposition, not to mention his reading of texts so far above his level would not necessarily get him in trouble, but it could bring him under scrutiny. Right about now, that was not something he could afford.

Bawb kept his findings to himself, pondering them as he drifted off to sleep. He wouldn't be able to think on them much, however. A new sort of water training was about to begin, and it would be unlike any they'd previously encountered.

The next morning after a hearty breakfast they were taken to a series of several chambers deep within the Ghalian compound in which to learn the basics of water infiltration, stealthy swimming techniques, and even some rudimentary water fighting tactics, though nothing too serious at this point. There was a seemingly never-ending choice of hidden chambers to torment them with, though they were slowly learning the whereabouts of more and more of them as their training progressed.

The idea behind their current torment was that they become comfortable in water. It was not their preferred means of infiltration or attack, but the Ghalian had spent more than their share of time in watery environments in the pursuit of their goals. And now it was time for the Aspirants to learn more than just treading water.

For this they were brought to a specialist even among Ghalian. Teacher Griggitz was his name, and he was not what any would have expected of a master of underwater fighting and stealthy techniques.

He wasn't exactly an enormous man, but he was so thickly

muscled that he looked as though he would sink like a rock if he ever so much as came near water, let alone submerged in it. This, of course, was part of what made him so good at it. No one ever suspected the likes of one like him to possess those skills. But to his targets' surprise, he was as agile as a sport fish and possessed their strength and endurance as well. Water, for him, was a second home.

The students were not expected to embrace the water as he had. Very few ever did. But they would learn from him. And it would not be easy.

Tough love, or in this case tough toughness, was the order of the day. He took his job *very* seriously, and as Albinius found out when he made an ill-advised joke, resulting in his being forced to tread water for three hours non-stop. Teacher Griggitz expected them to take their lessons as seriously as he took teaching them, regardless of their age.

"You are entering a new phase of your training," he told them when he first marched up and down their ranks, sizing up the fresh meat for his watery grinder. "Gone are the days of no consequences. You are Aspirants, training to be Ghalian, and you must perform as expected. If you do not, you will be reduced to Novice once more, if not expelled from the order. Is that clear?"

"Yes, Teacher," they replied in unison.

"I will teach you spells and techniques that may save your lives one day, so pay attention and take every instruction seriously. In water, you do not have the same luxuries as on land, and even a momentary lapse can be catastrophic."

With that, he sent them on swimming, diving, retrieval, and obstacle tasks, one after another, until they were all ready to drop from the effort. Water was *exhausting*, they quickly learned. Fighting a current could suck your energy, as could simply sitting in cold water. He was forcing them to learn firsthand just how dangerous water could be, but also drilling deep into their minds how that fact could be used to their advantage.

A wet opponent in heavy clothing would not only move slower, but they would tire faster, as the students learned on day two, forced to wear multiple layers for the entirety of their lessons. By the time they shed the heavy, soaked garments, their entire bodies felt as though they had been through a twenty-round sparring session with a grand champion.

But there was more.

Tepid water that felt as if it became colder the longer they spent in it, demonstrating how a body will try to heat what is around it.

"Even in relatively warm water, eventually, you will begin to shiver," Griggitz told them. "Your body will try to heat the entire ocean around you if it can, and you will burn through far too much energy when that occurs. For this, we have spells which you will be expected to learn and master. You will learn to cast a fine layer of magic around your body to keep your temperature stable."

"Will we be dry?" Albinius asked.

"No. It would be a waste of effort and magic to attempt to remain dry for most cases. But by limiting the water to what is directly on your skin, you will then only have to warm a small amount. Something your bodies can do easily. I know what you are wondering, and in response, yes, there are spells to keep you entirely dry. But those will be taught later, when you learn to make water ingress but also need to maintain a practical disguise's integrity. For now, you train."

He then proceeded to run them through drill after drill, swimming distances, treading water, and, of course, diving to retrieve even more items from water of various depth, clarity, and temperature.

Finally, after several days, he felt they were ready to progress beyond mere conditioning.

"There is a spell," he informed them. "A very specialized spell that is rather unconventional. One the Ghalian have used to great success. It will require practice and patience, but if you apply yourselves to your studies, you will find it comes as naturally as breathing. I will demonstrate."

He walked to the water's edge and uttered the spell, "*Oblio fama manititzi*."

The students saw nothing. The spell, it seemed, had failed.

Teacher Griggitz ignored that and stepped into the deep pool they had been training in, sinking straight to the bottom. And on the bottom he stayed.

"What's he doing?" Albinius asked.

"I don't know. It's been a long time," Zota replied.

"Do you think he's okay?"

Elzina crossed her arms. "He's a Master Ghalian. Of course he is okay," she grumbled.

But the longer he remained submerged, the more they began to doubt that was the case. Minutes stretched on and on.

"Should we get someone?" Zota asked after he had been down there for far longer than anyone could survive.

Before he could answer, Teacher Griggitz calmly stepped from the water, looking rested and not at all out of breath.

"How did you do that?" Zota marveled.

"As I said. A very specialized spell. Much as we can cast to create a thin layer of magic insulating our bodies, this spell is applied to form an air bubble around your head. How many breaths it contains is dependent on your power, your ability, and the strength of your intent."

The students were clearly in awe of this novel use of magic they had never even considered before. Fighting and their other daily tasks were normal, but this? This was something quite unusual.

"The key to this spell, as with all others, is your intent," Griggitz informed them. "Without intent, and I mean a *forceful*, well-defined intent without doubt or hesitation, you will fail. This is why the technique has only been used by the Ghalian and a very few select others with the requisite control over their emotions and thoughts to cast it. Anything less and you will find yourself without so much as a breath contained in it. We will begin practicing on land, but rest assured, you will be tested in water as well."

And so they did. The Aspirants trained and trained. Every day it was the same routine, exhausting them in water but now also having them cast the new spell in different environments. After seven days of practice, not without quite a few abject failures on all of the students' part, Griggitz felt they were ready for their next phase of training.

"You have all done a fair job," he told them. "But you must continue your practice on your own. For now it is time to move on to something different. You will learn to apply the basic wilderness survival skills you have learned from Teacher Demelza in a practical setting."

Bawb felt his heart beat a little faster. "Do you mean we will be going outside?"

"Indeed. Go put on dry clothes, then gather in the ground-level dining hall and feed yourselves well. When you are done, we will depart from there."

The Aspirants hurried to change, then rushed to the dining hall, where they eagerly filled themselves with a nutritious meal, their strained bodies glad for the energy to draw on.

Teacher Demelza was the one who came to gather them.

"Are you prepared?" she asked.

They nodded.

"Good. Follow. And remember, outside of these walls, you are simple Wampeh children. Act the part."

She was not wearing her Vespus blade, Bawb noted, a little disappointed he would not be able to see the weapon and feel its unusual draw. But it made sense. If they were just a group of Wampeh on an outing, overt weapons would be out of the question. He was sure, however, that she was well-armed in other ways.

They followed her out of the training house and into the streets. This time, rather than heading to the landing field on the outskirts, they were walking deeper into the busy core of the city. There was much for the young students to look at. All manner of alien life walked the streets, going about their daily routines, as well as the smells of a bustling society, both good and bad.

"We are taking a single ship large enough to accommodate us all," Demelza informed them as they emerged from a smaller street into a vast, open area. "Stay close."

Bawb gazed in awe at the large ships resting in a low hover in the busy transit hub. Some were smaller, but the majority appeared to be sizable cargo vessels. Demelza guided them to a medium-sized craft settled right in the middle of the others. Teacher Griggitz was waiting at the open entryway.

"Griggitz," she said with a nod.

"Demelza," he replied. "All ready to go."

"Excellent. Children, follow me."

She led them aboard, guiding them down a series of short corridors. One compartment had an open door through which they saw a small contingent of Drooks sitting in a circle, preparing to use their power for the flight.

Bawb felt a slight tug of familiar magic. Her Vespus blade was already aboard the ship. Of course she would have prepared for the trip ahead of time.

They kept walking until they reached a comfortable compartment with enough seats for all of them. She gestured to the seats.

"Relax. We will lift off momentarily."

Bawb remained standing a moment longer while the others sat. "Teacher Demelza?"

"Yes, Bawb?"

"I thought the Ghalian preferred to use a Drookonus to power their ships."

"We do."

"But I saw Drooks when we entered."

"Ah, yes. That. This group of Drooks work on any ship requiring power. They are freed Drooks with the ability to go as they wish, but as they do not have a particular vessel they call home, they prefer to stay here. As you know, Drooks are akin to working animals in that they only feel fulfilled when they have a purpose. And for their very specialized magic, flying a ship fills precisely that need. They suffer terribly when denied an outlet for their power."

"But they're free?"

"Yes. And paid for their services, though that is done through a shell entity to hide any Ghalian involvement. It is a good situation for all parties, though, admittedly, a little unusual."

"So this ship is just powered by Drooks rather than a Drookonus."

"Normally we use a Drookonus for this ship. Most are relatively weak, all told, but the Ghalian are in possession of particularly powerful Drookonuses, the most robust of which can easily power a large craft across the stars for months, if need be, depending on the size and demands of the ship."

"I am confused. Why are we using Drooks instead of a Drookonus?

Demelza sighed. "Because a certain thorn in our side went and stole it recently."

The students didn't gasp aloud, but they were all thinking the same thing.

"From the Ghalian?" Usalla marveled. "Who would be so foolish?"

"In this instance, we are not the only ones to use this ship. The Ghalian own it through many layers of entities, but others use it fairly often. It is how we keep it free of scrutiny. But Nixxa and her pirate friends did not know that. They just saw a prize and took it, much to our inconvenience."

*You can level up significantly if you retrieve the Drookonus*, Bawb's konus blurted. *It's quite an opportunity.*

"Retrieve it?"

"What was that, Bawb?" Demelza asked.

"Um, I mean, why don't the Ghalian find her and get it back?"

"While we would like to, it is not practical."

"Oh, so she is gone."

"No, Nixxa and her comrades are still in the system for now, but when she is pirating, she surrounds herself with powerful casters who use reveal spells to detect disguised intruders, making it problematic to sneak aboard without time to create a proper cover story and identity. I must admit, it is coin well spent and has kept her largely untouchable for some time. She may be trouble, but she is not an idiot."

*Idiot or not, that's a valuable piece of equipment.*

Bawb ignored the konus. "So she just keeps the stolen Drookonus? It seems she should be forced to return it. No one should be able to steal from the Ghalian."

Demelza smiled at the boy. "I appreciate the enthusiasm, Bawb, but it is not worth the risk or effort to retrieve it. We balance the costs, risks, and rewards, and in this case, it is not in the cards. Besides, while she causes chaos more often than not, she also makes life difficult for the Council of Twenty, which aligns with our desires. And despite her behavior, I do believe Nixxa means well. At least, mostly."

*I am telling you, this is your chance*, the onus persisted. *Find a way*.

"Quiet down," Bawb thought to the magical device, but in the back of his mind the seed had been planted. Maybe there *could* be a way to get it back. And with the thought of, *what if he did*, he couldn't help but wonder what rewards might await him.

# CHAPTER THIRTY-FIVE

Following a long jump to a different system, the ship descended from orbit and settled down in an open field beside a rocky set of ridges and a winding river. From what the Aspirants could see as they popped through the clouds and prepared to land, there was no civilization anywhere remotely near where they were going. As for what might be out there in the rest of the world, that was anyone's guess.

The twin suns were still high in the sky when they exited the ship, the orange-red glow bathing them in warm light. The grass in the field they had landed in was tall and amber, the ground soft and fertile.

The whisper of rushing water told of the swift river they had seen upon approach, but where they were there was nothing but solid ground and lush vegetation. The nearby cliffs must have been blocking the water's flow, keeping the faint sound from being louder.

"You will make camp here," Demelza instructed. "When you have finished preparing shelter, I suggest you set about putting your trapping lessons to use. You will find them most helpful in filling your bellies tonight if you do."

Finnia looked around. "How long are we going to be here?"

"That is not your concern. What is, is your being ready to strike your campsite and erase any sign that you were ever here, if needed. Is that clear?"

The students nodded their understanding.

"Good. Then I recommend you get to work. First shelter, then food. Once you have completed those tasks there should still be time for you to practice your spell casting. Teacher Griggitz has instructed you well. Practice what you have learned."

"What then?" Grayzin asked.

"Then? Then we will continue your training. For now, prepare."

With that she walked away to survey their campsite with Griggitz, who had just exited the ship to join her. "You heard her. Get to work!"

The students hopped to it, quickly gathering branches and leaves to make shelters. Most opted for a simple lean-to. It wasn't enough for a long stay, but seeing as Demelza told them to be ready to strike the location and mask their presence on a moment's notice, it was a fair bet that they would not be spending more than a few nights here, at most.

A few did decide to build more complex shelters, but those were proving time-consuming, and they still had the trapping and gathering for the evening's meal to consider.

Bawb had taken Demelza's words to heart, fashioning the smallest cover for himself he could, a snug little shelter barely big enough for him to squeeze into. He then hurried off to set snares and forage while the others continued their efforts.

*New Skill: Shelter Making. Level One*, the konus announced as he set his first snare. It was as he had been taught, but that was back in the cozy confines of the Ghalian training house. Here in the wild, however, there were many other factors in play. For one, his tool options were essentially none. What he could fashion with no more than a dagger would have to do. Then there was the uncertainty of what size game they would be attempting to capture.

He saw some prints on the ground near a barely visible trail of bent grass. Something had come this way. And if the grass was holding its misshapen form, that meant either it had come and gone repeatedly, or several of them were using this as a pathway. In either case, it was a good location to set a trap.

Carefully, he fashioned a noose out of a thin strip of reed that he braided into a slender but strong line. He then made a trigger mechanism out of a stick and a rock, attaching the far end to a bent limb from a stout shrub.

It wasn't perfect by any stretch of the imagination, but it should suffice.

*Level up: Snare and trap making*, the konus announced. *Well done.*

"Thanks. Now how about we go forage a bit?"

He set off in search of edibles as he had been instructed, leaving his snare to do its work. Elzina had been making one of her own not far away and eyed his with dislike. She looked around. No one was watching.

"*Pallinus*," she cast, the wind spell aimed directly at his snare.

The trigger rustled and released, the trap catching nothing but air. Elzina smiled to herself and continued her work, contented in the knowledge Bawb might be going to bed a bit hungry this night.

Elzina set her own trap and headed off toward the sound of rushing water in hopes of finding some berries. Bawb was already there, a decent haul piled up in the small container he'd made by securing a large leaf to itself in a cone.

"There is a bush with a lot of them over here," he said, putting their quarrel aside. They were all on the same team, after all, and this was just hunting and gathering, not some crazy combat scenario.

"I'm fine," Elzina replied, turning from him and heading in a different direction to find berries of her own.

Bawb shrugged and carried on. He had made the effort, and that was all that mattered. He rolled up several more leaves and loaded them all to overflowing, then headed back to the campsite.

"You found a lot!" Usalla noted as he passed her and Finnia heading the other way.

"I got enough for the three of us if you wish to share. See if you can find anything else out there."

"I will. A generous offer. We thank you, Bawb."

"See you two back at camp."

The two girls continued on their way while Bawb dropped off his haul back at his shelter, then went to check on his snare.

Triggered, but empty.

"Just my luck," he muttered, resetting the snare.

He returned several times, but each visit found his snare set off but without catching a thing. He glanced over at Elzina cleaning the small creature she had caught in her trap as she watched him with a look of slight amusement in her eyes.

Usalla walked over and saw his lack of luck. "Come share with us. Finnia and I caught a pair of large ones."

"Thank you. It is appreciated."

The trio made a small fire using the spell they had been taught, then roasted the animals whole. They were not terribly big, but there was enough meat on them to go around, and combined with Bawb's berry haul, it made a surprisingly satisfying meal.

They were digesting their meal, sitting around casually practicing their spell phrasing, when Teacher Griggitz called the group to attention. "Aspirants, come with me."

He stalked off through the long grass as the suns dropped lower in the sky. The students hurried after him, Demelza taking up the rear.

Griggitz led them through a small copse of trees to a clearing at the edge of a low cliff, where he had them line up. "You were lacking in proper intent just now. Each of you spoke the words, but your emphasis was not strong. I could feel the weakness of your spells, and that goes for all of you. Now, listen to the rushing water down below. Picture it all around you. Now think of the intent for your spell. How to cast your air bubble. You have done this in practice in the training house many times, so this should be no different."

They did as he said for several minutes to varying degrees of success and failure. Griggitz was not pleased with their progress, to say the least. He walked the line, staring at each of them as if he could sense their intimidation. Demelza stood back and watched. This was his specialty, not hers, and it was his to teach, though she did not always agree with his demeanor and methods.

"Emphasize your intent," he finally said. "Is it so hard?"

"It just feels forced," Albinius admitted.

"Forced? Turn and step to the edge. All of you." They did as he commanded. "Now, look down and think of your training. Can you smell the water? Can you feel its power?"

"I-I'm not sure," Albinus stammered.

Griggitz scowled and let out a frustrated sigh. "Very well. *Doxxalis pa!*"

The students found themselves slammed from behind with a powerful push spell, sending them all tumbling through the air, falling to the raging river below.

"What are you doing, Griggitz?" Demelza demanded, rushing to the edge.

"Only what needs to be done, Sister. No more coddling for

these Aspirants. You know better than most what comes next in their training. They must now fly without a net, whatever the consequences may be."

Much as she hated to admit it, she knew he was right. Eventually, all Ghalian youths transitioned from safety into the peril of training for real, and it seemed today was that day.

The Aspirants, however, were not aware of this shift as they plummeted into the rapids. They hit hard, most unable to align themselves for a clean entry. The impact was enough to knock the wind out of them, forcing each and every one to frantically paddle to the surface to try to suck in precious lungfuls of air.

Bawb tried desperately to cast his air bubble spell as he fell but failed, the impact with the water cutting his words short. He broke the surface but was immediately pulled under, having only just gulped down a gasp of air. He felt hands grabbing at him underwater and pivoted, pushing his feet against them, escaping their desperate grasp before they could pull him deeper in a panic while using the leverage to thrust himself above the surface.

"*Oblio fama manititzi*," he cast, his intent extremely clear in this moment of duress. The current pulled him back under, but he found the spell had actually worked. He had managed to cast a tiny pocket of air around his head. It was only enough for a couple of breaths, but that was all the difference he needed.

He hit the surface calmly this time, his lungs no longer on fire, and re-cast the spell, giving himself a few more water-free breaths as he was pulled under again. With the bubble, he could see around himself better as well. Usalla was close, struggling to swim upward. He made his way to her as quickly as he could, then wrapped his arms around her and kicked hard, pushing her above water.

She filled her lungs with glorious air and collected herself then began to swim for shore. Bawb followed behind, looking over his shoulder at the other Aspirants slowly making their way to the shallows.

*Level up: Casting, Water Skills. Rescue. Water Evasion.*

But Bawb didn't care about his konus. He was just happy to be safely ashore where Teachers Demelza and Griggitz were waiting for them.

Demelza ushered them to one side while Griggitz monitored the water, counting them as they emerged.

"One short," he noted after several minutes.

They did a quick head count.

"Where's Grayzin?" Finnia asked.

Griggitz squinted at the rushing waters. "We must search downstream. Aspirants, this way."

Tired and near drowned, they nevertheless moved as one, immediately jumping into action where one of their own was concerned. They walked for several minutes, scanning the water and shore before a pale form was spotted on the rocks.

"There!" Zota exclaimed.

Griggitz and Demelza hurried ahead, hauling the boy out of the water. The others reached them moments later to find their classmate's lifeless eyes gazing up from the ground.

Griggitz rose and turned to the group, not a hint of sympathy in his gaze. "*This* is why you must not think. Why you must cast and act with singular purpose and intent. You are not children anymore, and your training will reflect that." He pointed at the boy's body. "Look at him. He knew the spell. He had practiced it at length, I saw with my own eyes. But panic stopped him, and now see what has become of him. This could be any one of you if you allow fear to get the better of you."

Griggitz hefted the boy's body over his shoulder and began trekking back to the ship to put it on ice for later disposal. Demelza, however, stayed back, lingering a moment longer.

"Remember this lesson well," she said somberly. "I am sorry

you had to learn it in this manner, but this is the reality of Ghalian life. Tell me, what will you take away from this?"

Elzina stepped forward. "That you cannot cast while gasping for air, whether it is from water or from fear or from running hard. You cannot cast if you cannot breathe to say the words."

"Yes, that is the most obvious lesson. But what else? What applies to you as Ghalian?"

Bawb looked at the limp figure over Griggitz's shoulder as he trudged away and had to wonder, was that the person he had pushed off against? Had Grayzin's last moments been spent as Bawb's leaping-off point?

"There is more. Anyone? What else?" Demelza repeated.

"Teacher Demelza?"

"Yes, Bawb. What else have you learned?"

"That you cannot cast if you cannot breathe."

"I just said that," Elzina grumbled.

"You did not let me finish. You cannot cast if you cannot breathe, but neither can your enemy."

A slight grin crept onto Demelza's otherwise sad expression. "Very good, Bawb. *Anything* can be a weapon. Anything can be used to give you an advantage. Even something as seemingly benign as water. And not just a river. If a person is drinking, can they cast?"

"No."

"So if a power user is your target, what might be one method of gaining an advantage?"

"Attack when they have the greatest likelihood of being unable to cast a defense," he replied. "But I suppose they would probably have extra wards and defensive spells up when they are dining," he added in afterthought.

"A good observation and something for all of you to think about. Now, back to the campsite. Dry off and warm yourselves at the fire. We will pay our respects to Grayzin when we get home. Tonight we continue your training, just as you will continue your mission as Wampeh Ghalian. No death but your own will deter you from your goal. Is that understood?"

"Yes, Teacher," the group replied.

She managed a smile for the distraught youths. "Good. You have done well. Go warm up. We have much to do tonight."

# CHAPTER THIRTY-SIX

It was dark out in the wilderness.

The dead boy had been carefully stowed aboard the ship, and now the surviving Aspirants stood quietly beneath the moonless sky, the tall grass brushing against them as they waited in silence, pondering what had just happened.

Demelza had given them a little extra time to gather themselves after the traumatic experience of losing one of their own. Griggitz had thought she was being soft on them, but she reminded him that the delay was merely a matter of convenience, as their next lesson required waiting for the twin suns to fully set. Of course, the fact that it gave the students a chance to further process what had happened and recenter themselves was a bonus.

She had waited until the suns had dropped below the horizon but there was still a hint of light remaining. With their fires long extinguished, the Aspirants' eyes had adjusted to the low light naturally, making it easy for them to follow her as she led them out into the field on the far side of their ship.

Bawb felt the tug of her Vespus blade now strapped to her

back. It wasn't glowing, safely secured in its sheath, but the magical weapon's presence was as recognizable as the wafting aroma of fresh bread from a local bakery lingering in the air. He was wearing his own daggers, as their teacher had instructed, and Elzina was sporting her enchanted one as well, but none were carrying anything larger than that. They were training light this evening.

Demelza stopped at a flat area and instructed them to line up and wait, listening to their environment, taking in every sound.

"Hear the wind," she told them. "The sound of it rustling the grass. Can you hear the difference it makes in the open as opposed to where your classmates are standing? And the river nearby. How far is it, and which direction is the water flowing? Are there animals? Insects? Every sound is a clue to paint a picture in your mind of the world around you. Just listen."

She let them stand like that until the sky had become truly dark, the lingering hints of sunlight now long gone. The students had stood there listening for nearly an hour by the time she began the rest of the night's lesson, and after so long relying on senses other than their eyes, each and every one of them was acutely aware of every sound and smell around them.

"Bawb. Draw your blade," she instructed.

He did as he was told, his dagger ready in his hand.

"Now, try to cut me."

"Teacher?"

"You heard me. I want you to attack. Attempt to cut me."

"But—"

"*Try*."

She was one of the finest blademasters the order had, but he committed himself to the effort regardless while, in the back of his mind, the memory of their recently deceased classmate lingered. He could not help but wonder if this too might be a fatal lesson.

"*Lumaris*," he said, casting a minor illumination spell and running to attack her.

"*Phallistos*," she immediately counter cast, extinguishing the light in an instant.

Bawb's eyes had contracted from the light, leaving him fighting in even more pronounced darkness. Before he could cast his night-vision spell, he felt a sting on his arm and a kick to his rear, sending him tumbling through the grass.

"Usalla, you are next. Do not cast an illumination spell. Do not use a night-vision spell. You have been readying your senses for this. Now, attack!"

Usalla did as she was told and quickly reached the same outcome as Bawb, bleeding and sprawled out in the grass.

"Elzina, attempt to cut me."

She tried her best, switching her grip on her enchanted dagger mid-attack in hopes of fooling her teacher.

She failed, joining the others on the ground.

Demelza worked through the entire class one by one until all were left with a bloody mark from her blade, expertly applied to not be too deep, but to also make her point, literally as well as figuratively.

She cast a very minor illumination spell, affording them just enough light to see her.

"Darkness is not to be feared," she said, pacing before them as she spoke. "Darkness is not our enemy. It is the friend of the Ghalian as much as a shimmer cloak or any other means of subterfuge and disguise. You will learn to fight in it. To stalk in it. To perform any task required of you in total darkness, for one day you may not possess a konus to help illuminate your surroundings. But do not be afraid of the dark. Never be afraid of the dark. Instead, do as the Ghalian have done forever. What you have been told time and again. *Be* what people are afraid of in the dark. You are nimble killers, and with your daggers, you can move quietly and quickly, a key to remaining undetected. And you can achieve great accuracy with the lighter weapon as well," she added, gesturing to each of their matching cuts on their arms.

They realized then that she had somehow managed to land the exact same blow upon each of them, regardless of which side they had come at her from, and whether their attacks had been high or low.

"Teacher Demelza?" Zota asked. "What about swords. Would they not provide a more formidable method of attack in such circumstances?"

"A good question, Zota, and the answer is somewhat counterintuitive. A sword, while possessing greater reach and the capability to do greater damage, also creates more sound, both when unsheathed as well as when put to use. And fighting in the dark, some of them can even become a hindrance, despite their power."

She extinguished the illumination spell, plunging them all into darkness, a darkness replaced by a blue light as she drew her Vespus blade.

"This is a powerful weapon. A Vespus blade. In the hands of a trained Ghalian, there are few who can stand against it. And in the right circumstances it can end a conflict before it begins. Those who know what it is fear it and will sometimes flee or surrender. But to the less informed, it is just a source of light. A means to lock onto its user as a clearly defined target. Even the most powerful of weapons can have their drawbacks. Is that understood?"

"Yes, Teacher."

"Good. Now, train with your knives. Pair up and let us see what you can do."

"Teacher?" Bawb asked, feeling the pull of her blade more acutely now that it was exposed, free of its sheath.

"Yes, Bawb?"

"When will we be allowed to train more with swords?"

"When you are ready."

"But we have used them before. You know this; you were our teacher."

"Those were but dull facsimiles."

"I realize that. I just thought it would be beneficial for us to progress to using real ones."

The others glanced at him, disapproving looks on their faces. Bawb was making a mistake, and they all knew it. Even his konus reacted.

*Foolish boy. You push too far,* it chided, vibrating with a disapproving hum on his wrist.

Demelza, however, flashed an amused grin, though not a friendly one by any means.

"Wait here," she said, then sheathed her sword, jogging toward their ship, leaving the Aspirants straining their senses in the dark. They heard nothing.

A few minutes later a flash of blue light abruptly illuminated them again. Demelza had returned, and they had been none the wiser. And now she bore something else in her hands. A sword.

She tossed it to Bawb, the point embedding in the soil at his feet. This was not a dull training blank. This was the real deal.

"Take it," she commanded.

He pulled it free, holding it aloft, watching as she moved closer, casually twirling her blade.

"You wanted swordplay? Very well. Defend yourself."

Without hesitation Demelza launched herself at him, attacking him from all angles with her glowing sword. Bawb swung hard and fast, blocking as best he could, defending himself as he had been taught. Only this was not a dull training sword whistling through the air at his head, it was a very real and very sharp weapon.

Demelza forced him back on his heels, retreating from her onslaught. She paused, allowing him to regain his footing, then started again, relentlessly attacking with a barrage of blows. Bawb's arms were on fire, the muscles not accustomed to so fierce an attacker, and especially not one so skilled. It was all he could do to block, and there was no opportunity for him to make an attack of his own.

Demelza was toying with him, swinging just fast enough to keep him off guard but not so fast as to actually injure the boy. At least, not badly. She sliced him multiple times with expert precision, one on each arm and leg, mirror images of each other.

The sting of the cuts caused a visceral reaction, and Bawb felt a surge of something deep inside. His tired arms felt renewed, at least a little, and he pushed back as hard as he could, trying to move from a defensive to an offensive footing. Amazingly, it seemed to be working, as Demelza was taking steps back.

Bawb felt a flush of excitement and pressed on harder. Demelza blocked his blade with ease and pivoted aside, her foot casually tripping him as he rushed by, sending Bawb tumbling to the ground.

He felt the slightly warm metal of the Vespus blade resting on his neck. Demelza looked down on him a long moment then cast an illumination spell, sheathing her sword. Bawb got up and brushed himself off as he moved back into line with the others, leaving the sword where it lay.

Demelza paced before the line of students once more, assessing each of them as they passed.

"What did Bawb do wrong?" she asked.

"There are so many things to choose from," Elzina quipped, drawing a rare grin from their teacher.

"True, but more than his swordplay, which is expected to be lacking from one who has not fully trained in the arts, what did he do wrong?"

Usalla glanced at her bloodied friend then spoke up. "He got overconfident against a superior opponent."

"Good. Yes. But there is more. Bawb showed drive, no doubt, but he allowed his eagerness to prove himself overtake his better judgment. I defeated him with what? Was it my sword that bested him? Or was it merely my foot that sent him to the ground?"

The students muttered their understanding amongst themselves. Bawb had been too aggressive. Too cocky. Demelza held up a hand to silence them, then turned to Bawb.

"You must expect the unexpected, for as a Ghalian, it is you who will be using surprising tactics against your opponents."

"I understand," he said. "I will endeavor not to let it happen again."

"Oh, it will happen. You are an Aspirant and have much to learn. But take these words to heart. All of you. Do not focus on an enemy's blade alone. Do not tunnel vision to the point you become unaware of what is around you. Bawb was tripped not by some elaborate technique or high-level spell. I merely stuck out my foot. This sort of carelessness can, and will, cost you your life in real combat."

Bawb nodded but kept his mouth shut. Demelza stepped closer and examined his wounds.

"Minor," she said. "Though I am sure your arms and wrists are sore from the exercise. I assume you now realize there is more than just technique to swordplay. You must build those muscles until your grip is like a vise and your arms like sturdy branches. Even the most technically skilled will tire eventually."

She stepped back, allowing her illumination spell to start dimming. "Train with your knives for now and grow stronger. While I applaud your enthusiasm, your body is simply not yet ready for the likes of a proper sword. But one day, when you are, I will gladly teach you all I know. Now, back to training, the lot of you. The night is still young."

# CHAPTER THIRTY-SEVEN

"I am telling you, it would be a coup to succeed in such an endeavor."

Bawb was excited. Perhaps *too* excited, but his mind had been racing all night and most of the following day as he pondered how to make a good showing for the order, all while carrying out the various tasks the teachers foisted upon him and his cohort.

His ill-advised comment and subsequent beatdown by Teacher Demelza had left him the black sheep of the group for now, and while the others had wound up with a useful learning experience from it, Bawb had clearly pushed a boundary that he should have been smart enough to leave alone.

It was something Elzina, and a few others, were more than happy to point out to him repeatedly the following day.

But if he could achieve something grand, something that would help the Ghalian, he could regain standing and then some. And he had just the thing in mind.

It was crazy, of course. Risky and well beyond his very limited skills. But Bawb had latched onto the idea as soon as he'd heard of Nixxa's little escapade. Technically, his konus had first, but whatever the case, he had to run it by someone, and who better than Usalla? She was his friend, after all, and had been since his early days as a scared and culture-shocked Null.

"And I'm telling you it is madness," she replied, shaking her head. "You need to focus on the task at hand and forget about this foolish idea."

The task at hand was a deceptively simple one. They were to search out several marker points, noting the messages scrawled on each, then combine them to create the final message that would lead them to the day's prize.

Of course, Demelza and Griggitz would not make it as easy as just that. Any fool could stumble upon markers with enough aimless wandering. But it would require all they had learned in their codebreaking and hidden languages classes to successfully obtain the true location of their prize, whatever it might be.

Elzina had already claimed two of these precious additions to her personal kit recently, and she made no attempt to hide her certainty that she would get this one as well.

Bawb had other plans. But as Usalla was learning, not all of his thoughts revolved around their training.

"I can do it," he said, following her up a steep slope upon which they hoped to get a better view of the area and, perhaps, spot the next marker. "They said Nixxa is still in the system back home. If I can find her, I know I can retrieve the stolen Drookonus. You heard what they said. It has inconvenienced the order greatly."

"And they have not gone after it for a reason."

"But that reason is time and resources taken from other missions. I, however, am not part of that equation. They lose nothing by my actions."

"But you may lose your *life*, Bawb. You seem to forget the lesson Demelza taught you just last night. You do not have the skills. You were a Novice not that long ago. If you do this you will be killed."

"I strongly doubt it. An adult, perhaps. But me? People love kids. I am sure I can find a way. But first, I will need to find out which planet or moon Nixxa is currently on."

"Is that all? I think you forget a key element of this idiotic idea. The Ghalian will not lend you a ship, nor do you know how to fly one."

"Fine. Of course, I also need to figure out how to get a ride there."

"And how to exit the training house without drawing attention to yourself. And I would remind you, we have never been allowed outside on our own. We have only ever done so in the company of a teacher."

"Maybe I can disguise myself."

Usalla laughed as she pulled herself up over a large fallen tree stump on her way to the hilltop above. "Really? You?"

"Yes, me."

"Do you forget that we have only just begun learning the most basic of disguises? Bawb, you have clearly not thought this through."

"I have," he protested, scrambling up after her. "It is just this plan will, by its nature, have a lot of unforeseen variables."

"That could end with you punished, demoted, or killed."

"Again with the negativity. We are Ghalian."

"*Aspiring* Ghalian."

"And we are trained not to fear death."

"In the pursuit of our goals. But this? This is not sanctioned. This is you being impulsive and emotional. We have talked about this, Bawb. You said you would work hard to keep your feelings in check."

"And I have. You know this."

"Admittedly, you have come far since your arrival with us."

"Then admit that my plan is based in logic."

"Logic and good sense are not the same thing. Yes, it *could* work. But is it worth the risk?"

Bawb scanned the wooded area below them from their new vantage point, mulling over her words. He trusted her implicitly, which was why they were working together to find the markers. After they did, however, it would be each for themself when it came down to deciphering them and making a run for the prize.

He was about to posit something clever when something slightly out of the ordinary caught his eye. It was not in the tree line, however. Rather, there appeared to be a slight diversion in the flowing river. One that he had not noticed previously.

"Look," he said, taking care not to point lest any of the other Aspirants be watching them from below. "In the river just past the bend. Something is disrupting the flow."

"I see the whitewater around it," Usalla confirmed. "It must be the next marker."

"And with that, we would have all of them."

"Unless the teachers were lying about how many there were," she noted.

Bawb chuckled. "Well, yes, there is always that. Come on."

He quickly began descending the hill. They didn't know where the others were, but they were sure to be making good progress as well. They had been trained by the best, after all.

"Back to your idea," Usalla persisted when they hit level ground. "Tell me you see the folly in it. You have no way out of the training house, let alone off world."

"I just need to make it outside the walls. From there it should be simple."

"Simple? It sounds anything but," she said, hurrying her pace as they began descending toward the cliffs at the river's edge.

"I can sneak aboard a supply ship," Bawb replied as if it were the most normal thing in the world. "Or I can steal coin to buy passage the normal way."

"You will get caught."

"She stole something the order needs, and though I may not be a full Ghalian yet, maybe that can work to my advantage."

"How so?"

"We are not a threat. We are kids in their eyes. That might prove to be an advantage."

"You are also a lot smaller and weaker than an adult. If they catch you, there will be no defending yourself. Against one or two, perhaps you would stand a chance, but never against a group. And pirates always travel in groups."

*Ignore her*, the konus urged. *You know what you are capable of. Or are you going to let fear and uncertainty hold you back?*

They slowed down as they reached the edge of the cliffs, peering down at the water below. There, in the rapids just downriver, a small post rose from the water, the marker with the final clue.

"Nothing is holding me back," Bawb said, then leapt into the air, but this time his fall was fully intentional.

Usalla watched in momentary shock as he plummeted into the water, but unlike the night before, he was ready, and his air bubble spell was cast well before he hit the surface. He popped up unscathed and began swimming for the marker, their classmate's death pushed to the back of his mind. There would be time to dwell on that once they were back home.

"So that is how it will be," Usalla muttered, then jumped after him, not looking forward to the cold water but very much intending to win this challenge.

She broke the surface much as Bawb had done, her spell intact and her target acquired. She swam after him, pulling to a stop where he had braced his feet on an underwater rock.

"Step here," he said, pointing beside him.

She moved closer and found the foothold, locking in against the current.

Bawb had already reached up and exposed the clue. It was no more than a few words, and nonsense at that, but combined with the others it would somehow give them a map to the location of the prize. A prize they both intended to win.

"The last one," Usalla said. "Truce until we reach the shore?"

"Truce," he agreed.

They would compete hard once on dry land, but after the prior night, neither wanted to get into a competitive scrap in these waters. They swam close to one another, each ready to help if the other became caught in the current. But fortune was smiling upon them, and they reached the rocky shore at the foot of the cliff unscathed.

"I guess we part ways here," she said.

"I suppose we do. I would wish you good luck, but I fully intend to be the victor."

"As do I."

They hesitated a moment, each waiting for the other to say or do something, to make the first move. They had both read the clue and were each working over what it could mean in their minds. Finally, having apparently come to the same conclusion, they both made a run for the cliffs at the same time, scrambling up as fast as they could and grabbing handholds in a rush for the top.

The clue pointed them to the other side of the field beyond the ship, and the most direct way was straight up the sheer wall, then a beeline through the trees and grassy field. That meant a pretty significant climb. The pair stretched and reached, grasping handholds as they became apparent, their feet digging in as best they could with improvised toe holds.

It was obnoxiously slow going. So slow, in fact, that for a moment Usalla actually wondered if it would have been faster to have just run downstream until the terrain leveled out, then circled back around.

"You are perfectly welcome to descend and try the other way if you wish," Bawb joked, pulling ahead of her.

"Oh, I think I will be just fine where I am, thank you very much," she replied, closing the gap.

Bawb felt the pressure and moved faster, all but willing himself up the cliff face. Usalla knew he would beat her to the top, but it would not be by much, and the clue only gave them the general direction of the prize. There was still a chance even if he had a head start.

Bawb was thinking the same thing, pondering where, exactly, the prize would have been hidden, narrowing down the possibilities, when his handhold abruptly broke free just as he was pushing up with his legs to reach for the next one.

To his credit, he did not cry out as he peeled off the rock face, but the expression he bore told how serious he realized this was. He was falling down, not out, and he had no way to redirect to make himself hit the water.

Bawb was falling straight toward the shore.

Usalla watched in horror as her friend hit the rocks below with a sickening crack, bones audibly breaking from the impact.

"Bawb! Bawb! How badly are you hurt?" she called down to him.

Her friend just writhed in agony, teeth clenched and unable to speak.

Usalla hurried her pace, pushing her climb upward as fast as she could. Bawb was in trouble, competition be damned. She clawed her way to the top, standing at once and taking off at a sprint to find the teachers. She found Demelza and Griggitz reclining in the shade beside the ship.

"Don't you have a task to be—" Griggitz began.

"Bawb fell! He is badly injured!"

Demelza leapt to her feet. “Show me. Now!”

Usalla turned and ran. Demelza looked at her colleague, concern clear in her eyes. “Prepare for extrication and follow. We do not know how bad this will be,” she said, then ran after the girl.

They made it to the cliffs in no time, Usalla pointing down at the bent form of her friend below. Demelza jumped off into the open, falling straight down. At the last moment, she cast a powerful pressure spell in a most unusual way, the force of it arresting her fall just as her feet touched the ground.

She rushed to Bawb’s side, casting several spells at once to assess his injuries.

“How bad?” she asked him as she performed a rapid trauma assessment.

“It hurts,” he said through gritted teeth.

“Can you feel your limbs?”

“Yes. And they hurt too.”

“This is good. You have sensation, and that means you have not damaged anything vital. That said, you are a mess and in need of rapid attention.”

Demelza began casting healing spells, binding broken bones and keeping the sharp ends from causing any more damage when they moved him. Griggitz joined her a few minutes later, a small floating litter in tow. He lowered it down to her then descended to join her, loading Bawb into it and raising it to the top.

Usalla stood by watching with a terrible feeling of helplessness as Demelza rushed him to the ship. Griggitz stayed behind, watching as she took off to the skies.

“Is she flying home?” the girl asked.

“No, not home. The Ghalian train on this world often. There is a healing facility in a distant city. She will take him there for treatment then return immediately. Bawb may be out of the contest, but do not forget, there is a prize at stake."

Usalla followed his gaze and saw Elzina racing across the field in the general direction they were supposed to find the prize in. Griggitz looked at her and shrugged.

"Well? What are you waiting for?"

Putting her concern aside in an instant, Usalla took off in a sprint. Bawb would be okay, and Griggitz was right. Ghalian did not abandon a mission over injuries, or even death. And this was no exception.

He watched her run, nodding approvingly. She had learned well, he mused. Now to see if she might best Elzina for a change.

# CHAPTER THIRTY-EIGHT

Demelza was a solidly built woman, but she moved with impressive speed when there was a need for it. As a result, Bawb found himself aboard the ship and in flight before he realized what was happening.

She took to the air in a flash, the Drooks powering the ship more than able to provide the power for what would normally be considered excessive speed when in atmosphere. She picked up the ship's skree and called ahead to the healing house, fabricating a story about her nephew falling on a hike and injuring himself.

They were both Wampeh, and the age gap was right. No one would give them a second thought. It was a full-fledged city they were going to be in, but he was just a boy, and no one had a clue that this particular Wampeh was training to be an assassin.

Such a tiny fraction of Wampeh even possessed the innate ability required, let alone were invited to join the order. That meant that of the hundreds of millions of Wampeh spread across the stars, the odds of coming across a Ghalian among them were slim to none.

Demelza swung the ship in low and fast, dropping down to

the landing area closest to the healing house with both speed and precision. Today it would be okay to draw a little bit of attention. With the wounded boy in her care and her rush to seek attention for him, no one would think anything of it.

"Bawb, listen to me," she said as she prepared to guide his floating litter out of the ship. "We will land momentarily and you must follow the story we discussed. Do you remember it? Who I am?"

"You are my aunt Zinnia," he said. "We were hiking, and I fell a long way. Beyond that, I don't remember much."

"Perfect. That will be all you need to say, and only if asked. Ideally, keep your mouth shut and let them do their work."

"I understand," he replied, strangely calm after his brush with death. "Teacher?"

"Yes?"

"Do you know the story of Porrius?"

Demelza didn't flinch, but he noted her gaze grew more focused. "What do you know of that name?"

"I heard rumors in passing of a boy who perished within our home's walls and wondered how it happened."

Her features relaxed slightly. "Curiosity is natural, but this is one topic you should leave well enough alone. Rest. We have arrived. Time to play your part."

Bawb let it go, nodding his understanding and then laying back flat on the litter. Demelza cast the required spell and lifted it, making quick time out of the ship's airlock and through the city streets.

As expected, as soon as the bloodied and injured boy was seen, all interest in the ship that had come in so hot shifted from curiosity about who they were to chatter about seeing an injured child. They were hiding in plain sight, Bawb realized, blending in by being highly visible, as Ghalian often did.

This was turning out to be an impromptu lesson for Bawb whether he wanted it or not.

"Pay attention to the way this facility operates," Demelza instructed as she wove through the crowded streets. "You may be injured, but this is a good opportunity to learn about these places. What skills are used, what sort of patients they treat. All of this may be of use to you one day if you find yourself in need."

"I understand," he said, in pain but not to the point of inability to pay attention to his surroundings.

The building itself was nothing impressive. Low, round, with a domed roof allowing them to utilize natural light if desired, saving every bit of their magic for healing instead. Above the entryway were clear markings declaring its purpose to all.

Demelza pushed the floating litter into the entrance. A slender, wooden-skinned woman with vibrant green leaves for hair saw them come in and walked over to them on jointless but flexible legs. She was plant-based, Bawb realized to his surprise. He had never known such a thing was even possible. But here she was, coming right toward him.

"The boy, he is injured," the woman stated as fact, casting assessment spells as if on autopilot.

"Yes. We were hiking and he took a nasty tumble," Demelza said, her tone shifted from her all business Ghalian self to that of a doting family member who had surely never killed a man, let alone dozens, if not more.

"I'll say. He's broken a number of bones and damaged a few internal organs as well. How high did you fall from?" she asked him.

Bawb glanced over at Demelza, noting her slightest of nods.

"High enough, I guess," he said, cracking a pained little grin.

"Well, I can see you managed to stop much of the bleeding, but he will need far more intensive treatment."

"And that is why I brought him here. I was hoping perhaps

Healer Ashakaa was present. I hear wonderful things about her skills."

"You are in luck. She is on planet this solar cycle. I will summon her at once."

The woman scurried off, leaving the two alone for but a moment before a tall woman with thick black hair that looked like kinked wire, matching the ruggedness of her ash-gray skin, walked in. She looked like she could have been a fighter at one point in her life, but Healer Ashakaa was a master of the healing arts, and of some renown at that.

She strode to the newcomers, a warm smile on her face. "Thank you, Innix. I will see to our guests from here."

The wooden woman nodded once and returned to her duties.

Demelza reached out and shook the woman's hand, pressing her thumb square between two of her knuckles in a manner Bawb had never seen anyone do in a normal handshake. It was rather unnatural, but Ashakaa's expression remained neutral.

"A pleasure to meet you," Demelza said. "We hoped you might be able to help us. My nephew has taken a nasty fall. They say a shepherd is best suited to healing the flock."

She released the woman's hand and stepped back.

Ashakaa nodded slowly as she surveyed the two. "Indeed, that is often the case," she replied. "Come, follow me."

Demelza pushed the litter along, following as Ashakaa led them to a small room and closed the door behind them. She pressed what appeared to be just another spot on the wall. A hidden catch released, the entire wall pivoting aside.

"This way," she urged, leading her guests to the other side.

Bawb watched in amazement as the door closed without a sound, blending back in as if it had never been there. But that wasn't all that took him by surprise. A Ghalian was there, spread out in one of the beds, alive, but suffering from horrible injuries.

Anyone else might have simply taken the older woman as any other Wampeh, but Bawb had seen her before. A master he had not interacted with but knew on sight. A Ghalian, and a terribly wounded one at that.

"Ambushed," Ashakaa said, noting Bawb's stare. "Her contract went awry, and she was forced to face down more enemy than I would like to think about. It will take her a long time to heal fully from this, even with my help. But she is a fighter. I'm sure she will pull through."

"You know what she is?" Bawb marveled.

"I do, yes."

He looked around, concerned.

Ashakaa just smiled and patted his arm. "We are in a secure part of the facility, my young—is he an Aspirant or a Vessel?"

"Aspirant," Demelza replied.

"My young Aspirant. Only the initiated are allowed back here. We may speak freely. You see, the Ghalian fund much of our work, and we are quite grateful for this. Not to mention the fact they protect the innocent and most vulnerable of us. Despite the reputation, I have found your kind to be among the most honor-bound people I've come across. Adding in a strong dislike of injustice and a loathing of slavery, and you have the most misunderstood group of killers the galaxy has ever known. Now, let's get a better look at you and get you on the road to recovery."

She led them farther back toward an empty bed space, passing a pale-yellow-skinned man with long golden hair. He was sleeping, recovering from whatever treatments they had been giving him. Bawb's eyes grew wide at the sight.

"Is that an actual Ootaki?" he marveled. "I had only heard of them."

"Yes, he is."

"What happened to him? And why is he in the back area? Ootaki can't be Ghalian."

"No, they cannot. He was injured during a battle between his owner and another. Both powerful vislas, but with little care for the lives of others. This fellow was about to have his hair harvested to help power his owner's attacks when the enemy ambushed their group. It devolved into something of a mess, I can tell you, and most of the other Ootaki were either killed or taken prisoner. This one, however, managed to escape."

Bawb shifted uncomfortably on his litter to get a better look. "But how is he *here*?"

"Simple. A Ghalian spy was embedded in the victor's forces. They were able to sneak this man away from the site and hand him off to their underground network. And it was they who brought him here. It is tragic irony, really. So many Ootaki killed that day, and so much magic stored in their locks, yet sadly, they could not use any of it to defend themselves. This poor man was groomed. Raised in captivity, unshorn from childhood, his entire life designed to make him the perfect storage vessel. He and his kind are the most valuable among his people for that reason. A horrible trafficking of innocents."

"But why would they do that?"

"You know all of this, Bawb," Demelza interjected. "Let Ashakaa do her work. You are a very resilient, but very injured boy, and I would see you on the path to recovery sooner than later."

"I don't mind," Ashakaa said, guiding him onto his bed. "I can talk and work."

Bawb winced and clenched his teeth as she moved him, but he did not cry out. Even at his relatively young age, he had learned that much from the Ghalian.

"The first cut of Ootaki hair is the most powerful," she continued as she settled him into his bed. "And some people pour magic into their captives for decades, using them as a repository of magic to be drawn from or used as currency at a later time. Of course, the hair loses a lot of power when taken, and even freely given hair will lose some of its magic. But just a single strand of willingly gifted hair can possess a great deal of magic, depending on the donor."

"Just one strand?"

"Just one. That could be enough to block a control collar, as I have seen done in the past. Or power up a konus, or a great many other things," she replied, holding her hands over the injured boy, sensing his wounds. "All right, my young friend, we are ready to begin. This is going to hurt, I am afraid. The injuries you sustained must be mended, and that is never a pleasant sensation."

"I will be fine," he said, displaying admirable, if false, confidence.

"Very well," she said, handing him a leather strap. "You may wish to bite on this in case you find the pain too great. Once I start the process, I cannot stop midway."

"I would recommend listening to her on this," Demelza noted. "I speak from experience. The strap can help somewhat."

He wasn't terribly thrilled with their words of impending agony, but he didn't really have a choice about that. He slid the leather into his mouth and bit down, the smell of the freshly cured hide filling his nose with a surprisingly pleasant aroma.

Demelza nodded to Healer Ashakaa.

"And so it begins."

# CHAPTER THIRTY-NINE

Bawb slept for a day straight after Ashakaa had finished working on him. He had expended so much of his energy stores withstanding the horrible sensation of his bones and tissue knitting back together that he was drenched with sweat by the time she was done. Ashakaa provided him dry, loose clothing while his own garments were laundered, then left him to sleep and restore his energy.

He would be out for the rest of this training session, there was no way around that. But Demelza would test him when they returned to the training house to see if he needed to be held back to complete this bit of training or if he could advance. From what she had seen from him so far, she felt confident he would not require so drastic an action.

When he finally woke a day later, he opened his eyes to an unexpected visitor sitting beside his bed.

"Ah, you are awake. I am glad to see you have mended well."

"Master Hozark?"

"You took quite a fall from what Demelza tells me."

"It was. But the cliffs were the shortest route."

"Down, as well as up, you discovered."

"Most painfully. But it was worth the risk."

"Yes, the competition. I heard. I also heard you were poised to win it."

"Usalla and I were on equal footing. The opportunity was there for either of us."

"Of course, your friend. I understand you came to an arrangement to work together until the final challenge."

"Is that bad?"

"Quite the contrary. It shows you understand the value of maximizing your efficiency, as well as the tactic of forging alliances even with those you are working against. Sometimes, life is not as black and white as people would like it to be, even ours."

Bawb pushed himself up on his bed to a seated position and leaned back against the wall, rolling his shoulders and neck, feeling the formerly broken bones move smoothly as though they had never been damaged.

"How is it you are here?" he finally asked. "Are you helping Teachers Demelza and Griggitz?"

"Oh, no. Nothing of that sort."

"So you were on the planet for other reasons."

"No, but I was close enough."

"You came all this way for *me*?"

"I had business nearby, and when I heard you were injured, I thought it would be a good opportunity to visit Healer Ashakaa's facility. I'm sure you have learned by now that this is a safe place for our kind."

"I have."

"Always remember it. Over time, you will become privy to other secret locations that are welcome safe places for our order."

Bawb nodded his understanding. "It is a marvelous place, and she seems really skilled."

"That she is. But even she could not speed your recovery so much to allow you to rejoin your classmates. It is a shame, your not being able to complete this exercise with them. However, I would not want you to fall behind. You put in an exceptional effort, regardless of the results. I was thinking, perhaps we can salvage a lesson during your downtime."

"You think I can?"

"That depends entirely on you. Stand, Bawb. See how you feel."

Bawb pivoted on the bed and slid up to his feet, swaying a moment as he assessed his healed limbs. They felt good. Better than good, actually. He had mended fantastically. He jumped up and down a few times, feeling his legs absorb the shock easily.

"I feel good."

"Then you are able to participate."

"Participate in what?"

"Get dressed. Your clothes are clean and ready for you. I have a task to complete. Once you are clothed, you will accompany me."

Bawb almost did a double take but managed to keep his shock in check. He was going to get a one-on-one with a Ghalian master on a real mission? And one of the Five, no less? It was unheard of for an Aspirant.

"Master Hozark? There's an Ootaki here," he mentioned as he pulled on his clothes. "I'd never seen one before."

"Yes, they are typically either in captivity or well-hidden in a freehold settlement."

"What is a freehold?"

Despite being in a safe place, Hozark glanced around before answering nevertheless. "A freehold settlement is where we resettle the Ootaki we are able to rescue. We save them from their slavery whenever possible, using our network to transport them to hidden, safe communities located on distant worlds.

Places they will not be hunted, if we are fortunate. Where they can bond and raise families."

"Do they give each other their hair when that happens?"

"They do exchange a strand as part of the bonding ceremony. Ootaki only ever bond with their own kind, akin to Drooks and some other races. But despite receiving the gift of powered hair, they are entirely unable to use Ootaki magic, even that which is given to them."

"That is too bad. It could provide them a lot of comfort, being able to wield that kind of power."

"Yes, it is unfortunate. But at least they have the freedom to bond in safety if they so desire. Of course, we also provide false identities, as well as creating a few unusual, powerful disguises on rare occasion for those who wish to remain on more populated planets while retaining their anonymity."

"And they give you their hair as payment?"

"No, we do this not for payment but to right an injustice that plagues all worlds under the Council of Twenty's rule."

"Oh, I see."

"Though we have, on occasion, been gifted a few locks of hair as thanks, these gifts were freely given of their own accord. Take this dagger," he said, pulling an ornately handled blade from its sheath for Bawb to better see. "This was a gift. Quite a surprise, actually. Given to me by an Ootaki family I had personally saved from a particularly nasty visla working for the Council."

"It's beautiful," Bawb marveled, the detailed yet functional design of the weapon impressive even to his untrained eye.

"Not only beautiful, but powerful," Hozark added. "Each member of the family contributed a strand of hair, freely given and incorporated into the grip. It contains incredibly strong magic, which makes it a valuable tool, but also something quite dangerous if it were to fall into the wrong hands. For that reason, there is a spell woven into the very material of the weapon itself, known only to the Ghalian. One that when activated contains the power to unleash a self-defense mechanism. A safeguard. I will teach the words to you, Bawb."

He was flabbergasted by the offer. "You will?"

"You may be an Aspirant, but you are to become a Ghalian one day. This is the amount of confidence and trust I place in you, Bawb. I fully expect you to succeed in your endeavor. There will be many things you will learn beyond the confines of the training house walls in the coming years. Let today be one such occasion. Come with me."

Hozark led the boy through the hidden chamber, passing a few other beds, nearly all of them empty for the moment. This was a good thing, he said, as this area was typically frequented by those too injured to make it back to a Ghalian house for recovery. Seeing those beds vacant meant their brothers and sisters were doing well. Something they should be grateful for.

He paused at the far wall and gestured to the blank surface.

"What do you see, Bawb?"

"A wall?" he replied, wondering if this was somehow a trick question.

As it turned out, it was.

Hozark uttered a few words and a doorway appeared, and behind it, a long passageway. They stepped inside, the door sealing behind them.

*There is danger!* the konus exclaimed, the sound of fear in its voice ringing through Bawb's head.

Hozark turned to the boy and motioned for him to stay close. "This is a heavily fortified entry and exitway for our use alone. Pay attention to what I do. There are tripwire spells all throughout. I am temporarily deactivating them to allow us to pass. To any not in the order, making their way either into or out of the healing facility this way would prove to be a very unpleasant experience. For those who survived, that is. Not so much for the others. With the power of these spells, they wouldn't feel a thing."

Bawb moved closer to the Ghalian master, barely hearing the whispered words providing them safe passage. He was nervous, but the utter confidence with which Hozark moved inspired him to push aside his fear and follow. It was a decision which soon bore fruit as they stepped out another hidden doorway into a textiles stall in a marketplace.

The door vanished as soon as they passed through. The vendor sitting near the street entrance gave only the slightest of nods as the pale man and boy exited, the pair having never entered from the front in the first place.

They walked right out into a bustling marketplace, but Bawb was less shocked now that he had experienced such a thing back on the training house world. Nevertheless, it was still fascinating seeing so many diverse races all bustling about in the same place. The truly amazing part, however, was Hozark.

As soon as they stepped into the throng, he had become another man entirely. Jovial, smiling, greeting everyone as though they were a friend. And by the look of it, quite a few were, and even those who weren't were still responding with at least a courteous smile at the friendly man's salutations.

He was still one of the deadliest men in the galaxy, and certainly on this planet, but what they saw was not a stoic assassin, but rather a jovial merchant who didn't have an angry bone in his body.

This was Master Hozark's disguise. One of them, anyway. But from what he could gather, it was his most favored one. The one he could slip into at a moment's notice, as he and the other students had been told one day they would do as well.

He watched in awe at the display. Seeing a master at work

like this? Even without dramatic, magical alterations disguising his form, he was an amazing sight to behold.

"Come, my boy," Hozark said, clapping his arm around Bawb's shoulders. "Our ship leaves shortly."

He guided them through the streets with the ease of a man who had spent countless time navigating the city, and in no time at all they arrived at a commercial spaceport. There were all manner of craft available for hire, but Hozark guided them to a mid-sized transport ship.

It was powered by Drooks. Bawb could sense their power when they stepped aboard. It was a subtle thing, but he had found he had a knack for feeling the slight energy leaking off them even at rest.

Hozark led Bawb to a pair of empty seats away from other passengers. "These look fine," he said, flopping down with exaggerated relish. "Ah, it feels good to be off my feet. What a day!"

Bawb slid into the seat beside him, wondering what might come next.

The answer was simple. The ship took off, exited the atmosphere, then jumped to a new system. Immediately, Bawb felt something strange in his gut. His whole body, for that matter. It was unlike anything he'd ever experienced before. He looked at Hozark, wondering if he felt it too, only to find the man watching him with a curious expression.

"It is the sun," the assassin explained. "This system contains a dark sun, and for our kind, the power it radiates is particularly potent. Spend enough time here and you would find yourself feeling quite restored. In fact, I often visit such systems when in need of a boost."

"I thought I was getting sick."

Hozark laughed. "Oh, don't be self-conscious. This is a

lesson best experienced in person. No amount of classroom learning can replace the actual feeling."

He looked around the compartment. All the other passengers were still far from them. None had decided to take a stroll, which served his purpose well.

"You see, Wampeh are already particularly sensitive to the different types of power given off by different suns, and those with the traits necessary to become a Ghalian are even more so. Each variety of sun has its own unique properties, and we, as well as some other races, react to them, powering up casters and even konuses in unexpected ways. Be warned, though. Your spells may not act normally in these conditions. But then, so too will your adversaries find themselves affected. And this can be used not as an obstacle to overcome, but as a tool to use to your advantage. *Always* be aware of the sun and how it affects magic in a system you intend to visit *before* you travel there. It can mean the difference between life and death."

Bawb had questions. A *lot* of questions. But the ship's sudden lurch as it hit the edge of the atmosphere jolted them from his mind as he gripped the seat tightly.

"An inexperienced pilot," Hozark explained. "We should have passed into the atmosphere without feeling a thing. But that is why we got a reduced fare on this ship. Trainees cannot command full price. And for the same reason, we now fly with far fewer passengers aboard."

The ship dropped fast, heading toward a landing field near the center of the city they were approaching. It wasn't a huge place, but neither was it a rustic town. It was large enough for multiple landing sites, and that meant a thriving business in trade. It was likely why Hozark had selected it.

He enjoyed playing a trader, and the disguise afforded him the opportunity to learn much from the loose lips of his comrades in the business. Where there was coin to be had, you could always find a group of the often drunk and always eager interstellar salesmen. And with them, much information could be acquired, if one had the requisite skill.

Hozark most assuredly did.

The ship set down, settling into a gentle hover just above the ground. Passengers were gathering their things and disembarking, but Hozark held back a moment. He leaned in close.

"I have business to attend to, and you are coming with. Watch, but do not speak unless directed to. Learn what you can from this experience."

"What do I say if someone talks to me?"

"Never part from your cover story. I will interject and handle the rest."

"Cover story?"

Hozark grinned wide. "You are not a Ghalian trainee named Bawb. No. You are called Donnik, and you come from a merchant family."

"And you?"

"Today, I am called Alasnib, the trader. Your father, taking you with me to learn the family business."

"My father?"

"Yes, your father," he said, resting his hand on his shoulder. "Do you think you can play this role?"

Bawb felt a swell of pride that this legendary man would afford him this opportunity. And to incorporate him as family into his disguise? It was the highest honor he could imagine.

"I won't let you down," he said, a warm feeling of belonging spreading through his body.

Hozark squeezed his shoulder, his smile wide and bright. "I know you won't, *son*."

# CHAPTER FORTY

Bawb followed close behind Hozark, or Alasnib the trader, as he was currently being called. Apparently, he had quite a few friends in this city. Given his gregarious, outgoing nature, it was little wonder why.

He was loose with coin, happy to buy a drink for a friend if he happened upon one in the street, but equally likely to drink with a new trading partner after engaging in a fair, if not incredibly well-haggled, deal. Alasnib the trader was the kind of man it was hard to envision having any enemies. And it was that absolutely unthreatening air about him that made this the perfect cover.

"Alasnib, you never told me you had a son!" a stocky, deep-purple-skinned trader from a vending stall exclaimed when Hozark stopped by and made the introduction. "All this time and you kept something like that secret?"

"Yakka, my dear friend, you know our business. Trade is sometimes difficult on one's family. More than sometimes, if we're honest about it. That much time spent away, and often in distant systems? It's the kind of thing I wanted to allow him to decide for himself, if he wanted to become involved in when he was old enough."

"And?"

"Well, he's here with me now, isn't he?" Hozark said with a genuinely thrilled smile spread across his face. "To teach my boy the ropes of the trade? What father wouldn't *kill* for that kind of an opportunity?"

"Truer words have never been spoken," Yakka agreed.

"You know it, my friend, and I assume your boys are well?"

"Fantastic, if not a bit stubborn."

"Teenagers will be teenagers, eh? We'll catch up more later, but if you'll excuse us, I want to show him around."

"You mean show him off," Yakka said with a wink. "A fine-looking boy. Quite the resemblance."

"You say that about all Wampeh."

"Yes, but this time I actually mean it."

Hozark laughed deep and loud then put his arm around his son and merrily walked back into the flow of foot traffic, weaving through the crowd with practiced ease.

Bawb was almost giddy with the experience. He was being trained by Hozark himself. The privilege was priceless. And more than that, he was actually having fun. This felt more like an outing than a task, and he was relishing it.

"What do you say, son? You hungry?" Hozark asked with a grin.

"I suppose I am."

"Excellent! There's a tavern not far ahead that has wonderful travelers' meals, and pretty good drink as well. You'll love it."

He led him down a twisting path of roads and alleyways, greeting people and being the exact opposite of what one would expect of a Ghalian. He was the most gregariously visible person on the street, nothing at all like their reputation for impossible stealth. It was no wonder no one gave him a second thought.

"There it is!" he exclaimed in a loud, boisterous voice. "I love this place. C'mon, my boy, you're in for a treat." He leaned in close, embracing the youngster cheerfully while whispering in his ear. "Observe, listen, and learn," he said, then carried on as before, guiding them into the tavern.

Hozark's alter-ego bought food. A *lot* of food. And he bought quite a few drinks as well, not only for themselves, but also for a few familiar faces he spotted in the tavern, his generosity earning friendly waves and the occasional hug from a drunken friend.

Hozark just kept eating, drinking, and having a generally great time. Bawb tried to keep up, but after a few drinks he was starting to feel ill, while Hozark appeared to feel nothing of the sort. In fact, despite drinking many times what the boy had imbibed, the man seemed to be in pretty fair condition, conducting casual trades with his friends and arranging sales, deliveries, and payments in line with his cover identity.

"Your boy?" a red-skinned fellow with short horns and stout legs going by the name Orvit said, eyeing the youth. "I don't see the resemblance."

"That's because you always say that all Wampeh look the same, you bigoted fool," Hozark replied with a laugh.

"I'm not a bigot. I just can't see a difference, is all," he objected. "No offense, Alasnib."

"I'm just messing with you. Of course there's none taken. We've known each other far too long for that, am I right?"

"By the Goddess, that's how I see it. But my apologies for the boy. He's new to all this."

"Well then, you can buy him a drink to make up for it," Hozark said.

Bawb felt his stomach flip at the mere mention of another drink, but he smiled and nodded, playing it off as best he could.

Orvit flagged down the server and put in the order, then turned his attention back to the boy.

"So, what made you decide to join the old man in the trading game, young Donnik?"

"I saw how good my father was at it. I mean, I didn't *see* it, but I heard people talking about him. How Alasnib the trader was a friend to all anywhere in the galaxy. I don't know, it sounded like the kind of man I would want to grow up to be."

Hozark beamed at the words, and Orvit nodded his approval.

"Well said. *Damn* well said. Your boy has a gift for words."

"That he does."

*Level up: Subterfuge* his konus announced in his head.

Orvit let out a loud belch. "Must get it from his father. Donnik, remind me to tell you about the time old Alasnib here negotiated what should have been an impossible deal from some Tslavars."

"Tslavars? But aren't they really brutal?" Bawb asked. "Not good to trade with, I thought."

"Well, your father here got, shall we say, *creative,* with a few perks for them to sweeten the deal. Remind me, Alasnib, what were those delightful ladies' names again?"

Hozark's cheeks darkened as he threw his hands in the air. "Another time, my friend. The boy's still a bit green for that sort of thing."

Bawb was impressed at the Ghalian master's command over his blush reflex. Beyond spells and disguises, he was in complete control of his own body in ways Bawb could hardly imagine himself ever achieving.

Orvit let loose a deep belly laugh and gave the boy he called Donnik an amused slap on the back. "Later, then. But believe me, boy, it's a good story."

Orvit eventually took his leave, only to be replaced by

another after another in a long line of trade partners and acquaintances. Alasnib the trader seemed to know *everyone* in this place, and the drinks were flowing freely.

Finally, after many hours, Hozark rose to his feet, swaying unsteadily from the mass quantities he had imbibed, and said a loud farewell to all of his friends. With that, he led his son outside into the cool evening air. He led the way, weaving a bit as he walked until they rounded the nearby corner. There his demeanor shifted.

Hozark was not drunk. Not one bit.

He pulled Bawb close and pressed his back against the wall. "Breathe. Calm your mind," he instructed.

"How're you shober?" the boy asked with a little slur.

"In a moment. First things first. Who was seated at the table to your left?"

Bawb furrowed his brows a moment and came up empty. "I do not know."

"What about the large man at the door?"

"Whisch one?"

"The one employed by the tavern to keep things from becoming too rowdy."

Again, Bawb struggled to recall. "I don't remember."

"The woman seated behind you? What was her hair color?"

"She was *behind* me."

Hozark shook his head. "A Ghalian is *always* aware of his surroundings and who is in them."

"But we drank sooo musch."

"*You* did," he replied with an amused little grin. "And clearly you feel the effects of alcohol. A Ghalian must not become incapacitated. And now you understand what it truly is to be inebriated. To not be in complete control of your body. Of your mind."

"It's weird. I feel, I dunno... *fuzzy*."

"And in combat that can be the difference between life and death. But there is a way around that. Come. Let me show you something."

Hozark led the way down the street then turned into an alleyway. They weren't terribly far from the tavern as the crow flies, but the walk took them out of the line of sight and then some. Hozark pointed at a large puddle splashed across the ground. It reeked of alcohol so strongly Bawb almost gagged at the thought of another drink.

"Alcohol?" he marveled. "Where did that come from?"

"That, my boy, is what I drank. Or what it *appeared* I drank."

"I don't understand," Bawb said, his head pounding behind his aching eyes.

"It is a very specialized spell, Bawb. One that I will teach you."

"What sort of spell makes alcohol on a street?"

"The sort that allows you to drink endlessly and not become intoxicated. That was all an act. This spell takes what you swallow and deposits it a distance from your location. In this instance, this alleyway. This little trick is very helpful in times you have to drink much alcohol, or, on worse days, if you have to seem to be drinking poison to fool a would-be killer."

"It can let you drink poison?"

"You don't actually drink it. Once it enters your mouth the spell immediately deposits it elsewhere. Not a drop touches your tongue. This is a very advanced spell, Bawb. One that you normally would not learn for many years. But you handled yourself well in there, and I believe you are ready for it. However there is one very important caveat."

"What's that?"

"You must only practice this spell when you are by yourself. And I recommend using non-alcoholic liquids. As I said, this spell is far above what Aspirants learn, and you are sure to fail a great many times. One day, however, it *will* work."

Hozark took a moment, ensuring Bawb was steady on his feet, then instructed him in the casting of the spell. It was a subtle thing but of great power. As such, he would be required to cast without seeming to speak or move his lips. The quietest of casting but with deeply forceful intent.

Bawb repeated the words several times, trying to imagine something entering his mouth but going somewhere else. There was no tingle of magic and no sensation on his tongue, but his konus abruptly flashed to life, a new, blurred-out icon pulsing slowly.

"Konus, what is that?" he asked silently.

*You're attempting a spell far above your level.*

"And? Why's it all blurry?"

*One might say that's because you drank too much, fool. But no. In this case, it is simply because you are, frankly, terrible at it. You have a* lot *to learn before this spell will work for you.*

"Wonderful," he grumbled.

"What was that?" Hozark asked.

"Nothing. Just I think it's wonderful you're teaching me this."

He wanted to ask more. Why Hozark, one of the Five, would help him like this. But drunk as he was, he was aware enough to realize that was the sort of question that could end the aforementioned assistance if unartfully phrased.

He kept his mouth shut. At least, until he threw up a little.

Hozark handed him a small vial and a clean cloth from his pocket, as if he had been expecting this to happen. "Here," he said, handing him the cloth. "Clean yourself up, then drink this."

"What is it?" Bawb asked, wiping the sick from his lips.

"A little something I whipped up. It will reverse the effects of alcohol."

"Really?"

"Of course."

"Then why would I need that spell?"

"Because, you will not always have the ingredients to concoct the elixir, but magic will be with you at all times, so long as you have a konus. Now drink. Tomorrow is a busy day and you will need a clear head."

Bawb took the vial and popped the top open. The smell was quite pleasant. Almost appetizing, even. He downed it in a single gulp.

"That's not so ba—" he began to say before vomiting violently, every last drop of alcohol being sucked from his body and expelled out of his mouth.

Bawb hacked and coughed, doubled over, his hands resting on his wobbly knees. Finally, he stood up straight, stone-cold sober and a fair deal paler than even his normal Wampeh complexion. He looked at Hozark with a perturbed expression in spite of his best efforts not to.

"What seems to be the problem, Bawb?"

"That was horrible."

"I did not say that it would be pleasant. Only that it would remove the effects of alcohol from your system."

"Yes, but by violently pulling it out."

"Well, there is that," Hozark said with an amused chuckle. "The worst is over, so straighten up and follow me."

"Where are we heading now?"

"You will see."

They walked a few blocks over and took the lift disc to the top floor of a mid-height building. Hozark unlocked a secure door and led the way to the rooftop.

"What are we doing up here?" Bawb asked.

A little grin crept onto Hozark's lips. "We took public

transport to get here, but I think we can utilize my personal craft for the return."

He cast his spell quietly, as was his way, almost silently to any not directly beside him. A split-second later his shimmer ship's entry hatch, and the area directly around it, appeared, the shimmer spell fading away in an instant. Bawb was stunned. He had seen shimmer ships, yes. He'd even been in one. But to have an entire craft hidden in plain sight in the middle of town, and on a rooftop rather than a landing site, no less, well, it was rather amazing.

Hozark opened the door then re-cast the shimmer spell, only the opening remaining visible.

"Come," he said. "Time to depart."

Hozark stepped aboard, Bawb close behind, then sealed the door, the entire craft vanishing from sight entirely. He took a seat in the command chair and gestured for Bawb to take the seat next to him.

"Observe and learn," he said, then cast the spells to activate his Drookonus and lift off into the air.

Bawb watched, absorbing every detail in awe, thanking his good fortune for this incredible opportunity to learn from this master. Little did he know, there was more to come.

# CHAPTER FORTY-ONE

"It will just be a little detour. Nothing to worry about, I assure you. In fact, you might find it interesting," Hozark said as they exited their jump, activating the ship's shimmer spell immediately.

Bawb wasn't so sure about that, but he was hopeful. Hozark's last impromptu lesson had left his stomach sour and aching. He quietly prayed this would not be a repeat. Then he practiced the words to the spell he had been taught, just in case.

*Oh, definitely not. You are nowhere near ready,* the konus told him with a chuckle.

"What if I need it? I do not think my stomach can handle another round of drinks."

*Then you'll have to think of something else, because that spell? Not happening.*

"Aren't you supposed to be helping me? Powering my spells and all that sort of thing?"

*I power them, yes. I contain a vast quantity of magic, as a matter of fact. But you are not yet at a sufficient level of proficiency to tap into it. In fact, the rate you're going, I wonder if you ever will be.*

"Your vote of confidence is appreciated," the boy replied sarcastically.

He looked out the window as Hozark steered the shimmer ship toward their destination. They had jumped to a relatively unimpressive star system with only a few planets orbiting their sun, none of them habitable. One of the moons belonging to a gas giant, however, apparently was.

Hozark guided them closer, navigating his way through an asteroid field before making his final approach.

"The asteroids are just one more deterrent to keep this place undetected. With no planets of note, and a sun of only medium power, this system is a perfect place to avoid scrutiny."

He dropped into the exosphere, the shimmer spell barely holding up as he did. Most could not maintain it through atmospheric entry, but Hozark was not most people. Despite the effort required, he looked calm, and the ship did not so much as shudder as they popped into the moon's clear air.

He flew low, giving Bawb a tour of the lush surface of the little moon. It was a wet world, with ample water to support a vibrant ecosystem. Green and burgundy plant life grew everywhere, and herds of what appeared to be some sort of herbivorous animals roamed freely. It was an idyllic setting, made even more so by the utter lack of the ugly marks of civilization scarring the surface.

Hozark shifted course and headed toward what looked like a barren marsh area. On a world like this, Bawb had to wonder why he would choose to go there of all places. It was only when they were right upon it that he cast a powerful reveal spell, parting the illusion in front of them wide enough to pass through like opening curtains to another world.

They flew in through the gap, the illusion closing behind them. Bawb's eyes widened, awed by what he was seeing.

It was a pristine, beautiful valley, its rivers and natural hot springs running through the verdant landscape. Crops were laid out in neat rows, tended by hand and not industry. They flew on, arriving at a small town. From the air, it looked much smaller than any he had ever visited in his limited experience, but despite that, there was something unusual about it to his eyes.

"The Ghalian have established this as a refuge," Hozark said. "Powerful magic to keep it hidden by any prying eyes who might stumble upon this moon. And if someone did, they would still have to set down right beside the cover spell to detect it. Given the nature of the system, it is unlikely, but the Council of Twenty has been known to be rather persistent in their pursuits."

"Pursuit of what?"

"You will see," he replied, settling the ship down in the town's small landing zone.

Bawb followed Hozark off the ship, noticing that the deadly assassin seemed truly at ease here. He was always aware of his surroundings, of course, but he possessed an air of calm the likes of which Bawb had never seen on him. A moment later he realized why.

"Hozark! It is wonderful to see you, my friend!" exclaimed a tall man with golden hair so long it wrapped around his waist.

"Porticious, it has been too long," he replied, embracing him warmly. "How is the family?"

"Well, Zakkina will be thrilled to hear you are joining us. Gorrin is a teenager now; can you believe it?"

"Hardly. It is difficult to believe how he has grown."

"Indeed. But there is more."

"More?"

"Zakkina will show you." Porticious looked at the young Wampeh standing behind his friend. "And who is this?"

"This is Bawb. An Aspirant of the order, and a rather talented one at that."

The man embraced him just as he had Hozark. "Bawb, any

friend of Hozark's is a friend of ours. Welcome to our humble township."

"Thank you," the boy replied. "It is a lovely place."

"Isn't it, though? We are blessed. And it is all thanks to Hozark's hard work."

"There were others involved," the Ghalian noted.

"Yes, but it was you who put the plan into action, and we are all forever in your debt."

It was then that Bawb realized what it was about this place that felt so strange. What had unsettled him without realizing why.

Everyone here was the same. There were no mixed races. No settlers or travelers or traders from far-off worlds. Just a homogeneous society down to the last of them.

And they were all Ootaki.

This was a Ghalian safe zone, he realized. A place where freed Ootaki could live their lives without fear of capture and abuse. A place where their magic-storing hair was worth nothing, as they all possessed it, and none could use it. It was an Eden for their oppressed people.

"You must come join us for dinner," Porticious said. "I will tell the elders you are here. I am sure they will arrange a feast worthy of your visit."

"Please, my friend, do not make a fuss. I merely came to see how you and your family were adjusting to life here. I know the transition can be difficult for some."

"It can be, yes, but that we found it was more so for Gorrin than for my mate and I. He is of that age, and all he had known was suddenly different. For the better, by far, but it can still be unsettling for someone going through the change into adulthood. But he is quite well now, acclimated and happy, which is all any father could ask for."

"I am glad to hear it. I see there are a few familiar faces to visit, but for dinner, what do you say we keep this reunion smaller in scale this evening? Just your family and mine."

"Family, you say?" the Ootaki inquired, a curious look in his eye.

Bawb piped up. "We were just playing father and son on an intelligence-gathering mission."

"Ah. That makes sense. For a moment there I was quite confused. Ghalian do not bond."

"I should have been clearer, my friend. But come. Let us visit Zakkina and the boy. It will be wonderful to see them."

Porticious was more than happy to oblige. He owed this man his freedom, and his friendship meant the world. And as they walked and talked, Bawb noticed that Hozark's air lacked any trace of an act. He seemed genuinely engaged, happy to see this man and his family. It was a side of the Ghalian he didn't think existed. But here, in this moment, Hozark was, for a short while, at least, completely at ease.

They walked to a cozy house with a beautiful garden surrounding it and stepped onto the entry path. No one was crowded together here. This community was spacious enough for all to enjoy the pleasure of nature around their residences, no need to jam them close to one another. Compared to big cities, it was a truly refreshing change of scenery.

Their host led them into the warmly lit abode. A tall, skinny boy with waist-length golden hair was playing on a reed pipe. He stopped abruptly when they came in, rushing to Hozark and giving him a big hug.

"Hozark! You came to see us!"

"That I did," he replied with a genuine smile. "Allow me to introduce you to an Aspirant in the order. Bawb, this is Gorrin," he said.

"Great to meet you!" the Ootaki chirped.

"It is a pleasure to meet you as well."

"Is that visitors I hear?" a woman's voice called from an adjacent room.

"It is, love. Hozark and a friend have come to visit. I invited them to stay for dinner. I'm sure you don't mind."

"Mind? How could I ever?" she said, walking into the room. "Hozark, it is so good to see you."

She hugged him hard, but from an awkward position she had no choice but to assume. The surprise Porticious had spoken of was clear to see.

She was quite pregnant.

"Congratulations! I am thrilled for you both! But I must admit, this is tangible evidence I have been too long between visits."

"Nonsense," she said, her cheeks glowing with joy. "You are a busy man, and we do not expect you to put aside your regular duties over so trivial a thing as visiting us."

"You are not trivial."

"You know what I mean. Even if it is many cycles between visits, you will always be our most dear friend."

"I am flattered."

Zakkina looked at the young Wampeh at his side. "Hello, I am Zakkina."

"I am Bawb."

"Bawb. A good name, and a pleasure to meet you. Are you enjoying our home thus far?"

"It is a beautiful place. Honestly, I've never seen anything quite like it."

"Nor I until Hozark brought us here. Did he tell you how he rescued us from a Council depot, taking out their entire complement of guards single-handedly?"

Bawb glanced at the Master Ghalian, a little surprised by the tale of his impressive prowess. "No, he did not."

"We would not be free if not for him. We owe him

everything." She glanced at her mate. He nodded, a smile on his lips. "Hozark, with your permission, if our child is a boy, we would name him after you."

A hint of color crept to the stoic man's cheeks, and Bawb had to wonder if it was truly genuine this time.

"It would be an honor. And if it is a girl? Hozark is not a terribly feminine name."

"Perhaps Hozarka?" Porticious suggested.

"Dearest, that is a strange-sounding name," Zakkina said with a chuckle.

"Yes, I suppose it is."

"But we will keep the H in your honor. Perhaps Hoza? No, that's still not quite it."

Porticious laughed and kissed her on the head. "I will leave you to ponder for now. I know there are others who would like to see our guest."

"You go on then. Just be back for dinner. We have much to catch up on with our friend."

"As you wish."

Porticious walked to the door. "Gorrin, help your mother."

"She doesn't need my help thinking of a name."

He chuckled and ruffled his son's long golden hair. "You know what I mean."

"Okay. I'll help with dinner," he replied, heading to the kitchen to join her while his father and their guests stepped out into the fresh air. "Hey, Ma, how about Hunze?" he suggested as he washed his hands.

"Hm. Hunze. Perhaps. I've always liked that name," she replied. "Now come along and help me wash the vegetables."

Bawb was the last out, closing the door behind him as they headed off to greet the excited throng who had gathered when they heard Hozark had come to visit. It was a whirlwind of something he had not experienced much in his Ghalian training. Namely, unabashed joy and cheer. Where the Ghalian were trained to be stoic, these Ootaki were free and open with their emotions, and the happiness they expressed at Hozark's visit was almost contagious.

These people did not see one of the deadliest assassins in the galaxy. They only saw their friend. It was an eye-opener for the young Aspirant, to say the least.

They spent several hours making the rounds, Hozark introducing Bawb to every single person they encountered. He had an incredible memory, recalling names and faces as well as seemingly trivial details about each of their lives. Hozark had invested a lot of himself into saving these people, and the longer they were among them the more it showed.

Finally, after a long day and a delightful dinner, they declined the generous offer to stay the night and took their leave. As they lifted off into the night sky Bawb turned to his mentor, watching him masterfully guide the ship out of the atmosphere without so much as a bump.

"Master Hozark?"

"Yes, Bawb?"

"Why is it the Ghalian have gone to such lengths to protect the Ootaki? I mean, I understand you are keeping them from the hands of an enemy, and surely denying them the ability to harvest the power they had stored in their hair, but it seems against the Ghalian reputation."

"You know our feelings on slavery."

"Yes, that it is abhorrent, but it is something that happens in most conflicts."

"And you also know, then, that taking prisoners of war is commonplace, and willing combatants should expect as much. But innocents? The Council of Twenty's support of—no, their *active advancement*—of the slavery of people such as the Ootaki to expand their sphere of control is something the Ghalian do not abide, and this aggression will not stand."

"But what about the others whose power is taken. Like the Drooks?"

"They often prefer a life of service as their powers provide them a degree of comfort and a sense of belonging, even if they are technically enslaved. But you know of the freed Drooks."

"Yes, we flew with some on one occasion."

"Well, there are others out there, not many, but still far more than people would expect. Drooks we have freed and supplied their own ships."

"I thought that wasn't legal."

"We position a figurehead captain in place to keep them safe, and they are well paid for their efforts. But yes, the Drooks are the real parties in charge. It has proven a beneficial and very lucrative venture for them as well. So much so that they gladly provide us with powerful Drookonuses to power our ships as thanks. So you see, my boy, the Ghalian, while killers, are not defined by that alone."

With that he jumped the ship, Bawb paying close attention, learning all he could, his mind flooded with new information and his world view turned just a bit upside down.

# CHAPTER FORTY-TWO

Hozark's shimmer ship crossed the empty space between systems in the blink of an eye, his jump executed with the finesse of a man who had done the same in far more difficult situations. Simply getting from Point A to Point B was a cakewalk.

Alone, with no other classmates to distract him, Bawb was finally afforded the opportunity to look at the system he had been calling home for these past years. It was something he took for granted, living on a habitable world that was just the right distance from the sun to keep him from roasting alive or freezing to death, but he didn't know much else about it.

At least, that was what he told Hozark.

"It is amazing," he said, staring out of the empty space where the force spell created a window. "I have been wondering about this solar system we live in. The others have as well, but we have so far only taken a few trips off world, and on those, we jumped as soon as we hit space. There really was no chance to properly look around."

Hozark gave a little nod from his pilot's seat. "And what,

exactly, is it you wish to ask, Bawb? Be direct. You can always be direct with me."

"I was hoping to see more of what lies around our planet. What is in this system."

Hozark mimed looking around over both shoulders then leaned toward him and spoke with a conspiratorial whisper. "I think I can manage that," he said, a little grin on his lips. "But do not tell the others. There must be no appearance of favoritism."

"Of course."

"Very well, then. Let us get you home the *long* way."

Hozark altered course, taking the boy on an impromptu tour of the planets and moons of the system. Bawb reacted as one might expect. Namely, he was in awe as his tour guide showed him all eight planets in the system, each incredibly different from the next.

Bawb was fascinated by the function of interplanetary trade and asked endless questions about each world they passed. How big it was, how many people lived on it, if any, what sort of cities they had, and if they lay on any trade routes.

Hozark was pleased the boy was taking such an interest in more than just the basic details of the worlds. He wanted to know more. A hungry mind. And among the Wampeh Ghalian, a hungry mind would always be fed.

By the time they were close to wrapping up their little tour, Bawb knew more about the system and its internal trade, social networks, and governance, than many adults who had lived their whole lives there. The shimmer ship continued on, finishing their weaving loop of the worlds with the enormous showstoppers.

The two gas giants they were visiting last were Bawb's clear favorites, the slowly swirling mists creating dazzling displays of nature's strength. The boy watched them in awe, marveling aloud at the sheer power they must contain.

"How many moons do they have?" he asked. "There are so many."

"Dorus, which is the green-blue planet there, has one hundred fifty-three moons."

"Are any of them inhabitable?"

"Actually, twelve of them are."

"Amazing. What about the other one?"

"That planet is called Mitz. I know, not a terribly creative name, but it was given to it long before you or I were born."

"It is beautiful."

"Yes, it is. Also quite deadly. To take but one breath would be certain death. That is, if the pummeling winds did not smash your vessel to bits against the rocks contained within."

"There are rocks? It just looks like huge clouds."

"Looks can be deceiving. Just out of view are millions of small rocks tossed about in the wind. Maybe more than that. It is a rather enormous planet, after all."

"It looks like it has far fewer moons."

"Only five," Hozark replied. "Which is likely accounting for the quantity of rocks I mentioned. There were others in the past, but the planet slowly pulled them closer, dragging them out of orbit and devouring them, pulling them apart."

"So, no one lives on the ones still there?"

"Not major cities, but some do take refuge on the largest of them. It has a breathable atmosphere, though the soil is not suitable for farming and the water is quite limited."

"What is that one called?"

"Kardahn, though locals call it the Rock."

"The Rock. I suppose I can see why."

"It is not the most inviting of landscapes, but it is beautiful in its own way," Hozark mused. "And an interesting place to visit. One day soon, you and your cohort will find out for yourselves. But for now, we need to get you home."

"Thank you so much for taking the time to show me all of this. It has truly been a wonderful learning experience."

"I am pleased you have taken so much from this outing. Not all pay as close attention as you, even among the higher classes."

"I just wish to learn."

"Clearly. And now you will continue to do so back in the training house."

Hozark shifted their course back to the glowing marble in the sky with blues and greens visible even from this distance. The world Bawb now called home.

"Master Hozark?"

"Yes, Bawb?"

"You told me of the trade routes between worlds and planets, and we have seen a few ships in the distance, but I was wondering. What about pirates? I have heard talk that they can be a problem."

"In other systems, that is true. Pirates will always look for targets of opportunity. It is why you saw the cargo vessels traveling in groups for protection. But while many think there is safety in numbers, it also creates the opportunity to sneak in among them in their overconfidence."

"Really?"

"It requires skill and resolve, but it can be done, most definitely."

"So the pirates just sneak in?"

"Not typically. They most often employ more of a swarm-and-distract type of attack, utilizing many smaller ships to cause their target to miss the craft actually breaching their hull."

"And they go where they please?"

"Sometimes. Here, in this system, they tend to stay on Kardahn."

"The Rock?"

"The very same."

"But why?"

"That, my boy, is a complicated story. Let us just say that on Kardahn they can enjoy what the moon has to offer without the risk of upsetting people they should not."

"Like the Ghalian?"

Hozark chuckled. "Among others. Some do still venture out and commit small crimes, but in this system, it is fairly well known to all that drawing the attention of the Council of Twenty through foolish acts, be they violent or otherwise, will be met with a harsh reply from the other citizens. No one wishes for that sort of scrutiny to be brought upon them. And any who cause it? Well, let us just say they will have some significant problems on their hands."

"So Bud and Henni might stay on the Rock?"

"They could, but they are friends of the Ghalian and have no such need when our hospitality awaits in a far more pleasant environment."

"I can understand that. When I first met them they were talking about this other pirate, some woman they used to fly with. It sounds like she would be the sort to stay on the Rock."

"Nixxa," Hozark said, shaking his head. "A talented woman, but more trouble than she is worth. But she does not know of the Ghalian training house. Even if she did, and were to be granted access by some miracle, she would still choose Kardahn. They are more her sort of company."

"I see. Thank you for clarifying, Master Hozark."

"It is my pleasure, Aspirant Bawb."

The boy sat quietly as they flew the short distance to the landing site nearest home. He seemed to be pondering all he had seen and learned in his time with Hozark, and who wouldn't? But what could not be known was that something else that was brewing in his mind.

If she was still in the system, he now knew where Nixxa

would be. Where the stolen Drookonus could be found. Now he just had to figure out how in the world he would ever get there, let alone sneak onto her ship and steal it back. And all of that before she left for new adventures.

The clock was ticking, but he was at a loss for how to proceed. Bawb was, however, confident in one thing. He would find a way. Whatever it took.

# CHAPTER FORTY-THREE

Bawb's mind was churning from all he had learned during his time with Hozark, and once he had been returned to his group, it did not slow down. Not one bit. He had been going through the motions for years, progressing, but because it was what was expected of him, not much more.

But now he felt something new. He felt inspired. And if anything, his newfound sense of purpose only strengthened.

He knew where Nixxa was. Knew she was in the system and what moon she was on. But he still lacked the means to get to her, and as a lowly Aspirant, he couldn't just go leaving the training house whenever he pleased. He had the faintest beginnings of a plan, but there were so many obstacles to it that even in his exuberance, he found himself wondering if he was being irrational.

He had spent all of their short lunch break mulling it over in his head when they were abruptly interrupted.

"Drop your food and meet in the corridor," Teacher Rovos commanded. "Do not delay."

Albinius rolled his eyes and looked at his classmates with a sigh. "But we only just began—"

"You eat when you complete the task, no matter how long that may take. Ghalian do not have the luxury of casual meals whenever we wish."

The boy groaned and rose to his feet with the others. "Here we go again."

By this point, Rovos had pulled this little stunt enough times that the Aspirants were hip to his game. He would find them at rest or when their guard was down, then drag them off to run to the training dungeon for another session. It seemed to be at random, and for all they knew, it was. The only constant was the ever-shifting order of obstacles and the long run to get to the entry point.

The students gathered in the corridor as told and, to no one's surprise, were given their task.

"Time to train in the obstacle dungeon," their teacher said. "Today, there is a prize at the end."

"Is it a blade?" Elzina asked, anxious to add another to her collection.

"No," he said, to her disappointment. "At the end, the winner will claim a small bag of holding, capable of containing several times its apparent volume. Perfect for making a lot of coin seem like a little."

"That doesn't seem terribly useful," Albinius noted.

"To an Aspirant, perhaps not. But one day, and possibly sooner than you expect, you will be out in the real world, and flaunting your coin is a sure way to draw unwanted attention. Diminishing the appearance of it while keeping a large amount on your body is a tried-and-true Ghalian tactic. One that one of you will be able to begin learning ahead of the others." He sized up the students, all of them ready to go by the look of them. "Well? What are you waiting for? You know the way. I want you to run the dungeon three times each. Go!"

The Aspirants took off at a jog, heading for the nearest

staircase to the lower levels, where the long tunnel and cavern system leading to the dungeon maze was located. No one ran. There was no point. It would take hours to get there, and wearing oneself out in the approach would be foolhardy. The dungeon was more than enough to leave one exhausted.

The group reached the lower level and headed to the secret passageway entrance, filing in one after another. Bawb and Usalla were taking up the rear, in no hurry, especially having just eaten at least a bit of their lunch. No one wanted to feel nauseated, and a hard run right now would definitely do the trick.

"I bet Teacher Pallik is already there," Usalla said. "I still do not know how they always get there before us."

Bawb hesitated as they entered the tunnel, her words triggering a thought.

"What is it?" Usalla asked.

"Give me a moment."

He stood there, looking at the walls, the stone and wood and metal, along with the markings made long ago. They had made this trek many times, but today, something clicked into place in his mind.

It was the markings.

With more time in the dungeon and the long underground path leading to it, he had seen and noted all sorts of markings and runes. They were interesting but appeared to be of no use. But now, having taken codebreaking and deciphering classes, something stood out. A pattern he had simply not seen before, though it was right there in front of his eyes.

"What are you doing?"

Bawb walked to the wall and felt the surface around the symbol. "I have seen a variation of this at the dungeon entrance. I did not previously realize it was the same design, but it is. The same but hidden in a far more complex pattern."

"And? What does that mean?"

"It means," he said, pressing on a panel that looked just like all the others, save a tiny mark on it that could have passed for a scuff if not thoroughly examined, "that this should be—"

The wall silently slid open, revealing a clean, straight tunnel, well-lit and obstacle free.

"How did you know this passageway would be there? What is it?" she asked.

"This, if I am not mistaken, is how the teachers arrive there before us. A direct route that bypasses all the twists, turns, and assorted obstacles along the way. And as to how I knew it would be there, I did not. But haven't you wondered how many more hidden chambers might exist within these training house grounds? The teachers seem to keep revealing more to us just as we think we know them all. And on top of that, it struck me that the symbol on the wall was familiar. And what you said about them arriving there before us, well, it all just sort of clicked into place."

*Level up: Puzzle reading and magical sight,* the konus announced.

"So what do we do now?"

"Now? We take it. Come on!"

Elzina and the other Aspirants arrived at the dungeon entrance many hours later, winded but having conserved enough energy to speed run the dungeon if they were lucky enough to draw the easier of the obstacles.

What they found was Bawb and Usalla sitting against the wall, casually chatting, Bawb tossing the bag of holding from hand to hand. Elzina was not amused.

"That is the prize!"

"It is," Bawb replied with a calm grin.

"How did you get it?" Elzina demanded. "And how did you

get ahead of us? You were at the rear, and I know you did not pass me."

"All of those things are true," he said. "But we really should talk about that later. You do have to run the dungeon, after all."

Elzina glared at him but turned for the entrance, fuming at being one-upped.

"Oh, and do not forget, Teacher Rovos said to do so three times. We have already completed ours," Usalla added, her expression neutral but her eyes showing she was laughing on the inside.

"See you at dinner," Bawb said, managing to contain his mirth until his nemesis and the other Aspirants had entered the dungeon and begun their first of three run-throughs.

"That would have been worth it, even if there was no prize," he said with a wide grin.

"The look on her face."

"I know. I'm sure it will come back at us eventually. That is just how she is. But for today? For this moment? Absolutely worth it."

Rovos and Pallik emerged from the dungeon entrance where they had been observing the others' progress and sized up the two students.

"I see one of you figured it out," Rovos said. "Which one of you was it?"

"It was Bawb," Usalla replied. "He found the shortcut tunnel."

Rovos and Pallik both gave him a little nod. "Well done, Aspirant Bawb. And how did you find the entry mechanism?"

"It was the markings on the wall," he replied. "I'd seen similar ones elsewhere, but something Usalla said made me stop and look again. And suddenly they just made sense."

"That is how it is," Pallik said. "Once you absorb the lessons and truly integrate them into your daily life, you will see things without having to look for them. It will become second nature."

"So, we will all become proficient in puzzle and riddle solving?" Bawb asked.

Pallik looked at Rovos, sharing an amused glance. "Oh, far more than that. So much more. You have only just begun."

Bawb felt a little glow of warmth in his chest as he soaked up their praise. For the first time since he had arrived among the Ghalian, he could actually see this as more than just a profession he had been forced into. In fact, this was something he might grow to be quite good at, and that flare of hope inspired him to want to do even more.

All he needed now was the right opportunity.

# CHAPTER FORTY-FOUR

After dinner, Bawb decided to spend his rare free time walking the grounds of their expansive home. His spirits were high after his success, and it got him thinking.

"Konus, do you think there are many more hidden doors the teachers have been keeping from us?"

*That seems like a stupidly obvious question, wouldn't you agree?*

"I guess. But I have to wonder..."

*I know what you're thinking, and let me tell you, there's no way a mere Aspirant could hope to sniff out what the Masters don't want you to find.*

"Maybe, but then again—"

*Maybe not? You're predictable, you know. And you're going to fail miserably. But since you seem set on this idiotic waste of time, I suppose you might as well get on with it.*

"I think I will," the boy replied, setting off for the subterranean level just beneath them.

It was there he would have a bit of alone time at this hour. After dining, unless the teachers had some new sort of misery to inflict, the others would be relaxing in one of the upper common areas. Bawb had a rare chance to walk the corridors and chambers alone.

He started off with a quick descent of the curving stone stairwell nearest his location. There were others spread around the compound, but this one was closest. It was also one of his favorites. It may have been silly, his reason why, but the way the stone handrail had worn to a high polish over centuries of use as it spiraled downward appealed to him on a core level. An appreciation of the little details others might overlook that would one day be just one of the myriad instinctive traits that made him so skilled at his profession.

Bawb examined the walls, looking for hints of markings, be they seams or hidden runes. Anything to tell him this was the site of something different. He walked for over an hour, taking his time, running his fingers over the areas he suspected might hold some secrets hidden by the Masters. One even had the slightest trace of airflow trickling out from a crack. But try as he might, Bawb could not for the life of him figure out how to open it.

*I told you,* the konus said, self-satisfied and amused.

"But you felt it too, didn't you? That has to be a doorway."

*And if you can't open it? It might as well be a solid wall.*

Bawb was about to fire off a snarky reply when he caught a glimpse of a boy. Or was it a flicker of blue light? It was just an instant, and out of the corner of his eye, but Bawb knew he saw it. And the pale blue light had entered the stairwell. But unlike his previous encounters, a faint glow remained, though it was growing dimmer by the second.

He moved at once, pursuing it into the stairwell, spiraling down and down, the light always just out of sight, until its glow shifted course, exiting on subterranean level four. Bawb stepped out into the corridor in a rush, but the light was gone.

Bawb's gut told him something was there, but what was

anyone's guess. His teachers had noted h possessed some rudimentary skills one might find in a reader or empath. Maybe that was all this was, simply picking up on something he had no way of understanding. He drew the dagger on his hip and felt the edge. It was sharp and ready, but having the weapon did not put his mind at ease. The feeling in his gut was almost like an adrenaline surge, but also not. Like he was feeling someone else's energy and not his own.

But he knew for certain he was alone.

Or was he?

Bawb walked and walked, covering a great deal of the fourth subterranean level's corridors and the peripheral chambers he could access. He looked for signs, anything out of the ordinary, but found nothing. Whatever secrets were here, they were apparently beyond his skills to discern, and while he could visit these chambers alone, to delve into the interconnected tunnels on his own would be a foolish endeavor. Some could take all day to traverse, as he well knew.

Even so, he re-checked corridors and chambers as he walked back to the stairwell he'd used to access this level. But it seemed the deeper he went under their home, the more hidden the compound's secrets were.

*Finally done, thank the gods,* the konus griped. *You need to get back and get some sleep. Do you realize how long you've been at this?*

In truth, Bawb didn't. He'd lost track of time on his quest, immersed in the impromptu adventure. But now that he'd given up and was heading back, he felt the telltale exhaustion that always seemed to set in at the very end of the day. It was bedtime, and that was where he was headed. His body had other ideas. Namely, one thing he always did at about this time.

Fortunately, there was a small restroom chamber located near the stairwell, and it was there he headed for his pre-bedtime visit. Bawb relieved himself, his mind wandering to thoughts of his soft pillow as he washed his hands. Suddenly, the hair on the back of his neck stood up on end. He froze in place for but a second, then spun, his dagger ready in his damp hand.

There was nothing there. Or there *seemed* to be nothing there. But that tug in his gut had returned.

Bawb remained still, ready, ears listening for any sound of danger for nearly a full minute. None appeared.

"There is *something*," he mused, reaching out with his instincts rather than his eyes and ears. The konus, amazingly, didn't contradict him.

Bawb let the sensation guide him. The wall that had been behind him as he washed up, that was where it was coming from. But search as he might, he could find no sign of anything. The stones fit together with the characteristic precision of the rest of the chambers, and there was no sign of scraping or disturbance of the slight layer of dust on the floor nearest it. But he felt it. Something was there.

Bawb stepped back and unfocused his eyes, staring at one spot on the wall, letting the rest fade into a blur. It was only then that he saw it. The faintest of hints of the outline of an irregular-shaped door. One that, given the years upon years of minor settling of the stones, had not been opened in ages. He reached out as best he could with his senses, touching the hidden magic protecting the entryway.

"There's a door," he confirmed. "But it feels, I don't know, exactly. Warded, maybe? Locked? Somehow, it's sealed up tight."

*Which means you should leave it alone. Oh, damn, I know what you're planning, and for the record, I don't think it's a good—*

"*Pallus Orvix Imanna Rommus,*" Bawb recited, casting the odd words with the intent of unlocking the strange wards holding the door shut. It had dawned on him that if Porrius had figured out how to open it, the notes he had found could hold the key.

But the wall remained just as he found it, sealed up tight.

"I really thought that might work."

*Clearly not. Now, can we please get out of here?*

"No. I'm thinking."

Bawb stood there, pondering what had happened to Porrius. The boy had been studying fighting magic above his abilities, but he'd also made other interesting notes of a less martial nature. He had likely discovered this sealed chamber and, being the curious sort, had gone above and beyond and somehow figured out a way to gain access. In that, he and Bawb had much in common.

"Of course," Bawb muttered. "The *Rommus* spell. It has to be cast counter-clockwise."

It had made no sense when he'd found the scrawled note, the mix of spells an odd combination. But now it all seemed to fit into place. It was a tensioning spell, applied to the wall, and in the reverse direction it would normally be used. That, along with a rather arcane access spell, was a clever way of sealing the door without resorting to excessive magic. A Ghalian trick, using a spell in reverse, hiding the key in plain sight. Almost no one would figure this out, and to be fair, without the older boy's notes, Bawb likely wouldn't have either. Discovering it like this, however, was a lesson he would now take to heart and remember the rest of his days.

He fixed the new intent in mind, ready to use the *Rommus* spell in a most unusual way as he did.

"*Pallus Orvix Imanna Rommus,*" he recited, applying the pulling tension rather than pushing, counterclockwise against his every instinct. The magic felt wrong being used this way, but then the wall abruptly swung open, leaving no dust, nor any other trace on the floor, not even a hint of any magic having been used. It was impressive, the warding here, and within the hidden chamber the darkness beckoned, complete and silent.

*Level up: Hidden locks and doors*, the konus said, though Bawb could have sworn he heard a tone of reluctance in its admitting what he'd just done.

Bawb stepped toward the blackness.

*This is a bad idea.*

Actually, Bawb didn't entirely disagree with the konus on that point. He drew his dagger and cast a minor illumination spell and stepped forward over the threshold. A second later the door slid shut behind him, the ambient light gone. All that remained was his spell, a lone trace of light in the dark.

# CHAPTER FORTY-FIVE

Bawb felt his stomach sink and tighten as the door silently locked him inside. Standing alone in the dark, only a small illumination spell penetrating the inky black, he felt more vulnerable than he had in ages, and utterly alone.

"Keep it together, Bawb," he told himself, forcing his heart to slow as best he could. "*Pallus Orvix Imanna Rommus,*" Bawb recited, this time using the *Rommus* spell clockwise, reversing the force he had applied on the outside.

To his great relief, the door slid open, remaining so for a few moments before shutting once more.

"Okay. I am not trapped," he realized with relief, turning his focus forward into the cavern. "Let's explore."

There was vegetation at his feet, he noted, and even a few relatively small shrubs with odd, pale leaves that grew along the walls where moisture condensed and ran down in greater amounts than in the central area. There was no water source in this chamber that he could see, but knowing how many were interconnected in the maze of caverns beneath the training house, who knew where this one might lead.

Bawb walked the perimeter, taking stock of the place. It

wasn't terribly large, perhaps thirty meters across, if that. But so far as he could see, there was no pathway out. This appeared to be a standalone cavern. But if that was the case, where was Porrius's body? This chamber was empty.

A flash of movement at the edge of his illumination spell immediately changed his mind on that matter. There had not been anything in here with him when he made his survey of the cavern, of that he was certain. But now? Now he was definitely not alone, and his senses were screaming *danger* loud in his gut.

Bawb immediately dumped what extra magic he could into his illumination spell, widening the light surrounding him just as a massive lizard-looking beast lunged at him, its jaws snapping loud in the silence.

Bawb dove aside, his dagger swiping at the creature but meeting a tough hide the blade could not penetrate. His attacker didn't hesitate, spinning at once and rearing up for another attack, what looked like viscous venom dripping from its fangs.

Bawb wanted to flee, but the thing had positioned itself between him and the exit. It was nearly three meters long, not including its tail, running on four sturdy legs, its body and neck thick with muscles underneath its robust lizard skin. He was going to have to fight, but this was an adversary that showed no apparent weakness. And with only a dagger, he would have to be up close and personal if he hoped to land a blow. That meant he would be within striking range of the creature's claws and fangs.

*Focus!* the konus snapped at him. *Find a weakness.*

The beast lunged at him, jumping high, trying to bite his head, hoping to finish the fight in an instant. It was a ploy, Bawb realized, as time seemed to slow around him as he took in the details with a calm that surprised him. The creature clearly used its venom to disable its prey, so why make this seemingly wild attack?

It was then that he noticed the foreclaws had a sheen to

them that hadn't been there before. The animal had licked its claws, applying its venom to them when its first attack missed. An adaptive trait, no doubt, and very clever. Its prey would lock it up, holding its fangs at bay. But that left its foreclaws free to slash and cut, and once that poison entered its target's bloodstream, Bawb had a very good idea what would come next.

He reacted in a flash, moving on pure instinct, pushing aside what seemed to be the most logical to his conscious, planning mind, going instead with his gut no matter how wrong his brain warned him it was.

Bawb dove low, aiming at an angle that would take him beneath the foreclaws, allowing him to roll diagonally out of the lizard's path. His body obeyed his command, his years of training readying him for this more than he'd ever realized. In fact, he was on his feet on the other side of his attacker, already spun into a low crouch and ready for another go, before he even realized he'd done so. More than that, it seemed his other training had kicked in as well.

Only a trace of blood was on his blade, so quickly had he made his cut. But the attacking animal had exposed its one vulnerable spot in its gambit, and Bawb had instinctively taken full advantage of it.

The creature lay shuddering on the soil, unable to move as its guts spilled out, sliced open and emptying it of its precious life force. A moment later it was quite dead.

*That was unexpected,* the konus said. *Level up: Flow Combat.*

Bawb would ask what exactly that meant later, though given the way he'd fought without even thinking, he had a pretty good idea. He spun around, blade ready, scanning for other attackers. None were near, but this thing had come out of nowhere. He was not about to take his victory for granted. Bawb hustled around the chamber, his eyes looking for anything out of the ordinary. Nothing stood out.

Bawb turned to leave, but a strange feeling tugged his guts. Strange but familiar in its unusual sensation.

"I need to take one more look."

*You need to leave.*

"Not yet," he replied. Sure enough, it was on his second pass that he saw it. "A tunnel," he realized, crouching by a shrub growing almost against the cavern wall.

Behind it was a tunnel. Low, narrow, dark. Hidden from sight unless you were right up on it.

*Don't even think about it.*

"Too late. You read my mind, so you already know what I plan to do."

Bawb stretched out his arms in front, dagger ready, and began crawling. If there was another beast coming, at least he could hold it at bay. At least he hoped so. But after a thankfully short crawl, he exited into another chamber, and this one was illuminated with faintly glowing moss clinging to the walls and ceiling.

A few small tunnels dotted the walls, but none quite as large as the one he'd crawled through. Big enough for the beast, though. Undoubtedly how it hunted. Bawb spun a slow turn and took it all in.

The stench in the stagnant air was horrible, and it only took a glance to figure out why.

The lizard was typical of its kind, eating a large meal then digesting slowly. When it expelled its waste, almost everything had been digested for its nutrients, leaving behind a discharge most foul. He scanned the cavern. It was maybe a quarter the size of the other one. More importantly, he saw the bones of smaller versions of the thing that attacked him. Apparently, it was a cannibalistic species. And the one he'd encountered appeared to be an apex predator of its kind. Anything smaller would have been devoured. He was safe.

At least he hoped so.

A flicker in the light caught his eye as one pile of bones shifted. He pushed aside his disgust and began digging, sliding the bones apart. It only took a moment. This pile was old and had dried out long ago. It stank, but not nearly as bad as the fresh ones.

A tingle of magic buzzed in his fingertips as they brushed against something cool and hard. Something metal, not bone. Bawb cleared away the remains and pulled it out. It was a dagger, very banged up, but nevertheless containing the tiniest remains of magic. He dug a moment longer and uncovered what he both knew yet feared he would find.

A Wampeh skull, gouged and clawed, but clearly belonging to one of his own. He touched it, the odd power he'd been feeling only flittering hints of over the years clearly present. It was Porrius, there could be no doubt.

"Do you realize the hour, Aspirant Bawb?" Master Imalla asked as she opened her door.

The sight of the filthy boy caught her off-guard, though she didn't show it. Bawb held out the battered dagger. She took it from him, almost flinching as she felt the trace magic.

"Where did you find this?"

"I was exploring."

"There is very clearly an *and* coming after that statement."

"And I unsealed a hidden chamber down on level four. In the restrooms nearest the curved staircase."

Master Imalla just nodded once and immediately summoned several Masters and teachers despite the hour. All arrived in just minutes.

"Show us," she commanded, and Bawb did just that.

"A Ziffin lizard," Master Imalla said when her eyes fell upon the deceased creature. "You killed it?"

"I did."

"And without suffering so much as a scratch? Impressive for an Adept, let alone an Aspirant. They poison their claws in a most unusual way."

"I saw."

She gave him a look of actual surprise. "Did you, now? And in combat, no less." She nudged the beast's corpse with her boot. "The Ziffin are native beasts of this world, rarely seen, and rarely survived by those who do. They live in certain chambers, as you have discovered. Chambers the Masters sequestered from the rest many centuries ago, sealing them off to prevent unfortunate encounters."

"They are omnivorous, clearly," Bawb noted.

"Yes. And their venom is quite fatal. One bite is more than enough to do you in. It was for that reason the Master of this house sealed them away so long ago. They are dangerous, yes, but they are also just beasts living as they have since long before we arrived."

"Innocent, in their own way," a new arrival said from the doorway. "Their eradication was not warranted, but the Masters did see a need to ensure the safety of the students."

"Master Hozark?"

"Hello, Bawb. Is it true you fought this beast on your own?"

"Yes."

Hozark glanced at Imalla and the nearby Masters. "Impressive. But this particular chamber, why here? It was sealed and hidden ages ago. How did you come to find it?"

"I followed my gut. I cannot exactly explain it, but I just knew Porrius was here."

The Masters who had crawled into the adjoining chamber

had already confirmed that fact, retrieving what was left of the dead student's bones, placing them respectfully in a pile.

Imalla seemed unconvinced. "Where countless Masters had failed, you succeeded?"

"I mean no disrespect, Master Imalla. But yes, I did."

"Then you will surely not mind sharing with us how you managed this feat."

"Of course, though I admit I do not entirely understand all of the nuances," Bawb replied.

*You're gonna be in trouble for looking at spells above your level, you know.*

"Perhaps. But any punishment is worth it," he silently replied to his konus.

"Well?" Imalla said.

"I was in our study area, reading through spells."

"Your dedication to your studies is known, Aspirant, but how did you wind up *here*?"

Bawb swallowed but remained resolved. "I was reading spells that were, admittedly, above my level. Adept spells. Some Maven spells."

"Why would you do such a thing? You know that is—"

"I thought I might come to understand what Porrius had been doing. And, in fact, I came across some notes that I knew he had made."

"You knew? How?"

"I just knew. It felt almost as if he was there with me, if that makes sense."

The Masters shared a look but remained silent.

"Go on," Imalla urged.

Bawb went on to explain the unusual combination of spells he had found written in the margins, and given how one of them had actually gained him access to the chamber presumed sealed beyond the students' ability to open, it appeared he had been correct. And when he told them of the mixed combatives Porrius had been experimenting with, all became clear.

"Oh, yes. That is a foolish and powerful mixture of spells. If he attempted to cast those while he was dying, that would explain his unusual means of demise," Hozark said. He rested his hand on the filthy boy's shoulder, ignoring the grime and muck. "And now, because of you, Bawb, Porrius's remaining essence can finally be released. You have given him peace."

Bawb felt his eyes dampen but pushed his emotions down as best he could. He was a Ghalian, at least a student among them, and he had to keep those sorts of things under control. He nevertheless felt a mix of joy but also sadness. Joy that the spirit he'd sensed ever since his arrival would finally be free, but also an odd feeling of loss.

Imalla stepped closer, her expression hard to read, but at least not as displeased as it usually seemed. "Have you mentioned any of this to your classmates?"

"No."

"Good. It is for the best. We feel this should not be discussed with students, Bawb."

"I understand."

"*But* I will ultimately leave the final decision to you. You have done well, Aspirant, and have earned that trust in your judgment. Now, go get cleaned up and into bed. You have done well tonight, but you still have much ahead of you in the morning."

Bawb gave a respectful little bow and took his leave, doing exactly as Master Imalla asked of him. And once his clean head hit the pillow, he drifted off to sleep with a sense of happy satisfaction wrapping him in its warm embrace.

# CHAPTER FORTY-SIX

Elzina was still casting angry looks at Bawb after his unexpected victory the prior day, totally unaware of what else he had accomplished in the depths of their home compound, when several teachers came to interrupt the group's spell casting lesson the following day. All were kitted out in far more than they usually wore around the training house, though none had any visible weapons.

Knowing the likes of this group, however, they were all armed to the teeth.

"Gather your things," Teacher Griggitz hollered loud enough that all could hear. "Meet at the second-level sparring room. We are taking you on an outing."

"An outing?" Zota asked. "What sort of outing?"

"Be there and you will find out," was all he said.

The teachers followed him out of the chamber, leaving the Aspirants to wonder what was going on. That only lasted a moment, though. Griggitz said *out*, and that meant one thing for certain. They were leaving the compound walls.

The students hurried to collect their basic gear and rushed to the rally point, eager and ready to find out what sort of adventure they were being sent on today. Bawb hoped it was not another outing to a remote river. They had already lost one classmate that way, and he would really prefer not to lose another.

As it turned out, he was in luck.

"You will be sent out on a task," Griggitz told the gathered youths. "You will be competing against one another. Unlike your usual training, you will be doing this in the outside world."

"We have done outside training before," Albinius noted, drawing a sharp look from the teacher.

"Yes, you have. Pathetically, if I recall correctly. But today is different. Today you will be sent out into the city. Here. Into the population just outside these walls, though you will be working far from this compound."

The Aspirants managed to suppress the exclamations of excitement that were bubbling inside each of them. Outside. In a city, no less. It was thrilling.

Griggitz clapped his hands loudly, focusing their attention. "You are no longer children. You are Aspirants of the Wampeh Ghalian and are expected to act as such. This means, among other things, that you will maintain absolute silence about your Ghalian trainee nature, no matter what happens. Is that clear?"

"Yes, Teacher!"

"Good. Because if any of you slips up and lets that information out, you will be expelled from the order. No second chances. We take the security of our own *very* seriously. Even if it should cost you your life, you never betray the order." He surveyed the attentive faces staring at him with focused expressions. He had made his point. "Teacher Rovos will explain the task."

Rovos stepped forward, wearing lowly tradesman's clothes. A disguise, clearly.

"You are all likely wondering why I am in this attire. Because

I, and the other teachers, will be observing you from afar. You will not see us, but rest assured, we will be there. Watching."

"Will this require combat?" Elzina asked, her fingertips toying with the enchanted dagger she had tucked inside her clothing.

"No, but you are wise carrying a weapon. One never knows what situation may rear its head, and not all dangers are people. Beasts can kill or maim just as easily."

Bawb took it all in and felt adrenaline trickle into his bloodstream. It wasn't sounding like a truly dangerous task they were being sent out on—they were only Aspirants, after all—but this would be their first time walking the streets alone. Observed, yes, but for all other intents and purposes, on their own.

It was a chance to show off what they had learned these past years, but for Bawb, it would also be the opportunity he had been hoping for. A perfect way to learn how to better exit the training house and, if he was lucky, find a way to get off world and out to Kardahn's lunar city.

"The objective?" Usalla asked.

"A simple one, relatively speaking. You are to steal an item located somewhere in the city and bring it to a specified location to hand off to one of our agents under the guise of a sale. You will then receive coin for your efforts and return to the compound via the exit you are about to use."

"What sort of thing are we stealing?" Zota asked.

Pallik walked the ranks, handing each a small block of carved wood, all of them identical, blank on three sides and with runes and markings on the other three.

"That is for you to figure out," Rovos replied. "You work individually. No teaming up on this task. Ghalian work alone, and as you will be in a real city, it is time you put that into proper practice. Keep in mind, if you are caught, there will be real-world consequences. You may very well spend your night behind bars."

The teachers led the group down a hallway and out into a building entryway, sealing the wall behind them, the path to the training house hidden once more. The teachers then walked out a simple, plain door onto the street outside, leaving the Aspirants alone.

"I guess we have started," Zota said, rushing outside.

Elzina watched him leave with disdain then turned her attention back to the block in her hand. "Idiot. He does not even know where we are to go."

Bawb liked Zota, but in this instance, he couldn't help but agree with her. There was a puzzle here. A riddle. And both the location as well as the item's description were hidden in it. Rushing off without first figuring out the clues was just a waste of time.

The rest of the class stood quietly, studying the cubes, turning them over in their hands, applying all they had learned in their efforts. Some were better at this than others, naturally, and they were the first to head out. Bawb was among them.

The others followed, still working out the details but also allowing the efforts of their cohort to aid them in their task. If they could follow someone who knew where they were going, they could continue figuring out the mysteries of the cubes as they moved, keeping themselves within striking distance of the goal if they deciphered the riddle by the time they arrived.

As the Ghalian often said, work smarter, not harder. Allowing others to do the heavy lifting was a perfectly acceptable strategy in many situations, and this was one of them.

Bawb marveled at the city as he tried to appear nonchalant, weaving his way through foot traffic, avoiding the floating conveyances that sped past. He knew where he was going. The trick would be getting there before the others. That, and making it inside to steal the target item without bottlenecking at the entryway. With all of them after the same thing, getting there was only half the problem.

The hidden message of the cube had been simple enough. A riddle hidden in a rune. One that spoke in images rather than straight answers. But they had studied the city in class and knew it well on a didactic level. Practically, they had almost no time in the actual streets, but they were quite familiar with the layout of the city.

Once he had oriented himself as to where the exit had deposited them, it was a simple thing to plan a route. Past a small outdoor marketplace was the best one, though a bit crowded. He just needed to stay incognito and not draw attention to himself. Thieves were about, and as a result, there was a more robust security detail wandering that area looking for the out of the ordinary.

He had to be one with the crowd. To fit in and not appear out of place. It should be easy enough.

He was weaving between stalls when a loud crash just behind him made him turn. Two stalls had their wares tumble to the ground seemingly for no reason. The proprietors pointed in his direction and started yelling. Something about *thief* and *vandal.*

Bawb spun back around just in time to catch a glimpse of Elzina's amused face up ahead of him as she turned and bolted.

*An ambush*, he realized, quickly running laterally into an alley that would take him from the commotion but also off course. She had set him up, slowing him down while giving herself an advantage. Bawb knew it would take him too long going around this direction. He had a choice to make, and it was easy. Intellectually, anyway. In practice, in the real world, however, it was a little nerve-racking.

He ducked into a doorway, hiding from view as he quickly shed his tunic, turning it inside-out, the bright lining now on the outside making him *very* visible in a crowd. But it was Demelza who had mentioned this particular tactic in passing one day. How becoming the most easily spotted person could make you invisible to those seeking you out. No guilty party would actively draw attention to themselves. At least, not in the minds of normal people.

He took a deep breath and stepped back into the alleyway, walking tall and confident back the way he came. Bawb looked at the mess on the ground just like the other bystanders, going so far as to ask what happened.

"Damn thieves again," someone replied.

"That's not how people should behave. Someone needs to do something about them," he said as he walked away, embracing his character fully.

His heart was pounding in his chest, but his face betrayed no such worry. He forced himself to walk at a normal pace, pausing to look at items for sale before continuing. The marketplace's guard staff was rushing around, grabbing a few of his cohort in their haste to find the perpetrator. Whether they would wind up in custody for the night or not he did not know. But that was not his concern. In just moments he was clear of the ruckus and was on track once more.

*Level up: Adaptation and improvised disguise*, his konus announced. *Not a bad job of it, I have to admit.*

"Why, thank you," he replied.

*You've still fallen behind, though. And you haven't figured out the final part of the clue.*

"Yes, I have. Just now, in fact."

*Taking your mind off it allowed you to work on instinct. Melt me down and make me a doorknob, I think you might actually be getting the hang of this.*

"Your vote of confidence is appreciated," he scoffed. "Now, please be quiet. I have work to do."

For once, the konus listened, leaving him to his task without any further running commentary, which it seemed to enjoy distracting him with.

The last part of the task was to steal something, and he had figured out the location first. But the item itself? What it was had remained unclear until just now. It had to be portable, but that didn't help much. But when he stopped trying to figure out the meaning of the runes and instead just looked at their shape when he turned the block over in his hands, it all became clear.

Each of the three faces had a design with its own meaning, and he had been searching for a clear message in each of them. But when he pictured them in his mind's eye, combining the three into one, it was so simple it almost hurt his brain that he had missed it until now. He'd overthought it.

It wasn't a puzzle. It was a picture broken into three pieces. And when he envisioned them overlapped at the obvious junction points, he saw what he was looking for. A crystal bowl.

It was a strange thing to steal, but he wasn't going to argue with the teachers. If this was what he was to take, then he would take it. The difficult part would be gaining access to the residence it was kept in. At least it was not that far now if he hurried. Bawb moved to the less busy street he knew would take him there and shed his tunic as he walked, turning it back inside out again to its original muted color. He would not want to be visible for this next part.

When he arrived, he saw that the designated building was part of a row of squat homes, many of them sharing a common wall, but this one freestanding. That at least allowed a few more entry options, which would be good as other Aspirants were sure to be arriving shortly as well. He had to hurry.

The rear was the obvious choice, but that meant more

scrutiny as it faced several other homes. Instead, he opted for the side. It was still exposed, but if he pretended to be stopping to relieve himself, he could likely go unbothered by anyone who happened to glance his way. Only when climbing in a window might he draw attention, but if his spell worked as intended, the window would unseal and open without a sound, allowing him quick access.

Bawb reached the ground-level side window farthest to the rear when his nose detected something acrid in the air. Smoke.

Calls of alarm were being raised toward the front entrance. He saw a few of his classmates turn to retreat, but they were grabbed by adults who were now yelling about them being vandals and arsonists.

Bawb saw Usalla was one of them. She was doing her best to appear confused and scared. In reality, he knew she was keeping herself from drawing her dagger and making a bloody, if not quick, escape.

He had no time. He had to act at once.

While everyone was distracted at the front of the building, he hurried in through the window at the side, landing in a silent crouch, his ears straining.

No one was home.

Bawb hurried through the ground floor, searching for a crystal bowl. It would be in a protective box, but it was nowhere to be seen. He rushed upstairs, using his limited magic to sense crystal. It was a crude use of a spell intended for completely different task, namely, water purification by removing sediment, but crystal was related to those elements and was something he could shift the spell to draw. Unfortunately, he felt no pull. Not even the slightest tug. When he entered what appeared to be a study, he saw why.

"Damn," he grumbled. "Elzina."

The box was there, but its top was ajar, and when he peered

inside, it was quite empty. The fire made sense now. It was her diversion to make her escape. It also happened to get a few of their classmates nabbed in the process, not that she would care.

Bawb heard footsteps downstairs. Someone was in the building.

He raced to the nearest window and looked outside. There was a crowd gathered in front now as the fire was extinguished. The whole place would be under scrutiny now, with people running all around it, making sure no one was injured or trapped by the blaze. It had been extinguished quickly, but the smoke was still somewhat thick. It gave him an idea.

Bawb opened the window, but rather than drop to the ground where he would surely be seen, he climbed up to the rooftop. Without hesitation he ran and jumped, leaping across to the adjacent building through the obscuring smoke, using his force spell to add a little extra oomph to the effort. It was an unusual use of the spell, but it did the trick, carrying him easily across the gap.

*Level up: Novel use of magic.*

He didn't pause to look at the icons and see where his levels now stood. There was no time. He ran to the far side of the rooftop and dropped over the edge, rolling as he hit the ground hard, spreading the force of the impact as best he could. His feet hurt a bit, but he would survive. What's more, no one had seen him.

He took off around the corner to the rear of the building and began his long walk back home. He had gotten there too late. Elzina had, once again, played dirty and taken the prize. Of course, that was all part of the game, and the teachers would approve, but it still rubbed Bawb the wrong way.

One good thing, however, had come of this. He was afforded the chance to take the long way back, scoping out the landing area nearest the compound as he did. It would just look like he was avoiding the mess Elzina had stirred up, drawing no scrutiny from the teachers he knew were watching.

He would still have to be quick in his impromptu recon, but once he knew more about the area and the ships present, he would be better equipped come up with a plan to get aboard one and hopefully make his way to the Rock. To find Nixxa and steal back the Drookonus.

Bawb swiveled his head as he walked, looking as though he was amazed at seeing the world outside the training house walls. And, to a degree, that was true. But more than that, he was making note of all he saw, for anything could prove useful knowledge as he worked on his plan.

Crunching at his feet made him pause.

Crystal.

Shattered, pulverized crystal.

He noted where his roundabout path had taken him. It was close to where the handoff of the stolen item was to take place. But by the look of it, Elzina had lost hold of it somehow. Whether she was jostled or whatever, it didn't matter. What did was that she may have beaten him to the goal, but she had failed in the end.

A little grin tried to force its way onto his lips but Bawb held it back. Teachers were surely watching, and a Ghalian had to be in complete control of their emotions. With a calm expression, he continued on his way, appearing to any watching as if nothing had happened. But inside he was laughing. Elzina deserved it.

*Level unlocked,* the konus said, a little icon unblurring on his hidden display. *Deception and acting against skilled opponents. Ghalian, no less. Perhaps you are less hopeless than I thought.*

"You think?"

*This outing has proven you're far better in the real world than in training. Who knows? You might even survive to become a full Ghalian one day.*

Much as the konus could be an annoying little shit, a slight feeling of hope fluttered in his belly.

*Or you'll die a horrible death*, it added with a mocking laugh. *I guess we'll see.*

# CHAPTER FORTY-SEVEN

The next morning greeted the Aspirants with not another adventure in the city, but a mere crafting class. Teacher Warfin seemed thrilled to be conducting it once more, though the students were, for obvious reasons, less than enthused. After a night running the streets on a real-world mission, it was perfectly understandable that this felt like a letdown.

Elzina's mood was far more acidic than usual even for her, though she had good reason. She had both won and failed the task. Her backstabbing and scheming had achieved the primary goal—she had reached the objective first and secured the crystal bowl before anyone else had entered the building. But in her haste, she was careless, opting to leave the box as a decoy and make a quick exit with the bowl tucked away in her clothing.

It made sense to her at the time. The box was cumbersome and angular whereas the bowl was curved and could fit nicely under her attire. As a result, she rushed through the streets fleet of foot and light of spirit. She was going to win, and nothing pleased her more than that.

The large male alien had not taken her by surprise. She had seen him coming from down the street. How could she miss an enormous, green, pot-bellied thing with shiny silver wire for hair and a long neck that connected its bulbous head with its equally rotund body? She'd never seen anything like it, but there were so many races out there, it was hardly unexpected that she would not know them all.

What *had* taken her off guard were the tentacles trailing out from the long coat it was wearing. Apparently, this species ambulated on a cluster of the thick appendages rather than legs. She was so busy looking at the rest of its body she neglected to see the hazard.

The crystal bowl released a brief flash of light when it slid from her grasp under her tunic and shattered on the ground. It was apparently a magical vessel of some sort, possibly of great value. And she had just dropped it.

A *very* unamused Rovos had seemed to appear from nowhere, his scowl making his displeasure quite clear.

"Back to the compound," he growled. "And then *thirty* laps around the third-level training chamber."

She knew better than to say a word, heading off at a quick walk without looking back.

The others didn't know any of that, and only Bawb was privy to the bowl being broken at all. But even he was unaware of the circumstances, and the only hint he had of the consequence was Elzina's arriving back at their chambers well after him rather than before, drenched in sweat from her punishment, with a dark aura of angry frustration clinging to her like stink on overripe cheese.

It had lessened with a night's sleep, but compared to Warfin's joy, Elzina's ire seemed like a simmering waste fire hidden just beneath the surface of a dump site. One that would have to remain buried.

"Hello, Aspirants. I am glad to see most of you made it back from yesterday's outing in one piece."

They looked around. Indeed, a few were absent from the group. Not missing in action or at the healer, but simply detained by authorities, having been caught up in Elzina's diversions, Usalla among them.

"Today's crafting lesson will be expanding on what you have previously studied," he continued, carrying a wooden chair to the front of the class and taking a seat. "Some of you are more proficient than others, but all will have the opportunity to expand your knowledge. Do not hesitate to ask questions if you need assistance. That is the point of these classes. To fill in gaps in knowledge and help make you all better at your crafting skills."

"Crafting is boring," Elzina grumbled, not caring that this was a Ghalian master she was speaking to. "We've been out in the world. We've gone on tasks. But when do we get to go on a real mission? After all this training, I'm ready for it."

"You think your class is ready for a *real* mission?" Warfin asked, one brow arched with amusement.

"I did not say *we*. I said *I*."

"Of course you did," he replied dismissively.

He rose from his chair and retrieved a sparring dummy from the corner of the room, placing it against the far wall. It was something they had all practiced on, learning to commit to their attacks without having to worry about accidentally harming anyone, but they were using it less and less these days as their skills grew in parallel with their restraint.

"Okay, Elzina. You say you are ready for action. Fine. Let us assume you are on a mission and find yourself confronted by an adversary. You have no blades on you and your konus is out of magic. With what you have available within immediate reach, what would you use to kill them?"

She looked around. There was essentially nothing close by,

and that was obviously his point. It irked her being toyed with like that.

"The chair," she blurted, focusing in on the one thing near that she could lift.

"The chair? Interesting choice. And how would you kill your adversary with it?"

"I suppose I would beat them with it."

"A non-stunned, fully grown adult enemy and you think they would just allow you to pummel them with a chair until they were dead?"

"Do you have a better idea?" she fired back. The others were shocked she would dare talk like that to a teacher. "What would *you* use?"

The students restrained their gasps at her gall, but Warfin, however, seemed more amused than anything else.

"Oh, I would use the chair as well," he said, picking it up. "But my method is far more efficient than yours."

His hands were a blur as he ripped the chair apart, hurling piece after piece into the training dummy, all of them embedding deep, all of them fatal blows. He continued until the poor dummy looked like it had been attacked by a massive porcupine. The trainees were floored.

"*Anything* can be used as a weapon," he said, pleased with himself as well as the shocked expressions on the Aspirants' faces.

"How did you do that?" Bawb marveled. "They are all so perfectly pointed."

"Ah, now there is the right question, young Bawb," he said, pulling the pieces out one by one. "Anything can be used as a weapon, but sometimes we have the opportunity to prepare a little something in advance. To build weapons into a new item, or conceal them within an existing one, as you all know. I would remind you that this is where the crafting that many of you find so dull comes into play." He looked across the students' faces, pausing on Elzina longer than the rest. "Not so boring now, is it?"

He began sliding the pieces of the chair together with skilled hands, each of them locking into place as they once more started to form a whole. The framework, the legs, the back, were all designed to come apart with the right manipulation. It wasn't a chair; it was an arsenal of perfectly balanced throwing weapons. And the bits that had not broken down were just the right size and weight to be used as melee weapons if needed.

"Would you care to examine it?" he asked as the last piece locked into place.

The students nodded eagerly.

"Then come. See if you can discern the mechanism to release them."

The Aspirants gathered around. Even Elzina joined them, all of them running their fingers over the chair, looking for a seam or other means of accessing the throwing spikes. They tried for several minutes, all of them failing.

"It is not just about the weapon aspect, you know," Warfin said, holding the chair up and showing them how he depressed two areas and twisted a third to unlock the pieces. "Crafting is also about other uses. Take this chair leg, for example." He pulled it free, a melee club ready for action. "It seems like something to bludgeon with, yes? A brute force weapon. But in actuality, it is more than just that."

Again, he manipulated different parts of the wood until there was an almost imperceptible click. He pulled gently, sliding away a section to reveal a small vial hidden inside.

"This could be poison," he said, plucking it out. "Or coin. Or any number of things. The point is, many times practical hiding spots are used to avoid those seeking magical concealment spells. If there are no spells, one must learn to find them in other ways."

"But surely there are some spells to help detect voids in objects and that sort of thing," Bawb posited.

"Again, very good, Bawb. You seem to have something of a knack for this. Yes, there are spells that achieve roughly what you described. And, eventually, they will be taught to you. But for now, you are to rely on your eyes, your hands, your ears, and even your nose."

"My nose?" Albinius questioned.

"Yes, your nose. It is a tool, just like the rest of your body. What if there is a scent to the item you seek? Or if the hidden compartment is newly cut in wood, leaving a fresh smell to those bothering to look for it? My point is, think beyond what others perceive and you will excel. But there is more still."

"More than senses?"

"Yes. You must also use your mind. What you know of your target. If you know who constructed the hiding place and their motivation for doing so. If you learn to think like your target, you will eventually find you are able to deduct what methods they may have used to hide what you seek."

"We must learn their skills better than even they know them, essentially," Bawb mused.

"An astute observation. And if we know what someone will do under different circumstances, as well as the means they would employ, we can overcome them before the battle has even begun. And I would note that this applies to physical exchanges as well as battles of wits. Now, let us see what you might do with this lesson. Somewhere in this room I have fashioned a hiding place for my lunch. Knowing the size, as well as the crafter, can you find it before Elzina gets her wish?"

"My wish?" she asked.

"Yes. Though it has nothing to do with your little tantrum,

you are getting what you wanted this very day. After yesterday's outing, the masters have spoken and decided it is time to further elevate your training. And that means you work in the real world once more. You, and a handful of your classmates whom they feel are also ready. Be careful what you wish for, however. From what I understand, it should be quite the challenge, indeed. But for now, you have a task much closer at hand. To work, the lot of you. Find my lunch, if you can."

# CHAPTER FORTY-EIGHT

Elzina was positively giddy as she and the selected few were led out of the compound and into the city streets once more. There was only one teacher with them, Teacher Farpix, of whom they had seen less and less since they became Aspirants.

They were few in number, only Elzina, Bawb, Usalla, and Finnia, the four of them making up the entirety of their little outing group. The top performers had never been explicitly named, but now there were faces to place with the honor.

Bawb had expected Elzina, of course. She was still the best of them in most things, while Finnia surpassed them all in the ways of stealth and sneaky spy techniques. Bawb and Usalla tended to finish around the same in the pack and were both pleased to learn that meant they were each in the top four, not that it carried any honors or privileges. It was simply nice to have a bit of tangible proof that their efforts were paying off.

"This way," Farpix said, leading the youths to the landing area nearest the training house.

There were fewer ships there today, leaving the landing site feeling rather empty. Farpix explained that there was a convoy that left earlier, traveling in a group to help fend off any pirates who might get ideas. This batch was planning to jump as soon as they were clear of the atmosphere, but one could never be too careful, so the captains had come to an understanding, each lending the power of their casters to defend their group as a whole.

"That is our ride over there," he said, pointing to a windowless cargo transport.

"No windows?" Usalla asked.

"No. It may make for a less enjoyable flight, but this craft is an uninteresting one that will also avoid any suspicion. Now get aboard and take a seat. We leave at once, and it will be a long flight. The ship will only make a few jumps. A vessel of this nature would reserve its jump magic for emergency situations if possible."

"Like pirates?" Bawb asked.

"Among other things. All right. Get situated; we leave shortly."

They did as they were told, each settling in for the trip. Farpix left them and headed for the command chamber, closing the door to their compartment behind him. A few minutes later the ship vibrated slightly as it lifted off.

"I do not feel a Drookonus," Finnia noted. "I believe this is a Drook-powered ship."

Bawb felt the magic traces and had to concur. "It is weak, though. Likely a small crew of them. No wonder they conserve jump magic."

Finnia rose from her seat and walked the room, taking in the rather outdated design. "I do not see any markings that might tell us where this ship is from or who it belongs to."

"Not Ghalian, that much we know," Bawb stated plainly. "A regularly utilized transport, perhaps, but we know our flights are typically blended with aboveboard ones to mask any Ghalian presence."

"So, we are flying in the dark," Elzina noted. "Figuratively, if not literally, but only just. I am surprised this thing has the power to spare for illumination."

"I am simply glad for the opportunity to learn in a more advanced dynamic," Usalla chimed in. "Yes, the vessel may be a bit rundown, but this is exciting. We are going on an actual mission, and I, for one, am looking forward to whatever it may bring."

"She's right," Bawb said, rising to take a walk around the chamber. "This is something new. And new is good."

Even Elzina couldn't help but agree. "True. Now let us hope this flight is not as long as Farpix made it out to be."

Many hours and a few jumps later they were still flying through space, but where they were was anyone's guess. Time was passing painfully slow, the excitement finally worn off, having transitioned to boredom some time ago.

"I hope you are ready," Farpix said as he re-entered the compartment. "We should be arriving fairly soon. Then your task will begin."

Elzina toyed with her dagger, an expectant look in her eye. "Who do we kill?"

"No, you are not to kill anyone. You are but Aspirants, and youths are not expected to carry out those tasks. For one, you lack the requisite skills and training, though your enthusiasm is noted. But you are also still children, which makes you vulnerable in any physical confrontation. No amount of training can overcome that shortcoming, only time and growth."

"Then what are we supposed to do?" she asked.

"You are to use your age to your advantage. As children, you can go places without drawing attention. Observe without making people suspicious of your motives. At this age, you would be surprised just how much you can get away with before someone would actually take notice."

"So we are to do what? Watch?" Elzina asked, unimpressed.

"Yes," he replied, turning his attention to the spy-in-training. "Now, Finnia, this is more pertaining to your skills focus, but it applies to the rest of you as well. You are going to be deposited in a somewhat rough town and directed to a specific area to gather information for the order. We understand there may be some unrest brewing, and this is a location pivotal in the Council's hold on the region. We wish for you to look, listen, and report back. And above all, avoid conflict. You will be on your own. Well, not entirely on your own. You will partner with one another in teams of two. But otherwise, you are without support."

"Teams of two? But Ghalian work alone," Bawb noted.

"Yes, Bawb, that is correct. But as you pointed out, *Ghalian* work alone. You are on the path, no doubt, but you are still only Aspirants, and that is a long way to becoming full-fledged Wampeh Ghalian, so today you work in pairs. Now, you will need to come up with cover identities for yourselves should you be questioned. Make them second nature before we land. Finnia, you will pair with Usalla. Elzina, you are with Bawb."

With that he left them to prepare for their impending arrival.

"So, best of friends?" Finnia asked Usalla.

"A sound cover that should provide ample leeway to think on the fly," she replied.

Bawb looked at Elzina, whose distaste was almost palpable. But this was a mission, and they had to put aside their differences. It was a matter of being professional, no matter how unpleasant the task might be.

"We should do the same," she said. "Best friends."

"Or we could be dating," he suggested. "They will ignore a young couple sitting quietly by themselves. That will allow us plenty of opportunity for observation."

"I would rather just stab someone, myself, even. But you

have a point. A couple we shall be. I only pray this task ends quickly."

The ship landed an hour later, the hull rattling as it set down on the ground. No magic was wasted on a hover spell, reinforcing just how broke the captain truly was. That, or it was all an elaborate act by a Ghalian mastermind, but the youths had their doubts.

They exited the ship and split into two groups, making their way to the target area by different access routes. Farpix had given them further details and shown them maps of the area as they made their approach. It was an open marketplace they were to observe. It had the reputation of being something of a hub for illicit activity in this town, and as such would be the most likely place to overhear any worthwhile information.

The Aspirants kept their magic use to a minimum, using only a few basic spells to make sure there were no hidden dangers as they entered the marketplace and took up positions.

It was densely packed and pungent with the smells of spice, sweat, and drink, and dozens of cultures were represented in the brightly colored vendor stalls.

Food and merchandise were sold side by side, with no segregation of products discernible. Wherever someone set up shop, that was where they would remain. It was quite a shift from the clean and organized marketplace back on their homeworld.

A central plaza with a small fountain in the middle was the destination they had been given. It was a common reference point, and as such many handoffs and illicit deals were made there, any offworlder being able to find it relatively easily in the maze of the town's narrow streets.

Bawb and Elzina walked into the plaza hand in hand, smiles plastered on their faces, acting as young couples were expected to. They leaned close, laughed, and spoke in whispers in one another's ears. To anyone watching, there was nothing notable about them at all. They strolled over to the fountain and took a seat on a dry patch of stone, Elzina putting her disgust aside and leaning into Bawb affectionately, allowing them to have eyes looking in both directions, covering a full three-sixty of the marketplace.

Meanwhile, Finnia and Usalla achieved much the same result by presenting as best friends walking the marketplace, swapping stories and giggling with obvious mirth. Beneath it all, however, they were taking note of everything around them, from people present to conversations they could overhear, all the while listening for anything of importance to the Ghalian.

The two teams spent a long time in the plaza, shifting positions occasionally, following suspicious types to better hear their conversations, all while playing the roles they had chosen. Bawb and Elzina were working on positioning themselves closer to a rather burly woman, buxom, with coarse black hair and tusks protruding from her lower jaw. Her skin looked like dark wood, and the furrows in it resembled cracks of dried bark.

The two Aspirants did not hear what the tall, orange-skinned man said to her, but it was clearly something to which she took offense. In a flash they were locked in a brawl, fists flying as they tumbled into other patrons. Soon enough, nearly a dozen people were involved, the violence contained to the combatants for now while a few of those on the periphery saw an opportunity and began taking wagers on the outcome.

Elzina reached for her dagger, ready for a fight, but Bawb yanked her by the back of her clothing and dragged her out of the plaza before she could react.

"What do you think you are doing?" she hissed when he released her.

"We have a task, and that does not include engaging in a fight."

"But they were sloppy. I could have taken them."

"One or two, perhaps. But there were a dozen. And, again, that was not our purpose here."

"You have no drive, Bawb. No impetus to go beyond our mission parameters. You are so unmotivated, it sickens me. Why don't you just quit if you are unwilling to do what must be done?"

"I *am* motivated. I just choose to act in an intelligent manner."

"Intelligent?" she snarked.

"Just because you do not know what I plan does not mean I do not have any," he shot back.

Elzina looked as though she was about to ignore him and go rushing back toward the fray when Finnia and Usalla came running to join them.

"Did you see that mess?" Finnia said. "Good thing we got clear before it got *really* ugly."

Bawb glared at Elzina. "I was just thinking the same thing."

Finnia and Usalla noted the exchange but left that bit of drama alone.

"We need to get to the rendezvous point," Usalla urged. "Come on, follow me."

The others fell in behind her, hurrying through the maze of narrow streets, Bawb taking up the rear. It wasn't that he thought Elzina would turn and ditch them in favor of a fight, but this was their first true mission, and he wasn't going to take the risk. If she screwed this up for them, who knew how long it might be before they were trusted with such a task again?

And so they moved away from the sounds of fighting rather than toward them. A good thing, it would turn out. Good indeed.

# CHAPTER FORTY-NINE

The four Aspirants moved quickly through the winding path to the designated rendezvous point. It was a squat building, freestanding and with few exterior windows. It appeared to have been a storage facility at some point, but now it was simply a space for rent. And today, the Ghalian had taken possession, albeit through several false identities.

"Inside, all of you," Farpix said, leaning in the doorway as he awaited their arrival.

The group filed inside, the door shutting behind them at once.

"Over there. Line up."

They did as they were told. Farpix didn't pace in front of them, but that could just as well have been because there were only four present, rather than their entire class. He just stared. Stared and sized them up with a critical gaze.

"What happened? You were not to return this soon," he asked.

Finnia spoke first. "We were gathering information, as you instructed, but things got heated in the plaza."

"Heated?"

"A fight."

"These things happen, and they are not enough to end a mission. What of your task? What did you learn? Who was there? What sort of plans were being discussed? *This* was your only job for today. Are you telling me you failed at so easy a thing?"

"It was more than just a scuffle," Bawb interjected. "There were at least a dozen combatants in the altercation, and it looked as if it might grow even larger."

"A dozen, you say?"

"Yes. And all very large, very rugged fighters. We did manage to gather *some* information, but then the fight broke out."

"And what did you do?"

"Bawb turned tail and ran," Elzina said with a frustrated grumble.

"And you?"

"I wanted to stay and fight. We have trained for this. Bawb was a coward."

Farpix shook his head. "No, Bawb was correct. It would have been foolish to engage when not directly threatened. We often gather information, maintaining anonymity in the process even if it is not pleasant. Sometimes we even suffer a beating at the hands of those we could easily defeat rather than engage, all to preserve the lie we are convincing them to believe. To maintain our cover. Our disguise."

No sooner had the words left his mouth than the door burst open and the big, angry aliens they had seen fighting in the plaza stormed in.

The Aspirants jumped back, drawing their blades, readying for a very outnumbered fight against full-grown opponents. The leader of the pack, the woman who had started all the trouble in the first place, just stood there, laughing at them.

"What is so funny?" Elzina demanded, though she was in no position to back up her words or tone.

The black-haired woman with tusks strode forward, her image dissolving with each step until a quite different person stood before them.

"Teacher Demelza?" Usalla gasped.

She stared at her students, shaking her head. "*None* of you cast to detect disguise spells? Not one?"

The four of them dropped their heads slightly in shame. "No, Teacher," they said quietly.

"You know the spell. I have seen you cast it with some degree of proficiency. So why on this, of all occasions, did you not think to utilize this tool in your arsenal?"

"There was so much going on," Elzina rationalized. "It was easy to get caught up in keeping track of all the voices and faces."

"And if those faces were false? What good would that intelligence have been then, eh? You must always, and I do mean *always* remember that things are quite often not what they appear."

Bawb looked at the others who had followed her into the building. A rough-and-tumble group of ruffians if he had ever seen one. But her words, fresh on his mind, rang true. He looked closer. Not a single one was injured. Not so much as a scrape, let alone any more serious injuries.

"None of you were really fighting," he marveled as the realization hit. "*Claris morza*."

The spell was weak, but it made the faces of the nearest aliens glow slightly. It was a disguise, and a magical one at that.

The Ghalian released his spell, returning to his normal appearance. It was Teacher Donnik. One by one the rest of them did the same. All had been Ghalian. Not a single one was an alien at all.

"This whole excursion. It was just a training exercise," he said. "It was all a test."

*Level up: detect disguise magic*, his konus quietly announced, though he did not need anyone to tell him in this case. It was obvious. And it had been one hell of a learning experience. One that was now leaving him with a burning desire to learn to be as skilled at disguises as Demelza was. To one day pass as another as easily as breathing.

"Yes, it was," Demelza replied. "Very good, Bawb. But it would have been better had you thought to use your spells *before* you ran from the plaza." She nodded to the others, each reapplying their disguises then leaving the way they came in. Demelza, however, remained in her normal form. "Your lesson is done," she said, leading them outside.

Farpix sealed the door behind them then hurried off to prepare the ship. Demelza hung back a moment longer.

"All right, you four. Time to return to the training house," she said, pointing up into the sky.

The Aspirants all looked up at the distant orb hanging in space. A planet far off in the distance, as planets tended to be.

Bawb's mind was racing. "Wait. That is home?"

"Yes."

"Then the flight? All those hours of travel?"

"The ship was flying in circles around the system to give the impression of traveling a great distance. It even made a few small jumps to add to the illusion. But in reality, you never left. Did any of you notice the power from the sun?"

"It was overcast when we arrived," Elzina noted.

"Not the sunshine. The *power*. Day or night, overcast or clear, each sun radiates its own particular energy. And by now, this flavor of magic should be very familiar. So familiar, in fact, that you all failed to notice it at all. You are used to its feeling after all these years. But think about it. If you were in another system, with another sun sending off a new variety of power, you would have felt the difference. You failed to notice one of the most obvious parts of your environment. This whole time you could have realized it if you just paid attention."

"We have a lot more to learn," Bawb said quietly.

"Yes, you do. And you will, in time. You actually did quite well today. Better than most, in fact, so do not dwell on your shortcomings. You are still only Aspirants, and you have much time to grow both wiser and stronger in the coming years."

"But if we can see home from here, where are we?" Usalla wondered.

"This is a small moon orbiting Mitz, one of the two gas giants in the solar system."

"A moon?" she marveled.

"Yes. It is called Kardahn."

Bawb felt his stomach tighten at the name. He was on Kardahn. The Rock. The very place he had been trying to figure out how to reach. And now serendipity had taken him there. And somewhere in this place, Nixxa would be found, along with the stolen Drookonus.

"This is a somewhat rough place, but a fascinating one, nonetheless. You have earned a little time for yourselves to walk the area, if you wish, before we depart. Take in the sights and get a feel for a new town. You all know where the ship is located, and it will be waiting for a while yet, so go ahead and explore a little. But do not be late. The ship will not wait for you."

With that she left them to do something they hadn't been able to do since their first arrival among the Ghalian. They could walk the streets of a real city on their own.

"See you back there," Finnia said, already trotting off to see more of this exciting new place.

Usalla and Elzina followed suit, each peeling off in a different direction to go and do precisely what Demelza suggested, exploring with wide-eyed wonder.

Bawb, on the other hand, had other plans in mind. Plans he would have to hurry to set in motion if he hoped to succeed.

# CHAPTER FIFTY

While the others strolled the town with a sense of casual curiosity, Bawb was moving as fast as he could without drawing too much attention to himself. He was on a mission. A self-imposed one, but that didn't make it any less vital in his eyes.

He had to find Nixxa.

The fact that he had no idea where she might be or what she even looked like did occur to him, but if he was going to be a Ghalian one day he would need to learn to overcome problems like that, and there was no time like the present to start.

Bawb figured that, based on what he had learned from Bud and Henni's casual chatter, the pirating crowd would tend to group together in the rougher parts of town. Not because of any form of segregation, but because when you were a wanted person there was safety in numbers.

On Kardahn there would be no such issue, given the character of pretty much *all* the inhabitants. But even so, no matter how seemingly secure one might feel, a captain of Nixxa's reputation would undoubtedly be cautious no matter where she took her leisure.

He made his way through the winding streets and alleyways

to the largest of the three landing sites as he had memorized from the map Farpix had shown them in flight. If she had landed anywhere, that was where she would be. Her ship, anyway. If he found it, from there he could try to track her movements into the heart of the lunar den of iniquity.

A large, battle-scarred ship stood out from the others. It was more robust-looking for one, its magically sealed windows also protected by what appeared to be blast panels that could be slid into place if the spell sealing the ship's viewing portions was disrupted. Exactly the sort of thing one might expect to see on a pirate's raiding ship.

There were others, of course. Smaller, specialized craft of a wide variety of designs. But this one, for whatever reason, felt right. It was only after staring at it a long moment that Bawb realized he was feeling the energy of a Drookonus from within. Other ships would be using them as well, but this one was particularly strong.

"It has to be hers," he rationalized. "She is the most notorious of them, so it stands to figure that the most powerful ship would belong to her."

"Hey, kid, what are you doing? Get away from there before Nixxa has your hands," a guard shouted at him.

"Oh, so sorry," he said, scurrying away, hiding the smile on his face.

The threat had just confirmed his suspicion and saved him a lot of time in the process. Now to find Nixxa. And with his hands still attached to his body, no less.

"Who threatens to take a boy's hands?" he marveled. "What an unusual intimidation. But then, they are thieves and pirates, so perhaps it is related to how they are punished on other worlds?"

He thought about asking his konus, but the device, while actually rather knowledgeable about all sorts of things, seemed to only dole out information according to its own unpredictable whims.

"If I were the most notorious pirate on this moon, where would I go?" he mused, putting himself in the woman's shoes as best he could. "She would have an entourage, of course, but she would not need them for security. One does not become a captain of her reputation without having considerable skills of her own. And she would not frequent a small, out-of-the way establishment. In what is perceived as a safe haven, she would undoubtedly wish to be seen. To act like a queen holding court."

*Not bad, kid,* the konus abruptly chimed in. *Level up: Deduction.*

"Are you saying you know where she is?"

Silence.

"Konus, are you holding back information?"

*Do you really want me to level you back down?* it replied with more than a little sass.

Bawb wisely held his tongue. And besides, the konus had confirmed what he had suspected. He just had to find the biggest, most glitzy place on the Rock.

The relatively small size of the town made a survey of the likely places easier, though a bit time-consuming. He was on a ticking clock, after all, but there was no way to know where Nixxa might be without scoping it out himself. He could ask around, but with no time to plan a proper cover story he would just be drawing unwanted attention to himself if he asked the wrong thing. This may be a safe moon for pirates, but that did not mean they would lower their guard.

It was in the fourth tavern on his short list of likely targets that he found her.

The place was louder than the others by a long shot, which was saying something. On top of that, it seemed to be an all-around nicer joint, cleaner and more expansive, with a higher-priced selection of libations and delights, including those of the sensual variety. Bawb slid past the scantily clad men and woman at the door, not needing their enticements to come inside.

Nixxa stood out immediately. And now that he saw her in the flesh, it was easy to see how she had developed both her loyal following and notorious reputation.

She was long, lean, and wiry-strong, easily as tall as most males he knew in the training house. Her skin was a tan color with faint striping of a darker hue visible when the light hit it just right. Her fire-red hair was woven into tight braids, those then bundled together into a trio running down her back to mid-shoulder, where a medium-length sword was strapped.

Her clothing was unusual, her arms exposed but her torso and legs covered. He wondered why she would select such an outfit, but the long scar on her left arm answered that question. She was a fighter, and she wanted everyone to see the damage she had taken and survived, both bolstering her reputation while giving any would-be attackers second thoughts.

She could have had it healed entirely, but once the muscle and bone was mended, she apparently opted to leave the scar as a permanent reminder. A warning sign of flesh and blood. But for all her intimidating looks, she had an air to her. An aura of joviality and energy that boosted the moods of those around her. All were having a wonderful time, it seemed, and she was the center of attention.

"What'll it be, boy?" a gruff fellow with a globular, green-skinned body and six arms asked from behind the bar.

"Uh, nothing right now, thank you."

"Suit yerself. Nixxa's buying for the whole tavern, only a fool'd waste the opportunity."

"I didn't realize. I will take a light ale."

"Coming up," he said, one of his arms deftly filling a mug without even turning to look. He slid it across the bar to Bawb.

"Does she do this often? Buying rounds, that is."

"When she's had a good haul, yeah. Generous with coin, she is. Of course, that coin was someone else's not very long ago, but it all spends the same to me, and Nixxa's been a boon for those in need for a long time."

"Oh?"

"Yeah. Don't let appearances fool ya, lad. She may be the most feared woman in here, but she looks out for people. Has a sense of justice for the unfortunate, she does."

A spark of an idea caught in Bawb's mind. Perhaps there was a way to get aboard her ship after all.

"Thank you," he said, taking the drink and stepping back toward the door.

"Don't thank me. Thank Nixxa."

Bawb leaned against the wall, blending in as best he could as he sipped at his drink. He made one attempt at the spell Hozark had taught him, but he just didn't have the proper grasp of it yet. As a result, he left the drink almost entirely unfinished. He would need his full wits about him if he was going to pull this off. He put the mug down and stepped outside to wait, hoping she would not be too long.

It wound up being some time before Nixxa emerged with her little band of revelers. She waved her farewell to the uproarious reply of the grateful patrons, then took to the street, her stride only slightly off despite the amount she had imbibed. Say what you might about pirates, they could most definitely hold their liquor.

Bawb tore his tunic and rubbed dirt on himself, scruffing his hair a bit and improvising the look of a street urchin as best he could with what was to be had around him.

*Improvised disguise? Interesting choice*, the konus said. *Let's see where this takes you, eh?*

Bawb ignored it, but hearing it speak did remind him of the

band he was wearing. He tore a long strip from his clothing and wrapped it around his wrist and hand as if bandaging an injury. A beggar would not possess a konus. That one comment had just saved him from a terrible blunder, and he had to wonder, had it just given him a hint of its own accord?

Though the konus could read his thoughts, he received no reply.

Bawb hurried ahead, arriving at the last street leading to the landing site before the gregarious revelers, tucking into a doorway to wait. Soon enough he heard them approaching, Nixxa's clear voice cutting through the others with laugh and merriment. She was the life of the party even among her own crew, it seemed. It was no wonder they were so loyal to her.

He stepped out and walked toward the group, bumping into Nixxa as she passed.

"Excuse me," he said, then kept moving.

A vise-like grip wrapped around his arm, stopping him in his tracks. He turned to find himself facing the other side of Nixxa's personality. The one that had helped her claw her way to the top. Her eyes were blazing, an almost palpable energy coursing through her body as she gripped his arm hard. She held out her other hand.

"Give it back," she growled.

"I—"

"I said give it back."

Bawb cast his eyes low as he reached into his pocket and took out the coin pouch he had pickpocketed from her, placing it in her palm. She pocketed it and glared at him intensely.

"Do you know who I am?" she asked in a threatening tone.

Tears streamed down the boy's face as he looked up at her. He even managed to make his lip quiver a little.

"No," he whimpered. "Please don't hurt me. I'm sorry. I'm just so hungry."

The rage in Nixxa's eyes extinguished as if doused by his tears, her expression softening in an instant.

"What's your name, kid?"

"Boddik," he replied.

"Boddik, huh? When's the last time you ate?"

"A few days ago. I was mugged. They took everything. I haven't been able to sleep since then. It's not safe."

She looked at her crew and sighed. They knew what she was going to do. Deadly pirate or not, she had a soft spot for kids in distress.

"Okay, Boddik, come with me."

"Why? Y-you're not going to hurt me, are you?" he asked, wincing in fear in a most convincing way.

"You'll be fine," she said, her tone gentle and entirely unpiratelike. "Let's get you fed, cleaned up, and find you a cozy spot to get some rest, okay?"

Bawb hesitated, his reluctance slowly overcome by his exhaustion and hunger. "Okay," he said at last, quietly falling in with their group as they walked into the landing site and aboard her ship.

As part of the captain's away group, the guard didn't even look at him as he walked into the hatch. He was with Nixxa, and that put him above suspicion.

"I'm taking him to get cleaned up. Pollix, get him some clean clothes in his size," she instructed a short, yellow-and-black-skinned fellow with a deep orange mohawk of hair running from his head into his shirt and down his back.

"On it, Captain," he said, hurrying off to do as she requested.

Nixxa herself walked him to the bathing compartment and opened the door. "Take your time. No one will bother you. Pollix will be back with some fresh clothes for you shortly. Now, clean up, and then we'll see about getting you something to eat."

She turned and walked away, leaving the boy alone in the compartment to bathe in peace.

*Level up: Infiltration, deception, and acting,* the konus said. *Well done.*

Well done indeed, he mused. But the hardest part was yet to come.

# CHAPTER FIFTY-ONE

Bawb took his time bathing, not that he was particularly dirty, but more because he hadn't really expected his plan to work. But here he was, aboard Nixxa's ship and seen as a non-threat. It was as the teachers had said. Children are able to go places adults cannot simply because they are underestimated because of their age.

Bawb slid on the clean clothes and wrapped his konus and hand with a strip of washed cloth, making it appear to simply be an improvised bandage as before. When he stepped out of the bathing compartment, he found Pollix nearby, chatting with a massive, reptilian-looking creature in crew attire.

"Ah, Boddik, you're bathed. I hope the clothing fits. We don't normally keep many things around that are your size."

"Yeah, they're great. Thanks so much," he replied, making an effort to speak like any other youth.

"Oh, I want to introduce you to Zurk," the pirate said, gesturing to the huge creature beside him.

"Hey, little fella. Nice to meetcha," he said with a deep, rumbling voice.

"Uh, nice to meet you too," Bawb replied.

"I hear you tried to pickpocket the captain."

"Yeah. Not my proudest moment."

Zurk and Pollix laughed heartily. "You have no idea, Boddik," Zurk said. "Nixxa's known for having no tolerance for that sort of thing. Stealing from her is as good as a death wish. Fortunately for you, she's got a soft spot for kids in trouble."

"Good to know."

Pollix slapped him merrily on the shoulder. "Well, come on, then. Let's get you to the galley. We just re-stocked, so you're in luck."

He led the boy down the corridors, Bawb taking note of every twist and turn as he plotted an escape route in his mind. If things went good *or* bad, he would be needing one, though how soon he had no idea. He also noticed the crew they passed all spoke to one another in a slightly odd way. Nothing drastic, but a few words and expressions he hadn't heard used in that way before.

"That's a weird way of talking," he said innocently.

Pollix gave him a conspiratorial wink. "I'll let you in on a little pirate trick, kid."

"You will?" he replied, ramping up his look of amazement accordingly.

"Yep. You see, we have a code of sorts. A way to know who's really one of us. Not a problem normally, but during a raid, messages can get intercepted and this way we know it's really one of us talking."

"Wow, that's really smart!" Bawb marveled, making note to memorize absolutely everything he could of all aspects of their speech patterns, linguistic tics, and secret passphrases while he was among them. One never knew when it might come in handy, after all. "I can't believe you actually get to live here. This is a really nice ship. Do you fly a lot?"

"Oh, we do our fair share. But we had a busy time of late, so the captain's giving us a bit of an extended shore leave to unwind. She's good like that. Always looking out for her crew."

"It must be nice, seeing the stars."

"It can be, I have to admit. And we travel far and wide on our, uh, *business*."

"I bet. How many Drooks do you have on board?"

"Oh, we can't afford to risk using Drooks. Too much turmoil doesn't sit well with them. They fly better in tranquil conditions."

"But how do you fly without Drooks? I've never seen a ship that could do that."

Pollix chuckled, amused by the boy's enthusiasm. "Tell you what. I'll show you how we do it. But after we eat. The galley's just up ahead."

He opened the door to reveal several rough and tough pirates relaxing over a nice meal. It wasn't what Bawb had expected by a long shot. The galley was spotless, for one, the crew keeping it pristine as per Nixxa's orders. And the decor was tranquil and simple. None of the clutter and overtly macho trappings one would expect on a pirate ship. Again, Nixxa's influence setting the example for the crew.

As they gathered heaping plates of food in what he called an "around the world" sampler, Pollix explained that Nixxa was quite unlike the other captains. She was just as brutal and ruthless, when need be, even more than the others, truth be told. But she had an over-developed sense of right and wrong, and part of that had spilled over into the crew's common spaces.

No brawls were allowed aboard the ship, and while ribbing and casual insults were part of the lifestyle, she took pains to ensure all on her crew felt at home and valued for their contributions. And when they took a prize, the spoils were shared generously among her faithful. But more than that, apparently, Nixxa made a regular habit of spreading the wealth among the less fortunate and needy as well.

She was quite literally stealing from the rich and giving to the poor, Bawb marveled. He thought it was so unlikely a tale that had he not seen her generosity with his own eyes he would have believed it to be no more than a fairy tale.

Bawb and Pollix ate with the other crew, all of them seeming to take a liking to the boy, and the way he was shoveling down food only endeared him to them even more. Being a starving street urchin, he would be expected to eat ravenously. But as a Ghalian Aspirant who burned thousands upon thousands of calories a day with his rigorous training, Bawb found this was one part of the act he had no problem performing.

Finally, after a rather epic-sized meal, he pushed back from the table.

"I can't," he muttered. "Too full."

The pirates laughed uproariously. They were enjoying his discomfort, in a good-natured way. Since they couldn't challenge him with drink at so young an age, food would have to suffice.

"Okay, lads. Enough," Pollix said, pushing back from the table. "I'm giving him a tour of the ship. He's got a lot to learn about the world, it seems."

"You're a one to be teachin' 'im," an inebriated fellow said, lifting his head from the table just long enough for his pronouncement.

"Yeah, yeah. Sleep it off, Garrik," Pollix said with a laugh. "C'mon, boy. Let's show you around a bit. See you, lads."

Pollix led his guest out into the corridor and began a quick loop of the ship, showing off some of the more interesting features before finally reaching the command center. As they were parked, powered down, and not about to be going anywhere, the compartment was empty.

"When we're underway, this place is a buzzing hive of

activity," he said. "But since we're all on leave and the captain's taking a bit of a break, there's no need."

"Where do you sit?"

"Me? Oh, I'm not command crew. I'm more of a hands-on sort of fella. Most of this is beyond my skill set, though I do have certain priority overrides at my disposal just in case. But look at me digress. I almost forgot. This over here? It's what you were wondering about," he said, pointing out the Drookonus resting in its faintly glowing receptacle. "It's called a Drookonus," he added, uttering a few words to release it, pulling it free and holding it up for Bawb to examine.

"It's amazing. What does it do?"

"It powers the ship. Well, the flight and weapons systems, anyway. All ships have redundancies, but ours are a bit more robust than most, for obvious reasons. But this is what drives us. It contains quite a lot of Drook power in such a small package."

"Wow," Bawb said in awe. "I've never seen anything like it."

"Well, maybe you'll use one yourself one day. You think you might want to be a pirate? You're small, but when you grow up a bit—"

Bawb bent over fast, as if he had a sharp stomach pain.

"Are you all right?"

"I-I'm not used to eating so much. I think I may be sick. Or maybe something else."

"Both ends, eh? Perhaps you overdid it a little in the galley?"

"Maybe," he said, contorting with feigned discomfort.

"There's a head right through that door. Do your business. I'll wait for you in the corridor."

Bawb nodded his thanks and rushed through the door. He had hoped there was a toilet directly in the command center. It made sense that those crewing it would not wish to have to go far if they needed one, and that had given him what he needed.

He peeked out of the toilet. The command center was empty.

Without hesitation he ran to the Drookonus and repeated the words he had heard Pollix say, hoping they would work for him as well, lest this all be for naught.

The Drookonus released for him.

Bawb snatched it and tucked it into his clothing then raced back to the toilet. He waited a minute longer then flushed, not knowing if the walls were soundproof or if his guide would hear or feel the vibrations of it. Better safe than sorry, he figured.

"Better?" Pollix asked as Bawb stepped into the corridor to join him.

"Much. It was as you said. *Both* ends."

"Okay, kid, that's more information than I need, but good for you. Come on, Nixxa wants to see you."

Bawb felt a little surge of adrenaline but kept his cool, following close, his head on a swivel taking in all of the amazing sights around him as the character he was playing would.

They entered the galley to find Nixxa had arrived, joining the crew in meal and merriment despite having so recently eaten in the tavern. But this part of the crew had stayed aboard, and that meant they missed the festivities. It was only fair she should do what she could to bring the party to them instead.

"Boddik! Hey, you look much better!" she called out in greeting. "You were fed, yes?"

"Oh, yes. Thank you so much. I haven't eaten that much in, well, I can't remember how long."

"And your injury?" she asked, nodding to his wrist.

"Washed and wrapped. It's fine, I just try to keep it bound and clean."

"Smart thing when you don't have a healer on hand, isn't that right?"

The crew erupted in a chorus of agreement. They really were having a good time of it, and their affection for their captain seemed genuine.

"So," she continued, "Pollix tells me you want to be a pirate someday. You know, you could start now. Sweeping the decks, cleaning the head."

"Um, well, I—"

"I'm just playing with ya!" she said with a hearty laugh before digging into her pocket and retrieving the pouch the boy had failed to pickpocket from her earlier. She tossed it to him with a friendly grin on her lips. "Go on, take it and get out of here."

"I—are you sure?"

"No kid should ever go hungry," she said, her demeanor showing a flash of darkness.

It was only for an instant, but Bawb was certain of it. Something had happened to her in her youth, and she was going to do whatever she could to see to it other children did not face such a hardship. Bawb felt the Drookonus pressing against him under his clothes and almost felt guilty stealing from her. She had stolen it first, of course, but that was beside the point.

"Thank you," he said, tucking the coin in his pocket.

"Pollix, be a dear and show our new friend out. And, Boddik, you take care of yourself, okay?"

"I will," he replied. "Thank you for your hospitality."

"Yeah, yeah. Now get out of here before I change my mind," she said with a chuckle.

"C'mon, kid," Pollix said, leading the way.

A few minutes later he was back in the streets of Kardahn, wearing clean clothes, with coin in his pocket and a Drookonus hidden on himself. As soon as he was out of sight of the landing area, he ducked into a shop and bought some very basic clothes, ditching what they'd given him as he altered his appearance to blend in with the crowd.

He stepped out of the shop and took off running, excitement flowing through him. It had been his first real mission, and it was a success. All that was left was getting to the ship and heading home. The masters were sure to be pleased with what he had accomplished, and all on his own.

Visions of hearty congratulations and atta boys filled his head as he ran, but when he reached the landing site, they abruptly vanished. Vanished just as the ship had done.

Bawb felt a chill run through his body as he realized what had happened. It had taken too long. The ship was gone. He was too late, and now he was all alone.

"Shit."

# CHAPTER FIFTY-TWO

Bawb's shock was raging through his body, but his training kicked in, his face betraying none of what was going on in his mind. He had been abandoned. Left on a small moon, surrounded by ruffians and pirates, the most notorious of them all being someone he had just stolen a rather valuable item from.

It was enough to soil the trousers of anyone foolish enough to put themselves in that situation. Bawb, however, was not anyone. He was a Wampeh Ghalian. Well, an Aspirant Ghalian, anyway. And as such, he had the tools to make the most of this situation. He just had to slip away somewhere quiet to think without prying eyes wondering what the lone youth was doing standing around an empty space in the town's secondary landing site.

Bawb turned casually and walked to one of the small streets exiting into the landing area. There he bought a snack from one of the street vendors and sat against a wall, eating it slowly. He'd just been fed a massive meal, but this was what many of the ships' crews were doing, so he followed suit and blended in.

It also afforded him a little respite with which he could observe all around him, a solid wall to his back, and figure out exactly how the hell he was going to get out of this place, let alone back home.

He carefully counted the coin Nixxa had given him. It was a fair sum. She'd been quite generous in her gift. But it was not enough to buy passage all the way to where he needed to go. The transport was set to depart the following morning, so he had time, and if he could just make it aboard somehow, then he could find a quiet space to tuck away and wait out the night, just in case.

It turned out, the just-in-case scenario was already upon him.

A commotion was brewing across the landing site, the various crews talking about it amongst themselves. Nixxa's people were there, fanning out, searching. Searching for a boy wearing the clothes he had been given. The clothes he had wisely ditched as soon as he had been able.

Bawb casually slid into a nearby alleyway, pressing against the wall as he watched and listened. It seemed his theft had been noticed far sooner than he had anticipated. This was a decidedly bad turn of events. There was no time to try pickpocketing to steal enough to pay for a seat aboard the transport ship.

Worse, if he stayed on this moon he was going to get caught. There was simply no way he could pass without detection indefinitely. He had learned a lot, yes, but he was wise enough to realize he was not up to the task. Not yet.

Bawb tucked the coin pouch away and scanned the area. There had to be an option. He just needed to calm his mind and find it.

Nixxa's crew were moving fast. They were efficient, he had to give them that. And stealing from their captain, whom they all seemed to genuinely like, had put him square in the middle of their shit list. Bawb's stomach dropped when a tall figure strode into view, an angry look on her face and rage in her eyes. Nixxa herself had come to find him. This was getting out of hand, and fast.

"Anywhere other than here," he told himself. "It doesn't matter. Just get off this moon."

He moved fast, hugging the outskirts of the field and staying as much out of view as possible as he hurried to the nearest timetable posted at one of the larger landing area entrances. He scanned for the next ship leaving.

"Got it."

Bawb forced himself to walk normally. Fast, but unremarkable, as he made his way to the craft that was supposed to be leaving soonest. He was about to approach the man at the hatch to buy passage when Nixxa's people soured that plan, arriving before him.

"A Wampeh. Just a kid," the pirate said, describing the thief.

"No, haven't seen one," the man replied.

Bawb had unknowingly dodged a bullet. Had he purchased a fare he'd have been noted. And that applied to *every* ship, it seemed. Much as he hated the idea, he was going to have to stow away the hard way.

There was no time to try for another landing area. If Nixxa was already at this one, it meant her people had spread through the entire town in their hasty search for him. It was now or never. All he was lacking was a *how*.

Nixxa came striding toward the ship, her anger palpable from a distance.

"Anything?" she demanded.

"Not yet, Captain. But a few people did say they saw a boy of his size and age, but wearing different clothes than you gave him."

"Clever little thief, changing his appearance," she growled. "Find him. I'm going to see about locking down any ships until we do."

"Can you do that?" one of the pirates asked.

"I'll damn well try."

She turned slowly, her eyes scanning the crowd. Bawb ducked behind a medium-sized storage bin. It stank of pungent rot, making his eyes water. He peered inside. It was full of some sort of fermenting vegetables, and a *lot* of them, their fermentation powered by a slow-acting magic. A delicacy to some, no doubt, but to his uncultured palate it was no more than spicy, rotting trash.

He felt a whisper of magic tickle his senses, and it was moving closer. Nixxa was using some sort of spell to find him. No. Not to find him, but to find the Drookonus. He had to think fast. Using his limited spells, he cast hard and focused, sending a push spell across the open space, knocking over several stacked containers, causing a commotion.

Nixxa turned to look. He moved fast. He only had a moment before her attention shifted once more.

Bawb cast the air bubble spell around his head, lifted the lid, and slipped over the storage bin's edge, sliding beneath the surface of the foul concoction until he was completely submerged. He had no idea if it would work, but he hoped the ambient magic powering the fermentation would provide a masking effect, blocking out the traces of Drookonus energy Nixxa was seeking.

He held his breath, remaining completely still, conserving his oxygen. He would only have a few breaths in the bubble he had created, and he had to make them count. At least it was blocking most of the smell, but the air trapped in the bubble around his head was already rather ripe when he cast it.

He felt Nixxa's spell grow stronger, but then it gradually lessened. It was looking as though his ploy may actually have worked.

The container shook as it lifted into the air, a loading spell moving it into the cargo hold of the ship, workers locking it into place.

"Four more and we're loaded up, Cap'n," a man called out.

"I'll be in command," was the muffled reply. "We launch the moment you're done. Nixxa's got a bug up her ass about some kid, and I'd rather be out of here before things get out of hand. Says she's going to lock down all the landing sites."

"Can she do that?"

"It's Nixxa. If anyone's going to manage it, it'll be her."

"Aye, Cap. We'll hurry."

Bawb felt more containers slam into place in quick succession, followed by a lurching sensation as the ship took off in a rush, eager to get clear before Nixxa's rage affected their delivery schedule. Bawb popped his head above the surface and pushed up on the lid. It opened, but only partly. It was enough for him to press his lips to the gap and suck in some relatively fresh air.

He would not be able to exit his hiding spot until they landed and offloaded. But at least he was clear of Kardahn. What he'd do when they arrived wherever it was they were going was anyone's guess. At least he would still be alive to deal with that problem when he got there.

It was a short flight to their next destination, just a simple jump to another planet within the same system. To his delight, the storage bin was hauled out with the others and left on the landing field tarmac while the captain and his customer handled the final transfer details.

The securing spell released, Bawb managed to slip out and onto the ground. He was free, but now he had a different problem.

He stank. Badly.

"Water," he said, looking around for anything to wash himself with. There was an animal drinking trough abutting a market stall, but that was all he could find. It would have to suffice.

He stepped in, submerging himself completely as he shook his body, scrubbing off the foul concoction as best he could. Even so, he still smelled, but not nearly as strongly. He could walk about now without drawing too much attention, but he would, however, need to secure clean clothes sooner than later.

Without the fear of Nixxa hanging over his head, Bawb made his way through the city, taking it all in and stealing articles of clothing piecemeal as he could until he had a clean but mismatched outfit that was entirely stink-free.

Better yet, he managed to lift a small quantity of coin in the process. It wasn't a lot, but added to what he had already received from Nixxa, it should be enough. Enough to get home.

"One fare," he said to the male admitting passengers to the transport ship he had located.

"You okay, kid?" the alien asked, his stalked eyes looking the boy up and down. "Traveling alone?"

"Yeah, I'm just heading to visit my uncle. I can get my parents to talk to you if you want, but you'll need to hold the launch while I find them."

The man pondered a split second. "Take your seat. Next!"

Bawb did just that, sliding down into a form-fitting pod chair, his body finally relaxing from the continuous strain he had been under. The ship wasn't leaving for a little bit yet, but he wasn't worried about that. He had made it. He was safe. And he would be home soon enough. For now, he would do what he had been trained to do in these situations.

Bawb closed his eyes and slid into a shallow meditative state. He wasn't sleeping, not exactly, but was resting just on the edge of slumber, aware of his surroundings but also recharging his overtaxed body and mind.

Soon he would be back at the training house and all would be right.

# CHAPTER FIFTY-THREE

Bawb felt the stress slipping from his body the closer his transport came to his home planet. This sensation was further enhanced by the increasing vastness of empty space being placed between him and Nixxa's angry rampage on Kardahn.

By the time he landed and made his way to the training house door, Bawb was almost feeling back to normal. All he had to do now was face the masters. They would be mad. He had gone missing, wandered off, and failed to return on their transport, something he and the others had been expressly warned against.

Worse, he had nearly gotten himself killed, and undoubtedly riled up a world of hurt back on the little moon he had only just visited for the first time. All in all, it had turned into something of a mess.

He tried to open the door but found it locked, not budging an inch.

"That is odd," he mused.

The Ghalian had false entrances and hidden doors to the actual training house. This one merely led into one of the decoy entryways. And so far as he knew, it was never locked.

Until today.

He tried again, to the same results, or lack thereof. He stepped back, confused, then took off at a brisk pace for one of the other entrances on a different side of the block. It too was locked up tight. Now he was starting to get worried. These were the only entrances he knew for a fact contained an access point to a secret passageway.

Bawb stood there, perplexed a long moment, then decided to try the one thing anyone seeking a stealthy entrance would do their best to avoid. He began pounding on the door, making far more noise than he wanted.

Still nothing.

He stepped back, wondering what he might do next. What had happened.

"Konus?"

*What?* it replied with an annoyed sigh, even though it had no lungs with which to breathe.

"Have I been expelled from the order?"

*First smart question of the day, kid. I don't think you have, but you pretty well botched what should have been a quick in and out. All you had to do was steal the stupid Drookonus and get back to the ship before it left. How hard is that?*

"Apparently, harder than you make it out to be," he replied, his annoyance with the inanimate band on his wrist growing with his concern. "But you don't think I've been kicked out?"

*Who can say? The Ghalian are mysterious in their ways, as you well know. You really messed this up, didn't you?*

Bawb's cool was slipping, and he was about to give the konus a piece of his mind when the door abruptly opened. It wasn't a teacher standing there. It was Master Imalla, staring at him with cold eyes.

He stood still, not daring to breathe a word until spoken to. She was not a woman to be trifled with. In fact, she was the one who had suggested killing him when he had been unwilling to drink blood. And as a lowly Aspirant, he still had close to no value to her or the order. Losing him would not impact their daily activities one bit.

"Where have you been?" she finally asked, her words sending ice into his veins.

"I was on a mission."

"You had no mission. You had a training exercise. One you had performed only moderately well."

"Not that one. There was another."

"No, Aspirant Bawb, there was not. Your carelessness caused you to miss your transport. What if this had been a real task? If the lives of others had been on the line?"

"No, really. I *was* on a mission," he said, realizing that while it had been a difficult task, it was an unsanctioned one. That was likely to anger her even more.

"A mission I did not know of? Unlikely."

"It was," he said, dreading his next words. "It was just not an official one."

Master Imalla glared at him fiercely. Had they not been in public view he worried she might have struck him down on the spot. Quickly, he reached in his clothes and withdrew the Drookonus.

"I was getting this," he said, lowering his gaze and holding the device out to her with outstretched hands.

Imalla snatched it from him, examining it with a curious look. "Inside, Aspirant Bawb," she said flatly. "Come with me."

She led him inside, sealing the door behind her before opening the hidden passageway leading to the inner reaches of the compound. On and on they walked until they reached a small chamber he had never visited before. She opened the door and motioned for him to step inside.

Bawb looked around, noting the few seats in the small room

were already occupied. Masters and a few teachers were present. Even Master Hozark was there. None looked terribly pleased to see him.

"It would seem our overzealous Aspirant put it upon himself to steal something for us," Imalla said, handing Hozark the Drookonus.

He looked it over, his eyebrow arched with amusement. He turned his gaze to the boy.

"What did you do, Bawb? Why did you vanish, and how did you come by this Drookonus?"

"I wanted to help," he began. "When Nixxa stole the Drookonus from that ship we use, I thought if I could get it back it would help the order. Everyone else is busy on Ghalian business, but I'm just an Aspirant. Nobody would miss my labors if anything happened to me."

The adults shared what looked like surprised glances at one another, though Ghalian poker faces were second to none.

"You say you robbed *Nixxa*?" Imalla asked. "Not likely. How did you *really* come by this?"

"I told you. I took it from Nixxa's ship."

"Preposterous. With no preparation? No intelligence? You, an Aspirant, managed to overcome her guards, her defenses, and break into her command chamber? Lies within our order do not become a Ghalian, Aspirant Bawb."

"I am not lying. And I did not fight with anyone to get it."

Hozark leaned forward ever so slightly in his seat. "Interesting. Do tell us, Bawb. What did you do?"

"Well, people say that Nixxa has a generous streak. Gives to the unfortunate and that sort of thing. So I pickpocketed her, rather clumsily at that, and when caught, played up to her softer side in hopes that she would see not an unskilled thief, but a hungry boy down on his luck and in need of help."

Imalla's expression had shifted from angry disbelief to curiosity. "And this worked?"

"It did. She took me aboard her ship, allowed me to bathe—I had smeared filth on myself to enhance the impression I was trying to make—then she even gave me clean clothes and saw to it I was well fed."

"That does not explain how you came by this Drookonus."

"That was a little trickier, but I was not seen as a threat, so when I expressed interest in the workings of a pirate ship, I was given a tour. I took advantage of an opportunity by pretending my stomach was upset, and when they left me to use the restroom, I took the Drookonus."

"But a Drookonus is locked in place," Imalla noted.

"Yes, it was. But I said I had never seen one before, and the person showing me the ship removed it to show me."

Hozark laughed aloud, to the surprise of the others. "Oh, that is wonderful, Bawb. And let me guess, you memorized the release phrase?"

"Yes, I did," he replied, suddenly a lot less concerned about being kicked out of the order.

The masters huddled together, talking with great animation as they debated what to do with the boy. Finally, Master Hozark, as one of the Five and the ranking master present, stood up and approached him.

"You stole from a notorious pirate, Bawb. It was reckless and dangerous. Do you realize this?"

"I do. But she stole from the Ghalian. It seemed the right thing to do, getting the Drookonus back."

"And in that endeavor, you have rather outdone yourself, Bawb."

"What do you mean?"

"What I mean is, *this* is not the Drookonus that was stolen from us. No, that one, while a robust unit, was *far* less powerful than this one. You managed to replace what was taken with something of far greater value, and I am quite certain Nixxa will not be pleased. Not one bit."

"Good," Imalla interjected. "That woman is a menace who barely does more good than harm."

"But she is a thorn in the Council's side far more often than ours," Hozark noted. "I feel it is a fair trade-off in the long run."

Bawb watched the exchange in confusion, the two masters' demeanors more that of jovial colleagues than angry assassins ready to lay judgment upon him.

"Excuse me?" he said quietly.

"Yes, Aspirant?" Imalla replied.

"Does this mean I am not going to be expelled?"

Hozark chuckled, and even Imalla seemed to lighten up. "No, Bawb," he said. "You are not to be expelled. The masters and I have decided that you will stay. Foolish as your ill-advised attempt was, you actually succeeded, and in so doing proved yourself more than worthy of remaining in the order. You infiltrated a hostile force's home ship, gained their trust, stole an item of great value, and escaped without resources, making it all the way back several planets away. Frankly, it is an impressive feat for one so young as yourself."

"Well, I did not exactly have *no* resources."

"Oh?"

"Nixxa gave me a pouch of coin before I left."

Now Hozark and the others seemed truly amused, a few laughs breaking their normally stoic façades.

"And you had her give you coin. Exceptional, Bawb. Well done."

*Yeah, that was pretty great,* the konus said in his head. *Level up: enemy deception and theft. Keep it up and you might just make a Ghalian yet.*

Bawb noted that Hozark cracked a grin, almost as if he heard the silent words, but the master then dismissed him to join his classmates for dinner and a good night's sleep. He would surely need it after his adventure, and the others were undoubtedly going to have many questions for him.

The masters were still talking amongst themselves when he left, his mood elevated and his spirits high, looking forward to whatever his training might throw at him next.

This was where he belonged. This was home.

# EPILOGUE

Bawb enjoyed a moment of somewhat celebrity status among his Aspirant classmates following his successful, though ill-advised adventure. He had gone toe-to-toe with a notorious pirate and come out on top. It was the sort of thing that inspired people to do more. To try harder. And as a result, his classmates all began pushing themselves to succeed, and all because of Bawb's foolish escapade.

The masters were glad to see it. The added drive was a welcome change, especially as training was about to take a turn for the more serious now that they were progressing ahead of schedule. It would be grueling work, but, to his surprise, Bawb was actually looking forward to it.

"One day," he said to his konus, "I am going to be one of the Five."

*One of the Five? Ha! Not likely. Do you have any idea how hard it is just to become a master?*

"I do, actually. It will be quite a challenge."

*Yeah, it will. Now multiply that by a hundred and you might start to come close to how hard it is to become one of the Five. There is so much to learn. Way more than just a master, and that's a lot.*

The konus then did something unusual. For a moment, it flashed a massive list of spells and skills for Bawb to see. It was dizzying. Overwhelming. There was so much he didn't know, and it was all laid out for him in plain detail. The konus blurred the icons once more, hiding all from view, but Bawb had seen a lot in that glimpse, but rather than deter him, it had just made him desire his objective all the more.

He needed more information, though. Information about the Five. Only one person he knew was in the position to help him.

"Master Hozark?" he asked when he saw him next. "What does it take to become one of the Five?"

"Many years of hard work, but that is only the start," Hozark replied. "There is much to learn, and many of those things are not taught in classes or training sessions."

"Real-world knowledge," Bawb said.

"Yes. But why do you ask? You have performed your duties, but you never seemed terribly keen on advancing."

"I realize now this is something I can be good at. No, I can be *great*. It will be a lot of work, I know, but I am willing to put in the effort."

"It pleases me to hear you are embracing your skills."

"I am. But there is one somewhat unconventional thing I wanted to ask you."

"Yes?"

Bawb hesitated, suddenly a bit unsure. "Will you help me?" he finally asked.

Hozark's lips quivered a moment, a smile creeping onto his face and a look of pride growing in his eyes. "You wish to accelerate your training?"

"I do."

"Knowing it will require much effort?"

"Yes."

Hozark considered the request a moment. "I can set aside time to privately teach you when I am able. But if you commit to this, know it will mean less free time for you. You will need to devote yourself to your training and studies even when not in class."

"I will do it."

"You say that now, but friendships may suffer, as will your body."

"What do I have to do?" Bawb replied, resolute in his decision.

Hozark grinned. "Do? What I instruct you, without question or hesitation."

"I can do that."

Bawb didn't know why, but he could have sworn there was an almost cheerful air to the normally stoic Ghalian master. A gleam of happiness in his eyes.

"Go train with the others, Bawb. Strengthen your body and resolve. From time to time, when I deem you ready, I will add to your training with additional lessons. There will be no set schedule, but you must always be prepared. Sleeping, eating, resting after a days- or week-long mission, I may call upon you, and you will have to be ready at a moment's notice."

"I will be."

"You say that now, but this will be a long path. Becoming a master is attainable to many, but to go beyond? To become one of the Five. It requires more. Much more. That, and one of the Five must retire or die."

"But I thought Ghalian never retired."

"Exactly."

"When do we start?"

"We already have. Remember, Bawb, *a fire blazes, dead without embers. Storms rage, yet a feather floats.*"

"What does that mean?"

"One day, when the time is right, you will know. For now, I will leave you to your classes. I will be seeing you again, Bawb. Perhaps sooner than later. And here, this is for you."

He handed Bawb an item swaddled in cloth. Bawb unwrapped it and felt a little surge of familiar magic in his hands. It was Porrius's dagger. But it was no longer filthy and worn. It had been restored, its magic recharged.

"He would have wanted you to have that," Hozark said, resting his hand on the boy's shoulder. "You did right by a fallen Ghalian. You have potential, Bawb. I hope you live up to it."

With that, Hozark left him to his own devices, his cryptic words churning in the boy's mind. He thought about what Hozark said to him throughout dinner, during the animated conversations they had afterwards, and even as he reclined in his bed drifting off to sleep.

Bawb lay there in the dark, slumber overtaking him, sweet sleep beckoning, waiting to wash away the day's exhaustion. He let it come, welcoming it, at last happy in his life, and excited for what the new day would bring.

# PREVIEW: ASSASSIN'S APPRENTICE

Blood was dripping in a steady stream from Bawb's head, flowing off his chin in a crimson waterfall of sorts. He merely grit his teeth and waited his turn. Others were far worse off than he was and needed to be tended to before him. This was not the first time he would bleed, and it would certainly not be the last.

He was sitting quietly just outside the healer's chamber with several of his likewise-injured classmates. No one was safe from injury in the Ghalian training house, and this was one place in particular they had all come to know well as they moved up in the ranks from the greenest of the green all the way to where they found themselves now.

Vessels, in Bawb's class's case, each and every one of them. And after much blood and sweat, they were nearly ready to advance to the level of Adept. Soon they would be sent out on missions alone as Wampeh Ghalian, albeit of the lower ranks.

Naturally, they would be directed toward missions fitting their areas of proficiency at first, the early tasks tailored to their skills. But as they progressed, and once they each showed a solid grasp of their own unique fighting styles which they were now creating, they would then be allowed out on more dangerous contracts.

They had come far and excelled, but it had been a long, hard, and deadly road.

Of course, being a teenager was tough on any world. Growth spurts, hormones, and the usual drama that teens tended to find themselves ensnared in were all things one could expect at that age. Most teens, however, did not experience what the Vessels were going through, nor could they begin to fathom the difficulties they faced.

Their resilient bones were growing longer and stronger, while their body mass was simultaneously thickening with wiry muscles forged in the fires of hard work. Wampeh were a hardy race to begin with, but the intense Ghalian training molded them into fit and agile works of art.

They still had several years remaining in the Wampeh growth cycle, but their bodies had already taken on the basic form they would possess for the rest of their lives. Some were more wiry, others stocky. Some rounder while others lean. But one thing was universal among them. They were all willing and able to carry out their dangerous tasks without fear their bodies might fail them.

Years upon years of training and hard work had earned them as much, and they were tough, possessing ever growing confidence. They were good. Better than that, they were beginning to truly believe themselves to actually be *skilled*.

But this? This was a disconcerting reminder that no matter how much they had learned, they still had a *very* long way to go. The day had not begun easily, and it would only get worse.

During breakfast they were summoned by Teacher Griggitz and directed to stand outside a new chamber they had not yet trained in. They were then called in individually. Beyond that, none knew what the teachers wanted with them. They would, as always, find out soon enough.

The Vessels were each gone a fairly long time, eventually exiting in turn, Teacher Griggitz had sent them one-by-one on their way to the healer, a group of lower ranked aides helping when needed. Whatever challenge they were facing, it was unexpected, as was the norm with their instructors, but was also clearly not insignificant. It made for an unsettling situation, and as their classmates were hauled out in various states of agony, it only got worse.

Elzina had long been Bawb's de facto nemesis as the two jostled for rank as they grew. She was a fierce girl, and had an impressive level of drive that bordered on excessive. She fought hard and never gave up, but just like the others, she was soon carried out on a floating litter, battered and bloody, her left arm jutting out at an angle it was not meant to bend. Her nose was broken and her face was swollen, her lip split and trickling blood.

She glanced at the others with dazed eyes but said nothing as she was brought into the healer's chambers, just like the others.

"She's one of the best of us," Zota said in shock, notably disquieted despite his training.

"That is the fourth," Usalla added, shaking her head, her tightly-woven braids moving slightly though still tucked away and prepared for a fight. "This does not bode well for us."

"Not well at all," Finnia agreed, wondering if her spy training path might afford her any respite from the challenge.

Likely not.

This was a test. A test each of them would have to face, regardless of their particular area of proficiency or class rank. And so far, none had succeeded. Worst of all, those still waiting had no idea what it entailed. All they knew was that one by one they were called away, and one by one they returned in varying states of bloodiness.

"Bawb. You are next," Teacher Griggitz said, then turned and walked back into the chamber.

Bawb would follow, of course. They all would.

"See you soon," the boy said, then rose from his seat and left.

Zota shook his head with a hint of concern, something normally unbecoming a Ghalian. "I do not like this."

Usalla nodded somberly. "None of us do. But it is the way."

As they sat wondering what might lie in store for them, Bawb was finding out first hand.

"In here," Griggitz said, leading him through the new chamber and into a small room. "All you require for this task is present here."

Bawb looked around, taking in the items present. A few he would have expected were notably not present.

"There appear to be no weapons."

"That is correct. You are to infiltrate a tavern in town. A rough, dangerous place, as I am sure you have surmised by now."

"I have."

"Then you also realize the risk you face. You are to blend in, then find Teacher Demelza in the mix and hand her this," he said, giving him a plain wooden token with a basic symbol burned into it. "If you can accomplish that, you will have succeeded in this task."

"Magic?" he asked.

"You may attempt to use your konus to aid in your disguise, but be advised, you are still a Vessel and your casting has a long way to go yet. You may do more harm than good. But that decision is yours to make. You are no longer a child. I will now leave you to it. All you require to fashion a disguise is here.

When you are ready, head to the Rusty Kettle. You know the location, yes?"

Bawb, like all of the other students, had memorized every street, alley, shop, and tavern in the city over the last few years. It was one thing to quickly adapt on the fly in a new situation, but on their home turf they were expected to excel. To be better than just good.

"I know it," he replied, then immediately turned his attention to the wares spread out before him.

Griggitz nodded and left him to prepare. He would be situated near the tavern to collect him if things went wrong. And by the looks of Elzina and the others as they were carried home, there was a real likelihood that would be the case.

Bawb wasted no time, opting for a simple coloration spell to alter his skin tone to a light brown rather than the Wampeh's natural pale complexion. That was a spell he was actually becoming quite good at. The other disguise spells, however, were still somewhat lacking.

He used practical appliances to further change his appearance, giving his body additional bulk under his clothing and the semblance of a more muscular build. It wouldn't hold up to close inspection, but it might convince an aggressive interloper to just leave him alone.

Or not.

Some people sought out the more challenging adversaries in hopes of making a name for themselves. He just hoped this would not be the case today. He had to get in, find his zaftig teacher, and get out. The fact that the others to go before him were beaten so badly led him to believe this task would not be so simple.

Bawb noted a small bag of coin on the table and pocketed it. Griggitz had said everything was for his use, and he decided that applied to currency as well. The goodwill a round of drinks could purchase could often calm a rowdy crowd. At least, Master Hozark had told him as much, and had demonstrated in person on a few of their outings as well.

Bawb examined himself in the mirror spell. It wasn't perfect, and he was unarmed, but it would have to suffice.

*Not bad*, his konus said, the magical band on his wrist having developed even more of a personality in the years he had been wearing it. *Maybe you'll even make it out of this unscathed.*

"You think so?"

*No,* the device scoffed. *You're pretty much screwed and in for it like the rest, I'd wager.*

"We shall see about that, Konus."

*Oh, of that I'm certain.*

The device, a gift from Master Hozark himself, had a tendency to give him grief just before a challenging task, but Bawb had learned that this was just something it did when he might actually have a chance to level up in a skill. Sowing doubt and making him work harder for it, as the case may be.

But he had leveled up in many areas since he first received the device, and the icon list, visible only to his eyes, had slowly but steadily been unblurring new skills and levels as he progressed. He wasn't a Master, not by a long shot. Not even a Mavin or an Adept. But he was getting there. It would just take time.

Bawb took one last look at himself. "As ready as I'll be."

It was a short walk to the Rusty Kettle, a path he knew well. This explained how the others had been returned to the training house so soon after their failures. The teachers had selected a location close to their healer. Rather than making him worried, this only strengthened Bawb's resolve.

He strode into the tavern, cock-sure and full of confidence, exactly the attitude he would need to project lest he otherwise be perceived as an easy target. A few heads turned to look at him but most just carried on with their discussions and drinks.

As was the case on this world, all manner of races were present, but not a Wampeh among them. He knew that wasn't the case and that Demelza was here somewhere. And knowing the order, they had a few other Ghalian lurking around as well. But they were all masters and their disguises, magical or practical, were so expertly applied he would be unable to discern which was which.

He would have to use more than a simple reveal spell here. He would have to use what he knew of the target.

Teacher Demelza was a sturdily built woman. Curvy and strong. She was also among the best of them at disguises of all sorts. She could appear as male, female, or even another species entirely if she wanted to, but there were a few aspects that she had a somewhat harder time disguising. Her ample bosom was one of them.

Surprisingly, there were a number of people present fitting that description. A large man with yellow-brown skin who caught his attention initially. A violet-skinned woman with her cleavage on display, drawing the attention of many in the tavern. All manner of races that could conceal her true form. This would not be easy.

Bawb ordered a drink and walked the tavern, greeting those who seemed in a cheerful mood, buying them drinks and creating a somewhat safe bubble from which he could move and observe. He was not rushing this. He would have to be absolutely sure which one was her before he made his move. Elzina was as good as he was. Better, if he was being honest about it, and she had still failed at this task. Miserably at that. Bawb needed to think like she thought, then shift course where she went wrong.

If he could figure it out in time, that is.

He spent a short while making rounds of the tavern, taking note of the busty women and burly men of all races who most closely fit Demelza's description.

"That has to be her," he mused, his confidence in one woman in particular being his disguised teacher growing with every glance.

She was ignoring him, of course, paying attention to the two brutish Tslavar mercenaries she was talking to. By the look of them, that was likely how Elzina had taken a beating. She'd interfered with the green-skinned men's advances and reaped the whirlwind.

Bawb, walked toward her, planning how he would buy a round for the two men, pretending to know them from some trading excursion while ignoring the woman entirely. If it worked, his lack of interest in her would at least put them somewhat at ease. From there he could casually adjust course and hand her the token, ending the exercise.

He walked closer, a growing confidence in his plan, when a sense of unease tingled through his body, making the fine hair on the back of his neck rise. Something was not right. He looked at the woman closely and felt a twinge in his gut. His peripheral vision caught movement. Movement that just didn't seem right.

Misdirection was one of the Ghalian's favorite tricks, and he was walking right into it. He trusted his gut and threw himself aside, rolling hard into a group of revelers as a powerful kick swished through the air where he had just been standing.

"Watch it!" one of them growled, shoving him into an oncoming punch.

Bawb blocked most of the blow's force but still took a hit, spinning away as best he could as more attacks rained down on him.

Training kicked in without his having to think about it. He blocked and countered, lunging into an attack of his own, landing a solid elbow to the wiry man charging him, stunning him but not quite dropping him.

Some longed for a brawl and were always looking for an excuse. As such, two others joined in, the fight suddenly shifting to a very outnumbered and unbalanced attack.

Bawb blocked and fought, adjusting his style as fast as he could, shifting and flowing around the very different fighting styles being used against him. He recognized them, having trained at least a bit in each, but combined and overlapping they were just too fast. Too strong.

Bawb saw two of the attackers moving to pin him in an overlapped attack, the nearest throwing a powerful punch.

He feigned a block but instead ran right into the blow, absorbing it with a painful grunt but also using the momentum to pivot his body around the meaty fist, leveraging his forehead into the attacker's nose with a sickening crunch.

The man staggered back, blood pouring out of his nose. Bawb's own head was ringing from the impact but he carried on, spinning hard, his foot swinging high, the heel catching the other attacker on the jaw. Bawb knew he was going to wind up on the ground, but he was damned if he wasn't going to at least land a few good shots first.

A solid kick caught him in the ribs, sending him sliding into a stool, upending the large man atop it, his mass pinning the boy to the ground momentarily. Bawb was stuck. Defenseless. This was where he lost. He grit his teeth, waiting for the flurry of blows which never came.

"Not bad, Vessel Bawb," the barrel-chested man with yellow-brown skin and dirty dishwater colored eyes said, reaching down and offering him a hand.

He looked around. The other attackers had gone back to their places, though the one with the broken nose was busy applying a healing spell to set the bone back in place and stanch the bleeding.

"Teacher Demelza?" he asked, taking the large, dirt-stained hand.

"You performed above your usual abilities," she said, speaking in her own voice but not shedding her disguise.

"Out of necessity."

"Yes, but nevertheless, you adapted and improvised admirably. But tell me, you were about to approach the woman over there. Why did you stop?"

"She looks too much like I would expect you to look if you were in disguise. But that was all wrong. It is what you have taught us since the beginning. Misdirection is a great tool in our arsenal, and naturally, the person who most closely resembled you in form would be a decoy."

Demelza nodded, a grin flashing her yellow-stained teeth. It really was a disgusting disguise, and very effective, he had to admit.

"Well done, Bawb."

"Not well enough, though."

"In what way are you not satisfied with your performance? You did better than the others we have seen thus far."

"There was more to the lesson and I only realized that too late. The unspoken part. I was to find you, but I had seen the others return bloodied. Clearly there was an adversary here to slow my progress. But my mistake was expecting only one. And when I saw two I adjusted accordingly. But there were three. I should have been more alert."

She nodded her approval of his assessment. "Very astute. Yet, you speak freely of these things. Is that not against our way?"

Bawb looked around at the crowd and shook his head. "As do you," he said with a knowing grin creeping to his lips. "In fact, I would wager every last person here is of our order."

Heads turned, approving nods cast his way before the patrons went back to their performances.

*Level up: threat assessment and disguise detection*, the konus said. *For once. Not bad, Vessel.*

Demelza put her hand on his shoulder and walked him to the door. "You are but a Vessel, Bawb. Do not be too hard on yourself. The others did not make it as far as you did, and none of them identified that all present are Ghalian. Your magic is still weak, but we will work on that as well as your practical disguise techniques. That is the purpose of this lesson. To drive home what you must learn in a manner you will not forget."

"I will certainly not."

"I would expect no less of you. Do not be down on yourself, you have performed well."

"Thank you, Teacher."

"Now, go clean up. You still have a long day of training ahead of you, though you will have a bit of a break while waiting for the others' injuries to be healed."

He stepped outside, still walking on his own two feet, bloody and beaten, but not badly, much to Griggitz's surprise.

"I am ready to return if you are," Bawb said, holding back his grin.

Griggitz, normally stoic and gruff, actually let out a chuckle. "You are surprising, Bawb. And in good shape, I see."

"Thank you. I–"

"That means you will have your wounds repaired quickly. After, you can run laps while the others are healing up. Come on, now. Back we go."

Bawb followed, not looking forward to the run, but glad he was intact enough to do so. If Demelza's words were true, and they always were, it would be a busy day indeed.

# AFTERWORD

For all y'all who have been with me over all these years and all these books, thank you from the bottom of my heart. For those of you new to these characters, welcome to the madness.

Now, as for the business of indie author life. I don't want to be redundant, but I've got to reiterate how your ratings and reviews are so crucial to a book's success.

Your feedback not only helps stoke the creative fires and keep the stories coming, but it allows me the freedom to keep writing them. So, I'm asking pretty-please, if you can spare a moment, please leave an honest rating/review.

See you on Bawb's next adventure!

~ Scott Baron ~

# ALSO BY SCOTT BARON

**Standalone Novels**

Living the Good Death

Vigor Mortis

**The Clockwork Chimera Series**

Daisy's Run

Pushing Daisy

Daisy's Gambit

Chasing Daisy

Daisy's War

**The Dragon Mage Series**

Bad Luck Charlie

Space Pirate Charlie

Dragon King Charlie

Magic Man Charlie

Star Fighter Charlie

Portal Thief Charlie

Rebel Mage Charlie

Warp Speed Charlie

Checkmate Charlie

Castaway Charlie

Wild Card Charlie

End Game Charlie

**The Space Assassins Series**

The Interstellar Slayer

The Vespus Blade

The Ghalian Code

Death From the Shadows

Hozark's Revenge

**The Book of Bawb Series**

Assassins' Academy

Assassin's Apprentice

Assassin: Rise of the Geist

Assassin and the Dragon Mage

**The Warp Riders Series**

Deep Space Boogie

Belly of the Beast

Rise of the Forgotten

Pandora's Menagerie

Engines of Chaos

Seeds of Damocles

**Odd and Unusual Short Stories:**

The Best Laid Plans of Mice: An Anthology

Snow White's Walk of Shame

The Tin Foil Hat Club

Lawyers vs. Demons

The Queen of the Nutters

Lost & Found

# ABOUT THE AUTHOR

A native Californian, Scott Baron was born in Hollywood, which he claims may be the reason for his rather off-kilter sense of humor.

Before taking up residence in Venice Beach, Scott first spent a few years abroad in Florence, Italy before returning home to Los Angeles and settling into the film and television industry, where he has worked as an on-set medic for many years.

Aside from mending boo-boos and owies, and penning books and screenplays, Scott is also involved in indie film and theater scene both in the U.S. and abroad.

Made in United States
North Haven, CT
10 January 2025

64234224R00276